ABC's
of
Bumps & Bruises

A guide to home & herbal remedies for children

by Theresa K. Roberts

Author info: Theresa K. Roberts
c/o Natural Living Health Food Store
4376 W. Houghton Lake Dr.
Houghton Lake, MI 48629
989/366-8580

978-1-4357-0922-5

Acknowledgment

I wish to acknowledge my children and their children, who are the reason that this book has come to life. They have been my inspiration, support, guinea pigs and advisors. Much love my Kristal, Nathan, Hope, Cory, Katie, Denny, Becky, Eric David, Lanette, Martin, Vanassa, Deric, Naomi, Lauren Kate, Oberon, Aiyanna, Emily, Kortney, Kyle, Denielle, Craig, Chloe and Gabe. Photograph on cover is done by Lisa Winzeler of Naomi Jean Seneda. I would like to give special thanks to Donald Lee Torchia for the days of editing and his constant support. Also, my sister, Helen Macko, for her love and support. Special Thanks to Bella Brandt for her advice and mentoring over the years, and Gala & Hilton Muntz for their love and support. Dannie James Hummel, thanks for all your help with the front and back covers and for keeping me sane. To my mom, Nancy and Grandma Carol, I thank you for always being there for me and the children.

Author's Note

The information contained in this book are some of the things I used with my children. Now that they are grown, they use some of these remedies on their children and some new ones that they have discovered along the way. Not everyone is the same. So different things work better on some children than others.

I wanted to put this book together so that you could have a quick reference to children's aliments right at your finger tips. I know that for myself, I was tired of looking at so many books and going to the Internet to get information on one topic, so I decided to put my parenting experience of over 32 years, along with owning a Health Food Store for over 16 years, all the research that has come with owning a store and helping others, and what has worked really well for me over the years, into one book.

This book is in no means meant to replace your doctor. I believe that there are many really good doctors out there and I have some of the best that take care of my children. These days, it is not that difficult to find a good pediatrician or naturalistic physician, etc.

The information in these pages are for conditions that are not serious and that are very easy to remedy at home. Other conditions that are more serious will be described in this book for informational purposes only. Be sure you are working with the very best doctors to help your child live a healthy life. If you try any of these remedies that worked for my family, please check with your doctor first.

I cannot stress enough the importance of good nutrition and whole foods. Feeding your child well and giving them the best possible whole, natural, unprocessed foods will be some of the best medicine you can give them. I believe that a good multi-vitamin is very important for your child everyday. This way they are getting nutrients they may be missing in their diets. I believe it is important for children to play outside as much as possible, because exercise is a critical part of a child's healthy development.

I tried to keep this information as simple as possible. If you would like more detailed information, it can be very educational to go on your computer search engine and look at detailed information on the Internet.

The contents of this book are intended for informational and educational purposes only, and is not intended for medical advice. If you have any questions about your health, please consult a medical or health professional.

Contents

Allergies (Food)

Food allergies happen when the child's immune system responds in an inappropriate manner to a food that is not normally harmful to the body. Usually allergic responses will include coughing, shortness of breath, wheezing, itching, skin rashes, headaches, and fatigue. In an attempt to protect the body, the immune system produces IgE antibodies to that food which the child may be allergic to. Antibodies are special proteins the body makes that work to recognize a specific substance if the body starts seeing that substance as harmful or foreign. IgE antibodies then cause mast cells, which are allergy cells in the body, to release chemicals into the bloodstream, one of which is histamine. The histamine then acts on a person's eyes, nose, throat, lungs, skin, or gastrointestinal tract and causes the symptoms of the allergic reaction.

Once antibodies are made against a certain food, they will instantly recognize if that food is eaten and enters the digestive tract. So the next time that same food is eaten, IgE antibodies against it are activated, stimulating mast cells and causing histamine to be released into the bloodstream again. This creates the symptoms of the allergic reaction. In severe food allergies, reactions can occur even if that food is simply touched or if particles of it are breathed in through the nose. Most common allergic reactions in children come from eggs, milk, peanuts, wheat, and soy. Typically children outgrow these allergies. There are however, increasing concerns about food dyes and additives in our food these days and their possible negative reaction as an allergen. I have found these following nutrients to be helpful for my children:

Quercetin - a naturally occurring bioflavonoid that increases the immune system and decreases allergic reactions. From my experience, using quercetin has really been affective in helping with asthma symptoms. Some places that quercetin's bioflavonoid's are found is in lemons, cherries, blackberries, grapes, oranges, elderberries, and plums. You can get Quercetin in capsule, liquid and tablet form at your local health food store.

Bioflavonoids help reduce inflammation from allergic reaction. Bioflavonoids works really well when taken with vitamin C. It will help lessens histamine release.

DHA and EPA - is being added to baby cereal and formula because it is so good for babies brains and their development. It is a very good essential fatty acid. It also helps in inflammation and with the hypersensitive reaction so that an asthma or allergic condition is quelled.

Acidophilus - is an active good bacteria found in the intestinal track which increases the good flora and promotes a healthy immune system.

Homeopathy is based on the theory of "like cures like." I like homeopathic medicines because they do not have harmful side effects. The children do not get drowsy or act spacey. A few favorites we have used for Allergies are Apis mellifica, Rhus toxicodendron and Pulsatilla (the last one mentioned has stopped a runny nose very quickly).

Eucalyptus oil - will act as a decongestant. I have used it in the laundry to wash the bedding to kill dust mites which have been known to cause allergies.

Anemia

Anemia is usually caused by low iron or your body not absorbing iron. To understand anemia, it helps to start with breathing. The oxygen we inhale doesn't just stop in our lungs. It's needed throughout our bodies to fuel the brain and all our other organs and tissues that allow us to function. Oxygen travels to these organs through the bloodstream, specifically in the red blood cells. Iron deficiency, when the body's stores of iron are reduced, is the first step toward anemia. If the body's iron stores aren't replenished at this point, continuing iron deficiency can cause the body's normal hemoglobin production to slow down. When hemoglobin levels and red blood cell production drop below normal, a person is said to have anemia. Someone with anemia may appear pale and may be tired all the time.

Some of the things to look for in your children are fatigue, loss of appetite, headaches, weakness, feeling cold and or looking pale. If my children were fatigued for a period of time, then they were off to the pediatrician getting their iron check along with a general check-up. That way I knew what to do from there.

When my child was diagnosed with low iron, I have added extra eggs, dark leafy spinach, bananas, raisins and any other food that is high in iron to the children's diet until iron is no longer low. I extremely limit soft drinks, candy, sugar, etc., because these are know to lower iron absorption.

Sickle cell anemia is a hereditary condition that affects thousands of people. It is a rare blood disease that causes red blood cells to become brittle and mis-shaped. This causes many painful conditions that need medical attention. This condition affects mostly people of African-American and Mediterranean descent. I have adopted several children and some of them are of African-American decent, so I had them tested for Sickle cell anemia as part of their over all child wellness check-up.

Anemia is a symptom of something gone wrong elsewhere in the body. For example, there could be blood loss, infection, thyroid, and deficiencies in the diet, etc. That is why it is important to see your family doctor.

Some of the supplements I have used for low iron are:

Iron – is a very important mineral that is needed for anemia. I have used gluconate form to replace Iron. Use iron under your doctors care and advice, because too much iron can be toxic.

B Complex - B complex works best when you have all the B's combined. B complex is very important in red blood cell production, cell repair and energy.

Vitamin C - Needed to help iron absorb.

Dandelion – Is very high in iron. It also makes a very nice tonic. Dandelion comes in tea, tincture, and capsule form.

Blackstrap Molasses – is high in iron and B vitamins.

Alfalfa – is high in iron and minerals.

Cherries, purple grape skins, plums, raisins, and red raspberries are also very good for anemia. Adding beans, peas, yams and whole grains, which are high in iron, is very helpful also.

Anthrax

You may be wondering why I would add this to a book on children's ailments. Well, when it was in the news so much a while back, all I could do is wonder how this would effect my children and my grand babies. Then I decided to educate myself about anthrax. I believe the more we know about all subjects, the less fear we have about it, and the more empowered we become in our lives about our health and how to treat it.

Anthrax is an infection caused by a bacterium, a type of germ, called Bacillus anthracic. Although it's most commonly seen in grazing animals like sheep, pigs, cattle, horses, and goats, anthrax can also occur in humans, although it's very rare. In the environment, the anthrax causing bacterium forms spores which is a version of the germ covered by a hard protective shell that can live in the soil for years. People can become infected by coming into contact with these spores through a break in the skin, such as a cut or scrape, by eating food contaminated by them, or by inhaling spores, and breathing them into the lungs. But anthrax is not contagious, which means that it can't spread from person to person.

It's extremely unlikely that you or someone you know could get anthrax. In fact, there are usually only a few reported cases of anthrax per year. Most of these have been in people who work with animals or animal products. Anthrax that occurs naturally in the environment isn't a huge threat. But B. anthracis can be grown in a laboratory and some people are worried about anthrax germs being grown as a weapon.

The issue of laboratory-grown B. anthracis received lots of attention in 2001 after an anthrax outbreak in the United States. The outbreak scared a lot of people, in part because five people died and also because the outbreak coincided with the September 11 terrorist attacks. However, bioterrorism experts believe that it is technologically difficult to use anthrax effectively as a weapon on a large scale.

The three main types of anthrax are cutaneous or skin anthrax, can occur if someone with a cut or scrape handles contaminated animals or animal products. More than 95% of anthrax cases are of the cutaneous type, which is the least dangerous form. A person with cutaneous anthrax will notice a small sore that develops into a painless ulcer with a black area in its center. If left untreated, the infection can spread to other areas of the body. Intestinal anthrax can occur if someone eats undercooked contaminated meat.

Intestinal anthrax is far less common than cutaneous anthrax, but it can make someone much sicker. Intestinal anthrax symptoms include severe abdominal pain, nausea, vomiting, severe diarrhea, and bleeding from the digestive tract. Pulmonary, or inhaled, anthrax is the rarest form of anthrax, but it's also the most dangerous. Pulmonary anthrax can only occur if someone breathes thousands of anthrax spores into the lungs. Pulmonary anthrax usually seems like a common cold or the flu at first, but it rapidly turns into severe pneumonia and requires hospitalization.

If you worry when you hear about anthrax, remember that it's very rare, and it's unlikely that you will ever be exposed to the germs that cause anthrax. If you're worried about it, talk to a medical professional, who can help you find the answers to any questions you may have about anthrax.

Anxiety

At one time or another children become anxious. Anxiety is a natural human reaction that involves mind and body. It serves an important basic survival function. Anxiety is an alarm system that is activated whenever a person perceives danger or threat. They may be fearful of going to the doctor, school, being in crowds, a new baby added to the family, and excess stress, to name a few. If a child's anxiety seems to be extreme, than be sure to have them checked out by their pediatrician.

When the body and mind react to danger or threat, a person feels physical sensations of anxiety, things like a faster heartbeat and breathing, tense muscles, sweaty palms, a queasy stomach, and trembling hands or legs. These sensations are part of the body's fight-flight response. They are caused by a rush of adrenaline and other chemicals that prepare the body to make a quick getaway from danger. They can be mild or extreme. Although everyone experiences normal anxiety in certain situations, most people, even those who experience traumatic situations, don't develop anxiety disorders. And people who develop anxiety disorders can get relief with proper treatment and care. They can learn ways to manage anxiety and to feel more relaxed and at peace.

Enough cannot be said about a good balanced diet and exercise. Avoid caffeinated pop and chocolate because these can be stimulating and cause a child to feel out of sorts adding extra stress to the body. It is also important to watch for allergies. Teas that help with anxiety are catnip, passionflower, skullcap and valerian. Some other supplements that have worked well for us are:

Calcium & Magnesium - This has a calming effect. One of my favorite ways to use it is to heat purple grape juice on the stove then add powered Cal/Mag to it and stir. It taste like a cream cycle and has an immediate calming effect on the children. It is best to take Calcium with Magnesium because they work synergistically well together to relieve anxiety and nervousness.

Multivitamin and mineral complex – is needed to correct chemical imbalances due to poor nutrition.

B - Complex - It helps with stress, nerves and provides energy.

Vitamin C – helps with anxiety, stress, and immune system.

Melatonin - Is a great sleep aid and especially helps when child is having night fears and night anxiety.

Calms Forte - It is a homeopathic blend by Hyland's. We have used this for years. It helps with nervousness and sleeplessness.

Catnip – helps with anxiety and to relax.

Passion Flower – helps with stress and anxiety. Also has a calming effect.

Valerian - Helps with sleeplessness and anxiety.

Fennel – helps with stomach upset caused by anxiety and has a nice licorice taste.

Apnea

Everyone has brief pauses in his or her breathing pattern called apnea, even your child. Usually these brief stops in breathing are completely normal. Sometimes, though, apnea or other sleep-related problems can be a cause for concern. Find out what it means when your child's doctor mentions apnea.

The word apnea comes from the Greek word meaning "without wind." Although it's perfectly normal for everyone to experience occasional pauses in breathing, apnea can be a problem when breathing stops for 20 seconds or longer. The three types of apnea are obstructive, central, and mixed.

A common type of apnea in children, obstructive apnea is caused by an obstruction of the airway, such as enlarged tonsils and adenoids. This is most likely to happen during sleep because that's when the soft tissue at back of the throat is most relaxed. As many as 1% to 3% of otherwise healthy preschool-age children have obstructive apnea. Because obstructive sleep apnea may disturb sleep patterns, these children may also show continued sleepiness after awakening in the morning and tiredness and attention problems throughout the day. Sometimes apnea can affect school performance. One recent study suggests that some children diagnosed with ADHD actually have attention problems in school because of disrupted sleep patterns caused by obstructive sleep apnea. Treatment for obstructive apnea involves keeping the throat open to aid air flow with surgical removal of the tonsils and adenoids, or continuous positive airway pressure, which involves having the child wear a nose mask while sleeping.

When the part of the brain that controls breathing doesn't start or maintain the breathing process properly it's called central apnea. It's the least common form of apnea except in very premature infants, in whom it's seen fairly commonly because the respiratory center in the brain is immature and often has a neurological cause. An example of normal central apnea would be the short pause that occurs following a deep a sigh.

Mixed apnea is a combination of central and obstructive apnea and is seen particularly in infants or young children who have abnormal control of breathing. Mixed apnea may occur when a child is awake or asleep.

Apnea of infancy occurs in children who are younger than 1 year old and who were born after a full-term pregnancy. Following a complete medical evaluation, if a cause of apnea isn't found, it's often called apnea of infancy. AOI usually goes away on its own, but if it doesn't cause any significant problems such as low blood oxygen, it may be considered part of the child's normal breathing pattern.

Infants with AOI can be observed at home with the help of a special monitor prescribed by a sleep specialist. This monitor records chest movements and heart rate and can relay the readings to a hospital apnea program or save them for future examination by a doctor. Parents and caregivers will be taught CPR before the child is sent home.

If you suspect that your child has apnea, call your child's doctor. Although prolonged pauses in breathing can be serious, after a doctor does a complete evaluation and makes a diagnosis, most cases of apnea can be treated or managed with surgery, medications, monitoring devices, or sleep centers. And many cases of apnea go away on their own.

Appendicitis

Your appendix is a small, finger-shaped pouch connected to your large intestine, in the lower right part of your abdomen. The appendix manufactures white blood cells and assists in producing antibodies. When your appendix gets inflamed, or swells up, it's called appendicitis. Both children and adults can get appendicitis. There isn't always an obvious reason why appendicitis happens. Sometimes it happens after there is an infection in the intestine.

Appendicitis can occur when the opening of the appendix to the large intestine gets blocked. Blockage can be due to hard rock-like stool, inflammation of lymph nodes in the intestines, or even parasites. Once the appendix is blocked, it becomes inflamed and bacteria can overgrow in it. Appendicitis is not contagious. This means you can't catch it from anyone who has it. But there isn't much you can do to prevent appendicitis from happening.

If the infected appendix is not removed, it can eventually burst or rupture from the buildup of pressure. This may happen as soon as 48 to 72 hours after symptoms start. The infection from a ruptured appendix is very serious, it can form an abscess, a walled-off infection of pus, or spread throughout the abdomen. An appendectomy generally has few complications, with a hospital stay of 1 to 3 days. However, if the infected appendix ruptures before surgery, the person usually stays in the hospital longer to receive antibiotics that will help kill bacteria that may have spread to the abdominal cavity. Even if the appendix has not ruptured, the doctor may prescribe antibiotics because they can decrease the risk of infection after surgery.

Children have different types of symptoms when they have appendicitis. Someone with appendicitis might feel as if he or she is having stomach cramps or really bad indigestion. Usually, the first symptom is a bellyache around the belly button. Sometimes, throwing up follows. After a few hours, the pains tend to move down to the lower right side of the belly. Sometimes the pain can become sharp and intense in this area, enough to keep a child up at night.

A child with appendicitis will not feel very hungry and might have a slight temperature. Do not put a heating pad over area since this may cause the appendix to rupture. Some children do not want to move around because they feel better if they lie down and curl up. If the doctor decides that a child has appendicitis, the appendix will need to be removed. Without immediate attention, the infected appendix can burst sending poison throughout the body. Prevention is the best medicine. Make sure there is plenty of fiber and whole grains in your child's diet.

Fiber – absorbs toxins, adds bulk and helps clean the intestines.

B Complex – helps nutrients absorb in body and cell repair.

Vitamin C – detoxifier, inflammation, helps with infection, and immune system.

zinc – helps build immune system and speeds healing.

Multivitamin and mineral complex – is needed to correct chemical imbalances due to poor nutrition.

Arsenic Poisoning

Arsenic is a heavy metal that can be found all over the place. It can be found in paint, pesticides, rodent killer products, naturally in rocks and soil, water, air, and plants and animals. It can be released into the environment through natural activities such as forest fires, or through human actions.

Approximately 90 percent of industrial arsenic in the U.S. is currently used as a wood preservative, but arsenic is also used in paints, dyes, metals, drugs, soaps and semi-conductors. High arsenic levels can also come from certain fertilizers and animal feeding operations. Industry practices such as copper smelting, mining and coal burning also contribute to arsenic in our environment. You may be exposed to arsenic by breathing sawdust or burning smoke from arsenic-treated wood.

Because arsenic targets a number of metabolic processes, it affects nearly all organ systems of the body.

Exposure to arsenic can cause both short and long term health concerns. Minor effects can occur within hours or days of exposure. Long or chronic effects occur over many years. Long term exposure to arsenic has been linked to cancer of the bladder, lungs, skin, kidneys, nasal passages, liver and prostate. According to the Agency for Toxic Substances and Disease Registry (ATSDR), an agency of the U.S. Department of Health and Human Services, arsenic is strongly associated with lung and skin cancer in humans, and may cause other internal cancers. Skin lesions, peripheral neuropathy, and anemia are hallmarks of chronic arsenic ingestion.

A few things that I do know that help with any kind of heavy metal poisoning are:

Apple Pectin – helps remove heavy metals from the body.

Activated Charcoal – absorbs poisons and toxins. I always have activated charcoal in the medicine cabinet and the first aid kit. It is very good to keep on hand in case of accidental poisoning.

Acidophilus - is an active good bacteria found in the intestinal track which increases the good flora and promotes a healthy immune system. It helps so that bad bacteria can not take over.

Vitamin C – is an important antioxidant that helps remove toxins and bacteria from the body.

Garlic – detoxes the body and works like a natural antibiotic and has antiviral properties.

Colloidal Silver – is a natural antibiotic. Kills fungi, viruses and bacteria. Helps in healing.

Minerals – to replace the ones lost during diarrhea and to balance the electrolytes in the body.

Fiber – removes toxins from the colon walls so that they do not enter the bloodstream.

Kelp – high in minerals that are needed to restore electrolyte imbalance.

Multivitamin and mineral complex – is needed to correct chemical imbalances.

If you are concerned about heavy metal poisoning, you can get a Hair Analysis done. This will tell you how much heavy metals are in your system and which ones they are.

Keep the number of your local Poison Control Center near your telephone.

Asthma

If you have ever seen a child having an asthma attack, you know how scary that can be and how helpless you feel. Asthma can be a life threatening disease, so it is very important to get a child's asthma under control as soon as possible. An Asthma attack is when the muscles surrounding the small airways in the lungs constrict making breathing difficult. An Asthma attack can last for several minutes or a couple hours or more.

My daughter would cough for hours and nothing I gave her seemed to help so I took her to her pediatrician where they ran tests on her and she was diagnosed with asthma. I did not know that persistent coughing was a symptom of an asthma attack. Some other symptoms are wheezing, tight feeling chest, and difficulty breathing. Two of my children grew out of their asthma by the time they were teenagers.

There are several things that can trigger an asthma attack, a few are allergies, animal dander, pollens, mold, dust mites, food allergies, dairy products, nuts, anxiety, pollution, fumes from paints, exercise, and cold temperatures, etc. It is very hard to prevent asthma but there are a lot of things you can do to cut down on attacks. One of the first things that I had done was remove the carpeting in my home. Now I have wood floors and use throw rugs that can be easily washed. This cut down asthma attacks by 75%. I also covered mattresses and pillows with special coverings, and limited stuffed animals.

Here are a few supplements that help:

Quercetin – good for the immune system, antihistamine, and helps with inflammation.

Vitamin C – protects lungs, helps with infections and inflammation.

Calcium and Magnesium – relaxes muscles and helps with lung capacity.

Lobelia – soothes bronchial muscles and gets rid of excess mucus.

Mullein – helps congestion, coughs, and breathing.

Belladonna – is a homeopathic that relaxes the bronchial tubes and stops wheezing.

Essential fatty acids (EFA) – are anti-inflammatory.

Fenugreek tea – helps get rid of mucus.

zinc – helps to speed healing and helps with infections.

Colostrum – is an immune system builder and speeds healing.

Eucalyptus oil - will act as a decongestant. I add a few drops in water on the stove and it seems to help with breathing. I have used it in the laundry to wash the bedding to kill dust mites which have been known to cause allergies which can bring on an asthma attack. I also put eucalyptus in a mister bottle with water and mist pillows and mattresses to kill dust mites. I have mixed several herbs together such as ginger, licorice root, echinacea and elderberry and made a tea which helped calm an asthma attack.

Multivitamin and mineral complex – is needed to correct chemical imbalances due to poor nutrition.

Athlete's Foot

Athlete's foot or Tinea pedis is a fungal infection of the epidermis of the foot. It is typically caused by yeast that grows on the surface of the skin and then into the living skin tissue itself, causing the infection. It usually occurs between the toes, but in severely lasting cases may appear as an extensive moccasin pattern on the bottom and sides of the foot. Athlete's foot more commonly affects males than females. Tinea pedis is estimated to be the second most common skin disease in the United States. Up to 15% of the U.S. population may have tinea pedis.

Athlete's foot causes scaling, flaking and itching of the affected skin. Blisters and cracked skin may also occur, leading to exposed raw tissue, pain, swelling and inflammation. Secondary bacterial infection can accompany the fungal infection, sometimes requiring a course of oral antibiotics. The infection can spread to other areas of the body, such as the armpits, knees, elbows, and the groin, which usually is called jock itch.

It is typically transmitted in moist environments where people walk barefoot, such as, gyms, swimming pool areas and locker rooms. It can also be transmitted by sharing socks and shoes with an infected person, or less commonly, by sharing towels with an infected person.

Hygiene plays an important role in managing athlete's foot infection. Since fungi thrive in moist environments, it is very important to keep feet and footwear as dry as possible. Spray tub and bathroom floor with disinfectant after each use to help prevent reinfection and infection of other household members. Wash sheets, towels, socks, underwear, and bedclothes in hot water (at 60 °C / 140 °F) to kill the fungus.

Onion extract – destroys fungus.

Hydrogen peroxide – apply 3% hydrogen peroxide and or rubbing alcohol after bathing will help in killing the fungus on the skin and will help prevent a secondary infection from occurring.

Baking soda – make a baking soda paste and apply to foot and also sprinkle baking soda in the shoes. This will help change the pH balance.

Colloidal Silver – is a natural antibiotic. Kills fungi, viruses and bacteria. Helps in healing.

Lamisil – antifungal medication.

Tea Tree Oil – is an antifungal.

Acidophilus – builds friendly flora, builds immune system and helps with fungal infection.

Essential fatty acids – helps the skin to heal.

Caprylic acid - is an antifungal and kills candida fungus.

Garlic - a natural antibiotic and immune enhancer. Garlic has antifungal properties.

Comfrey salve - is soothing and helps healing.

Fiber – removes toxins from the colon walls so that they do not enter the bloodstream.

ADD/ADHD
Attention Deficit Disorder / Attention Deficit Hyperactivity Disorder

ADD is a disorder that affects the central nervous system. It seems like just about every family knows of, or has a child with ADD. We have dealt with this disorder in our own family. A whole book could be written on this disorder itself. Our goal is to make information simple and at your finger tips. Many years ago, one of my sons was diagnosed with ADD/ADHD and was prescribed Ritalin. For some children this works very well, but it did not work well for my son. He was tested and had an above average IQ and was very creative, but his performance level was low because he had trouble concentrating. So working with the pediatrician, nutritionist and chiropractor, these are some of the things that worked best.

Diet - Nothing with dyes, preservatives, sugar, or processed. If it came in a box, we didn't get it. Lots of fruit, vegetables, whole grains, fish, salmon, herbal ice teas in place of fruit juices and soda. Sometimes we sweetened the tea with stevia, which is a plant sweetener that is good for blood sugar and has zero calories. We made a rinse with food grade hydrogen peroxide and water and rinsed all fruits and veggies to get rid of pesticide residue and bacteria.

By changing his diet we saw dramatic changes almost immediately. It may seem like there is nothing you can feed your child, but don't become discouraged, because you will be surprised at what a child will like to eat. Let your child help pick out healthy foods to eat, this way they are more likely to enjoy trying it.

Calms Forte - This is one of our all time favorites. It is made by Hylands an you can get it in just about any health food store. I gave 1 to 2 tablets to my son before school and he usually stayed calm until around 2 in the afternoon. It is good to use for occasional sleeplessness also.

Grapeseed extract – is also know as OPC. It is a very strong antioxidant and it helps the child to focus and seems to calm them down.

Cal-Mag - relaxes and has a calming effect. One of my favorite ways to use it is to heat purple grape juice on the stove then add powered Cal/Mag to it and stir. It taste like a cream cycle and created a calming effect on the children. It is best to take Calcium with Magnesium because they work synergistically well together to relieve anxiety and nervousness.

GABA – is important for brain metabolism and inhibits nerve cells from over firing. Helps with anxiety, stress, and depression without side effects. Be sure and work with your doctor before using GABA with your child.

Multivitamin/Mineral - is needed to correct chemical imbalances due to poor nutrition.

DHA – is an omega-3 essential fatty acid. It boosts intelligence and is very important for the brain. It is now being added to babies formulas and babies cereals. Low levels of DHA has been linked to depression.

Fiber – removes toxins from the colon walls so that they do not enter the bloodstream.

Acidophilus – builds friendly flora, builds immune system.

Quercetin – good for the immune system.

Autism

One of my daughters that I adopted came to me with Autism. Any parent that has a child with autism will tell you how frustrating it can be, to not be able to communicate and interact normally with your child. Autism causes a child to experience the world differently from the way most other children do. It's hard for children with autism to talk with other people and express themselves using words. Children who have autism usually keep to themselves and many can't communicate without special help.

They also may react to what's going on around them in unusual ways. Normal sounds may really bother someone with autism. Being touched, even in a gentle way, may feel uncomfortable.

Children with autism often can't make connections that other kids make easily. For example, when someone smiles, you know the smiling person is happy or being friendly. But a child with autism may have trouble connecting that smile with the person's happy feelings.

A child who has autism also has trouble linking words with their meanings. Imagine trying to understand what your mom is saying if you don't know what her words really mean. It is doubly frustrating then if a child can't come up with the right words to express his or her own thoughts.

Autism causes children to act in unusual ways. They might flap their hands, say certain words over and over, have temper tantrums, or play only with one particular toy. Most children with autism don't like changes in routines. They like to stay on a schedule that is always the same. They also may insist that their toys or other objects be arranged a certain way and get upset if these items are moved or disturbed.

Autism affects about 1 in every 150 children, but 1 in 97 boys. Boys seem to out number girls with autism and no one knows what causes it. Some scientists think that some children might be more likely to get autism because it or similar disorders run in their families. Others believe it is the mercury in immunizations or a child having a yeast infection at the time of their immunization, so a brain chemical imbalance happens. Knowing the exact cause of autism is hard because the human brain is very complicated.

You will get a lot of help in so many ways and on every level with your child's treatment, from your child's team of doctors. Here is a list of nutrients that your may find helpful.

Yeast Cleanse – helps kill the overgrowth of yeast and removes parasites from body.

DHA - is an omega-3 essential fatty acid. It boosts intelligence and is very important for the brain. It is now being added to babies formulas and babies cereals. Low levels of DHA has been linked to depression.

Parasite Cleanse – kills parasites in the body and removes them. Renew Life has a very good cleanse.

MSM – helps to concentrate, helps with being more alert and for calmness.

Acidophilus - builds friendly flora, builds immune system and helps with fungal infection.

Autism
Asperger

This is the form of autism my daughter has been diagnosed with. Most children with Asperger's tend to speak in a flat emotionless voice. Their conversation will revolve around themselves. They will also be obsessed with a single topic and seem eccentric. A child with Asperger's will have some kind of learning disability and usually lack common sense. Usually their movements will be clumsy and they will have odd movements of hand waving or finger flicking. Asperger children are a high functioning autistic and are normal in appearance in social situations but display inappropriate interactions. Depression and bipolar disorder are often reported in those with Asperger's syndrome as well as in family members.

At this time, there is no prescribed treatment regimen for individuals with Asperger's syndrome. In adulthood, many lead productive lives, living independently, working effectively at a job. Many are college professors, computer programmers, dentists, and raising a family.

Sometimes people assume everyone who has autism and is high-functioning has Asperger's syndrome. It appears that there are several forms of high-functioning autism, and Asperger's syndrome is one form.

Diet - Nothing with dyes, preservatives, processed or sugar. If it came in a box, we didn't get it. Lots of fruit, vegetables, whole grains, fish, salmon, herbal ice teas in place of fruit juices and soda. Sometimes we sweetened the tea with stevia, which is a plant sweetener that is good for blood sugar and has zero calories. We made a rinse with food grade hydrogen peroxide and water and rinsed all fruits and veggies to get rid of pesticide residue and bacteria.

Calcium & Magnesium – very important for brain and nervous system function.

Coenzyme Q10 – a strong antioxidant and improves brain function.

DMG – is an oxygen carrier to the brain. Good for brain and nervous system function. I was able to find a chewable tablet that seems to work pretty good.

Yeast Cleanse – helps kill the overgrowth of yeast and removes parasites from body.

DHA - is an omega-3 essential fatty acid. It boosts intelligence and is very important for the brain. It is now being added to babies formulas and babies cereals. Low levels of DHA has been linked to depression.

Parasite Cleanse – kills parasites in the body and removes them. Renew Live has a very good cleanse.

MSM – helps to concentrate, helps with being more alert and for calmness.

Acidophilus - builds friendly flora, builds immune system and helps with fungal infection.

Multivitamin and mineral complex – is needed to correct chemical imbalances due to poor nutrition.

Autism
Savants

Autistic savant means a person with autism who has a special skill. Around 10 per cent of people with autism show special or even remarkable skills. For example, a person with autism, who may be intellectually disabled in most ways, could have an exceptional memory for numbers or very good playing the piano, etc.

Savant skills are occasionally found in people with other types of intellectual disability and in the non-disabled population, so most researchers use the term 'savant syndrome' instead of autistic savant. Autistic savant behavior is so far unexplained. Some researchers think it might have something to do with the right hemisphere of the brain.

CT and MRI scans of the brains of autistic savants suggest that the right hemisphere is compensating for damage in the left hemisphere. It seems that the right hemisphere of an autistic savant focuses its attention on one of the five senses. If the brain concentrates on hearing, then the autistic savant may have a special skill in music. Research is ongoing.

My child is not a savant, but she is into letters and can spell way beyond her years even though she is developmentally delayed in all other areas of learning and she had no idea what the words mean that she is spelling..

Diet - Nothing with dyes, preservatives, processed or sugar. If it came in a box, we didn't get it. Lots of fruit, vegetables, whole grains, fish, salmon, herbal ice teas in place of fruit juices and soda. Sometimes we sweetened the tea with stevia, which is a plant sweetener that is good for blood sugar and has zero calories. We made a rinse with food grade hydrogen peroxide and water and rinsed all fruits and veggies to get rid of pesticide residue and bacteria.

Calcium & Magnesium – very important for brain and nervous system function.

Coenzyme Q10 – a strong antioxidant and improves brain function.

DMG – is an oxygen carrier to the brain. Good for brain and nervous system function. I was able to find a chewable tablet that seems to work pretty good.

Yeast Cleanse – helps kill the overgrowth of yeast and removes parasites from body.

DHA - is an omega-3 essential fatty acid. It boosts intelligence and is very important for the brain. It is now being added to babies formulas and babies cereals. Low levels of DHA has been linked to depression.

Parasite Cleanse – kills parasites in the body and removes them. Renew Live has a very good cleanse.

MSM – helps to concentrate, helps with being more alert and for calmness.

Acidophilus - builds friendly flora, builds immune system and helps with fungal infection.

Bad Breath
(Halitosis)

Bad breath is the common name for the medical condition known as halitosis. Many different things can cause halitosis, from not brushing your teeth to certain medical conditions.

Sometimes, a child's bad breath can blow you away and he or she may not realize there's a problem. There are tactful (nice) ways of letting someone know about bad breath. You could offer mints or sugarless gum without having to say anything. Although everyone gets bad breath sometimes, if your child has bad breath a lot, you may need to visit your dentist or doctor.

Poor oral hygiene leads to bad breath because when you leave food particles in your mouth, these pieces of food can rot and start to smell. The food particles may begin to collect bacteria, which can be smelly, too. Plus, by not brushing your teeth regularly, plaque (a sticky, colorless film) builds up on your teeth. Plaque is a great place for bacteria to live and yet another reason why breath can turn foul.

Not just poor oral hygiene leads to bad breath. There could be tooth decay, gum disease, infection in the throat, lungs, nose, and sinusitis. There could also be bad diet, diabetes, constipation, indigestion and over growth of bad bacteria in the colon.

Brushing – brush at least twice a day and floss once a day. It is important to brush your tongue also, because bacteria can grow there. It is important to visit your dentist twice a year for regular checkups and cleanings.

Fiber – needed for removing toxins from the colon that can result in bad breath.

Chlorophyll – fights bad breath and controls body order.

Alfalfa – loaded with minerals and is high in chlorophyll and will help fight bad breath.

Vitamin C – fights infections, helps in healing, gum disease, bleeding gums, and helps with immune system.

Acidophilus - builds friendly flora, builds immune system and helps with fungal infection.

Garlic – acts as a natural antibiotic, antibacterial, detoxes the body.

zinc – is antibacterial and neutralizes sulfur compounds which is a common cause of mouth oder.

Propolis – good for healing sores or infections in the mouth, antibacterial, works great for sore throat.

B Complex – needed for cell repair and proper digestion.

Parsley – is rich in chlorophyll.

Keep your toothbrush clean by storing it in food grade hydrogen peroxide between uses. This will kill viruses and bacteria. Rinse well before using.

Bee Stings
&
Bug bites

Most bug bites and bee stings can be handled at home. Some children are severely allergic and should be seen by their pediatrician. Some times a prescription for an Epi Pen is prescribed. An Epi Pen is a pre-measured dose of epinephrine. You will need to be sure to carry an Epi Pen on you if your child is highly allergic.

If your child is stung by a bee, remove the stinger by scraping with the edge of a credit card. Then apply a cold pack to numb the area, and apply a paste of charcoal or baking soda or hydrocortisone cream to reduce pain and swelling. Take oral Benadryl to reduce symptoms of allergic reaction.

These are some other remedies that I have used with great success:

Charcoal - Make a paste using a few drops of water added to Activated Charcoal. This will draw out the poison from the bite. A lot of people have used mud with good results.

Ice - apply ice to the bite area to help reduce swelling and help with pain.

Lavender oil - reduces inflammation and pain.

Tea Tree oil - repels insects, stops itching, simply add to jojoba oil and apply. Do not get near Eyes because it will burn.

Black tea bag - Put a few drops of water so that tea bag is wet. Then put it in a microwave for a couple of seconds until very warm. Then apply it to bite until the tea bag cools and then reheat and apply again until swelling is reduced. This will draw out the toxins.

Antihistamine - A antihistamine like benadryl will relieve itching and hives caused by the bite.

Meat tenderizer - Make a paste and apply. This will help with pain and swelling and drawing out poison .

Buffered C with Bromelain - This has anti-inflammatory properties.

Quercetin - good for the immune system, antihistamine, and helps with inflammation.

Insect repellent - We mix different oils together to make a pretty good insect repellent. We will mix citronella, cedar, tea tree, lemon grass, and jojoba oil together and apply. This works on our pets as well.

Vitamin C – protects lungs, helps with infections and inflammation.

Calcium and Magnesium – relaxes muscles and helps with lung capacity.

Mullein – helps congestion, coughs, and breathing.

Belladonna – is a homeopathic that relaxes the bronchial tubes and stops wheezing.

Essential fatty acids (EFA) – are anti-inflammatory.

Bell's Palsy

Bells Palsy is a condition that causes the facial muscles to weaken or become paralyzed. It's caused by trauma to the 7th cranial nerve, and is not permanent. Bells palsy affects about 1 of every 5000 people, and 40,000 Americans every year. The percentage of left or right side cases is approximately equal, and remains equal for recurrences. The incidence of Bells palsy in males and females, as well as in the various races is also approximately equal. The chances of the condition being mild or severe, and the rate of recovery is also equal.

Children tend to recover well from Bell's Palsy. Diabetics are more than 4 times more likely to develop Bells palsy than the general population. The symptoms are dry eye or tingling around their lips that progress to classic Bell's palsy during that same day. Occasionally symptoms may take a few days to be recognizable as Bells palsy. It is not contagious. Approximately 50% of Bells palsy patients will have essentially complete recoveries in a short time. Another 35% will have good recoveries in less than a year.

Regardless of the trigger, Bell's palsy is best described as trauma to the nerve. As with any other injury, healing follows. The quality and duration of recovery is dependent on the severity of the initial injury. If the nerve has suffered nothing more than a mild trauma, recovery can be very fast, taking several days to several weeks.

Impaired immunity, whether temporary stress, lack of sleep, minor illness, physical trauma, upper respiratory infection, etc., or long-term autoimmune syndromes, chronic disease, etc. are strongly targeted as the most likely triggers.

Garlic – has antibacterial and antiviral properties and stimulates the immune system.

Multivitamin & Mineral - is needed to correct chemical imbalances due to poor nutrition.

B 12 – aids in the rebuilding and healing of nerve cells.

Quercetin - good for the immune system, antihistamine, and helps with inflammation.

B Complex – are needed for stress, normal brain function, absorption of nutrients and energy.

Calcium - very important for brain and nervous system function.

Vitamin C – is an important antioxidant that helps make you less susceptible to infections.

Oregano – discourages the growth of microorganisms, viruses and parasites.

Diet – is very important for keeping your immune system strong. Sugars, processed foods and a diet high in fat suppresses the immune system. Make sure to eat foods that are high in nutrition and include lots of fresh fruits and vegetables. Include nuts, seeds, whole grains and other food that is high in fiber.

Sleep – is very important for good health when you get the proper amount. It also helps keep the stress levels down.

Acidophilus - builds friendly flora and builds immune system.

Belly Pain

Sometimes a child can have a stomachache so you need to run through a lot of questions to find out why. Belly pain can be the most frustrating to figure out because it could be something as simple as being nervous to something as serious as an appendicitis attack.

Inside your abdomen, you have your stomach and your intestines, along with other organs: bladder, kidney's, liver, spleen, pancreas, gallbladder, appendix, and adrenal glands. If you're a girl, your abdomen also includes your uterus and ovaries. So there is a lot to figure out when your child says their belly hurts.

Some reasons for belly pain are constipation, diarrhea, vomiting, food poisoning, over eating, allergies to a food, lactose intolerance, appendicitis, urinary tract infection, bacterial infection, virus, heartburn and stress, to name a few. If the belly pain is serious, see your doctor. If the belly pain is not something that you feel is to serious, then here are some things that may help.

Diet – it is important to not over eat. A child's stomach is only so big and it is better to give your child several small meals throughout the day along with a couple of healthy snacks.

Fiber – is very important so that there are regular bowel movements. Fiber also helps clean out toxins from the body. Many fruits and vegetables are high in fiber along with whole grains, nuts and beans. Fiber also adds bulk and helps clean the intestines.

Hand washing – washes away germs and viruses that otherwise could get into a child's system when they put their hands in their mouths.

Sleep – this way the body does not get run down. Sleep is very important for good health when you get the proper amount. It also helps keep the stress levels down.

Acidophilus - is an active good bacteria found in the intestinal track which increases the good flora and promotes a healthy immune system.

Vitamin C – is an important antioxidant that helps make you less susceptible to infections.

Activated Charcoal – absorbs poisons and toxins. I always have activated charcoal in the medicine cabinet and the first aid kit. It is very good to keep on hand in case of accidental poisoning.

Garlic – detoxes the body and works like a natural antibiotic.

Multivitamin and mineral complex – is needed to correct chemical imbalances due to poor nutrition.

B - Complex - It helps with stress, nerves and provides energy.

Colloidal Silver – is a natural antibiotic. Kills fungi, viruses and bacteria. Helps in healing.

Diet is very important for keeping your immune system strong. Sugars, processed foods and a diet high in fat suppresses the immune system. Make sure to eat foods that are high in nutrition and include lots of fresh fruits and vegetables. Include nuts, seeds, whole grains and other food that is high in fiber.

Bladder Infection

A bladder infection is also called a urinary tract infection (UTI) by most medical people. If you hear both names don't get scared or confused. It's a bacterial infection that affects any part of the urinary tract. Although urine contains a variety of fluids, salts, and waste products, it normally does not have bacteria in it. When bacteria get into the bladder and multiply in the urine, it causes a urinary tract infection. Most of the time it is the bacteria that is found inside the intestines and sometimes on the skin around the rectal and vaginal areas. Yes, that means from fecal contamination.

Girls are more likely than boys to get a UTI. That's because their urethra's are much shorter than boys' urethra's. The shorter urethra means bacteria can get up into the bladder more easily and cause an infection there. The bacteria that cause UTIs normally live in your intestines. Each time you have a bowel movement, some of these bacteria come out of your body. If they aren't wiped away properly, they stay on your skin. In girls, this means they can grow near the opening of the urethra because their urethra's are closer to where they wipe. From there, bacteria can get inside the urethra, causing irritation to the urethra. This is called urethritis. If the bacteria go there, they can cause a bladder infection. You may also hear a bladder infection called cystitis, which really means an irritation of the bladder.

If your child has any symptoms of a urinary tract infection, you'll need to take them to a health care professional right away. The symptoms won't go away if you ignore them, they'll only become worse. The quicker treatment begins, the less uncomfortable your child will be. If you get help right away, a UTI should completely clear up within 10 days to 2 weeks.

Water – it is important to drink lots of water during and after an infection. Six to eight glasses of water a day will keep your bladder active and bacteria free.

Cranberry – is antibacterial and acidifies the urine and prevents bacteria from sticking to the walls of the bladder. If pure cranberry juice is not available, cranberry capsules can be substituted. Pure cranberry juice will help keep the urine acidic and bacteria don't multiply as well in that kind of environment.

Vitamin C – has antibacterial properties and helps build the immune system.

Hygiene – good hygiene practices can help prevent urinary tract and bladder infections. It is also important after going to the bathroom to wipe from the front to the back to prevent bacteria from the rectal area from getting to the bladder area.

Vitamin and Mineral - is needed to correct chemical imbalances due to poor nutrition.

Vitamin C – is an important antioxidant that helps make you less susceptible to infections.

Colloidal Silver – is a natural antibiotic. Kills fungi, viruses and bacteria. Helps in healing.

Garlic – a natural antibiotic and immune enhancer.

Acidophilus – is needed to restore friendly bacteria. Acidophilus is very important if antibiotics are prescribed. Acidophilus and antibiotics should not be taken at the same time so that they do not cancel each other out. Take acidophilus two hours after you take your antibiotics.

Blisters

A blister is an area of raised skin with watery liquid inside. Blisters form on hands and feet from rubbing and pressure, but they form a lot more quickly than calluses. You can get blisters on your feet the same day you wear uncomfortable or poor-fitting shoes. You can get blisters on your hands if you forget to wear protective gloves when you're using a hammer, a shovel, or even when you're riding your bike.

Blisters are pretty common and easy to prevent. They happen because of friction, which means that two surfaces rub against each other. Areas on a child's body that form blisters and continue to be rubbed every day, like their feet, because of the same pair of uncomfortable shoes a child wears to school, may go on to form calluses.

The best way to deal with blisters, calluses, and corns is to avoid getting them altogether. To avoid getting blisters and calluses on hands, wear the right kind of gloves or protective gear. For instance, your child might use palm protectors called grips for gymnastics.

To keep feet callus free, choose shoes wisely.   Even if they look really cool, don't get them if they don't feel right. Often, a different size or width can make a big difference. If any skin gets red, inflamed, or looks infected, you will want to check with your doctor. But more often blisters, calluses, and corns can be cared for at home.

Blisters need a few days to heal on their own. Keep a blister clean and dry and cover it with a bandage until it goes away. Try not to put pressure or rub the area where it is healing.

Colloidal Silver – is a natural antibiotic. Kills fungi, viruses and bacteria. Helps in healing.

Vitamin C – has antibacterial properties and helps build the immune system.

Garlic – a natural antibiotic and immune enhancer.

Acidophilus – is needed to restore friendly bacteria. Acidophilus is very important if antibiotics are prescribed. Acidophilus and antibiotics should not be taken at the same time so that they do not cancel each other out. Take acidophilus two hours after you take your antibiotics.

Black tea bag - Put a few drops of water so that tea bag is wet. Then put it in a microwave for a couple of seconds until very warm. Then apply it to the blister until the tea bag cools and then reheat and apply again until swelling is reduced. This will draw out the toxins.

Lavender oil - reduces inflammation and pain.

zinc – aids in healing and helps the immune system.

Flax – ground and made into a paste can be used as a compress.

Fenugreek – ground, mix with flax and add warm water to use as a hot compress.

Suma – boosts the immune system.

Essential fatty acids – helps the skin to heal.

Activated Charcoal – absorbs poisons and toxins.   Make a paste using warm water and then apply to blister.

Boils

There are many causes of boils. Some boils can be caused by an ingrown hair. Others can form as the result of a splinter or other foreign material that has become lodged in the skin. Others boils, such as those of acne, are caused by plugged sweat glands that become infected. Boils are round pus filled nodules on the skin that result from bacterial infection. The skin is an essential part of our immune defense against materials and microbes that are foreign to our body. Any break in the skin, such as a cut or scrape, can develop into an abscess should it then become infected with bacteria.

Most simple boils can be treated at home. Ideally, the treatment should begin as soon as a boil is noticed since early treatment may prevent later complications. The primary treatment for most boils is heat application, usually with hot soaks or hot packs. Heat application increases the circulation to the area and allows the body to better fight off the infection by bringing antibodies and white blood cells to the site of infection. As long as the boil is small and firm, opening the area and draining the boil is not helpful, even if the area is painful. However, once the boil becomes soft it can be ready to drain.

Antibiotics are often used to eliminate the accompanying bacterial infection if there is an infection of the surrounding skin. However, antibiotics are not needed in every situation. In fact, antibiotics have difficulty penetrating the outer wall of an abscess well and often will not cure an abscess.

Any boil that is associated with a fever should receive medical attention. There are some measures that you can take to prevent boils from forming. The regular use of antibacterial soaps can help to prevent bacteria from building up on the skin. This can reduce the chance for the hair follicles becoming infected and prevent the formation of boils. When the hair follicles on the back of the arms or around the thighs are continually inflamed, regular use of an abrasive brush (loofah brush) in the shower can be used break up oil plugs that build up around hair follicles.

Colloidal Silver – is a natural antibiotic. Kills fungi, viruses and bacteria. Helps in healing.

Garlic – a natural antibiotic and immune enhancer.

Vitamin C – has antibacterial properties and helps build the immune system.

zinc – aids in healing and helps the immune system.

Flax – ground and made into a paste can be used as a compress.

Fenugreek – ground, mix with flax and add warm water to use as a hot compress.

Suma – boosts the immune system.

Tea Tree Oil – antiseptic and antibacterial.

Botulism

Did you know that you can be poisoned by food, especially food that wasn't cooked or preserved properly. Botulism is a serious kind of food poisoning, but fortunately it's also very rare. Only about 100 people get it every year in the United States.

Botulism can be caused by foods that were canned or preserved at home. Maybe you've had fruits or vegetables that someone picked from the garden in the summer and jarred so they could be eaten during the winter months. These foods need to be cooked at very high temperatures to kill the germs.

If food is not heated to a correct temperature, bacteria could cause botulism in the people who eat the food. You can't see, smell, or taste this bacteria, but it releases a poison, also called a toxin. This toxin travels through the blood to attach to the nerves that control muscles.

Many botulism cases occur in infants, and experts think that's because their digestive systems can't protect them from germs the way an older child's or an adult's digestive system can. Infant botulism can happen if a baby younger than 1 year eats honey, so it's important that babies don't eat honey until they're older.

Botulism stops the muscles from working, so a child with botulism needs medical care right away. Poison control center can be called twenty four hours a day and can help you with any information regarding poisoning. It is a good idea to always have the number close to the phone. Botulism is not the only way to get food poisoning. Salmonella is the most common type of food poisoning. Symptoms of food poisoning are nausea, vomiting, abdominal pain and diarrhea.

Prevention – wash your hands and make sure foods that are canned were heated properly to the correct temperature before serving to children. Also, do not give raw honey to babies.

Activated Charcoal – give at the first sign of illness. This will remove toxins from the colon and bloodstream. It will also help with upset stomach and diarrhea. You can get Activated Charcoal at any Health Food Store or Pharmacy. I always make sure I have plenty in the first aid kit as well as in the medicine cupboard.

Garlic – detoxes and kills bacteria in the colon.

Minerals – to replace the ones lost during diarrhea and to balance the electrolytes in the body.

Vitamin C – detoxes and helps in removing bacteria and toxins from the body.

Acidophilus – builds friendly flora and replaces important intestinal bacteria.

Fiber – removes bacteria from the colon walls so that they do not enter the bloodstream.

Kelp – high in minerals that are needed to restore electrolyte imbalance.

Hydration – is important if there has been vomiting and diarrhea. Add electrolytes that have been especially designed to rehydrate to water and sip.

Ipecac – useful for inducing vomiting that can help get toxins out of body quickly. You can get Ipecac at any drug store. Be sure you talk with Poison Control Center before giving to your child.

Bronchitis

Bronchitis is usually caused by viruses or bacteria and may last several days or weeks a condition that occurs when the inner walls that line the main air passageways of your lungs become infected and inflamed. Bronchitis often follows a respiratory infection such as a cold.

Most cases of acute bronchitis disappear within a few days without lasting effects, although coughs may linger for weeks. If you have repeated bouts of bronchitis, see your doctor. You may have a more serious health problem such as asthma or chronic bronchitis and that needs medical attention. Bronchitis is an inflammation of the lining of the bronchial tubes. This delicate, mucus producing lining covers and protects the respiratory system, the organs and tissues involved in breathing. When a child has bronchitis, it may be harder for air to pass in and out of the lungs than it normally would, the tissues become irritated and more mucus is produced. The most common symptom of bronchitis is a cough.

When you breathe in, small, bristly hairs near the openings of your nostrils filter out dust, pollen, and other airborne particles. Bits that slip through become attached to the mucus membrane, which has tiny, hair-like structures called cilia on its surface. But sometimes germs get through the cilia and other defense systems in the respiratory tract and can cause illness.

Acute bronchitis is usually caused by viruses, and it may occur together with or following a cold or other respiratory infection. Germs such as viruses can be spread from person to person by coughing. They can also be spread if you touch your mouth, nose, or eyes after coming into contact with respiratory fluids from an infected person.

Prevention - washing your hands often helps to prevent the spread of many of the germs that cause the condition, especially during cold and flu season.

Colloidal Silver – antiviral, antibacterial and helps in healing.

Quercetin – very good for allergic bronchitis and works like an antihistamine.

Vitamin C – immune builder, works like an antihistamine.

MSM – improves lung problems aids in healing of lungs.

Garlic – antiviral, antibacterial, detoxifier and natural antibiotic.

Chickweed – improves lung and bronchial congestion.

Elderberry – improves lung and bronchial congestion.

Mullein – improves lung and bronchial congestion.

Horehound – works as an expectorant.

Slippery Elm Bark – sooths a sore throat and helps with a cough.

Echinacea & Goldenseal – works as an immune builder, natural antibiotic, and helps to fight viruses, inflammation of the mucous membranes. Use goldenseal under your doctors care.

Calcium and Magnesium – relaxes muscles and helps with lung capacity.

Lobelia – soothes bronchial muscles and gets rid of excess mucus.

Mullein – helps congestion, coughs, and breathing.

Bruising

Children get bruises at the drop of a hat. They fall off their bikes, collide while they are skate boarding, playing sports, etc. We all recognize the black and blue marks of a bruise. A bruise is also called a contusion, and it forms because the soft tissues of your body have been bumped. Some people bruise easily, whereas others may have tougher skin tissue. When these soft tissues are injured, small veins and capillaries under the skin sometimes break. Then red blood cells leak out of these blood vessels.

These red blood cells that collect under your skin cause that bluish, purplish, reddish, or blackish mark. That's where black and blue marks get their name, from their color under the skin. When a child first gets hurt and it looks like a pretty good bruise is going to appear, try to get ice on the area to constrict blood vessels. This way it helps the bruise not get so large. At this point the bump will look red or purple and be tender. There will also be some swelling. After a couple of days, the bruise will look blue or even black and after five to ten days it will look greenish or yellow. From there the bruise will turn a light brown and then fade away.

Bruises go through color changes as the body begins to heal itself. The color changes mean that your body is metabolizing, or breaking down, the blood cells in the skin. This is the process that your body goes through to repair itself.

Diet – some children do not eat enough fresh fruits and vegetables to supply the body with needed nutrients and because of this they bruise easily. Vitamin C deficiencies can make the blood vessel walls very thin and delicate, causing them to rupture with even the slightest amount of bumping.

Arnica - helps prevent bruising.

Cal/Mag with D - protects the skin.

Ice - to help reduce swelling and pain. Sometimes I use a frozen bag of veggies. You just shake the bag up a little to loosen the veggies and apply. I have also used one part rubbing alcohol and two parts water and put it in a freezer baggie and pull it out of the freezer when I need it.

Vitamin and Mineral - is needed to correct chemical imbalances due to poor nutrition.

Vitamin C – is an important antioxidant that helps make you less susceptible to infections and it helps to prevent bruising by supplying oxygen to the injured cells.

Alfalfa – high in minerals and vitamin K, which helps with blood clotting and healing.

DMG Dimethylglycine – improves oxygen metabolism in the cells and tissues.

Comfrey salve – helps reduce swelling and pain and discoloration in the bruised area.

zinc – strengthens the blood vessel walls and aids in blood clotting.

Colloidal Silver – antiviral, antibacterial and helps in healing.

MSM – aids in healing.

Kelp – high in minerals and helps in healing.

Bruxism

Bruxism is the medical term for the grinding of teeth or the clenching of jaws, especially during deep sleep or while under stress. Three out of every 10 children will grind or clench, experts say, with the highest incidence in children under 5. Though studies have been done, no one knows why bruxism happens. But in some cases, children may grind because the top and bottom teeth aren't aligned properly. Others do it as a response to pain, such as an earache or teething. Children might grind their teeth as a way to ease the pain, just as they might rub a sore muscle. Most children outgrow these fairly common causes for grinding.

Usually nervous tension or anger, is another cause. For instance, your child may be worrying about a test at school or experiencing a change in routine. Even arguing with parents and siblings can cause enough stress to prompt teeth grinding or jaw clenching. Some children who are hyperactive also experience bruxism. Generally, bruxism doesn't hurt a child's teeth. Many cases go undetected with no adverse effects, though some may result in mild morning headaches or earaches. Most often, however, the condition can be more bothersome to you and others in your home because of the grinding sound. In some extreme circumstances, nighttime grinding and clenching can wear down tooth enamel, chip teeth, increase temperature sensitivity, and cause severe facial pain and jaw problems.

Lots of children who grind their teeth aren't even aware of it, so it's often siblings or parents who identify the problem. If you think your child is grinding his or her teeth, visit the dentist, who will examine the teeth for chipped enamel and unusual wear and tear, and spray air and water on the teeth to check for unusual sensitivity. Most children outgrow bruxism, but a combination of parental observation and dental visits can help keep the problem in check until they do.

In cases where the grinding and clenching make a child's face and jaw sore or damage the teeth, dentists may prescribe a special night guard. Molded to a child's teeth, the night guard is similar to the protective mouthpieces worn by football players. Though a mouthpiece may take some getting used to, positive results happen quickly. Whether the cause is physical or psychological, children might be able to control bruxism by relaxing before bedtime, for example, by taking a warm bath or shower, listening to a few minutes of soothing music, or reading a book. For bruxism that's caused by stress, try to find out what's upsetting your child and find a way to help. In rare cases, basic stress relievers aren't enough to stop bruxism. If your child has trouble sleeping or is acting differently than usual, your child's dentist or doctor may suggest a psychological assessment. This can help determine the cause of the stress and an appropriate course of treatment.

Childhood bruxism is usually outgrown by adolescence. Most children stop grinding when they lose their baby teeth because permanent teeth are much more sensitive to pain. However, a few children do continue to grind into adolescence. And if the bruxism is caused by stress, it will continue until the stress is relieved. Because some bruxism is a child's natural reaction to growth and development, most cases can't be prevented. Stress-induced bruxism can be avoided by talking with a child regularly about their feelings and helping them deal with stress.

Burns

We are talking about first degree burns in this chapter. Anything more severe you need to see your family doctor. First degree burn is usually a mild sunburn or when your child bumps fingers against hot pan, or a little hot chocolate gets spilled on your child. The area will be red and sensitive.

Some people get a sunburn faster than others because of their coloring. If you have blond or red hair, light-colored skin, and light-colored eyes, you'll tend to get a sunburn more quickly than someone with dark eyes and skin. That's because you have less melanin. Melanin is a chemical in the skin that protects the skin from sun damage by reflecting and absorbing UV rays. People with darker skin have more melanin, but even if you have dark hair, dark eyes, or darker-toned skin, you can still get a sunburn. It will just take a little bit longer.

Sunburns look bad and feel worse. They can cause blisters on your skin. They can keep you inside feeling sore when everyone else is outside having fun. They increase your chance of getting wrinkly when you get older. And worst of all, they can lead to skin cancer when you get older. Because getting wrinkles and getting sick don't happen right away, they can seem like things that could never happen to you. But you still need to be careful.

Use a sunscreen with an SPF rating of 15 or higher. Put on sunscreen 15 to 20 minutes before going out in the sun. If you are fair skinned, you should use a sunscreen with a higher SPF rating such as SPF 30. The letters SPF stand for sun protection factor, and the number rating tells you how much longer you can stay in the sun without getting sunburned. So if you normally burn after 20 minutes and you put on a sunscreen with an SPF rating of 15, this sunscreen may give you 15 times the protection. That's 15 times 20 minutes, or 300 minutes (5 hours).

But this isn't always true, so reapply sunscreen at least every 2 hours, just to be safe. Do this more often if your child has been swimming or sweating a lot - even if the sunscreen is waterproof. And remember that you can get sunburned more quickly when you're swimming or boating because the reflection from the water intensifies the sun's rays.

Water – it is important to replace fluids lost from sweating while exercising.

Aloe Vera - apply directly to burn. This helps in pain relief and speeds healing.

Colloidal Silver - a natural antibiotic that helps wounds heal quickly by applying to burn.

Garlic - Natural antibiotic and helps with tissue repair.

Beta Carotene – helps with skin repair.

B Complex - important for skin repair, cell repair and stress.

C with Bioflavonoids – is an antioxidant that helps in the formation of collagen and healing.

Cool water - It does help with the pain and cools the burn to apply cool water.

zinc – aids in healing and helps the immune system.

Flax – ground and made into a paste can be used as a compress.

Suma – boosts the immune system.

Callus

A callus is an area of thick skin. Calluses form at points where there is a lot of repeated pressure for a long period of time, such as the hours spent raking leaves. The skin hardens from the pressure over time and eventually thickens, forming a hard tough grayish or yellowish surface that may feel bumpy.

Calluses can be a form of protection for the hands. Gymnasts who perform on uneven parallel bars and other apparatus often get calluses on their hands, which take a lot of abuse. Guitar players also get calluses on their fingers from manipulating the strings. Once formed, calluses may make it easier for the person to swing around the bars or play the guitar.

Calluses on the feet, however, can be painful because you have to step on them all the time. They usually form on the ball of the foot. The ball is the roundish part on the bottom of your foot, just behind your big toe. Some calluses also form on the outside of the big or little toe or the heel. Tight shoes often cause calluses because they put a lot of pressure on your feet at points that aren't used to all of that stress.

To keep feet callus free, choose shoes wisely. Even if they look really cool, don't get them if they don't feel right. Often, a different size or width can make a big difference. If any skin gets red, inflamed, or looks infected, you will want to check with your doctor. But more often blisters, calluses, and corns can be cared for at home.

Pumice Stone – has a rough surface and can be used to rub dead skin off after soaking the callus in warm, soapy water for about ten minutes or longer.

Vitamin and Mineral - is needed to correct chemical imbalances due to poor nutrition.

Vitamin C – is an important antioxidant that helps make you less susceptible to infections.

Colloidal Silver – is a natural antibiotic. Kills fungi, viruses and bacteria. Helps in healing. Soak callus in a mixture of one part Colloidal Silver five parts warm water for ten or more minutes and then rub callus with a pumice stone.

Garlic – a natural antibiotic and immune enhancer.

Beta Carotene – helps with skin repair.

B Complex - important for skin repair, cell repair and stress.

Essential fatty acids – helps the skin to heal.

Vitamin and Mineral - is needed to correct chemical imbalances due to poor nutrition.

C with Bioflavonoids – is an antioxidant that helps in the formation of collagen and healing.

Vitamin E - 400 IU cut open and apply directly to the callus and cover with gauze.

Zinc - 50mg a day speeds healing.

Astragalus – builds the immune system and has antiviral and antibacterial properties.

Aloe Vera - applied directly 3 - 4 times a day and then cover with a band aid will soften a callus.

Tea Tree Oil – placed directly on a callus and then covered with gauze.

Cancer

Cancer is a scary word. Almost everyone knows someone who got very sick or died from cancer. I have had my share of family members who have fought cancer. Most of the time, cancer affects older people. Not many children get cancer, but when they do, very often it can be treated and cured. Cancer is actually a group of many related diseases that all have to do with cells. Cells are the very small units that make up all living things, including the human body. There are billions of cells in each person's body.

Cancer happens when cells that are not normal grow and spread very fast. Normal body cells grow and divide and know to stop growing. Over time, they also die. Unlike these normal cells, cancer cells just continue to grow and divide out of control and don't die. Cancer cells usually group or clump together to form tumors. A growing tumor becomes a lump of cancer cells that can destroy the normal cells around the tumor and damage the body's healthy tissues. This can make someone very sick. Sometimes cancer cells break away from the original tumor and travel to other areas of the body, where they keep growing and can go on to form new tumors. This is how cancer spreads. The spread of a tumor to a new place in the body is called metastasis.

A tumor can be either benign or malignant. Benign tumors are not cancerous. They can appear anywhere in the body and usually do not pose a threat to your child's health. They also do not metastasize or spread to other parts of the body. Nor do they grow back after they have been removed. Malignant tumors are cancerous and they are usually serious and can be life threatening because they grow out of control and invade other tissues.

It can take a while for a doctor to figure out if a child has cancer, because the symptoms of cancer can cause weight loss, fevers, swollen glands, or feeling overly tired or just feeling sick. These symptoms can be symptoms of so many other illnesses. When a child has these problems, it's often cased by something less serious, like an infection. With medical testing, the doctor can figure out what's causing the trouble. Tests can determine what kind of cancer it is and if it has spread to other parts of the body. Based on the results, the doctor will decide the best way to treat it. The sooner cancer is found and treatment begins, the better someone's chances are for a full recovery and cure.

No one really knows exactly what causes the cell damage that starts the cancer process. Some believe it could be genetic, environmental toxins, lifestyle, diet, parasite infestation, etc., that turn normal cells into abnormal cells that become cancerous. What we do know is that there are many things that we can do to lower the risk of getting cancer such as changing diet, exclude exposure to cigarette smoke, and limit time of sun exposure, to name a few.

Cancer is treated with surgery, chemotherapy, radiation, alternative medicines, or sometimes a combination of these treatments. The choice of treatment depends on the type of cancer someone has and the kind of abnormal cells causing the cancer, and the stage of the tumor, meaning, how much the cancer has spread within the body, if at all. There are many alternative treatments also and there are some special Hospitals that combine traditional along with alternative treatments with great results.

Cancer – Continued

Surgery - is the oldest form of treatment for cancer. Three out of every five people with cancer will have an operation to remove the cancer. During surgery, the doctor tries to take out as many cancer cells as possible. Some healthy cells or tissue may also be removed to make sure that all the cancer is gone.

Chemotherapy - is the use of anti-cancer medicines or drugs to treat cancer. These medicines are sometimes taken as a pill, but are usually given through a special intravenous line, also called an IV. An IV is a tiny catheter, a straw like tube that is put into a vein through someone's skin, usually on the arm. The catheter is attached to a bag that holds the medicine. The medicine flows from the bag into a vein, which puts the medicine into the blood, where it can travel throughout the body and attack cancer cells. Chemotherapy is usually given over a number of weeks to months. Often, a permanent catheter is placed under the skin into a larger blood vessel of the upper chest. This way, a person can easily get several courses of chemotherapy and other medicines through this catheter without having a new IV needle put in. The catheter remains under the skin until all the cancer treatment is completed.

Radiation - therapy uses high energy waves, such as X-rays which are invisible waves that can pass through most parts of the body, to damage and destroy cancer cells. It can cause tumors to shrink and even go away completely. Radiation therapy is one of the most common treatments for cancer.

With both chemotherapy and radiation, children may experience side effects. A side effect is an extra problem that's caused by the treatment. Radiation and anticancer drugs are very good at destroying cancer cells, but unfortunately they also destroy healthy cells. This can cause problems such as loss of appetite, tiredness, vomiting, or hair loss. With radiation, a person might have red or irritated skin in the area that's being treated. But all these problems go away and hair grows back after the treatment is over. During the treatment, there are medicines that can help a child feel better along with quality nutritional supplements.

While treatment is still going on, a child might not be able to attend school or be around crowds of people. The child needs to rest and can't risk getting infections, such as the flu, when he or she already isn't feeling well. It is important to keep the immune system as strong as possible at this point. Remission is a great word for anyone who has cancer. It means all signs of cancer are gone from the body. After surgery or treatment with radiation or chemotherapy, a doctor will then do tests to see if the cancer is still there. If there are no signs of cancer, then the child is in remission.

Remission is the goal when any child with cancer goes to the hospital for treatment. Sometimes, this means additional chemotherapy might be needed for a while to keep cancer cells from coming back. And luckily, for many children, continued remission is the very happy end of their cancer experience.

Essiac – is an Ojibwa (Native American) herbal blend that is used for cancer. It has sheep sorrel, burdock root, slippery elm bark, and turkey rhubarb root in it. There are many books about Essiac on the market and they are very informational about cancer. I use Essiac with my family, because I feel it is a very good immune builder and the children seem to not get colds, etc. while they are drinking it.

Cancer – Continued Types

Leukemia - is the most common type of cancer Children get, but it is still very rare. Leukemia involves the blood and blood forming organs, such as the bone marrow. Bone marrow is the innermost part of some bones where blood cells are first made. A child with leukemia produces lots of abnormal white blood cells in the bone marrow. White blood cells fight infection, but the white blood cells in a person with leukemia don't work the way they're supposed to. Instead of protecting the person, these abnormal white blood cells multiply out of control. They fill up the bone marrow and make it hard for enough normal, infection-fighting white blood cells to form. Other blood cells such as red blood cells which carry oxygen in the blood to the body's tissues and platelets that allow blood to clot also get crowded out by the white blood cells of leukemia. These cancer cells may move to other parts of the body, including the bloodstream, liver, spleen, and lymph nodes. In those areas, cancer cells can continue to multiply and build up.

A brain tumor - is a group or clump of abnormally growing cells that can be found in or on the brain. They're rare in children. Of the more than 73 million children and teens in the United States, about 3,100 are diagnosed with brain tumors every year. Brain tumors can either start in the brain or spread there from another part of the body. Some cancers that start in other parts of the body may have cells that travel to the brain and start growing there. When cancer starts in another part of the body and then is found in the bones or brain then this is known as a secondary cancer.

Lymphoma - is a general term for a group of cancers that start in the body's lymphatic system. The lymphatic system is made of hundreds of bean-size lymph nodes, also sometimes called glands, that work to fight off germs or other foreign invaders in the body. Lymph nodes are found throughout the body. When we get colds or the flu, we can sometimes feel our lymph nodes along the front of the neck or under the jaw. That's because when the body is fighting off these germs, the lymph nodes grow larger. The spleen, an organ in your stomach that filters blood, and the thymus, a gland in the upper chest, are also parts of the lymphatic system. Lymphoma happens when a lymphocyte, a type of white blood cell, begins to multiply and crowd out healthy cells. The cancerous lymphocytes create tumors, masses or lumps of cancer cells that enlarge the lymph nodes.

Carcinomas – are cancers that affect the skin, mucous membranes, glands, and internal organs.

Sarcomas – are cancers that affect muscles, connective tissue and bones.

These are just a few out of the hundred or so varieties of cancer. But cancer is cancer. According to some studies I have read, 1 out of 2 people will get cancer in their lifetime. That is just crazy. There are so many elements people have to deal with when dealing with cancer. You have genetic, behavioral, diet, environmental exposure to toxins, and lifestyle can possibly turn healthy cells to abnormal ones that start to divide out of control. Studies show that the highest amounts of cancer are caused by diet and lifestyle. This is bad news and good news. Bad news in that we take care of ourselves very badly and good news is that we can change our diet and lifestyle and have some control over our health and well being. Diet and prevention are very important in our fight against cancer.

Cancer - Supplementation

Now that we know that when we keep our bodies healthy, and avoid known cancer causing agents, we have a good defense against cancer. But if there is cancer, then it is very important to stay in the best health you can possibly be in and take supplements to keep the immune system strong.

Colostrum – is an immune system builder and speeds healing.

CoQ10 – is a strong antioxidant, puts oxygen into the body, has anticancer properties.

Garlic – is an immune builder, antiviral, antibacterial, anti-parasite, and anticancer properties.

IP6 (Inositol hexaphos phate) – increases natural killer cell activity and anticancer properties.

MSM – helps prevent cancer.

Shark cartilage – inhibits and reverses the growth of some types of tumors, especially those in the brain and it stimulates the immune system.

Beta-1, 6-glucan – a powerful immune builder that stops the growth of cancerous tumors.

Acidophilus - builds friendly flora and replaces important intestinal bacteria.

Flaxseed – is an antioxidant that protects the body from cancer and prevents the spread of cancerous cells.

Grape seed extract – is a strong antioxidant.

Multivitamin and mineral complex – very important for normal cell division. Use a whole food supplement.

B Complex - important for skin repair, cell repair and stress.

Astragalus – is a cancer fighter and immune booster. It increases your bodies natural killer cell activity.

Cat's Claw – is anti-tumor and strengthens the immune system.

Green tea – has cancer fighting properties and contains a compound that has been found to cut off blood vessels that feed cancerous tumors.

Essiac – is an Ojibwa (Native American) herbal blend that is used for cancer. It has sheep sorrel, burdock root, slippery elm bark, and turkey rhubarb root in it. There are many books about Essiac on the market and they are very informational about cancer. I use Essiac with my family, because I feel it is a very good immune builder and the children seem to not get colds, etc. while they are taking it.

Rosemary – antioxidant, anti-inflammatory and cancer fighting properties.

Diet - Nothing with dyes, preservatives, sugar, or processed. If it came in a box, we didn't get it. Lots of fruit, vegetables, whole grains, fish, salmon, herbal ice teas in place of fruit juices and soda. Sometimes we sweetened the tea with stevia, which is a plant sweetener that is good for blood sugar and has zero calories. We made a rinse with food grade hydrogen peroxide and water and rinsed all fruits and veggies to get rid of pesticide residue and bacteria.

Candida

(yeast)

Most of us have seen the white pasty looking tongue of an infant. This is known as thrush. Yeast which is a fungus overgrowth can also be in the form of a diaper rash, athlete's foot, and jock itch. Oral thrush in a baby usually spreads to the mother during nursing. Some of the symptoms of Candida (yeast) are rash, itching, and burning.

Lots of children get fungal infections. Children love to share and hang out together. Some fungal infections are contagious, which means they easily spread from person to person. Close contact or sharing a comb or hairbrush with someone who has a fungal infection can spread the fungus from one person to another. Because fungi need a warm, dark, and humid place to grow, public showers, pools, locker rooms, and even the warmth of shoes and socks can give fungi the perfect opportunity to strike. Some of the symptoms of this kind of yeast overgrowth are digestive upsets, constipation, diarrhea, fatigue, mood swings, muscle pain, canker sores, headaches, and depression.

Taking antibiotics can cause some children to get a yeast infection. Antibiotics get rid of germs that make us sick, but they can also kill many of the harmless bacteria in our body. These harmless bacteria normally fight with the yeast for a place to live, but when antibiotics kill them, the yeast is free to grow. Yeast thrives on sugar, so if your diet is high in processed, refined sugar, and low nutritional value, you could end up with a yeast overgrowth in no time at all. It usually takes a few weeks to clear up a yeast overgrowth. Here are some things that have help my family.

Acidophilus - builds friendly flora and replaces important intestinal bacteria.

Caprylic acid - is an antifungal and kills candida fungus.

Garlic - a natural antibiotic and immune enhancer. Garlic has antifungal properties.

Colloidal Silver - is soothing and helps healing.

Grapefruit seed extract - Rids the body of harmful micro organisms.

Colostrum - A very strong immune builder.

Yogurt - Live active cultures help build the friendly flora in the body.

Diet - should be low in sugar since Candida/Yeast grows quickly when you consume junk food. Nothing with dyes, preservatives, processed or sugar.

Aloe vera – helps the white blood cells to kill yeast cells and helps remove them from the body.

Cinnamon – helps with thrush.

Lavender – helps get rid of yeast infections on the skin, such as athlete's foot, etc.

Tea Tree Oil – helps get rid of yeast infections on the skin and has antifungal properties.

Oregano – is a strong antifungal.

Canker sores

Canker sores are small, round, white sores on the inside of the mouth. It is usually white or yellow with a red border surrounding it. A canker sore usually burns especially if you eat something acidic like orange juice. A canker sore may spring up if a person's diet doesn't contain enough vitamins and minerals. The inside of your mouth is delicate, so mouth injuries, such as biting the inside of your lip or brushing your teeth too hard, also seem to bring on canker sores. But anybody can get a canker sore and it is usually not something to be to concerned about. A canker sore will usually go away on its own and it is not contagious.

Most canker sores don't hurt as much after the first few days, but it may take 2 weeks for the sore to heal. While you're waiting, you'll want to be careful when eating and brushing your teeth. Scraping the sore can make it hurt worse. If your canker sore is large, lasts longer than a week, or is keeping you from eating, you should see your doctor so he or she can check it out. There's no guaranteed way to prevent canker sores, but it's a good idea to eat healthy and get enough sleep.

Salt water rinse – add enough sea salt to water to make a saline solution. Then rinse mouth several times a day.

Acidophilus - is an active good bacteria found in the intestinal track which increases the good flora and promotes a healthy immune system. It can also help prevent and clear up canker sores. If there is thrush, you can swab the mouth with acidophilus and this helps the sore go away faster.

L Lysine - is an amino acid. By adding lysine, you will decrease the out breaks of sores in and Around the mouth.

B Complex - immune function, stress, and cell repair. Canker sores have been linked to a deficiency of B vitamins.

C with Bioflavonoids - Builds immune system and fights infection.

Tea Tree oil - Anti Viral and Anti bacterial. Add a couple of drops to your saline solution and rinse and spit out.

Wintergreen oil – add a couple of drops to your saline solution and rinse and spit out.

Yogurt / Kefir - is high in active good bacteria found in the intestinal track which increases the good flora and promotes a healthy immune system.

Myrrh oil – this stops soreness and helps with any swelling. Just add a couple of drops to your saline solution, rinse and spit.

Quercetin – helps with inflammation.

Multivitamin and mineral complex - is needed to correct chemical imbalances due to poor nutrition.

Diet – a lot of people with celiac disease, which mean they are allergic to the gluten in grains, have a higher rate of canker sores. By eliminating gluten from the diet seems to eliminate canker sores from returning. So if you are getting high rates of canker sores, it may not be a bad idea to get tested for allergies to wheat and other grains.

Celiac Disease

Celiac disease is a digestive disease that damages the small intestine and interferes with absorption of nutrients from food. People who have celiac disease cannot tolerate a protein called gluten, found in wheat, rye, and barley. Gluten is found mainly in foods but may also be found in products we use every day, such as stamp and envelope adhesive, medicines, and vitamins.

When children with celiac disease eat foods or use products containing gluten, their immune system responds by damaging the small intestine. The tiny, finger like protrusions lining the small intestine are damaged or destroyed. Called villi, they normally allow nutrients from food to be absorbed into the bloodstream. Without healthy villi, a child becomes malnourished, regardless of the quantity of food eaten. Because the body's own immune system causes the damage, celiac disease is considered an autoimmune disorder. However, it is also classified as a disease of malabsorption because nutrients are not absorbed.

Celiac disease affects children differently. Symptoms may occur in the digestive system, or in other parts of the body. For example, one child might have diarrhea and abdominal pain, while another child may be irritable or depressed. In fact, irritability is one of the most common symptoms in children. Many children are diagnosed with the problem between 6 months and 2 years of age. It makes sense because, at this time, children are getting their first taste of gluten in foods.

Anemia, delayed growth, and weight loss are signs of malnutrition. The body is just not getting enough nutrients. Malnutrition is a serious problem for children because they need adequate nutrition to develop properly. Recognizing celiac disease can be difficult because some of its symptoms are similar to those of other diseases.

Diet - The only treatment for celiac disease is to follow a gluten-free diet. This can be difficult because gluten is in many foods. It is important not to start a gluten-free diet unless you are truly diagnosed with celiac disease. Someone with celiac disease needs to learn how to read ingredient lists and identify foods that contain gluten in order to make informed decisions at the grocery store and when eating out. For most people, following this diet will stop symptoms, heal existing intestinal damage, and prevent further damage. Improvements begin within days of starting a gluten free diet. The small intestine is usually completely healed in 3 to 6 months in children and younger adults.

Quercetin – helps with allergies and inflammation.

Omega-3 Fatty Acids - are anti-inflammatory.

There are many companies out there that make gluten free mixes. You can get bread mixes, cookie mixes, and a whole variety of other mixes. Nearly all of the foods we eat can be made gluten-free. There are also many support groups for people with celiac that can help with recipes, new up to date information, and a great place to meet other children with celiac. In addition to foods that contain gluten, you'll need to watch out for foods that may have been contaminated with gluten. That means a food that doesn't contain gluten as an ingredient, but came into contact with gluten containing foods. This is most likely to occur at home in your own kitchen. For instance, wheat bread crumbs in the toaster, butter, or peanut butter.

Cerebral palsy

Cerebral palsy is a condition that affects thousands of babies and children each year. It is not contagious, which means you can't catch it from anyone who has it. The word cerebral means having to do with the brain. The word palsy means a weakness or problem in the way a person moves or positions his or her body. A child with CP has trouble controlling the muscles of the body. Normally, the brain tells the rest of the body exactly what to do and when to do it. But because CP affects the brain, depending on what part of the brain is affected, a child might not be able to walk, talk, eat, or play the way most children do. There are three types of cerebral palsy, spastic, athetoid, and ataxic. The most common type of cerebral palsy is spastic. A child with spastic CP can't relax his or her muscles or the muscles may be stiff. Athetoid CP affects a child's ability to control the muscles of the body. This means that the arms or legs that are affected by athetoid CP may flutter and move suddenly. A child with ataxic CP has problems with balance and coordination.

A child with CP can have a mild case or a more severe case, it really depends on how much of the brain is affected and which parts of the body that section of the brain controls. If both arms and both legs are affected, a child might need to use a wheelchair. If only the legs are affected, a child might walk in an unsteady way or have to wear braces or use crutches. If the part of the brain that controls speech is affected, a child with CP might have trouble talking clearly. Another child with CP might not be able to speak at all.

No one knows for sure what causes most cases of cerebral palsy. For some babies, injuries to the brain during pregnancy or soon after birth may cause CP. Children most at risk of developing CP are small, premature babies and babies who need to be on a ventilator for several weeks or longer. But for most children with CP, the problem in the brain occurs before birth and doctors don't know why. Doctors who specialize in treating children with problems of the brain, nerves, or muscles are usually involved in diagnosing a child with cerebral palsy. These specialists could include a pediatric neurologist, a doctor who deals with problems of the nervous system and brain in children.

A case of cerebral palsy often can be diagnosed by the age of 18 months. For example, if a child does not sit up or walk by the time most children should be doing these things, the child might have CP or some other problem that is causing development to go more slowly. Doctors follow infant and child development closely and look for problems with muscle tone and strength, movement, and reflexes. For a child with CP, the problem with the brain will not get any worse as the child gets older. Children with CP usually have physical, occupational, or speech therapy to help them develop skills like walking, sitting, swallowing, and using their hands. There are also medications to treat the seizures that some children with CP have. Some medications can help relax the muscles in children with spastic CP. And some children with CP may have special surgeries to keep their arms or legs straighter and more flexible.

Children with cerebral palsy are just like other children, but with some greater challenges that make it harder to do everyday things. More than anything else, they want to fit in and be liked. Be patient if you know someone or meet someone with CP. If you can't understand what a person with CP is saying or if it takes a person with CP longer to do things, give him or her extra time to speak or move.

Chemical Poisoning

Children shouldn't work with poisons, chemicals, or fertilizers. But how do you know if something is dangerous to touch? The label may say "caution," "poison," or "danger" and some of these chemicals are toxic or poisonous.

Teach children to stay away from areas where these dangerous substances are stored and never open the containers. If they have easy access to them, you might want to store them somewhere else or lock them up, where little hands can't reach them. Some times no matter how hard you try, a child will still find a way to get into these things. Be sure to always have the **Poison Control** number at your fingertips. It is also a good idea to keep ipecac syrup in the medicine cabinet as long as there are young children in the home. I have had my share over the last 30 plus years of children drinking or tasting stuff they were not suppose to be getting into, no matter how high up they were put, and ipecac has come in pretty handy at these times. Always talk with the Poison Control Center first before giving ipecac to your child.

Some of us live close to farms and visit them often. Manure is often used on farms as fertilizer for the soil. Although many people consider it to be safer than chemical fertilizers, in large quantities and in enclosed spaces, manure can produce deadly gases. Children shouldn't work with manure or be around manure pits or storage areas because this can make some children pretty sick.

Ipecac – useful for inducing vomiting that can help get toxins out of body quickly. You can get Ipecac at any drug store. Be sure you talk with Poison Control Center before giving to your child.

Activated Charcoal – give at the first sign of illness. This will remove toxins from the colon and bloodstream. It will also help with upset stomach and diarrhea. You can get Activated Charcoal at any Health Food Store or Pharmacy. I always make sure I have plenty in the first aid kit as well as in the medicine cupboard.

Garlic – detoxes and kills bacteria in the colon and cleanses the bloodstream.

Minerals – to replace the ones lost during diarrhea and to balance the electrolytes in the body.

Vitamin C – detoxes and helps in removing bacteria and toxins from the body.

Acidophilus – builds friendly flora and replaces important intestinal bacteria.

Fiber – removes bacteria and toxins from the colon walls so that they do not enter the bloodstream.

Kelp – high in minerals that are needed to restore electrolyte imbalance.

Hydration – is important if there has been vomiting and diarrhea. Add electrolytes that have been especially designed to rehydrate to water and sip.

Grape seed extract – is a strong antioxidant and works as a free radical scavenger to protect body cells from damage.

Diet – avoid foods that have been sprayed with pesticides, added dyes, and supplements with petroleum, to name a few.

Chicken Pox

Chicken pox is a type of Virus. There is usually an itchy rash with fluid filled blisters. Chicken pox is spread by direct contact with an infected person or when the person with chicken pox coughs or sneezes. Most of our children have had chicken pox and have done their fair share of spreading it before we knew they had it. Someone who has chickenpox is most contagious during the first 2 to 5 days that he or she is sick. That's usually about 1 to 2 days before the rash shows up. So you could be spreading chickenpox without even knowing it. Now they have an immunization to prevent your child from getting it. I have talked to a few people who said their children have gotten Chicken pox any way but it wasn't as severe as if they wouldn't have gotten the vaccine and one of my sons got Chickenpox twice.

It is important not to pick at the blister or scratch the rash. This way you minimize scaring and possible infection. The blisters and scabs are contagious. Once the blisters and scabs are gone the child is no longer contagious. It usually takes about 2 weeks for the chicken pox to clear up. It is important to keep your child isolated. It also helps to dim the lights in the room, since bright lights seems to hurt their eyes while they are broke out. We do not give our children aspirin at this time since their immune systems are down and we are concerned about Reye Syndrome, which is a rare disease that can be fatal in young children.

Chickenpox may start out seeming like a cold and a child might have a runny or stuffy nose, sneezing, and a cough. But 1 to 2 days later, the rash appears, often in bunches of spots on the chest and face. From there it can spread out quickly over the entire body and sometimes the rash is even in a person's ears and mouth. The number of pox is different for everyone. Some people get just a few bumps, others are covered from head to toe.

Beta Carotene - very good for the immune system and repairs tissue damage.

Vitamin E – is a free radical scavenger and promotes healing. Make sure you use a food grade supplement and not one with petroleum in it. You want it to say d-alpha-tocopherol.

Goldenseal - Anti viral and anti bacterial. We have put the tea in a bath along with oatmeal and Soaked the child in it.

Calamine Lotion – is very soothing when applied to the rash and helps with itching.

Tea Tree oil - antibacterial and antiviral.

Vitamin C with bioflavonoid – builds the immune system.

Multivitamin and mineral complex – all nutrients are need for proper body function and healing.

Catnip tea – is good for fever.

Baths – add uncooked oatmeal to the water to help stop itching.

Antiviral medication – you can receive an antiviral medication from your doctor to shorten the duration of chickenpox.

Aloe Vera – is antiviral and is very soothing when smoothed over the rash.

Cold

A cold is an infection of the upper respiratory system. This just means it affects the nose, throat, and ears. There are over 200 viruses that cause colds. The rhinovirus is the most common cold virus. Because there are so many, there isn't a vaccination, or shot, to prevent you from getting colds. The immune system defends your body against illness. White blood cells are the immune system's main warriors. They're your own private army working to help you feel better. White blood cells charge to the nose's rescue and cause cold symptoms, while also killing the virus that caused the cold. Runny noses and sneezing actually help to prevent viruses from invading other parts of your body.

When someone sneezes or coughs, mucus drops float in the air. Breathing in these droplets can spread a cold from one person to another. You can also catch a cold if you touch your eyes or nose after handling something with cold viruses on it. Video games, the doors at the mall, and your school desk are all hot spots for viruses.

Symptoms are signs or clues that tell you that your sick. Some of the symptoms of a cold are sore throat, headache, nasal congestion, coughing, watery eyes, running noses, low grade fever, and sneezing. Once you've been in contact with a cold virus, it takes 2 to 3 days for cold symptoms to begin. Hot drinks soothe coughs and sore throats while also clearing mucus. Also a humidifier will help with a stuffy nose. Antibiotics will not help a cold because they do not work on viruses. It is important to wash hand frequently during cold and flu season.

Propolis – helps get rid of a sore throat. Get the liquid form and drizzle it down the back of the throat and gargle.

Echinacea – helps speed recovery.

Fenugreek tea – helps get rid of mucus.

Eucalyptus – helps relieve congestion. Add a few drops to a humidifier.

zinc – helps to speed healing and helps with infections.

Vitamin C – is antiviral, shortens the life of a cold, and helps build the immune system.

Chicken soup – seems to help a cold and my kids love it.

Colostrum – is an immune system builder and speeds healing.

Garlic – is an immune builder and antiviral.

Multivitamin and mineral complex – very important for normal immune system function. Use a whole food supplement.

B Complex - important for cell repair, immune system, and stress.

Homeopathy is based on the theory of "like cures like." I like homeopathic medicines because they do not have harmful side effects. The kids do not get drowsy or act spacey. A few favorites we have used for colds are **Apis mellifica**, **Rhus toxicodendron** and **Pulsatilla** (the last one mentioned has stopped a runny nose very quickly).

Acidophilus - is an active good bacteria found in the intestinal track which increases the good flora and promotes a healthy immune system.

Cold Sores

A cold sore is a small blister that is reddish or purple. They are usually on the outer edge of the lip, on just one side. Cold sores can appear one at a time or in little bunches, and they are sometimes filled with fluid. They usually crust over and form a scab before they go away. They last a week or 2 and usually don't require any special treatment Although they're called cold sores, you don't need to have a cold to get one. Some people call them fever blisters, but you don't have to have a fever to have one, either. Cold sores are caused by a virus called herpes. Herpes is one of the most common viral infections in the world. HSV-1 (herpes virus) is so common that most Americans get infected with it, although many never have any symptoms. People can catch HSV-1 by kissing a person with a cold sore or sharing a drinking glass or utensils, so it's easy to see why there are so many cold sores around.

Children who get infected with HSV-1 may get cold sores occasionally for the rest of their lives. That's because even after the sores themselves dry up and go away, the virus stays in the body, waiting around for another time to come out and cause more sores. When a cold sore reappears, it is often in the same place as the previous one.

If you've had cold sores before, it can be hard to tell what might make them come back. For some children, too much stress, too much time in the sun, or getting sick can cause cold sores to reappear. Eating well, getting enough rest, and learning how to deal with stress are important things for any child to do, especially a child who is likely to get cold sores. Putting on sunblock lip balm and sunscreen on the face before going out in the sun may help prevent cold sores from reappearing in children who tend to get them.

For most children, the sores go away on their own without any special treatment from a doctor. While you're waiting for the cold sore to go away, wash your hands regularly and don't pick at it. Picking at a cold sore can spread the virus to other parts or your body, like your fingers or eyes. Worse yet, you might spread the virus to other people. Cold sores are contagious. As soon as swelling and or redness appears, put tea tree oil on a cotton swab and apply it to the cold sore. If you repeat this through out the day, cold sore is usually gone within 24 hours.

Black tea bag - Put a few drops of water so that tea bag is wet. Then put it in a microwave for a couple of seconds until very warm. Then apply it to the cold sore until the tea bag cools and then reheat and apply again until swelling is reduced. This will draw out the toxins.

L Lysine - fights the herpes virus

B Complex - Builds the immune system, cell repair and stress.

zinc - needed for immune function.

Acidophilus - is an active good bacteria found in the intestinal track which increases the good flora and promotes a healthy immune system.

Colloidal Silver - a natural antibiotic that helps wounds heal quickly by applying to burn.

Tea Tree Oil - antibacterial and antiviral.

Garlic – antibacterial and antiviral.

Concussion

A concussion is a temporary change in the way the brain works when it is suddenly moved or jarred in this way. The brain is made up of soft tissue and it's cushioned by blood and spinal fluid. When someone gets a blow to the head or hits something very hard, the brain suddenly shifts inside the skull and can knock against the skull's bony surface. Sometimes this can happen with a lot of force.

Sometimes, concussions last just a few moments. Other times, a person can be unconscious for a couple of minutes or longer. But even concussions that seem to last just a few moments can be serious.

Every year, more than 400,000 children are sent to the emergency department for serious brain injuries. Injuries from car crashes, playgrounds, or sports are the most common ways that children get concussions. Most of the time, after a mild head injury, people return to normal even if the injury caused a concussion. But getting more than one concussion can lead to more serious problems. You may have heard of football players and boxers who have medical problems because of repeated concussions.

Severe concussions can happen after a bad blow to the head, like from a bad bike accident or a car crash. A severe concussion is a medical emergency. The person will need to go to the hospital right away. If the brain is seriously injured, someone could have long-lasting problems with movement, learning, or speaking. Most people who have a concussion will feel groggy and dazed for at least a little while. They may feel like they are in a fog. They may be shaky or dizzy if they try to walk or do normal activities right away. Some people feel nauseated or may even throw up right after a concussion. Many people will have a mild headache that lasts for a few days or longer. Sometimes, with a severe concussion, there may be bleeding inside of the head or bruising of the delicate brain.

Anyone with a head injury, especially children, should get checked by a doctor. Someone who is knocked unconscious should get immediate care in the emergency department as soon as possible. Here are some things that may help after being checked out by your family doctor.

DLPA – DL Phenylalanine – is in the amino acid family and helps with pain relief. Take under supervision of your doctor.

5-HTP – 5-Hydroxy L-tryptophan – helps with headache pain.

Glucosamine Sulfate – is an alternative to aspirin and an anti inflammatory.

MSM Methylsulfonyl-methane – helps relieve pain.

Primrose oil – helps with inflammation and relieves pain.

B complex – aids in the workings of the nervous system and reduces swelling by removing excess fluid from the body.

Ginger – helps relieve pain.

Lavender – using lavender as an aromatherapy and smelling it has been know to relieve headaches.

Conjunctivitis

Conjunctivitis is the most common eye problem children can have. It can cause redness, itching, inflammation or swelling, and a clear or white, yellow, or greenish gooey liquid to collect in the eyes. It's called pinkeye because the white part of the eye and inside the eyelids become red or pink when you have it. Pinkeye may start in one eye, but many children get conjunctivitis in both eyes at the same time. Conjunctivitis usually doesn't hurt, but itching can be annoying. Sometimes it feels like you have an eyelash or a speck of sand in your eye and can't get it out.

Children get conjunctivitis for different reasons. Most children get it from bacteria or viruses. This is called infectious conjunctivitis. Bacteria can be seen only with a powerful microscope, and viruses are even smaller than bacteria. Bacteria live on your skin or in your nose or mouth all the time and you never know it. Most don't ever bother you, but certain kinds of bacteria can cause infections like conjunctivitis.

Sometimes children get ear infections when they have conjunctivitis because the same bacteria can cause both problems. Viruses, like the kind that can give you a cold, can cause conjunctivitis, too. Conjunctivitis is easy to catch just through touching. You can get conjunctivitis by touching the hand of an infected friend who has touched his or her eyes. If you then touch your eyes, the infection can be spread to you. Washing your hands often with warm, soapy water is the best way to avoid being infected with conjunctivitis.

Children can get conjunctivitis because of allergies or because they get something irritating in their eyes, but these kinds of conjunctivitis are not contagious. If your child has conjunctivitis caused by bacteria, the doctor will probably prescribe antibiotic eye drops or ointment. Babies are usually given the ointment and children and adults get the eye drops. Try not to touch the eyes and remember to wash hands often. These two things will help keep pinkeye from spreading to friends and family members. I have made an eyewash using a cup of diluted eyebright tea and a pinch of sea salt and it worked quickly in clearing up pink eye.

Vitamin A – helps to speed healing in viral conjunctivitis.

Vitamin C with bioflavonoids – helps with inflammation and healing.

zinc – speeds healing.

Eyebright tea – make a compress or eyewash and apply to eyes. Helps with eye irritation and inflammation.

Goldenseal tea – can be used in place of eyebright tea for an eyewash. It also is antibacterial and antiviral.

Compresses – make warm compresses and apply to eyes because the microorganism that cause conjunctivitis cannot survive the heat. This will also help clear away the gunk that collects in the eyes and help them to open better.

Multivitamin and mineral complex – all nutrients are needed in balance.

L-Lysine – antiviral properties.

Constipation

Most children experience constipation at one time or another. Constipation is when a child has difficulty passing stool. Usually changing the diet helps. Adding extra water during the day is helpful also. Add more fiber rich foods. Fiber rich foods are fruits, veggies and whole grains like oats, brown rice and beans. Sometimes babies become constipated because of extra iron added to the baby's formula. Medicines such as cough syrup with codeine can cause constipation. Some signs of constipation include bad breath, headaches, gas, upset stomach, etc. Toxic buildup in the intestines can cause other health problems also.

Normal bowel movements should be soft and easy to pass. They shouldn't be dry, hard, or painful. If your child is constipated, this means changing the foods you eat, at least for a while. You may need to eat fewer fatty and greasy foods like fried chicken and french fries and fewer sugary foods like soda and candy.

Sometimes, being worried or upset can give you either diarrhea or constipation. You might even have some combination of tummy pain, bloating, gas, diarrhea, and constipation.

Fluid - drinking water and other liquids keeps stool soft as it moves through your intestines. When you don't drink enough, stool can get hard and dry, and you might get stopped up.

Exercise -Moving around helps food move through your digestive system.

Fiber - found in fruits, vegetables, and whole grains - can keep your stool from getting hard and dry. Also, absorbs toxins, adds bulk and helps clean the intestines.

Flax - is a fiber that is high in omega 3. Flax will help soften stools

Aloe Vera - Cleansing and soften stools

Garlic - kills bacteria and removes toxins.

C with bioflavonoids - healing, detoxifier, inflammation, helps with infection, and immune system.

B complex - digestion of fats and helps nutrients absorb in body and cell repair.

Alfalfa – detoxifies the body

Acidophilus - is an active good bacteria found in the intestinal track which increases the good flora and promotes a healthy immune system.

Ginger Tea – soothing to the stomach and in tea form will add extra fluid to the body.

Senna tea – is an herbal laxative.

Cascara Sagrada – an herbal laxative that may cause cramping in a small number of people.

zinc – helps build immune system and speeds healing.

Multivitamin and mineral complex – is needed to correct chemical imbalances due to poor nutrition.

Aloe Vera – works as a mild laxative and detoxes.

Crib Safety

Your baby will spend a lot of time in the crib, napping during the day and sleeping at night. It's important to make sure it's always a safe environment. In addition to always placing your baby to sleep on his or her back to prevent sudden infant death syndrome (SIDS), there are a number of steps you can take to ensure the safety of your littlest sleeper.

Before placing your baby in any crib, whether it is a new crib or a hand-me-down at home or in a child-care setting, or at a relatives home,make sure that the slats are no more than 2-3/8 inches apart and aren't cracked, loose, splintered, or missing. Also make sure that there are no decorative cutouts on the headboard or foot board in which the baby could become caught. There should be no sharp or jagged edges, the sides should latch securely, drop-side latches can't be released by the child, there are no protruding screws and all screws are accounted for, and that there are tightly attached corner posts are no more than 1/16 inch high.

Make sure the crib sheet snugly fits the mattress and never use an adult sheet in the crib so that the excess material does not gather around the baby's face. The mattress needs to fit snugly against the sides of the crib and there are no big gaps between the mattress and the crib and the mattress is kept at its lowest position once your child can stand.

Also, soft toys, comforters, blankets, and pillows, adult pillows, throw pillows, or infant donut pillows, are never kept in the crib. If crib bumpers are used, it's best to use the kind that tie at the top and bottom. You can also buy mesh bumpers that keep the baby's head and limbs inside the crib. Once the baby becomes more active make sure there are no mobiles or toys with strings or ribbons longer than 7 inches hanging above the crib and mobiles are removed once the baby begins to push up on his or hands and knees, or by 5 months, whichever comes first because of the risk of strangulation once he or she can reach the mobile. To prevent strangulation once the baby is mobile, remove cords from drapes or cut the ends and move crib away from drapes or window shades out of the baby's reach. Check to make sure that the crib hasn't been recalled by the U.S. Consumer Product Safety Commission (CPSC).

If you're expecting a baby or you already have a child, it's a good to learn cardiopulmonary resuscitation (CPR) and the Heimlich maneuver. Keep the following numbers near the phone for yourself and caregivers such as the toll free poison control number, child's doctor's number, work, cell phone numbers, close relatives number, close neighbors number, because in an emergency, it is better to see the number and dial, than trying to remember it. Make a first-aid kit and keep emergency instructions inside and install smoke detectors and carbon monoxide detectors. To maintaining a safe, child-friendly environment, check your childproofing efforts. Get down on your hands and knees in every room of your home to see things from a child's perspective. Be aware of your child's surroundings and what might be potentially dangerous. Completely childproofing your home can be difficult. If you can't childproof the entire house, you can shut the doors to any room a child shouldn't enter to prevent wandering into places that haven't been properly childproofed. Supervision is the very best way to help prevent children from getting injured. Whether you have a baby, toddler, or school-age child, your home should be a haven where your little one can explore safely. After all, touching, holding, climbing, and exploring are the activities that develop your child's body and mind.

Croup

Croup is a viral infection. There is a distinct barking cough along with trouble breathing, tightness in the lungs, and mucus build up. The term croup does not refer to a single illness, but rather a group of conditions involving inflammation of the upper airway that leads to a cough that sounds like a bark, particularly when a child is crying.

Most croup is caused by viruses, but similar symptoms may occasionally be caused by bacteria or an allergic reaction. The viruses most commonly involved are para influenza virus. Most children with viral croup are between the ages of 3 months and 5 years old. Croup is most likely to occur during the winter months and early spring, and symptoms are most severe in children younger than 3 years of age.

Most croup due to viruses is mild and can be treated at home, though rarely, viral croup can be severe and even life-threatening. Some children are more prone to developing croup, especially those who were born prematurely or with narrowed upper airways. The term spasmodic croup refers to a condition similar to viral croup, except that there are no accompanying symptoms of an infection. The cough frequently begins at night with a sudden onset. The child usually has no fever with spasmodic croup. The symptoms are treated the same for either form of croup.

At first, a child may have cold symptoms like a stuffy or runny nose for a few days and may also have fever. As the upper airway becomes progressively inflamed and swollen, the child may become hoarse, with a harsh, barking cough. Symptoms of croup often worsen at night and when the child is upset or crying. Frequent hand washing and avoiding contact with people who have respiratory infections are the best ways to reduce the chance of spreading the viruses that cause croup.

Humidify - the air with a cool-mist humidifier. Having your child breathe in the moist air through the mouth will sometimes break a croup attack. Or try running a hot shower to create a steam-filled bathroom where you can sit with your child for 10 minutes or more. Try cuddling and reading a bedtime story while doing this to help calm your child. The symptoms of croup generally peak 2 to 3 days after the symptoms of infection start. Croup resulting from viral infection usually lasts less than a week.

Quercetin – good for the immune system, antihistamine, and helps with inflammation.

Vitamin C – protects lungs, helps with infections and inflammation.

Calcium and Magnesium – relaxes muscles and helps with lung capacity.

Lobelia – soothes bronchial muscles and gets rid of excess mucus.

Mullein – helps congestion, coughs, and breathing.

Belladonna – is a homeopathic that relaxes the bronchial tubes and stops wheezing.

Essential fatty acids (EFA) – are anti-inflammatory.

Eucalyptus oil - will act as a decongestant. I like to add a few drops in water on the stove and it seems to help with breathing.

Cuts

Cuts, scratches, and abrasions are a part of growing up. Cuts are injuries to the skin caused by something sharp, like a knife. Scratches are slight injuries that happen when a sharp object, like a fingernail or thorn, scrapes along your skin the way a pencil scrapes across paper. Abrasion is a scrape that happens when the skin is rubbed away. For example, your child might get a rug burn while wrestling with their brother or a board burn if they wipe out on their skateboard when they weren't wearing kneepads.

After getting a cut, scratch, or abrasion, the skin may start bleeding. This happens because the injury breaks or tears the tiny blood vessels that live right under the skin's surface. Your body wants to stop the bleeding so the platelets in your blood come to the rescue.

At the site of a wound, platelets stick together, like glue. This is called clotting, which works like a plug to keep blood and other fluids from leaking out. A scab, a hardened and dried clot, forms a crust over the wound. This protects the area so the cells underneath can have time to heal.

Underneath the scab, new skin cells multiply to repair the wound. Damaged blood vessels are repaired, and infection-fighting white blood cells attack any germs that may have gotten into the wound. You can't see it under the scab, but a new layer of skin is forming. And when the new skin is ready, the scab falls off. A scab usually falls off within a week or two. If you pick at a scab, the new skin underneath can be ripped and the wound will take longer to heal and may leave a scar. So try not to let your child pick at scabs.

Stop any bleeding by pressing a clean, soft cloth against the wound. If the wound isn't very bad, the bleeding should stop in a few minutes. Then you'll want to clean the wound, using warm water and a gentle soap. Most small cuts, scrapes, or abrasions will heal well without any special care. For extra protection, use an antibacterial ointment or a bandage. Antibacterial ointment will kill germs. A bandage will keep the wound from getting irritated and will prevent germs from getting inside. If you use a bandage, it should be changed daily and when it gets wet or dirty.

If a wound is very long or deep or if its edges are far apart, then your child may need stitches. The doctor will use some type of anesthetic on your child's skin to numb it . This numbing medicine might be applied directly or through a shot. For more minor cuts, the doctor might use a special kind of glue, instead of stitches, to close the cut. This glue holds the sides of the cut together so the skin can begin to heal. The glue will dissolve over time. But more often, cuts, scratches, and abrasions go away on their own, thanks to the body's amazing ability to heal itself.

Quercetin – good for the immune system, antihistamine, and helps with inflammation.

Vitamin C – protects and helps with infections and inflammation.

Vitamin K – helps the blood to clot.

Garlic – helps fight infection.

Arnica gel – helps with cuts and bruises.

Cystic Fibrosis

Cystic Fibrosis is an inherited disease that causes thick, sticky mucus to build up in the lungs and digestive tract. It is the most common type of chronic lung disease in children and young adults, and may result in early death. Cystic fibrosis is caused by a defective gene which tells the body to produce abnormally thick and sticky fluid, called mucus. This mucus builds up in the breathing passages of the lungs and the pancreas, the organ that helps to break down and absorb food. This creates a place where bacteria can easily grow and cause infections.

This collection of sticky mucus results in life threatening lung infections and serious digestion problems. Millions of Americans carry the defective Cystic Fibrosis gene, but do not have any symptoms. That's because a person with Cystic Fibrosis must inherit two defective CF genes, one from each parent. The disease is the most common, deadly, inherited disorder affecting Caucasians in the United States.

Most children are diagnosed with CF by their 2nd birthday. A small number, however, are not diagnosed until age 18 or older. These patients usually have a milder form of the disease. A blood test is available to help detect CF. The test looks for variations in a gene known to cause the disease. An early diagnosis of CF and a comprehensive treatment plan can improve both survival and quality of life. Specialty clinics for cystic fibrosis may be helpful and can be found in many communities.

There is no way to prevent cystic fibrosis. Screening of family members of a cystic fibrosis patient may detect the cystic fibrosis gene in between 60 and 90% of carriers, depending on the test used. The pancreas produces enzymes that help digest food and hormones that help absorb sugar. When thick mucus in the pancreas clogs up the narrow passageways, it can make it difficult for people to digest food and get all the vitamins and nutrients they need. A child with CF will work with a medical team, including doctors, nurses, nutritionists, physical therapists, social workers, and respiratory therapists. A respiratory therapist knows a lot about breathing and how the lungs work. He or she can teach a child with CF to do special breathing exercises that help get rid of extra mucus. Breathing treatments also help by adding moisture and delivering medicine into the lungs.

Enzymes – to replace those that are missing. Enzymes help break down nutrients and get them into the body.

Vitamin A – helps to speed healing.

Vitamin C with bioflavonoids – helps with inflammation, healing, protects lungs, and helps with infections .

zinc – speeds healing.

Multivitamin/Mineral - is needed to correct chemical imbalances due to poor nutrition.

Quercetin – good for the immune system, antihistamine, and helps with inflammation.

Calcium and Magnesium – relaxes muscles and helps with lung capacity.

Lobelia – soothes bronchial muscles and gets rid of excess mucus.

Mullein – helps congestion, coughs, and breathing.

Dandruff

First you should know that a person's entire body surface continuously sheds dead skin cells. The skin itself sheds every twenty-four days. Dandruff is the result of the normal growing process of the skin cells of the scalp. In a normal scalp, the process of sloughing off old cells and manufacturing of their replacements is very orderly and complete. In the dandruff scalp, there is mass disorder and often the departing cells are not dead before leaving the scalp.

Dandruff is usually seasonal. It is most severe during the winter and mildest during the summer. Other common allergens which provoke dandruff are chocolate, nuts and shellfish. Dandruff scales usually occur as small, round, white-to-gray patches on top of the head. Dandruff can affect many different people in every age group. There is still controversy over whether dandruff is caused by fungus or by excessive sebum production of the scalp. Dandruff can manifest as either very dry and flaky scalp or very oily scalp with flakes.

The good fats, found in nuts and flax seed benefit the body and promote healthy scalps. Garlic and oil of oregano are also excellent for fighting dandruff. You can take it internally or externally depending on what seems to work best for your situation. Both are sold in health food stores as capsules or tablets.

Eggs - provide vitamin B6 in addition to supplying sulfur which is nature's beauty mineral for the scalp. Sometimes an allergy to dairy products may cause dandruff in which case alternative food sources of vitamin B6 are preferred.

Cabbage - provide vitamin B6 in addition to supplying sulfur which is nature's beauty mineral for the scalp. This is an alternative to dairy.

Flax seed – high in omega 3 and good for the hair, skin and nails.

Garlic - excellent for fighting dandruff and has antifungal properties.

Oil of oregano - excellent for fighting dandruff and has antifungal properties.

Vitamin C with bioflavonoids – helps with inflammation, healing, and helps with infections .

zinc – speeds healing.

Multivitamin/Mineral - is needed to correct chemical imbalances due to poor nutrition.

Omega 3 fatty acids – helps to stop itching, inflammation and good for hair, skin and nails.

Kelp – loaded with minerals and good for scalp and hair growth.

B vitamins – are good for cell repair, stress, healthy skin and hair.

Aloe vera – added to shampoo has antiseptic and anti inflammatory properties.

Vinegar – add to water and rinse hair after shampooing.

Antifungal dandruff shampoo – helps to clear up dandruff.

Vitamin A – prevents dry skin and helps tissues to heal.

Selenium – is an antioxidant and controls dry scalp.

Acidophilus - increases the good flora and promotes a healthy immune system.

Deafness

Hearing loss is generally described as slight, mild, moderate, severe, or profound, depending upon how well a person can hear the intensities or frequencies most greatly associated with speech. Generally, only children whose hearing loss is greater than 90 decibels (dB) are considered deaf for the purposes of educational placement.

There are four types of hearing loss. Conductive hearing losses are caused by diseases or obstructions in the outer or middle ear, the conduction pathways for sound to reach the inner ear. Conductive hearing losses usually affect all frequencies of hearing evenly and do not result in severe losses. A child with a conductive hearing loss usually is able to use a hearing aid well or can be helped medically or surgically.

Sensorineural hearing losses result from damage to the delicate sensory hair cells of the inner ear or the nerves which supply it. These hearing losses can range from mild to profound. They often affect a child's ability to hear certain frequencies more than others. Thus, even with amplification to increase the sound level, a child with a sensorineural hearing loss may perceive distorted sounds, sometimes making the successful use of a hearing aid impossible. This is the type of hearing loss my son has.

A mixed hearing loss refers to a combination of conductive and sensorineural loss and means that a problem occurs in both the outer or middle and the inner ear. A central hearing loss results from damage or impairment to the nerves or nuclei of the central nervous system, either in the pathways to the brain or in the brain itself.

Some children who are hard of hearing will find it much more difficult than children who have normal hearing to learn vocabulary, grammar, word order, idiomatic expressions, and other aspects of verbal communication. I have a son with a hearing loss and you would never be able to tell. He plays every kind of instrument under the sun, and has absolutely no speech impediment. For children who are deaf or have severe hearing losses, early, consistent, and conscious use of visible communication modes such as sign language, finger spelling, and Cued Speech, and/or amplification and oral training can help reduce this language delay.

By age four or five, most children who are deaf are enrolled in school on a full-day basis and do special work on communication and language development. It is important for teachers and audiologists to work together to teach the child to use his or her residual hearing to the maximum extent possible, even if the preferred means of communication is manual. Since the great majority of deaf children (over 90%) are born to hearing parents, programs should provide instruction for parents.

Hearing loss, or hearing impairment, happens when there is a problem with one or more parts of the ear or ears. A child who has hearing loss or impairment may be able to hear some sounds or nothing at all. Impairment means something is not working correctly or as well as it should. People also may use the words deaf, deafness, or hard of hearing when they're talking about hearing loss.

Magnesium – prevents damage to the hair cells in the inner ear.

B complex – is important for hearing and lowers ear pressure.

Deafness (Hearing Impairment)

About 3 in 1,000 babies are born with hearing impairment, making it the most common birth defect. A hearing problem can also develop later in life. To understand how and why hearing loss happens, it helps to know how the ear works. The ear is made up of three different sections: the outer ear, the middle ear, and the inner ear. These parts work together so you can hear and process sounds.

The outer ear, picks up sound waves and the waves then travel through the outer ear canal. When the sound waves hit the eardrum in the middle ear, the eardrum starts to vibrate. When the eardrum vibrates, it moves three tiny bones in your ear. They help sound move along on its journey into the inner ear. The vibrations then travel to the cochlea, which is filled with liquid and lined with cells that have thousands of tiny hairs on their surfaces. There are two types of hair cells: the outer and inner cells. The sound vibrations make the tiny hairs move. The outer hair cells take the sound information, amplify it, and tune it. The inner hair cells send the sound information to your hearing nerve, which then sends it to your brain, allowing you to hear.

Hearing loss can happen because a child was born with parts of the ear that didn't form correctly and don't work well. Other problems can happen later because of an injury or illness, middle ear fluid, serious ear infections, head injury, listening to very loud music, etc.

If a doctor thinks that a baby or child may have hearing loss, the doctor will recommend that the parents take him or her to an audiologist. An audiologist is someone who is specially trained to test and help with the problems related to hearing loss. A pediatric audiologist tests a child's hearing by doing different types of tests. They even have hearing tests for babies. If an audiologist finds that a child has hearing loss, he or she will recommend treatment and suggest the family work with a special team. This team can help figure out the best way for the child to learn and communicate.

The kind of treatment depends on the type of hearing loss, how severe it is, and the child's other needs. Common treatments include medicine, operations, hearing aids, or listening devices, which emphasize voices and help kids hear better in noisy settings. With treatment, most children will be able to hear normally again.

Hearing aids are tiny amplifiers. They help someone hear sounds better and can even pick up the sounds so that what a child hears is more clear. Hearing aids deliver amplified sounds from the eardrum and middle ear to the inner ear or cochlea. Hearing aid technology is available that can adjust the volume of sounds automatically.

For some children who are not able to hear or understand words even with the help of hearing aids, there is a device called a cochlear implant. This is a very tiny piece of electronic equipment that is put into the cochlea during an operation. It takes over the job of the damaged or destroyed hair cells in the cochlea by turning sounds into electrical signals that stimulate the hearing nerve directly.

Ginkgo – has been shown to help hearing loss along with ringing in the ears.

Antioxidants – such as E, C, A, and CoQ10 protect the inner ear from age related hearing loss.

Dehydration

When it's hot outside and you've been sweating, you get thirsty. Thirst is a sign of dehydration. Dehydration means that your body doesn't have enough water in it to keep it working right. A child gets water by drinking and eating. You lose water when you sweat, urinate, have diarrhea, or throw up. You even lose a little water when you breathe.

Our bodies need water to work properly. Usually, you can make up for the water you lose, like when you come in from outside and have a long, cool drink of water. If you don't replace the water your body has lost, you might start feeling sick. And if you go too long without the water you need, you can become very ill and might need to go to the hospital.

Many times children get dehydrated when they are playing hard and having fun. Children also can get dehydrated when they're sick. If you have a stomach virus, you might throw up or have diarrhea. On top of that, you probably don't feel like eating or drinking. If you have a sore throat, you might find it hard to swallow food or drink. And if you have a fever, you can lose fluids because water evaporates from your skin in an attempt to cool your body down. Some signs of dehydration are feeling lightheaded, dizzy, tired, rapid heartbeat, dry lips, mouth, and not urinating enough. That's why it is important to drink a lot of fluids when you're sick.

It is best to prevent getting dehydrated in the first place. If you're going to be going outside, it's a good idea to drink water before, during, and after you play, especially if it's hot. Dehydration can happen along with heat-related illnesses, such as heat exhaustion and heat stroke. In addition to drinking water, it's smart to dress in cool clothes and take breaks indoors or at least in the shade.

If your child's sick, keep taking small sips of drinks and soups, even if they are not that thirsty or hungry. Eating an ice pop is a great way to get fluids. The warmth in your mouth and stomach turns the pop-cycle from a solid to a liquid. Other foods, such as fruits and vegetables, contain water, too. Some cases of dehydration can be handled at home. But sometimes, that isn't enough to get a child feeling better. A child may need to go to the doctor or emergency department if he or she has a heat-related illness or a virus with vomiting or diarrhea that just won't quit.

At the hospital, an intravenous line can get fluids into their body fast. An IV line is a special tube that goes right into their veins, so the liquid goes right to where their body needs it most. It may pinch a little when the nurse is inserting it, but it often helps a child feel much better.

Limit soda and other sugary drinks, such as fruit punches, lemonades, and iced teas. These drinks contain a lot of sugar that your body doesn't need. Some of them also contain caffeine, which is a diuretic. This means that caffeinated drinks cause you to urinate more often than normal. In other words, they tell your body to get rid of fluids, and as you know, that's the opposite of what your child needs to do if they are dehydrated.

Hydration – is important if there has been vomiting. Sip slightly salty liquids and add electrolytes that have been especially designed to rehydrate to water and sip.

Bitter Orange tea – helps maintain electrolyte balance.

Dermatitis

A rash can also be called dermatitis, which is any swelling, puffiness, or irritation of the skin. It can be red, dry, scaly, and itchy. Rashes also can include lumps, bumps, blisters, and even pimples. Most people have had a rash or two. When you were a baby, you probably had diaper rash. But some rashes, especially combined with a fever, can be signs of serious illnesses. Hives, also called urticaria, also can be serious because they can be a sign of an allergic reaction and the person may need immediate medical attention. Hives, which are reddish or pale swellings, appear on a person's body when a chemical called histamine is released in response to an allergen. The trigger could be a certain food, medicine, or insect bite. A virus also can cause hives.

Do not let your child scratch. If you do, the rash may take longer to heal and they will be more likely to develop an infection or scar. A visit to the doctor is a good idea if your child has a rash. Although all rashes may look alike to you, a skin doctor, called a dermatologist, knows the difference. And knowing which kind of rash your child has can help the dermatologist choose the best treatment to heal the rash.

For eczema, the doctor may suggest special moisturizers. Emollients retain the water in their skin, keeping it soft and smooth while soothing the itchy feeling. With poison ivy, the doctor may prescribe cool showers and calamine lotion. In more severe cases, a liquid or pill medicine called an antihistamine may be needed. It decreases itching and redness.

For rashes that are caused by an allergen, including hives, the doctor will probably want more information. He or she will want to find out which food, substance, medicine, or insect caused your child's rash or hives. He or she may recommend a medical test to determine which allergens are causing the trouble. It's important to find this out because the best way to prevent rashes and hives caused by allergens is to avoid the problem food, substance, medicine, or insect.

Betaine – is a form of hydrochloric acid and people with dermatitis usually have low levels of this acid.

B Complex – is needed for cell repair and makes healthy skin.

Essential Fatty Acid – is good for the skin.

Vitamin C with bioflavonoids – has anti inflammation properties.

Vitamin E – is an antioxidant and relieves dry, itchy skin.

Flaxseed oil – is good for the hair, skin, and nails. It help the skin retain moisture.

Shark cartilage – reduces inflammation.

Vitamin A – is good for the skin.

Emulsified Cod Liver Oil – is good for smooth skin and prevents dryness.

Chamomile tea – reduces inflammation.

Oregon grape root – detoxifies and reduces inflammation.

Gluten free diet – eliminate gluten for a few days to see if rash clears up.

Diabetes

Diabetes mellitus occurs when specialized cells of the pancreas, a gland located behind the stomach, does not produce adequate amounts of the hormone insulin. Insulin permits the body to process proteins, fat and sugars in food to make body tissues, produce energy, and store energy. In children without diabetes, insulin is produced as needed to process food. But in children with diabetes, who have a reduced supply of insulin or none at all, the nutrients cannot be used by the cells but remain in the blood.

Without a source of energy, the cells think they are starving. In an attempt to nourish the starving cells, the liver makes sugar from the body stores of protein and fat. This leads to weight loss and weakness, because muscle is being broken down and is not getting the energy it needs. The body tries to flush out the excess sugar circulating in the blood by making more urine. This is why children who have diabetes urinate more frequently and can become very thirsty as they try to replace the loss of fluids. Without insulin, fat breaks down to form ketones, which also are excreted in the urine.

The tendency to develop diabetes is inherited, although most children with insulin-dependent diabetes, called Type 1, don't have any close relatives with the disease. The destruction of the cells that make insulin results from a process in which the body views these cells as foreign invaders and mounts an immune response against them. This autoimmune process starts years before the first symptoms of diabetes show up. The trigger for this process may be viruses or other agents in the environment.

Type 1 diabetes is very different from non-insulin-dependent diabetes (called Type 2). Type 2 diabetes is much more common and occurs in most adults with diabetes (more than 90 percent). Because Type 2 is so different from that which occurs in children, the advice intended for people who have non-insulin-dependent diabetes is not appropriate for children.

Diabetes can appear at any time, even in the first year of life. The diagnosis is often delayed in infants and toddlers until the child is very sick, because the symptoms at this age are not terribly specific. If your child is failing to grow, gain weight, losing weight, increased thirst, increased urination, dehydration, sores that do not heal in the normal time that they should, weakness, tiredness and on going vomiting then it is important to notify your pediatrician immediately.

Chromium picolinate – improves insulin's efficiency and lowers blood sugar levels.

Garlic – improves the immune system, stabilizes blood sugar levels, decreases blood sugar levels, and improves circulation.

L-Glutamine – reduces cravings for sugar.

Taurine – aids in the release of insulin.

Biotin – improves the metabolism of glucose.

zinc – diabetics have been shown to be low in zinc.

CoQ10 – improves circulation, stabilizes blood sugar, and is a strong antioxidant.

Diarrhea

Diarrhea is when your child has loose, watery stoles. This can cause loss of fluids and electrolytes. The large intestine, also known as the colon, absorbs water and nutrients from the partially digested food that enters the colon from the small intestine. Anything that is not absorbed is slowly moved on a pathway out of the body. These undigested and unabsorbed food particles are also known as stool.

Stress can speed up the colon and slow the stomach down. Stressful feelings also can be a trigger for IBS-Irritable bowel syndrome. Let's say a child has a big test at school the next day and really worries about it, that's stress. Or if a child sees his or her parents fighting and begins to feel worried, that's stress, also. A child in this situation can learn to handle stress in other ways, so symptoms of diarrhea will go away or at least be less severe.

What children eat can also be a trigger, but this can be different for each child. For example, a high-fat diet may bother some children, while an extremely low fat diet may cause diarrhea in other children. Eating big meals and spicy foods often cause problems, so if your child has a problem with diarrhea, try to avoid those.

The best solution is to learn what makes the symptoms worse and avoid whatever it is. Sometimes it is a big meal, spicy foods, high fat foods, chocolate, dairy products, food poison, allergies, certain medicines, bacteria, virus, etc.. Sometimes it could just be your child eating to many fruits and one time or foods that are to high in fiber for them. Fiber is very good for children, but if they have to much of it, or are not use to fiber in their diets and then it's added, it could cause loose stools. Do not drink apple juice while rehydrating, because it could make diarrhea worse.

Fluids – to prevent dehydration.

Gelatin water – to prevent dehydration.

Apple pectin – absorbs toxins from the colon and helps with diarrhea.

Charcoal - Absorbs toxins from colon and stops diarrhea. This is one of the first thing we grab when a child has diarrhea.

Minerals - replaces minerals lost from diarrhea.

Acidophilus - builds friendly bacteria.

Garlic -kills bacteria and parasites.

Marshmallow root tea -calms stomach and intestine.

Wild oregano oil - antibacterial, antifungal, kills parasites, and antiviral.

Kelp – replaces minerals lost from diarrhea.

Fenugreek tea – lubricates the intestines and reduce fever.

Marshmallow root tea – calms the stomach and soothes intestinal problems.

Homeopathic – Arsenicum album, Podophyllum, and Sulfur are some good homeopathics to use for diarrhea.

Dog bites

A dog bite can be very scary. Children usually want to hug and play with just about any animal they see. Sometimes, though, the animal doesn't want to play with them and the child gets bit or scratched. A bite that breaks the skin can become infected. An estimated 4.7 million dog bites happen every year in the United States. Of those, nearly 800,000 required medical treatment. Also, how about the word "Rabies". This can be very scary for any parent. Thank goodness most pets are vaccinated by their vets.

Dogs are a part of life. Millions of people have dogs as pets. Like many kinds of pets, no matter how small or cute they are, dogs need to be respected as an animal that, under certain conditions, could hurt you. Even the nicest, most well-trained family dog may snap if it's startled, scared, threatened, agitated, angry, or hungry. Our family has had their fair share of dog bites, like the time my son got between two fighting dogs to break them up. You can respect a dog by giving it space and following certain rules. These rules not only keep the dog happier, they can protect your child from getting bit.

It is important to teach your child not to tease a dog, to pet a dog only when the owner says it is all right, do not get between or try to separate dogs that are fighting, and be careful when feeding a dog by hand, because it may think little fingers are part of the treat.

If you own a dog than you have a lot of responsibility for preventing dog bites. If your family has a dog, make sure to keep its immunizations up to date and have regular checkups with a veterinarian. Also, have it spayed or neutered. Consider taking your dog to obedience school since this will make it less aggressive and more obedient, and thus less likely to bite someone.

When you take your dog out in public, always keep it on a leash so you can be in control if your dog's behavior gets out of hand. And if you have children, closely supervise them while they're around the dog. Never leave an infant or toddler alone with a dog. If your child is bitten by a dog and the bite breaks the skin, contact your doctor, particularly if the dog is not yours.

Wash wound throughly with antibacterial soap. Place colloidal silver on a gauze and cover wound. Check with the animal's owners to make sure the dog has had vaccinations. It is important to teach your child how to be around animals.

C with bioflavonoids - fights infection, repairs collagen and connective tissue.

Colloidal Silver - natural antibiotic and reduces infection. Apply topically and take internally.

Garlic -is a natural antibiotic.

B complex – aids in antibody production, stress, and cell repair.

Goldenseal salve – is a natural antibiotic and helps fight infection.

Acidophilus – is important if your doctor has put child on antibiotics. This will replace the friendly bacteria that the antibiotic destroy. Take acidophilus a couple of hours after you have taken the antibiotic. That way the two are not canceling each other out.

Ear Infection

Ear infections are very common in babies and children. Usually an ear infection comes on when a child has been teething, allergy, or has a cold. It is important to check with your doctor concerning allergy testing if ear infections are common.

Signs of an ear infection are throbbing pain, pressure, child pulling on ear, and or fever. Constant ear infections cause hearing loss. Most children have at least one middle ear infection before they are 2 years old. These infections can cause ear pain and fever. Middle ear infections are one of the most common childhood problems. An infection happens when germs like bacteria and viruses get inside the body and cause trouble. The middle ear is a small pocket of air behind the eardrum. You have a middle ear infection when germs get into the middle ear and the area fills up with fluid, which contains germ-fighting cells. When the pus builds up, your child's ear starts to feel like a balloon that is ready to pop, which can really hurt. If the doctor thinks bacteria is causing the problem, he or she might prescribe an antibiotic.

Children develop ear infections more frequently in the first 2 to 4 years of life because their Eustachian tubes are shorter and more horizontal than adults. This allows bacteria and viruses to find their way into the middle ear more easily and makes them more prone to blockage. Also, a child's immune system is not full developed so it is more difficult for them to fight infections. Ear infections also occur more commonly in boys than girls, in children whose families have a history of ear infections, and more often in the winter season when upper respiratory tract infections or colds are most frequent.

To try and prevent ear infections, stay away from people who have colds, if possible. Make sure your child washes their hands regularly and try not to touch their nose and eyes.

Ear Candles – will remove excess wax and relieve pressure.

Colloidal Silver - natural antibiotic, use orally and topically.

Vitamin C with bioflavonoid - immune booster and fights infection.

Zinc – speeds healing and an immune builder.

Garlic - natural antibiotic, reduces infection and inflammation.

B complex - immune builder, cell repair.

Echinacea – helps build the immune system.

Warm garlic oil - few drops in ear helps relieve pain.

Earache tablets - is a homeopathic blend by Hyland's that really helps with pain and fever.

Onion poultices – relieves pain.

Olive Leaf Extract – helps the body fight infections.

Impacted earwax can cause pressure and pain in the ear canal. Ear Candles can remove the excess wax and relieve pressure. Sometimes children get ear infections when they have conjunctivitis because the same bacteria can cause both problems.

Eczema

Eczema is also called atopic dermatitis. Atopic refers to someone who is likely to develop an allergy to something. Dermatitis means that the skin is inflamed, or red and sore. Eczema makes your skin dry, red, and itchy. Sometimes you may even break out in a rash. It's a chronic condition, which means that it comes and goes.

About one out of every 10 children develops eczema. Most children who have eczema got it before they turned 5 years old, but you can get it when you're older than 5. The good news is that more than half of the children who have eczema today will be over it by the time they are teenagers.

Skin has special cells that react when they come in contact with anything that irritates them. They make the skin inflamed to protect it. If you have eczema, you have more of these special cells than other people do. These cells overreact when something triggers them and they start to work overtime. That's what makes your skin red, sore, and itchy.

No one is really sure why children get eczema. It's not contagious. Children who get eczema often have family members with hay fever, asthma, or other allergic conditions. Some scientists think these children may be genetically predisposed to get eczema. About half of the children who get eczema will also someday develop hay fever or asthma themselves. Eczema is not an allergy itself, but allergies can be a trigger factor for eczema. That means that if your child has allergies, their eczema may flare up sometimes.

You may need some moisturizing lotion or cream to control the dryness and itchiness. Some children need stronger medicines called corticosteroids. Steroid ointment or cream is rubbed on their skin to help calm the inflammation. Your doctor might suggest you try an antihistamine, a medicine that comes in pill or liquid form, to help control the itching. And if all that scratching leads to an infection, you may need an antibiotic. None of these eczema medicines will cure your child forever, but they can help make their skin more comfortable and less red.

Betaine – is a form of hydrochloric acid and people with dermatitis usually have low levels of this acid.

B Complex – is needed for cell repair and makes healthy skin.

Essential Fatty Acid – is good for the skin.

Vitamin C with bioflavonoids – has anti inflammation properties.

Vitamin E – is an antioxidant and relieves dry, itchy skin.

Flaxseed oil – is good for the hair, skin, and nails. It help the skin retain moisture.

Shark cartilage – reduces inflammation.

Vitamin A – is good for the skin.

Emulsified Cod Liver Oil – is good for smooth skin and prevents dryness.

Chamomile tea – reduces inflammation.

Oregon grape root – detoxifies and reduces inflammation.

Epilepsy

Epilepsy is a general term that includes various types of seizures. Children with diagnosed epilepsy have had more than one seizure, and they may have had more than one kind of seizure. A seizure happens when abnormal electrical activity in the brain causes an involuntary change in body movement or function, sensation, awareness, or behavior.

About 300,000 American children under the age of 14 have epilepsy. It affects children at different ages, and in different ways. For some, it will be a temporary problem, easily controlled with medication, outgrown after a few years. For others, it may be a lifelong challenge affecting many areas of life. Medical treatment of childhood epilepsy is getting better, and research towards a cure continues. More medications are now available. For children whose seizures are not controlled by medication or who experience unacceptable side-effects, several treatments including surgery, the ketogenic diet, and the vagus nerve stimulator (VNS) may be effective in treating their seizures. Epilepsy is a disorder of the brain.

A child's brain contains billions of nerve cells. They communicate with each other through tiny electrical charges that fire on and off in random fashion. When some or all of these cells suddenly begin to fire together, a wave of electrical energy sweeps through the brain, causing a seizure. Seizures interfere with the child's normal brain functions. They produce sudden changes in consciousness, movement, or sensation.

Some people use the term "seizure disorder" instead of "epilepsy" to describe this condition. Both mean the same thing, an underlying tendency to experience seizures. Having a single seizure does not mean a child has epilepsy. Epilepsy is the name for seizures that happen more than once without a known treatable cause, such as fever or low blood sugar.

Pinpointing the cause of epilepsy is difficult at any age. In seven out of every ten cases, there is no known cause and they are labeled as having idiopathic epilepsy. "Idiopathic" is a Latin word meaning "of unknown cause."

There are many possible causes in children. These include problems with brain development before birth, lack of oxygen during or following birth, a head injury that leaves scaring on the brain, unusual structures in the brain, tumors, a prolonged seizure with fever, or the after-effects of severe brain infections such as meningitis or encephalitis. When a cause can be identified, these children are labeled as having symptomatic epilepsy. The seizures are felt to be a symptom of the underlying brain injury.

L-Tyrosine – is important for proper brain function.

Magnesium – is needed to calm the nervous system and muscles spasms.

Taurine – is an important building block for all other amino acids and levels are often low in people with seizure disorders.

B complex – is very important in the function of the central nervous system and cell repair.

Calcium – is important in normal nerve impulse transmission.

zinc – protects brain cells and speeds healing.

Stress management – being over stressed can bring on a seizure for those with this disorder.

Eye
Pink Eye/Conjunctivitis/Stye

Pink eye, also known as conjunctivitis, is an inflammation of the membrane that lines the eyelid. It also covers most of the white of the eye. Symptoms of pink eye are blood shot eyes, itchy, swollen, and irritated. As the infection progresses the eye lids fill with pus and the eyelids stick together, especially in mornings after child has slept all night and lids have remained closed. It is the most common eye problem kids can have.

It's called pinkeye because the white part of the eye and inside the eyelids become red or pink when you have it. Pinkeye may start in one eye, but many people get conjunctivitis in both eyes at the same time. Conjunctivitis usually doesn't hurt, but itching can be annoying. Sometimes it feels like you have an eyelash or a speck of sand in your eye and can't get it out.

Children get conjunctivitis for different reasons. Most children get it from bacteria or viruses. This is called infectious conjunctivitis. Bacteria can be seen only with a powerful microscope, and viruses are even smaller than bacteria. Bacteria live on your skin or in your nose or mouth all the time and you never know it. Most don't ever bother you, but certain kinds of bacteria can cause infections like conjunctivitis. Sometimes children get ear infections when they have conjunctivitis because the same bacteria can cause both problems. Viruses, like the kind that can give you a cold, can cause conjunctivitis, too.

Conjunctivitis is easy to catch just through touching. Your child can get conjunctivitis by touching the hand of an infected friend who has touched his or her eyes. If you then touch your eyes, the infection can be spread to you. Washing your hands often with warm, soapy water is the best way to avoid being infected with conjunctivitis. Children also get conjunctivitis because of allergies or because they get something irritating in their eyes, but these kinds of conjunctivitis are not contagious. Washcloths and towels used to clean or dry the child's eyes should go right into the laundry so no ones else gets infected.

Vitamin A – helps to speed healing in viral conjunctivitis.

Vitamin C with bioflavonoids – helps with inflammation and healing.

zinc – speeds healing.

Eyebright tea – make a compress or eyewash and apply to eyes. Helps with eye irritation and inflammation.

Goldenseal tea – can be used in place of eyebright tea for an eyewash. It also is antibacterial and antiviral.

Compresses – make warm compresses and apply to eyes because the microorganism that cause conjunctivitis cannot survive the heat. This will also help clear away the gunk that collects in the eyes and help them to open better.

Multivitamin and mineral complex – all nutrients are needed in balance.

L-Lysine – antiviral properties.

Colloidal Silver - natural antibiotic and reduces infection. Apply topically and take internally.

Fever

A fever is when your body temperature rises above normal body temperature which can range from 97 to 99. A fever is a symptom of something else that is wrong in the body. It is the bodies way of defending itself from bacterial or viral infection. A low grade fever is not to much to worry about unless it lasts more than 3 days. Then you should see your pediatrician. If your child's fever is more than 102, then it is time for you to contact your child's doctor.

Why does the hypothalamus, which controls the temperature in your body, tell your body to change to a new temperature? Researchers believe turning up the heat is the body's way of fighting the germs and making your body a less comfortable place for them. After the cause of the fever disappears, your hypothalamus will set everything back to a normal temperature. When your child's strep throat medicine starts to work, for instance, their body will begin to cool down and they will no longer have the chills.

For almost all children, fevers aren't a big problem. Once the cause of the fever is treated or goes away on its own, their body temperature comes back down to normal and they feel like their old self again. Most doctors say that children with a fever less than 102° Fahrenheit don't need to take any special medication unless their fevers are making them uncomfortable.

It's a different story for newborns and very young infants, though. They should be evaluated by a doctor for any fever that reaches 100.4° Fahrenheit or higher. The two medicines most often recommended are acetaminophen or ibuprofen. The medicine blocks the chemicals that tell the hypothalamus to turn up the heat. Children should never take aspirin to treat a fever because it can cause a rare but serious illness call Reye Syndrome.

Fluids - important because as your body heats up, it's easy for it to get dehydrated, which means there isn't enough water in your body. You have a lot of choices when it comes to fluids, juice, water, sports drinks, soup, flavored gelatin, and even ice pops.

Tepid Bath – will help lower a fever. If the water is to hot is will raise the temperature.

Feverfew – reduces a fever.

Moltrin – helps with aches and pains and reduces a fever.

Catnip tea - good for lowering fever

Vitamin C – flushes out toxins and reduces fever.

Garlic – is a natural antibiotic and helps build the immune system.

Poultice – making a poultice from echinacea, hyssop, thyme, feverfew, lobelia, and yarrow will help lower a fever.

Hydration – is important if there has been vomiting. Sip slightly salty liquids and add electrolytes that have been especially designed to rehydrate to water and sip.

Homeopathic – Belladonna and Aconite napellus are both good for reducing fevers.

Bitter Orange tea – helps maintain electrolyte balance.

Olive Leaf Extract – helps the body fight infections.

Flu

Stomach flu is an illness called gastroenteritis, which is usually caused by a virus. Someone who gets gastroenteritis might have stomach cramps, nausea,throwing up, and diarrhea. He or she will probably feel pretty sick for a day or two but will then get better. Gastroenteritis is contagious, which means that someone who has it can spread it to other people. That's why it's important to wash your hands.

If your child has gastroenteritis, you'll want them to rest until they feel better. If they are throwing up, don't eat solid food. Instead, sip fluids, such as water, or chew on bits of ice. Once they stop throwing up, drink more clear foods and drinks such as warm chicken broth, Popsicles, and gelatin. When they start to feel better, try feeding bland foods like toast, pretzels or crackers, bananas, and plain noodles. As their digestive system returns to normal, you can gradually go back to feeding them what you usually do.

Influenza is also called the flu. It's an infection that causes fever, chills, cough, body aches, and headaches. The flu is caused by the influenza virus. A virus is a microorganism, which means it's so small that you can't see it without a strong microscope. The flu goes away in a week or two. But for babies and children under age 5 or children with health problems such as diabetes and asthma, the flu can make them very sick. Anyone who's at risk of getting really sick needs to get a flu shot, or vaccine.

This virus gets around in little drops that spray out of an infected person's mouth and nose when he or she sneezes, coughs, or even laughs. You can catch the flu from someone who has it if you breathe in some of those tiny flu-infected drops. You can also catch the flu if those drops get on your hands and you touch your mouth or nose.

Prevention - washing your hands often helps to prevent the spread of many of the germs that cause the condition, especially during cold and flu season.

Acidophilus - is an active good bacteria found in the intestinal track which increases the good flora and promotes a healthy immune system.

Vitamin C – is an important antioxidant that helps make you less susceptible to infections.

Activated Charcoal – helps stop diarrhea and absorbs toxins. I always have activated charcoal in the medicine cabinet and the first aid kit.

Garlic – detoxes the body and works like a natural antibiotic and has antiviral properties.

B - Complex - It helps with stress, nerves and provides energy.

Colloidal Silver – is a natural antibiotic. Kills fungi, viruses and bacteria. Helps in healing.

Minerals – to replace the ones lost during diarrhea and to balance the electrolytes in the body.

Acidophilus – builds friendly flora and replaces important intestinal bacteria.

Fiber – removes bacteria from the colon walls so that they do not enter the bloodstream.

Kelp – high in minerals that are needed to restore electrolyte imbalance.

Hydration – is important is there has been vomiting and diarrhea. Add electrolytes that have been especially designed to rehydrate to water and sip.

Food Allergies

Food allergies occur when your immune system makes a mistake. Normally, your immune system protects you from germs and disease. It does this by making antibodies that help you fight off bacteria, viruses, and other tiny organisms that can make you sick. But if you have a food allergy, your immune system mistakenly treats something in a certain food as if it's really dangerous to you.

The same sort of thing happens with any allergy, whether it's a medicine, pollen in the air, or a food, like peanuts. So the thing itself isn't harmful, but the way your body reacts to it is. If a child with peanut allergy would have eaten that peanut topped brownie, here's what would happen. Antibodies to something in the food would cause mast cells, a type of immune system cell in the body, to release chemicals into the bloodstream. One of these chemicals is histamine. The histamine then causes symptoms that affect a child's eyes, nose, throat, respiratory system, skin, and digestive system.

A child with a food allergy could have a mild reaction or it could be more severe. An allergic reaction could happen right away or a few hours after the child eats it. Some of the first signs that a child may be having an allergic reaction could be a runny nose, an itchy skin rash such as hives, tightness in the throat, wheezing, nausea, vomiting, stomach pain, diarrhea, or a tingling in the tongue or lips.

In the most serious cases, a food allergy can cause anaphylaxis. This is a sudden, severe allergic reaction in which several problems occur all at once and can involve the skin, breathing, digestion, the heart, and blood vessels. A person's blood pressure can drop, breathing tubes can narrow, and the tongue can swell. Children at risk for this kind of a reaction have to be very careful and need a plan for handling emergencies, when they might need to get special medicine to stop these symptoms from getting worse. Many children outgrow allergies to milk and eggs as they grow older. But severe allergies to foods like peanuts, certain kinds of fish, and shrimp often last a lifetime.

Many children react to a certain food but are not actually allergic. For example, children with lactose intolerance get belly pain and diarrhea from milk and other dairy products. That doesn't mean they're allergic to milk. They don't feel good after drinking milk because their bodies can't properly break down the sugars found in milk. Some of the most popular foods children are allergic to are peanuts, nuts, seafood, shrimp, milk, eggs, soy, and wheat.

Skin Testing - allergist will make a little scratch on your skin and drop a little of the liquid extract on the scratched spot or spots. Different extracts will go on the different scratch spots, so the doctor can see how your skin reacts to each substance. If you get a reddish, raised spot, it shows that you are allergic to that food or substance.

The plan - should spell out what to do, who to tell, and which medicines to take, if you have a reaction.

Epinephrine - epinephrine injection comes in an easy-to-carry container that looks like a pen and will stop a severe attack that affects breathing.

Quercetin - a naturally occurring bioflavonoid that increases the immune system and decreases allergic reactions.

Food Poisoning

Food poisoning is when bacteria grow in the food left in the fridge or on the counter to long, and those bacteria made you sick. Food poisoning can be mild and last just a short time or can be more serious. Foods from animals, raw foods, and unwashed vegetables all can contain germs that cause food poisoning. The most likely source is food from animals, like meat, poultry, eggs, milk, and shellfish.

A few signs that your child has food poisoning are an upset stomach, nausea, stomach cramps, diarrhea, and a fever. Sometimes feeling sick from food poisoning shows up within hours of eating the bad food. At other times, someone may not feel sick until several days later. With mild cases of food poisoning, your child will not feel sick for very long and will soon be feeling fine again. If there is blood in your child's diarrhea, then it is important to see the pediatrician.

Sometimes it's hard to tell if your child has food poisoning or something else. You might do a little detective work and see who else gets the same sickness. Did they eat the same thing you did? If only children who ate that food got sick, food poisoning could be the problem. It's one thing to get food poisoning from something in your fridge, but imagine how many children could get sick if a restaurant served food that had these bad germs in it. When that happens, people from the health department would get involved and try to figure out what happened and make sure everyone gets the medical care they need. Some of the most common bacteria are, salmonella, listeria, campylobacter, and E. coli. The best way to not get food poisoning is prevention, so it is important to make sure food is prepared, cooked, and stored properly. Wash fruits and vegetables well before eating them and make sure meat is cooked throughly before feeding to children.

Prevention - washing your hands often helps to prevent the spread of bacteria that cause the condition.

Acidophilus - is an active good bacteria found in the intestinal track which increases the good flora and promotes a healthy immune system. It helps so that bad bacteria can not take over.

Vitamin C – is an important antioxidant that helps remove toxins and bacteria from the body.

Activated Charcoal – helps stop diarrhea and absorbs toxins. I always have activated charcoal in the medicine cabinet and the first aid kit.

Garlic – detoxes the body and works like a natural antibiotic and has antiviral properties.

Colloidal Silver – is a natural antibiotic. Kills fungi, viruses and bacteria. Helps in healing.

Minerals – to replace the ones lost during diarrhea and to balance the electrolytes in the body.

Fiber – removes bacteria from the colon walls so that they do not enter the bloodstream.

Kelp – high in minerals that are needed to restore electrolyte imbalance.

Hydration – is important if there has been vomiting and diarrhea. Add electrolytes that have been especially designed to rehydrate to water and sip.

Psyllium – removes bacteria and toxins from the colon walls so that they do not enter the bloodstream.

Fractures

Your bones are tough stuff, but even tough stuff can break. Like a wooden pencil, bones will bend under strain. But if the pressure is too much, or too sudden, bones can snap. Your child can break a bone by falling off a skateboard or crashing down from the monkey bars.

When a bone breaks it is called a fracture. There's more than one way to break or fracture a bone. A break can be anything from a hairline fracture to the bone that's snapped in two pieces like a broken tree branch. A complete fracture is when the bone has broken into two pieces. A greenstick fracture is when the bone cracks on one side only. A single fracture is when the bone is broken in one place. A comminuted fracture is when the bone is broken into more than two pieces or crushed. A bowing fracture is when a child's bone bends but does not break. A open fracture is when the bone is sticking through the skin. A spiral fracture is when the bone is twisted and broke.

Breaking a bone is a big shock to your whole body. It's normal for you to receive strong messages from parts of your body that aren't anywhere close to the fracture. You may feel dizzy, woozy, or chilly from the shock. A lot of children cry for a while. Some children pass out until their bodies have time to adjust to all the signals they're getting. And other children don't feel any pain right away because of the shock of the injury.

The worst thing for a broken bone is to move it. This will hurt the child and it can make the injury worse. If you're not sure what bone is broken or you think the neck or back is broken, do not try to move the injured child. Wait until a trained medical professional has arrived.

With breaks in larger bones or when a bone breaks in more than two pieces, the doctor may need to put in a metal pin, or pins, to help set it. When the bone has healed, the doctor will remove the pin, or pins. After your bone has been set, the next step is usually putting on a cast, the special bandage that will keep the bone in place for the 1 to 2 months it will take for the break to mend. Casts are made of bandages soaked in plaster, which harden to a tough shell. Sometimes casts are made of fiberglass or plastic, and some are even waterproof, which means you can still go swimming and get them wet. And sometimes they come in cool colors or patterns that children can choose.

Your bones are natural healers. At the location of the fracture, your bones will produce lots of new cells and tiny blood vessels that rebuild the bone. These cells cover both ends of the broken part of the bone and close up the break until it's as good as new.

Calcium – important for bone repair.

Magnesium – balances calcium and helps it absorb in the body.

Boron – increases calcium uptake and helps in healing bones and bone health.

Silica – helps in calcium absorption and connective tissue repair.

Horsetail – helps in calcium absorption and connective tissue repair.

Vitamin D - needed for calcium absorption and bone repair and makes bones stronger.

Amino acid complex – speeds healing and cell repair.

Fungal Infection

This germ is harmless most of the time, but sometimes it can cause a problem called a fungal infection. A lot of children get fungal infections, but they're usually easy to treat because a fungus rarely spreads below the skin. Fungi, the word for more than one fungus, can be found on different parts of the body.

Tinea is a type of fungal infection of the hair, skin or nails. When it's on the skin, tinea usually begins as a small red area the size of a pea. As it grows, it spreads out in a circle or ring. Tinea is often called ringworm because it may look like tiny worms are under the skin but of course, they're not. Because the fungi that cause tinea (ringworm) live on different parts of the body, they are named for the part of the body they infect. Scalp ringworm is found on the head, and body ringworm affects the arms, legs, or chest.

Athlete's foot is another type of fungal infection that usually appears between the toes but can also affect toenails and the bottom or sides of the feet. Jock itch is a fungal infection of the groin and upper thighs. You might think only men and boys get it, but girls and women can get it, too. Candida is a yeast, similar to a fungus. It most often affects the skin around the nails or the soft, moist areas around body openings. Diaper rash in babies can be from one type of candida infection, as can thrush which are white patches often found in the mouths of babies. Older girls and women may develop another form of candida infection in and around the vagina. This is called a yeast infection.

Taking antibiotics can cause some children to get a yeast infection. Antibiotics get rid of germs that make us sick, but they can also kill many of the harmless bacteria in our body. These harmless bacteria normally fight with the yeast for a place to live, but when antibiotics kill them, the yeast is free to grow. Sometimes, a fungus may infect children if they have an immune system disorder, this means their bodies can't fight certain types of infections.

Acidophilus - builds friendly flora and replaces important intestinal bacteria.

Caprylic acid - is an antifungal and kills candida fungus.

Garlic - a natural antibiotic and immune enhancer. Garlic has antifungal properties.

Colloidal Silver - is soothing and helps healing.

Colostrum - A very strong immune builder.

Yogurt - Live active cultures help build the friendly flora in the body.

Diet - should be low in sugar since Candida/Yeast grows quickly when you consume junk food. Nothing with dyes, preservatives, processed or sugar.

Aloe Vera – helps the white blood cells to kill yeast cells and helps remove them from the body.

Cinnamon – helps with thrush.

Lavender – helps get rid of yeast infections on the skin, such as athlete's foot, etc.

Tea Tree Oil – helps get rid of yeast infections on the skin and has antifungal properties.

Oregano – is a strong antifungal

Growth

Growing pains is not a disease. But they can hurt. Usually they happen when children are between the ages of 3 and 5 or 8 and 12. Growing pains stop when children stop growing. By the teen years, most children don't get growing pains anymore. Children get growing pains in their legs. Most of the time they hurt in the front of the thighs, in the calves, or behind the knees. Usually, both legs hurt.

Growing pains often start to ache right before bedtime. Sometimes a child will go to bed without any pain, but wake up in the middle of the night with their legs hurting. The best news about growing pains is that they go away by morning.

Growing pains don't hurt around the bones or joints, the flexible parts that connect bones and let them move, but in the muscles. For this reason, some doctors believe that children might get growing pains because they've tired out their muscles. When you run, climb, or jump a lot during the day, you might have aches and pains in your legs at night.

If your child has a fever, limping when they walk, or their leg looks red or is swollen, you should go to the doctor. Growing pains should not keep your child from running, playing, and doing what you normally do.

Vitamin A – needed for proper growth.

Vitamin D – needed for proper growth and strong bones.

Cod liver oil – contains vitamin A and D and are needed for proper growth and strong tissues and bones.

Lysine – is needed for normal growth and bone development.

Essential Fatty Acids – needed for normal growth.

Calcium and magnesium – is for normal bone growth.

Amino Acid complex – needed for proper growth.

L-Ornithine – promotes the release of growth hormone. Use under a doctor's supervision.

Diet – Make sure you child gets good sources of protein since it is necessary for proper growth. Nothing with dyes, preservatives, processed or sugar. Lots of fruit, vegetables, whole grains, fish, salmon, herbal ice teas in place of fruit juices and soda. Sometimes we sweetened the tea with stevia, which is a plant sweetener that is good for blood sugar and has zero calories. We made a rinse with food grade hydrogen peroxide and water and rinsed all fruits and veggies to get rid of pesticide residue and bacteria. Let your child help pick out healthy foods to eat, this way they are more likely to enjoy trying it.

DHA and EPA - is being added to baby cereal and formula because it is so good for babies brains and their development. It is a very good essential fatty acid.

Multivitamin and mineral complex – is needed to correct chemical imbalances due to poor nutrition.

Sleep – is very important for good health and proper growth when you get the proper amount. It also helps keep the stress levels down.

Hair Loss
(Alopecia)

Anyone can have hair loss, even children. The medical name for hair loss is alopecia. Every hair on your head is made of keratin, the same protein that makes up your nails. Hairs grow from follicles, which are very tiny holes deep in your skin. Each follicle contains a hair root, the part of the hair that is alive and growing. The part of the hair you can see, the part above the skin, is dead. That's why it doesn't hurt to get a haircut.

This alive and growing part is called the hair shaft, and it's the part of your hair that can get long. Most children's hair grows about half an inch a month. About 85 out of 100 hairs on your head are growing at any time. When a hair is done growing it goes into its resting phase and eventually falls out. Usually, 15 out of 100 hairs on your head are in the resting phase.

So why do some children lose their hair? A child's hair may fall out if he or she uses harsh chemicals to dye, bleach, straighten, or perm their hair. Even drying hair with very high heat can hurt it and cause it to fall out. Too-tight braids, ponytails, and barrettes can also make hair fall out. Hair also can be lost if a person combs or brushes the hair too hard, especially when it's wet. A fever, stress, or surgery can cause this change in your hair.

Children who have a fungus called ringworm on their scalp might lose their hair. This infection causes the hairs to break close to the scalp. If your thyroid gland isn't working right, it can also cause hair loss. Severe problems with nutrition also can result in unhealthy hair that falls out or breaks easily. Most people think about cancer when they see a child who is bald. Cancer does not cause hair to fall out, but the powerful drugs and treatments used to kill cancer cells, kill the cells that make hair grow. A child getting chemotherapy may lose a lot of hair quickly, but the hair will grow back when the treatment is stopped.

Being bald can be upsetting and scary. Some children wear wigs or hair extensions while they wait for their own hair to return. Others feel more comfortable just wearing a baseball cap, bandanna, or scarf. It's always tough to be different, especially in a way that's easy for people to notice. Friends and classmates can make all the difference to someone who's dealing with hair loss. They can tease the person and make him or her feel even worse, or they can support the person, be kind, and remember that a person is more than just his or her hair.

Essential Fatty Acids – good for texture of hair and prevents dry, brittle hair.

Flaxseed oil – is good for hair, skin, and nails.

Silica – helps in calcium absorption and connective tissue repair and makes your hair stronger.

B complex – helps cell repair and the growth of healthy hair.

Vitamin C – is good for hair follicles.

zinc – stimulates hair growth.

Apple Cider Vinegar – use as a rinse to help hair growth.

Sage tea – use as a rinse to help hair growth.

Halitosis
(Bad Breath)

Bad breath is the common name for the medical condition known as halitosis. Many different things can cause halitosis, from not brushing your teeth to certain medical conditions. Certain foods can cause bad breath such as garlic and onions. Poor oral hygiene leads to bad breath because when you leave food particles in your mouth, these pieces of food can rot and start to smell. The food particles may begin to collect bacteria, which can be smelly, too. Plus, by not brushing your teeth regularly, plaque (a sticky, colorless film) builds up on your teeth. Plaque is a great place for bacteria to live and yet another reason why breath can turn foul.

Teach your child to take care of their mouth by brushing their teeth at least twice a day and flossing once a day. Brush the tongue also, because bacteria can grow there. Flossing once a day helps get rid of particles wedged between the teeth. Also, visit your dentist twice a year for regular checkups and cleanings. Not only will your child get a thorough cleaning, the dentist will look around their mouth for any potential problems, including those that can affect breath. For example, gum disease, also known as periodontal disease, can cause bad breath and damage your teeth.

The way a child's breath smells can be a clue to what's wrong. For instance, if a child has uncontrolled diabetes, his or her breath might smell like acetone, the same stuff that's in nail polish remover. Sinus problems and liver or kidney problems can cause bad breath. If it is persistent in your child, you may want to see your pediatrician.

Brushing – brush at least twice a day and floss once a day. It is also important to brush your tongue also, because bacteria can grow there. It is important to visit your dentist twice a year for regular checkups and cleanings.

Fiber – needed for removing toxins from the colon that can result in bad breath.

Chlorophyll – fights bad breath and controls body order.

Alfalfa – loaded with minerals and is high in chlorophyll and will help fight bad breath.

Vitamin C – fights infections, helps in healing, gum disease, bleeding gums, and helps with immune system.

Acidophilus - builds friendly flora, builds immune system and helps with fungal infection.

Garlic – acts as a natural antibiotic, antibacterial, detoxes the body.

zinc – is antibacterial and neutralizes sulfur compounds which is a common cause of mouth oder.

Propolis – good for healing sores or infections in the mouth, antibacterial, works great for sore throat.

B Complex – needed for cell repair and proper digestion.

Parsley – is rich in chlorophyll.

Keep your toothbrush clean by storing it in food grade hydrogen peroxide between uses. This will kill viruses and bacteria. Rinse well before using.

Hay Fever

Hay fever is the name of a type of allergy that people have to natural things like pollen from plants and flowers. If you have hay fever, you don't really get a fever, but you will experience a runny, red, itchy nose and eyes. These symptoms are almost the same as a cold, but a cold lasts for a few days, where hay fever lasts for weeks.

Pollen is a fine powder produced by certain plants. During the spring, summer, and fall seasons, it is released into the air and picked up by the wind. The wind carries it to other plants so they can make seeds. But while it's traveling in the wind, pollen gets into the air we breathe. Many children are allergic to it, including children who have asthma. When they breathe in pollen, it can trigger their asthma symptoms.

Children who have allergies get runny noses when they're around the thing they're allergic to like pollen or animal hair. That's because their bodies react to these things like they're germs. Histamine is a substance in the body that's released during an allergic reaction. It can cause allergy symptoms that affect the eyes, nose, throat, skin, digestive system, and lungs. When histamine affects the lungs, a child who has asthma may have breathing problems.

Antihistamines are medicines that block allergy symptoms. They can make your child stop sneezing, and stop their nose from running when their allergies are acting up. When they are itchy or have hives, they can work, too.

If you think that your child might have hay fever, a special doctor called an allergist can help figure out what they are allergic to by giving them a skin test. For this test, the doctor will use different liquids, each containing a small amount of stuff that a child can be allergic to, such as pollen or certain foods. The doctor puts a drop of each liquid on their arm or back and then lightly pricks the skin. If they get a red, itchy bump there, you'll know they are allergic.

Bromelain – reduces inflammation associated with hay fever symptoms.

Quercetin – works like an antihistamine.

Vitamin B – are necessary for proper functioning of the immune system.

Vitamin C – helps with inflammation and it helps with the immune system.

zinc – increases immune function.

Grape Seed extract – acts as a free radical scavenger and has anti inflammatory properties.

Eucalyptus oil – helps relieves congestion. Use a few drops in a humidifier.

Eyebright – helps sooths eyes when they are red, itchy, and sore.

Horehound – helps prevent hay fever reaction.

Stinging nettle – helps prevent hay fever reaction and gets rid of excess mucus.

Turmeric – has anti inflammatory properties.

Nettle leaf – helps prevent hay fever reaction.

Horseradish – is good for runny nose and congestion.

Homeopathic – Sabadilla and Wyethia are very good for hay fever.

Headache

Lots of children have headaches from time to time. In fact, it's more unusual for someone not to have had a headache at least once before his or her early teens. Although it may feel like it, a headache is not a pain in your brain. Your brain tells you when other parts of your body hurt, but it can't actually feel pain. Most headaches happen outside your skull, in the nerves, blood vessels, and muscles that cover your head and neck. Sometimes the muscles or blood vessels swell. They also can tighten or go through other changes that stimulate or put pressure on the surrounding nerves. The nerves send a rush of pain messages to your brain, and you end up with a headache.

The most common type of headache is a tension headache. This happens when head or neck muscles keep squeezing too hard. When you get this kind of headache, the pain is usually dull and constant. It might feel as though something is pressing or squeezing on the front, back, or both sides of your head.

Pain that's especially sharp and throbbing can be a sign of a different kind of headache called a migraine. Migraine headaches aren't as common as tension headaches, especially in children, but they can still happen. Sometimes, just before a migraine happens, the person sees wavy lines or bright spots of light. This is called an aura. Also, children who get migraines often feel sick to their stomachs and sometimes throw up.

Sometimes a headache is just a part of another illness, such as a cold or flu or strep throat. Staying up too late, skipping a meal, or playing in the hot sun too long can set off a headache. Some foods can cause headaches in some children, such as bacon, bologna, and hot dogs. The caffeine in sodas, chocolate, coffee, and tea may cause headaches, too. Children don't need caffeine, so it's a good idea to limit it in their diet.

Most headaches will go away after your child has rested or slept awhile. It helps to have your child lie down in a cool, dark, quiet room and close their eyes. Put a cool, moist cloth across their forehead or eyes. Acetaminophen or ibuprofen can help with headache pain. You want to avoid giving your child aspirin for a headache because it may cause a rare but dangerous disease called Reye syndrome.

Calcium and magnesium – helps with muscular tension and low levels of magnesium may cause a migraine.

Bromelain – an enzyme that has anti inflammatory properties.

DLPA DL-Phenylalanine – is a pain reliever.

5-HTP – helps with all variety of headaches.

Glucosamine sulfate – is a natural pain reliever and helps with inflammation.

L-Tyrosine – helps with headaches.

Primrose Oil – helps with headaches and helps with inflammation.

Ginger – is a natural pain reliever.

Homeopathic – Belladonna, Natrum muriaticum, Arsenicum album, and Sanguinaria.

Hearing Loss

Hearing loss, or hearing impairment, happens when there is a problem with one or more parts of the ear or ears. Someone who has hearing loss or impairment may be able to hear some sounds or nothing at all. Impairment means something is not working correctly or as well as it should. People also may use the words deaf, deafness, or hard of hearing when they're talking about hearing loss.

About 3 in 1,000 babies are born with hearing impairment, making it the most common birth defect. To understand how and why hearing loss happens, it helps to know how the ear works. The ear is made up of three different sections: the outer ear, the middle ear, and the inner ear. These parts work together so you can hear and process sounds. The outer ear, picks up sound waves and the waves then travel through the outer ear canal. When the sound waves hit the eardrum in the middle ear, the eardrum starts to vibrate. When the eardrum vibrates, it moves three tiny bones in your ear. These bones are called the hammer, anvil, and stirrup. They help sound move along on its journey into the inner ear.

The vibrations then travel to the cochlea, which is filled with liquid and lined with cells that have thousands of tiny hairs on their surfaces. There are two types of hair cells: the outer and inner cells. The sound vibrations make the tiny hairs move. The outer hair cells take the sound information, amplify it, and tune it. The inner hair cells send the sound information to your hearing nerve, which then sends it to your brain, allowing you to hear.

There are four types of hearing loss. Conductive hearing losses are caused by diseases or obstructions in the outer or middle ear, the conduction pathways for sound to reach the inner ear. Conductive hearing losses usually affect all frequencies of hearing evenly and do not result in severe losses. A person with a conductive hearing loss usually is able to use a hearing aid well or can be helped medically or surgically.

Sensorineural hearing losses result from damage to the delicate sensory hair cells of the inner ear or the nerves which supply it. These hearing losses can range from mild to profound. They often affect the person's ability to hear certain frequencies more than others. Thus, even with amplification to increase the sound level, a person with a sensorineural hearing loss may perceive distorted sounds, sometimes making the successful use of a hearing aid impossible. This is the type of hearing loss my son has.

A mixed hearing loss refers to a combination of conductive and sensorineural loss and means that a problem occurs in both the outer or middle and the inner ear. A central hearing loss results from damage or impairment to the nerves or nuclei of the central nervous system, either in the pathways to the brain or in the brain itself. Lots of children have had ear infections, which also can cause hearing loss. Permanent hearing loss is rare from an ear infection.

If a doctor thinks that a baby or child may have hearing loss, the doctor will recommend that the parents take him or her to an audiologist.

Ginkgo – has been shown to help hearing loss along with ringing in the ears.

Antioxidants – such as E, C, A, and CoQ10 protect the inner ear from age related hearing loss.

Magnesium – prevents damage to the hair cells in the inner ear.

Heat Exhaustion

If you're out in the hot sun, or you're exercising on a hot day, it's easy to get heat exhaustion. Children get heat exhaustion when their bodies can't cool themselves fast enough. A child with heat exhaustion might feel overheated, tired, and weak. Heat exhaustion can come on suddenly. A child may just collapse when playing soccer or tennis, for example. It can leave a child feeling really tired for days after it happens.

Heat stroke is a more serious heat-related illness and can cause a child to stop sweating, to have red, hot skin, and to have a high temperature. The child might become uncoordinated, confused, or even lose consciousness. It requires emergency medical attention.

We normally cool ourselves by sweating and radiating heat through our skin. Under certain circumstances, such as unusually high temperatures, high humidity, or vigorous exercise in hot weather, this natural cooling system may begin to fail, allowing internal heat to build up to dangerous levels. The result may be heat exhaustion or heatstroke.

Heat cramps are brief, severe cramps in the muscles of the legs, arms, or abdomen that may occur during or after vigorous exercise in extreme heat. The sweating that occurs with vigorous exercise causes the body to lose salts and fluids. And the low level of salts causes the muscles to cramp. Children are particularly susceptible to heat cramps when they haven't been drinking enough fluids. Although painful, heat cramps aren't serious. Most heat cramps don't require special treatment. A cool place, rest, and fluids should ease your child's discomfort. Massaging cramped muscles may also help.

Heat exhaustion is a more severe heat illness that can occur when a person in a hot climate or environment hasn't been drinking enough fluids. Symptoms may include dehydration, fatigue, weakness, clammy skin, headache, nausea, vomiting, rapid breathing and irritability. If your child is showing any of these symptoms, bring them indoors or into the shade, loosen your child's clothing, and encourage them to take sips of cool water with a little salt added. If left untreated, heat exhaustion may escalate into heatstroke, which can be fatal.

The most severe form of heat illness, heatstroke is a life-threatening medical emergency. The body loses its ability to regulate its own temperature. Body temperature can soar to 106 degrees Fahrenheit or even higher, leading to brain damage or even death if it isn't quickly treated. Prompt medical treatment is required to bring the body temperature under control.

Heatstroke can also happen when a child is left in, or becomes accidentally trapped in, a car on a hot day. When the outside temperature is 93 degrees Fahrenheit, the temperature inside a car can reach 125 degrees Fahrenheit in just 20 minutes, quickly raising a child's body temperature to dangerous levels.

Kelp – high in minerals that are needed to restore electrolyte imbalance.

Hydration – is important if there has been vomiting. Sip slightly salty liquids and add electrolytes that have been especially designed to rehydrate to water and sip.

Bitter Orange tea – helps maintain electrolyte balance.

Magnesium – is needed to calm the nervous system and help with muscles spasms.

Hepatitis

It's sneaky, it's silent, and it can permanently harm your liver. Some people have hepatitis for many years without knowing it and then discover they have liver damage because of it. Twenty-four hours a day, nonstop, your liver which is an internal organ on the upper right side of your abdomen, performs many tasks to keep your body running smoothly.

Your liver cleans out poisons from your blood, it stores vitamins and minerals and makes sure your body gets the right amounts, it produces the right amount of amino acids to build strong, healthy muscles, it keeps your body fueled up with just the right amount of glucose. Your liver also regulates the levels of medicine you are taking. Before some medicines can work, the liver has to start them up. It also regulates hormones in your body and produces an important digestive liquid called bile.

Hepatitis is an inflammation or infection of the liver. If the liver is affected by or gets scarred from inflammation or infection, it can't effectively do all of its jobs. There are different ways you can get hepatitis. The two most common forms are toxic hepatitis and viral hepatitis. Toxic hepatitis can occur if someone drinks a lot of alcohol, takes certain illegal drugs or medications, or is exposed to poisons. Then there is viral hepatitis A virus to hepatitis G. Though the viruses differ, they have one thing in common: They cause infection and inflammation that is harmful to liver cells.

For children, hep A is the most common type of hepatitis to get. The virus lives in feces from people who have the infection. That's why it's so important to wash your hands before eating and after going to the bathroom. If you don't, and then go make yourself a sandwich, hep A virus might end up on your food, and then in you.

Vegetables, fruits, and shellfish can carry hepatitis if they were harvested in contaminated water or in unsanitary conditions. Hepatitis A affects people for a short time and when they recover, does not come back. Getting vaccinated helps a person's body make antibodies that protect against hepatitis infection. The hepatitis A vaccine is now given to all children between the ages of 1 and 2 years, and to people who are traveling to countries where the virus easily gets into the food and water supply. Although hep A is a short-term illness that goes away completely, hep B and C can turn into serious long-term or chronic illnesses for some people. Teens and young adults are most at risk for getting these two viruses. Today all babies routinely get vaccines against the hep B virus. There is not yet a vaccination for hep C.

Hep B and C get passed from person to person the same ways that HIV does, through direct contact with infected body fluids. Hepatitis B and C are even more easily passed in fluids and needles than HIV. Even when infected people don't have any symptoms, they can still pass the disease on to others. Sometimes mothers with hep B or C pass the virus along to their babies when they're born. Hep B and C also can get passed in ways you might not expect, such as getting a manicure or pedicure with unsterilized nail clippers or other dirty instruments.

Some people with hepatitis show no signs of having the disease, but others may have tiredness without any reason, flu-like symptoms, yellowing of skin and whites of eyes, dark brown pee and poor appetite for days in a row or weight loss.

Milk Thistle – has been shown in scientific studies to protect, heal, and detox the liver.

Hepatitis B

Hepatitis is a disease of the liver. It is usually caused by a virus, although it can also be caused by long-term overuse of toxins. Although there are several different types of hepatitis, hepatitis B is a type that can move from one person to another through blood and other body fluids. It can be transmitted through sexual intercourse and through needles by those who have the virus, or tattoo needles that haven't been properly sterilized. A pregnant woman can also pass hepatitis B to her unborn baby. You cannot catch hepatitis B from an object, such as a toilet seat.

Someone with hepatitis B may have symptoms similar to those caused by other viral infections, such as the flu, tiredness, nausea, loss of appetite, mild fever, and vomiting as well as abdominal pain or pain underneath the right ribcage where the liver is. Hepatitis B can also cause jaundice, which is a yellowing of the skin and the whites of the eyes, and may cause the urine to appear brownish.

Someone who has been exposed to hepatitis B may have symptoms 1 to 4 months later. Some people with hepatitis B don't notice symptoms until they become quite severe. Some have few or no symptoms, but even someone who doesn't notice any symptoms can still transmit the disease to others. Some people carry the virus in their bodies and are contagious for the rest of their lives.

Hepatitis B can be very dangerous to a person's health, leading to liver damage and an increased risk of liver cancer. Of babies born to women who have the hepatitis B virus, 90% will have the virus unless they receive a special immune injection and the first dose of hepatitis B vaccine at birth.

To help prevent the spread of hepatitis B, health care professionals wear gloves at all times when in contact with blood or body fluids, and are usually required to be immunized against the hepatitis B virus. There is an immunization against hepatitis B. The immunization is given as a series of three shots over a 6-month period. Newborn babies in the United States now routinely receive this immunization series. Teens who see their health care provider for yearly exams are also likely to be given the hepatitis B immunization if they haven't had it before. Immunization programs have been responsible for a significant drop in the number of cases of hepatitis B among teens over the past 10 years.

If someone has been recently exposed to the hepatitis B virus, a doctor may recommend a shot of immune globulin containing antibodies against the virus to try to prevent the person from coming down with the disease. For this reason, it's especially important to see a doctor quickly after any possible exposure to the virus.

Silymarin – Milk Thistle extract – has been scientifically proven to repair and rejuvenate the liver.

Garlic – detoxifies the liver.

Burdock root – aids in liver repair and cleanses the bloodstream.

Red Clover tea – aids in liver repair and cleanses the bloodstream.

Hives

Hives are pink or red bumps or slightly raised patches of skin. Sometimes, they have a pale center. Hives usually itch, but they also can burn or sting. Hives can occur anywhere on the body and vary in size and shape. Hives also might look like rings or groups of rings joined together. Hives can appear in clusters and might change locations in a matter of hours. A bunch of hives might be on a person's face, then those might go away. Later some more may appear on a person's arms. They are usually harmless, though they may occasionally be a sign of a serious allergic reaction.

The medical term for hives is urticaria. When a child is exposed to something that can trigger hives, certain cells in the body release histamine. This causes fluid to leak from the small blood vessels under the skin. When this fluid collects under the skin, it forms the blotches, which we call hives. One common reason for getting hives is an allergic reaction. Some common allergic triggers are certain foods like milk, shellfish, berries, nuts, medications such as antibiotics, and insect bites. A case of hives can last for a few minutes, a few hours, or even days. Sometimes, doctors will suggest a child take a type of medication called an antihistamine to relieve the itchiness. In many cases, hives clear up on their own without any medication or doctor visits. Less often, hives can be a sign of a more serious allergic reaction that can affect breathing and other body functions. In these cases, the child needs immediate medical care. Some children who know they have serious allergies carry a special medicine to use in an emergency. This medicine, called epinephrine, is given by a shot. Ordinarily, a nurse gives you a shot, but because some allergic reactions can happen really fast, many adults and children carry this emergency shot with them and know how to use it, just in case they ever need it in a hurry.

Acidophilus – Reduces allergic reaction and builds friendly flora.

Flaxseed oil – has anti inflammatory properties.

Garlic – antibacterial, antiviral, immune builder and natural antibiotic.

Multivitamin and mineral complex – helps in nutrition imbalance.

B complex – helps with cell repair and nervous system, immune system and skin.

Vitamin C – has anti inflammatory properties.

Vitamin D3 - is good for the skin and helps with hives.

Quercetin – works as an inflammatory.

Alfalfa – is high in minerals, blood tonic, and cleanses the blood of toxins.

Burdock root tea – cleanses the blood of toxins.

Aloe Vera – is soothing to the skin and helps with rashes.

Nettle – helps with hives.

Echinacea – is an immune builder and helps with hives.

Homeopathic – Bovista, Cantharis and Rhus toxicodendron help alleviate symptoms of hives.

Hypoglycemia
(Low Blood Sugar)

Hypoglycemia is the medical word for low blood sugar level. When blood sugar levels go lower than they're supposed to, you can get very sick. No matter what we're doing, even when we're sleeping, our brains depend on glucose to function. Glucose is a sugar that comes from the foods we eat, and it's also formed and stored inside the body. It's the main source of energy for the cells of our body, and it's carried to each cell through the bloodstream.

The blood glucose level is the amount of glucose in the blood. When blood glucose levels, also called blood sugar levels, drop too low, it's called hypoglycemia. Very low blood sugar levels can cause severe symptoms that need to be treated right away.

There are a bunch of symptoms that a child with low blood sugar might have. It's not the same for everybody. The symptoms are as minor as feeling hungry and as serious as having seizures or passing out. If you have low blood sugar you may feel hungry, feel shaky, feel sweaty, pale skin color, headache, feel sleepy, weak, dizzy, and confused.

The warning signs of hypoglycemia are the body's natural response to low blood sugar levels. When blood sugar levels fall too low, the body releases the hormone adrenaline, which helps get stored glucose into the bloodstream quickly. Becoming pale, sweating, shaking, and having an increased heart rate are early signs of the adrenaline being released. If the hypoglycemia isn't treated, more severe symptoms may develop, including drowsiness, confusion, seizures, and loss of consciousness.

When blood sugar levels are low, the goal is to get them back up quickly. Most children who have low blood sugar need to eat, drink, or take something that contains sugar that can get into the blood quickly. Skipping meals can cause blood sugar levels to drop, so it is important to make sure children eat meals on time and have lite snacks in between.

Chromium picolinate – improves insulin's efficiency and lowers blood sugar levels.

Garlic – improves the immune system, stabilizes blood sugar levels, decreases blood sugar levels, and improves circulation.

L-Glutamine – reduces cravings for sugar.

Taurine – aids in the release of insulin.

Biotin – improves the metabolism of glucose.

zinc – diabetics have been shown to be low in zinc.

CoQ10 – improves circulation, stabilizes blood sugar, and is a strong antioxidant.

B Complex - B complex works best when you have all the B's combined. B complex is very important in red blood cell production, cell repair and energy.

Multivitamin and mineral complex – is needed to correct chemical imbalances due to poor nutrition.

Impetigo

It's an infection of the skin caused by bacteria. Impetigo is commonly found on the face, often around the nose and mouth, but it can show up anywhere the skin has been broken. If you have a cut or scrape or if you scratch your skin because of a bug bite, eczema, or poison ivy, germs may find a way to get inside. Once inside, the bacteria cause small blisters to develop on the skin. These blisters burst and ooze fluid that crusts over, a condition called impetigo. Sometimes impetigo is called 'school sores' because so many school age children get it. Children seem to get it more than adults do, but impetigo can affect anyone.

We all have bacteria living on our skin and in our nose, but most of the time they don't cause any trouble. Two types of bacteria can cause impetigo are Group A streptococcus and Staphylococcus aureus. It doesn't matter which bacteria caused your impetigo, the treatment will be similar. Impetigo usually starts as small blisters that quickly burst and ooze fluid that crusts over. The crust is yellow-brown, or honey-colored, making impetigo look different than other scabs. In a less common kind of impetigo that affects babies and younger children, the blisters are larger and take longer to burst. The fluid in these blisters may start out clear and then turn cloudy.

A doctor usually can tell if your child has impetigo by examining their skin. If your child has mild impetigo, your doctor probably will prescribe an antibiotic ointment. If the impetigo has spread to a lot of places or if the antibiotic ointment is not working, your child may need to take an antibiotic as a pill or liquid for ten days. Impetigo might itch, but your child should try not to scratch or touch the sores. Touching them can spread the sores to other parts of their body or to someone else. If they do touch the area, be sure to wash their hands. Gently wash the infected areas with mild soap and water, using a piece of clean gauze. If a sore is very crusted, you can soak it in warm, soapy water to loosen the crust. You don't have to get it all off, but it's good to keep it clean. Cover the sores with gauze and tape or a loose plastic bandage. Impetigo is contagious, which means that you could spread it to other people. That's why someone with impetigo should stay home from school until they have used their medicine for about 24 hours. By then, the impetigo is no longer contagious. After 3 days, the sores should begin to heal. Call the doctor if your child develops a fever or if they don't get better after taking the medicine for a couple days.

Acidophilus – Reduces allergic reaction and builds friendly flora.

Flaxseed oil – has anti inflammatory properties.

Garlic – antibacterial, antiviral, immune builder and natural antibiotic.

Lavender – helps get rid of infections on the skin.

Tea Tree Oil – helps get rid of infections on the skin and has antifungal and antibacterial properties.

Oregano – is a strong antifungal and antibacterial.

Hydrogen peroxide – apply 3% help in killing the bacteria on the skin and will help prevent a secondary infection from occurring.

Immune System

The immune system is made up of a network of cells, tissues, and organs that work together to protect the body. White blood cells, also called leukocytes, are part of this defense system. Lymphocytes allow the body to remember and recognize previous invaders and get rid of the invading germs. These are two basic types of germ-fighting cells.

Leukocytes are found in lots of places, including your spleen, an organ in your belly that filters blood and helps fight infections. Leukocytes also can be found in bone marrow, which is a thick, spongy jelly inside your bones. Your lymphatic system is home to these germ-fighting cells, too. Lymph nodes contain clusters of immune system cells. Normally, lymph nodes are small and round and you don't notice them. But when they're swollen, it means your immune system is at work.

Lymph nodes work like filters to remove germs that could hurt you. Lymph nodes, and the tiny channels that connect them to each other, contain lymph, a clear fluid with leukocytes (white blood cells) in it. Beside your neck, lymph nodes are behind your knees, in your armpits, and in your groin, just to name a few.

Sometimes a child has a problem with his or her immune system. Sometimes the immune system overreacts and treats something harmless, like peanuts, as something really dangerous to the body and they end up having an allergic reaction.

With certain medical conditions, such as lupus or juvenile rheumatoid arthritis, instead of fighting germs, the immune system fights the good cells and this can cause problems. You can't prevent most immune system disorders. But if they happen, they can be treated with medicine and in other ways to help the child feel good and be healthy again. If your child has an immune system problem, your doctor can help teach them ways to take care of themselves so they stay strong and are able to fight off illness. Immunologists are doctors who specialize in immune system problems.

Colostrum – is an immune system builder and speeds healing.

CoQ10 – is a strong antioxidant, puts oxygen into the body, has anticancer properties.

Garlic – is an immune builder, antiviral, antibacterial, anti-parasite, and anticancer properties.

Beta-1, 6-glucan – a powerful immune builder.

Grape seed extract – is a strong antioxidant.

Multivitamin and mineral complex – very important for normal cell division. Use a whole food supplement.

B Complex - important for skin repair, cell repair and stress.

Essiac – is an Ojibwa (Native American) herbal blend that is used for cancer. It has sheep sorrel, burdock root, slippery elm bark, and turkey rhubarb root in it. There are many books about Essiac on the market and they are very informational about cancer. I use Essiac with my family, because it is a very good immune builder and the children seem to not get colds, etc. while they are taking it.

Immunizations

Shots protect you by giving you only a small part of a disease-causing germ or by giving you a version of the germ that is dead or very weak. But giving only this tiny, weakened, or dead part of the germ does not give you the disease. Instead, just the opposite happens. Your body responds to the vaccine by making antibodies. These antibodies are part of your immune system, and they can fight the disease if you ever come in contact with that nasty germ.

When your body is protected from a disease in this way, it's called being immune to an illness. In most cases, it means you won't get the illness at all. But sometimes, you can still get a mild case of the illness. This can happen with chickenpox. Even children who get the shot to prevent chickenpox can still get a case of it. The good news is that they usually don't get a very bad case of it. Milder cases mean fewer spots and less itching.

Shots are given by injection with a needle. Shots are usually given in your arm or sometimes your thigh. There are a few shots given when children are between the ages of 4 and 6 years. The next set of shots isn't usually until children are about 11 or 12 years old. Some children will get a flu shot each year. Shots are great for individual children because it means that they won't get those serious diseases. When almost all children have received these shots, it means that these illnesses do not have much of a chance to make anyone sick. Because most children in the United States get all their shots, you rarely meet anyone who has had diseases like measles or mumps.

Sometimes, after a shot, your child's arm will hurt, look red, or have a small bump where the needle went in. They may also could have a fever. Usually, the pain goes away quickly, or after taking a pain reliever, like acetaminophen or ibuprofen is given. It is very important to make sure your child is healthy when they go get their immunizations. If they are not well at the scheduled time for the immunization, then wait until they are, because their bodies are going to have enough to do building up antibodies, and they should be well for that. I have also read many studies, that if a child has a yeast infection during the 1 year and 18 month vaccination, and they receive the shot, it puts them at a higher risk of autism because of the chemical reaction in the brain from the vaccine and the yeast. I know a lot of people thought it was the mercury in the vaccine, but autism is on the rise since it was removed, and the studies are showing there is a correlation between yeast and the vaccine. Personally, I would play it safe and make sure my child didn't have a yeast problem at the time of immunizations, and do what ever I could to be sure it was under control.

Acidophilus - builds friendly flora and replaces important intestinal bacteria.

Caprylic acid - is an antifungal and kills candida fungus.

Garlic - a natural antibiotic and immune enhancer. Garlic has antifungal properties.

Colloidal Silver - is soothing and helps healing.

Grapefruit seed extract - Rids the body of harmful micro organisms.

Colostrum - A very strong immune builder.

Diet - should be low in sugar since Candida/Yeast grows quickly when you consume junk food. Nothing with dyes, preservatives, processed or sugar.

Indigestion

Indigestion is just another name for an upset stomach. Indigestion usually happens when children eat too much, too fast, or foods that don't agree with them. Heartburn is a burning feeling that travels from a child's chest up to the neck and throat. It's caused by stomach acid, which isn't a problem unless it gets out of the stomach. With heartburn, stomach acid splashes up and irritates the esophagus, the tube that carries food from the mouth to the stomach. Also called acid indigestion, this usually leaves a sour or bitter taste in the child's mouth.

Indigestion and heartburn are common problems for both children and grownups. That's why you see all those commercials for heartburn and indigestion medicines on TV. Digestive problems, such as ulcers, can cause the symptoms of indigestion and heartburn, too. But they're not common in children. If your child has indigestion, they will most likely have pain in their belly, nausea, bloating and gas. Usually, indigestion only happens once in a while, like after eating one too many hot dogs. But you'll want to see the doctor if they get indigestion even when they are eating healthy foods, exercising, and getting enough sleep.

Some children can eat anything and they never get upset stomachs. But other children are more sensitive to food and they might find certain ones just don't agree with them. If you discover one of these foods, it's best not to give them to your child or skip them entirely. In addition to avoiding problem foods, it's a good idea to eat several smaller meals instead of a couple really big ones.

Glucomannan – is a fiber that cleanses the colon and aids stool formation.

Enzymes – helps nutrients break down in the body and improves absorption.

Papaya enzyme – comes in chewable form and helps nutrients break down in the body and aids in digestion.

Acidophilus – helps with digestion.

Garlic – kills unwanted bacteria in the bowel.

Omega 3 Fatty Acids – helps with proper digestion.

Vitamin B – important for proper digestion.

Activated charcoal – absorbs intestinal gas.

L-Carnitine – puts fats into cells for energy.

Lecithin – helps break fat down.

Peppermint – aids in digestion.

Ginger – helps with nausea.

Parsley – helps relieve indigestion.

Pineapple – contains bromelain which is a digestive enzyme.

Hydrochloric Acid – is needed to digest foods properly.

Insect Allergy

Insects and other creatures like bees, wasps, spiders, scorpions, and hornets usually attack when they feel they're in danger. Sometimes they are protecting their territory, web, or nest. Other insects such as mosquitoes and ticks suck blood in order to survive. The female mosquito needs blood so that she can lay her eggs. Ticks are parasites, which means they live on other animals and need to suck blood to live.

Insects and other bugs can inject venom into your skin when they bite or sting you. It will make a small, itchy bump no bigger than a pea form on your skin. When you scratch, your skin becomes red and more itchy. A tick bite can cause a red rash that looks a little like a bull's-eye. In the case of bee stings, the area becomes swollen and a stinger might be left in the skin.

Some children have an allergic reaction to the venom that certain insects, such as bees, inject. If your child has trouble breathing, breaks out in hives, or feels like they are going to throw up after a bee or wasp has stung them, they could be having an allergic reaction. Once you know your child is allergic to bee stings, your doctor will provide you with a special kit. The kit is called an epinephrine kit and will contain a shot of epinephrine. You should keep this kit with you at all times, especially when you are outside.

You can keep from getting stung by staying away from bee or wasp nests. Keep sweet-smelling food or drink covered when you are eating outdoors. Don't swat at flying insects, it just makes them angry, causing them to bite or sting. If you go hiking, wear a long-sleeved shirt and pants tucked into your socks and shoes to avoid ticks. The best way to avoid being bitten by spiders or scorpions is to avoid places where they like to make their homes, like woodpiles.

In most cases bug bites are not serious and only hurt for a little while. The itching is the most irritating part of most bites and stings. Some bites or stings, such as a bite from a scorpion or a black widow spider, may require a trip to the emergency room. But this doesn't happen very often.

Charcoal - Make a paste using a few drops of water added to Activated Charcoal. This will draw out the poison from the bite. A lot of people have used mud with good results.

Ice - apply ice to the bite area to help reduce swelling and help with pain.

Lavender oil - reduces inflammation and pain.

Tea Tree oil - repels insects, stops itching, add to jojoba oil and apply. Do not get near eyes because it will burn.

Black tea bag - Put a few drops of water so that tea bag is wet. Then put it in a microwave for a couple of seconds until very warm. Then apply it to bite until the tea bag cools and then reheat and apply again until swelling is reduced. This will draw out the toxins.

Antihistamine - A antihistamine like benadryl will relieve itching and hives caused by the bite.

Meat tenderizer - Make a paste and apply. This will help with pain and swelling and drawing Out poison .

Buffered C with Bromelain - This has anti-inflammatory properties.

Insomnia

Not only is sleep necessary for your body, it's important for your brain. Though no one is exactly sure what work the brain does when you're asleep, some scientists think that the brain sorts through and stores information, replaces chemicals, and solves problems while you sleep.

Most children between 5 and 12 get about 9.5 hours a night, but experts agree that most need 10 or 11 hours each night. Sleep is an individual thing and some children need more than others. When your body doesn't have enough hours to rest, you may feel tired or cranky, or you may be unable to think clearly. Researchers believe too little sleep can affect growth and your immune system, which keeps you from getting sick.

As you slowly fall asleep, you begin to enter the five different stages of sleep. Stage 1, your brain gives the signal to your muscles to relax. It also tells your heart to beat a little slower, and your body temperature drops a bit. In stage 2, you can still be woken up easily. Stage 3, you're in a deeper sleep, also called slow-wave sleep. Your brain sends a message to your blood pressure to get lower. Your body isn't sensitive to the temperature of the air around you, which means that you won't notice if it's a little hot or cold in your room. It's much harder to be awakened when you're in this stage, but some people may sleepwalk or talk in their sleep at this point. Stage 4, is the deepest sleep yet and is also considered slow-wave sleep. It's very hard to wake up from this stage of sleep, and if you do wake up, you're sure to be out of it and confused for at least a few minutes. Like they do in stage 3, some people may sleepwalk or talk in their sleep when going from stage 4 to a lighter stage of sleep. REM, stands for Rapid Eye Movement. Even though the muscles in the rest of your body are totally relaxed, your eyes move back and forth very quickly beneath your eyelids. The REM stage is when your heart beats faster and your breathing is less regular. This is also the stage when people dream.

While you're asleep, you repeat stages 2, 3, 4, and REM about every 90 minutes until you wake up in the morning. For most children, that's about four or five times a night. For most children, sleeping comes pretty naturally, but others have a hard time falling asleep for more than one or two nights or have worries that are keeping them from sleeping. Just talking about it with your child could help them relax just enough that they will be ready to sleep.

Try to go to bed at the same time every night; this helps your body get into a routine. Limit foods and drinks that contain caffeine, like sodas, ice tea, and other drinks. Follow a bedtime routine that is calming, such as taking a warm bath or reading. Use your bed just for sleeping, not doing homework, reading, playing games, or talking on the phone. That way, you'll train your body to associate your bed with sleep.

Melatonin - Is a sleep aid, especially helps when child is having night fears and night anxiety.

Calms Forte - It is a homeopathic blend by Hyland's. We have used this for years. It helps with nervousness and sleeplessness.

Catnip – helps with anxiety and to relax.

Passion Flower – helps with stress and anxiety. Also has a calming effect.

Skullcap – helps with sleep, stress and anxiety.

Valerian - Helps with sleeplessness and anxiety.

Irritable Bowel Syndrome

The large intestine absorbs water and nutrients from the partially digested food that enters the colon from the small intestine. Anything that is not absorbed is slowly moved on a pathway out of your body. These undigested and unabsorbed food particles are also known as stool.

Here's why an intestine gets irritable. To have a bowel movement, the muscles in the colon and the rest of the body have to work together. If this process is somehow interrupted, the contents of the colon can't move along very smoothly. It sort of stops and starts, doesn't move, or sometimes moves too fast. This can hurt and make a child feel awful. Doctors also believe that children with IBS may have more sensitive bowels, so what might cause a little discomfort in one child causes serious pain for someone with IBS.

Between 5% to 20% of children have IBS, and about one in five adults do, too. It's not fun, but the good news is that IBS doesn't lead to more serious problems. It's irritating, but it can be managed and children can do whatever activities they like in spite of it.

Stress can affect children with IBS. Stress can speed up your colon and slow your stomach down. Stressful feelings also can be a trigger for IBS.

The best solution is to learn what makes the symptoms worse and avoid whatever it is. Sometimes it is a big meal, spicy foods, high fat foods, chocolate, dairy products, food poison, allergies, certain medicines, bacteria, virus, etc.. Sometimes it could just be your child eating to many fruits and one time or foods that are to high in fiber for them. Fiber is very good for children, but if they have to much of it, or are not use to fiber in their diets and then it's added, it could cause loose stools. Do not drink apple juice while rehydrating, because it could make diarrhea worse.

Fluids – to prevent dehydration.

Gelatin water – to prevent dehydration.

Apple pectin – absorbs toxins from the colon and helps with diarrhea.

Charcoal - Absorbs toxins from colon and stops diarrhea. This is one of the first thing we grab when a child has diarrhea.

Minerals - replaces minerals lost from diarrhea.

Acidophilus - builds friendly bacteria.

Garlic -kills bacteria and parasites.

Wild oregano oil - antibacterial, antifungal, kills parasites, and antiviral.

Kelp – replaces minerals lost from diarrhea.

Fenugreek tea – lubricates the intestines and reduce fever.

Marshmallow root tea – calms the stomach and soothes intestinal problems.

CoQ10 – is a strong antioxidant and removes toxins from the body and builds the immune system.

Jaundice

Jaundice is a common condition in newborns, jaundice refers to the yellow color of the skin and whites of the eyes caused by excess bilirubin in the blood. Bilirubin is produced by the normal breakdown of red blood cells.

Normally bilirubin passes through the liver and is excreted as bile through the intestines. Jaundice occurs when bilirubin builds up faster than a newborn's liver can break it down and pass it from the body. A newborn baby's still-developing liver may not yet be able to remove adequate bilirubin from the blood and more bilirubin is being made than the infant's liver can handle.

High levels of bilirubin, usually above 20 mg, can cause deafness, cerebral palsy, or brain damage in some babies. The American Academy of Pediatrics recommends that all infants should be examined for jaundice within a few days after being born.

Jaundice usually appears around the second or third day of life. It begins at the head and progresses downward. A jaundiced baby's skin will appear yellow first on the face, followed by the chest and stomach, and finally, the legs. It can also cause the whites of an infant's eyes to appear yellow. Since many babies are now released from the hospital at 1 or 2 days of life, parents should keep an eye on their infants to detect jaundice.

In mild or moderate levels of jaundice, by 5 to 7 days of age the baby will take care of the excess bilirubin on its own. If high levels of jaundice do not clear up, phototherapy, treatment with a special light that helps rid the body of the bilirubin by altering it or making it easier for your baby's liver to get rid of it, may be prescribed.

It is also possible for older children to get jaundice, which could be a symptom of anemia, parasitic infestation, viral, bacterial, or a bite from an insect that carries a virus.

Milk thistle (Silymarin) – repairs liver damage and detoxes.

Burdock root – cleanses the blood.

Red Clover – cleanses the blood.

Dandelion – cleanses the blood.

CoQ10 – is a strong antioxidant and removes toxins from the body and builds the immune system.

Colostrum – is an immune builder and protects the liver.

Grape Seed Extract – is a strong antioxidant and removes toxins from the body.

Garlic – detoxes the liver.

Vitamin B – is needed for proper absorption of nutrients and formation of red blood cells that protect the liver.

Oregano – helps get rid of jaundice.

Vitamin C – helps the body to get rid of toxins.

Turmeric – is a liver cleanser.

Kidney Disease

Your kidneys are tucked under your lower ribs on either side of your spine. Each one is about the size of your fist and shaped like a bean. Most people have two kidneys, but they work so effectively that a person can be happy and healthy with only one. Each day your kidneys act like high-powered filters for about 200 quarts of fluid in your flowing blood. That's enough fluid to fill 100 of those big soda bottles that hold 2 liters each.

Your kidneys remove waste and excess fluid that naturally builds up in your blood after your body breaks down food. The kidneys collect that stuff and send it on to the bladder as urine, so you can get rid of it when you go to the bathroom. Besides taking out your body's waste, your kidneys help balance your body's vitamin and mineral levels so your other organs and bones can do their best work. They help in the production of red blood cells and produce a form of vitamin D, which promotes healthy bones. If that's not enough, they help keep your blood pressure at a healthy level.

Like any complicated machine, not all kidneys work perfectly. When someone's kidneys have problems for a long time, doctors call it a chronic kidney disease. Children's kidney problems are either congenital or acquired. The difference is that a congenital problem exists from the day someone is born. An acquired kidney problem develops over time, often due to an injury, kidney infection, or other illness. Many congenital kidney problems are hereditary, which means it's something that is passed down through your genes. Acquired kidney problems are not hereditary.

Kidney problems are often not noticed at an early stage. As the illness progresses, a person with a kidney disease may feel tired, nauseated, itchy, or dizzy. The child also might have puffy eyes, ankles, or feet because the child's body has trouble getting rid of extra fluid. A child who has these problems needs to go to the doctor.

The treatment for chronic kidney problems depends on how well the kidneys are working. It may include vitamins, minerals, and medications to help with growth and to prevent bone disease. Sometimes unhealthy kidneys have problems producing a hormone that helps make red blood cells, the cells that carry oxygen to your body's tissues. Children with kidney problems are more likely to get high blood pressure, which can be harmful if it isn't controlled. For kidneys that need even more help, doctors might suggest dialysis, a process that cleans the blood artificially. A kidney transplant is another possibility. In this operation, doctors replace a kidney that doesn't work with a healthy kidney from another person.

Coenzyme A – is a strong antioxidant and removes toxins from the body.

B complex – is needed for cell repair and helps get rid of excess fluid.

Mutimineral complex – helps with mineral depletion.

Celery seed tea – is a natural diuretic and helps get rid of uric acid.

Cranberries – causes the urine to be acidic destroying bacteria. Do not use the sweetened drink mixes, only pure cranberry juice.

Uva Ursi tea – is a natural diuretic and kills germs.

Knee

Osgood-Schlatter disease is one of the most common causes of knee pain in children who play sports. Usually only one knee is affected, but both can be. There may be a slightly swollen, warm, and tender bony bump at the top of the lower leg, about 2 inches below the kneecap. The bump hurts when pressed. It also hurts when a child kneels, jumps, runs, squats, or does anything that bends or fully extends the leg.

The quadriceps tendon attaches the large, powerful quadriceps muscle to the kneecap. Another tendon, the patellar tendon, attaches this big thigh muscle to the shin bone. Your muscles and tendons work together when you move your legs. A child who plays sports uses their knees and legs a lot. All this activity means the patellar tendon pulls at the attachment to the shin bone a lot. That's what causes the pain of Osgood-Schlatter disease.

Although boys are more likely to develop the condition, many girls involved in sports, like gymnastics or soccer, develop it, too. If your doctor suspects Osgood-Schlatter disease, he or she may arrange for X-rays of your knee just to make sure that there isn't another problem. Your doctor also might send you to an orthopedist, a doctor specially trained to understand bones, joints, ligaments, tendons, and muscles.

If it's Osgood-Schlatter, resting the knee may be helpful in getting the pain to settle down. Applying ice directly to the painful area after vigorous activities can help along with pain-relieving medicine, such as ibuprofen or acetaminophen. Learning how to properly stretch your hamstring and quadriceps muscles is also an important part of the treatment of this condition. With rest, stretching, and time, the pain usually goes away. Children with Osgood-Schlatter don't have to give up sports, but they may have to limit their activities for a few weeks or months until the pain improves.

Robert Bayley Osgood, a U.S. orthopedist, and Carl Schlatter, a Swiss surgeon, were the two doctors who described this knee problem in 1903. The condition was named after them and that is how a little knee condition got a very big name.

Boron – increases calcium uptake and helps in healing bones and bone health.

Silica – helps in calcium absorption and connective tissue repair.

Horsetail – helps in calcium absorption and connective tissue repair.

Amino acid complex – speeds healing and cell repair.

Calcium and magnesium – helps with muscular tension.

Bromelain – an enzyme that has anti inflammatory properties.

DLPA DL-Phenylalanine – is a pain reliever.

Glucosamine sulfate – is a natural pain reliever and helps with inflammation.

L-Tyrosine – helps with pain.

Primrose Oil – helps with inflammation.

Ginger – is a natural pain reliever.

Lactose Intolerance

People who have lactose intolerance have trouble digesting lactose, a type of sugar found in milk and other dairy foods. Lactose intolerance does not mean you are allergic to milk, but you will probably feel bad after drinking milk or eating cheese, ice cream, or anything else containing lactose.

As with everything else you eat, your body needs to digest lactose to be able to use it for fuel. The small intestine normally makes a special substance called lactase, an enzyme that breaks lactose down into simpler sugars called glucose and galactose. These sugars are easy for your body to absorb and turn into energy.

People who have lactose intolerance do not make enough of the lactase enzyme in their small intestine. Without lactase, your body can't properly digest food that has lactose in it. This means that if you eat dairy foods, the lactose from these foods will stay in your intestines, where it can cause gas, cramps, a bloated feeling, and diarrhea.

Between 30 million and 50 million people in the United States have lactose intolerance. Most of them do not show signs of it before they are old enough to start school. Many cases of lactose intolerance are genetic. The condition is more common among some groups of people - about 90% of Asian Americans are lactose intolerant, and up to 75% of African Americans, Hispanic Americans, and Native Americans get symptoms whenever they eat dairy foods. If you belong to one of these groups, you're also more likely to develop lactose intolerance while you're young.

Even if your child doesn't have trouble with lactose now, there's a chance they might someday, because your body starts making less lactase when you're around 2 years old. The older you get, the more likely it is that you could have trouble digesting dairy foods.

Yogurt - contains live cultures and is more easily digested because it contains healthy bacteria that produce lactase. Even if you are lactose intolerant, you may be able to handle smaller portions of your favorite dairy products.

Calcium and mineral complex – nutrients that are needed for optimal health and strong bones.

Vitamin D – needed for calcium uptake.

Charcoal – absorbs toxins and helps with diarrhea.

Lactaid – supplies the enzyme lactase that is needed for digesting milk sugar.

Soy milk – is a good substitute to use in place of milk. There is also soy cheese and other products on the market if your child is lactose intolerant.

Rice milk – is a good substitute to use in place of milk.

Diet – it is important to eat foods that are high in calcium such as broccoli, greens, salmon, spinach, tofu, and yogurt.

Magnesium – needed to help break calcium down and get it into cells and balance pH.

Multivitamin/Mineral - is needed to correct chemical imbalances due to poor nutrition.

Cod liver oil – contains vitamin A and D and are for proper growth, strong tissues, and bones.

Laryngitis

At the top of your windpipe is your larynx, or voice box. It's the source of your voice. Inside your larynx are two bands of muscles called vocal cords, or vocal folds. When you breathe, your vocal cords are relaxed and open so that you can get air into and out of your lungs. But when you decide to say something, these cords come together. Now the air from your lungs has to pass through a smaller space. This causes your vocal cords to vibrate. The sound from these vibrations goes up your throat and comes out your mouth.

You can make different sounds by lengthening or shortening, or tensing or relaxing, the vocal cords. Although you don't even think about it, every time you want to talk with a deeper voice you lengthen and relax these vocal muscles. When you talk with a higher pitched voice, you tighten the vocal cords and make them smaller.

When your cords become inflamed and swollen, they can't work properly. Your voice may sound hoarse. This is called laryngitis. In children, laryngitis often comes from too much yelling and screaming. They may be hollering at their younger brother or sister. Or they may be in a group of noisy children and have to talk loudly to be heard. Even a lot of loud singing can irritate their vocal cords and cause laryngitis. Over time, children who yell all the time may develop nodules, or little bumps, on their vocal cords. This can make their voice hoarse, rough, and deeper than usual.

Although it sounds odd, sometimes your stomach can cause laryngitis. Just like you have a tube for air to go into and out of your lungs, you have a tube for food to go into your stomach. Sometimes the stomach acid that helps break down that food comes back up your swallowing tube. The acid can irritate your vocal cords. Infections from germs are a very common cause of laryngitis in children as well as adults. Sometimes bacteria can infect the vocal cords, but most of the time it's viruses.

A raspy voice is the main symptom or sign of laryngitis. Your child may also have no voice at all or maybe just little squeaks come out when they try to talk. They may need to cough to clear their throat, or they may feel a tickle deep in their throat. These are all signs that they may have laryngitis. They may have this strange voice for a few days, but if they have it longer, you probably will need to go to the doctor.

To prevent laryngitis, try not to let your child talk or yell in a way that hurts their voice. A humidifier that puts more water into the air may also help keep their throat from drying out.

Bee propolis – protects the mucous membranes in the mouth and throat. Do not use if allergic to bee stings.

Colloidal silver – is a natural antibiotic. It is also soothing to the throat to gargle with.

Garlic – builds the immune system.

Vitamin C – has antiviral properties.

Blackberry tea – soothes and heals a sore throat.

Licorice – soothes a sore throat and helps with the hoarseness.

Fenugreek tea – relieves a sore throat when you gargle with it.

Lead Poisoning

If you have young children, it's important to find out whether there's any risk that they might be exposed to lead, especially if you live in an older home. Long-term exposure to lead, a naturally occurring metal used in everything from construction materials to batteries, can cause serious health problems, particularly in young children. Lead is toxic to everyone, but unborn babies and young children are at greatest risk for health problems from lead poisoning because their smaller, growing bodies make them more susceptible to absorbing and retaining lead. Each year in the United States 310,000 1- to 5-year-old children are found to have unsafe levels of lead in their blood, which can lead to a wide range of symptoms, from headaches and stomach pain to behavioral problems and anemia. Lead can also affect a child's developing brain. You can protect your family from lead poisoning. If your child is between 6 months and 3 years of age, talk to your doctor about potential lead sources in your house or anywhere your child spends long periods of time. And it's important for children to get tested for lead exposure at age 1 and again at age 2, as many with lead poisoning don't show any symptoms.

When the body is exposed to lead by being inhaled, swallowed, or in a small number of cases, absorbed through the skin, it can act as a poison. Exposure to high levels of lead in a short period of time is called acute toxicity. Exposure to small amounts of lead over a long period of time is called chronic toxicity.

Lead is particularly dangerous because once it gets into a child's system, it is distributed throughout the body just like helpful minerals such as iron, calcium, and zinc. And lead can cause harm wherever it lands in the body. In the bloodstream, for example, it can damage red blood cells and limit their ability to carry oxygen to the organs and tissues that need it. Most lead ends up in the bone, where it causes even more problems. Lead can interfere with the production of blood cells and the absorption of calcium that bones need to grow healthy and strong. Calcium is essential for strong bones and teeth, muscle contraction, and nerve and blood vessel function.

Some of the health problems that lead poisoning causes are decreased bone and muscle growth, poor muscle coordination, damage to nervous system, kidneys, hearing, speech, language problems, developmental delay, and in cases of very high lead levels, seizures.

Most commonly, young children get lead poisoning from lead-based paint, which was used in many U.S. homes until the late 1970s, when the dangers of lead became known and the government banned the manufacture of paint containing lead. That's why children who live in older homes are at a greater risk for lead poisoning. Also at risk are those who immigrate to the United States or are adopted from a foreign country that doesn't regulate the use of lead. Another big concern is toys coming from countries that do not regulate the use of lead.

Apple pectin – binds toxins and metals and removes them from the body.

Garlic – helps to cleanse and detox the body and remove metals from the body.

Kelp – removes unwanted metal deposits.

MSM – helps the body remove toxic metals.

Alfalfa – helps detox the body and is high in vitamin and minerals.

Lice

Every year millions of children worldwide get head lice. Any child who goes to school has probably already heard about lice. They can spread easily at schools, so if one child gets them, the rest of the class might get them, too. Lice are very small insects. In fact, they are so tiny that you can barely see them. Each louse is brown and gray and only about the size of a sesame seed.

Lice are parasites, which means that they live off other living things. Head lice need to be next to skin to survive and the warmth of your skin is a perfect place for them to live. Lice eat tiny amounts of blood for their nourishment and use their sticky little feet to hold on to hair.

When lice start living in hair, they also start to lay eggs, or nits. Lice can survive up to 30 days on a person's head and can lay eight eggs a day. Lice attach their nits to pieces of hair, close to the scalp. If you see a small, oval blob on a strand of hair, that's probably a nit. If these little eggs are yellow, tan, or brown, the lice haven't hatched yet. If the eggs are white or clear, the lice have hatched.

Although they don't hurt, lice sometimes can irritate the skin and make it itchy, especially at night. Too much scratching can lead to scalp infections. Because lice are parasites, they will set up house on anyone's head, whether that person is clean, dirty, in second grade, in fifth grade, black, or white. Anyone who says that people who get lice are dirty doesn't know that lice love everyone and that includes the cleanest children in the class. Lice spread in classrooms and schools because children play together closely and often share more stuff than adults do.

Lice cannot jump or fly. They spread when people's heads touch or when they share hats and other clothing, combs, brushes, headbands, barrettes, and bedding, sheets, blankets, pillowcases, and sleeping bags. If lice are stuck on any of these things and that thing touches another person's head, that person may also get lice. Although lice can live for only 1 to 2 days off a person's head, it's a good idea to wash all your bedding, hats, clothing, and stuffed animals in hot water. Or seal these things in airtight bags for 10 days. That also will kill the lice and their eggs.

Vacuuming the carpets, upholstery, and car seats will take care of any lice that fell off before treatment. Combs, brushes, and hair accessories need to be soaked in hot water, washed with medicated shampoo, or thrown away.

Tea Tree Oil – kills lice on contact. It is important not to get it in a child's eyes, because it will be very irritating. Speaking from experience, if it gets in the eyes, rinse with warm water mixed with a little vegetable oil and dry with a towel. Add a fourth of an ounce of tea tree oil to your shampoo and wash your child's hair as usual when there is a lice out break going around school, because lice will stay away as well as mosquitoes, flies, flees, and other insects.

Meat tenderizer – make a paste out of it and apply to hair and leave on for several minutes to remove eggs from hair shaft. The meat tenderizer has enzymes in it that eat away at the glue that holds the eggs to the hair.

Lyme Disease

Ticks hang out in wooded, grassy areas, so cover up. If you find a tick on your child, remove it with needle nose tweezers by grabbing the head or mouth parts and not the body. Then pull firmly outward and place the tick in alcohol to kill it and then take it to your child's pediatrician. Watch for a rash that looks like a ring around the original bite. If a rash appears or there is fever, joint pain, chills or fatigue, then call your doctor. Ask your doctor about preventive antibiotics within 72 hours after a tick bite if you live in an area where Lyme disease is common.

In the spring and summer, you might hear about something called Lyme disease, a bacteria that ticks carry. If the bacteria gets in a person, it can cause the infection Lyme disease. The bacteria are called spirochetes. The best way to prevent Lyme disease is to prevent tick bites. Ticks feed on mice, dogs, horses, and sometimes people. They have eight legs, but are so tiny, they might look like a speck of dirt or the head of a pin. You're most likely to run into them in grassy or wooded areas. In spring and summer, you're more likely to have a lot of skin exposed, so it gives ticks a lot of opportunity to latch on to your skin.

You don't feel anything when the tick first bites you. You probably won't even know the tick is feeding. After an infected tick bites you, it pumps some water back into your body. In this way, it can spit the spirochetes into you. If the tick has been there a more than a day or two, there is a small chance that you can get Lyme disease. If your child has symptoms of feeling tired and achy all over, flu like symptoms, and a bull's eye rash around the area the tick was attached, then it is important to go see your doctor. If you wait too long, your child may start to feel even worse. In some cases, a person's face muscles might stop working properly. That means the person wouldn't be able to smile on that side or close that eye. It's called Bell's palsy, or facial nerve paralysis. Other people might develop swelling or pain in their knees or another joint a few months after the tick bite. Once the doctor knows for sure, he or she will prescribe an antibiotic, a medicine that kills the spirochetes.

Essential fatty acids – helps with inflammation and joint pain.

Primrose oil – is an essential fatty acid and helps with pain and inflammation.

Garlic – acts as an antibiotic and a strong immune builder.

Kelp – removes toxins from the body.

Selenium – is a free radical scavenger.

Vitamin C with bioflavonoids – helps build the immune system.

Horsetail – helps rebuild blood and damaged tissue.

Bromelain – helps reduce inflammation.

Pineapple – enzymes in pineapple help to reduce inflammation.

Echinacea – helps build the immune system.

Goldenseal – acts as a natural antibiotic and immune builder.

Red Clover – cleanses the bloodstream.

Malnutrition

We all feel hungry at times. Hunger is the way the body signals that it needs to eat. Once a person is able to eat enough food to satisfy the body's needs, he or she stops being hungry. Teens can feel hungry a lot because their rapidly growing and developing bodies demand extra food.

Children with malnutrition lack the nutrients necessary for their bodies to grow and stay healthy. A child can be malnourished for a long or short period of time, and the condition may be mild or severe. Malnutrition can affect a child's physical and mental health. Children who are suffering from malnutrition are more likely to get sick; in very severe cases, they may even die from its effects.

Children who are malnourished don't grow as tall as they should and they are underweight as well. Children suffer from hunger because they don't get enough food, and not getting enough food over the long term can lead to malnutrition. But someone can become malnourished for reasons that have nothing to do with hunger. Children who have plenty to eat may still be malnourished if they don't eat food that provides the right nutrients, vitamins, and minerals.

Some children become malnourished because they have a disease or condition that prevents them from digesting or absorbing their food properly. For example, someone with celiac disease has intestinal problems that are triggered by a protein called gluten, which is found in wheat, rye, barley, and oats. Celiac disease can interfere with the intestine's ability to absorb nutrients, which may result in nutritional deficiencies.

Children with cystic fibrosis have trouble absorbing nutrients because the disease affects the pancreas, an organ that normally produces chemical substances called enzymes that are necessary for digesting food. Children who are lactose intolerant have difficulty digesting milk and some other dairy products. By avoiding dairy products, they are at higher risk of malnutrition because milk and dairy products provide 75% of the calcium in America's food supply. In the United States, food manufacturers fortify some common foods with vitamins and minerals to prevent certain nutritional deficiencies. For example, the addition of iodine to salt helps prevent some thyroid gland problems, the folic acid that's added to foods can help prevent certain birth defects, and added iron can help prevent iron-deficiency anemia.

Malnutrition harms children both physically and mentally. The more malnourished someone is and the more nutrients they're missing, the more likely it is that the child will have physical problems. The signs and symptoms of malnutrition depend on which nutritional deficiencies a child has. Some children may have fatigue and low energy, dizziness, poor immune function, dry skin, bleeding gums, tooth decay, underweight, poor growth, muscle weakness, and brittle bones. When a pregnant woman is malnourished, her child may weigh less at birth and have a smaller chance of survival.

Acidophilus – is needed for the breakdown of many nutrients.

Multivitamin and mineral complex - is needed to correct chemical imbalances due to poor nutrition.

Malnutrition Deficiency – Continued

Vitamin A deficiency is the biggest cause of preventable blindness in the developing world. Children in developing countries who have a severe vitamin A deficiency as a result of malnutrition have a greater chance of getting sick or of dying from infections such as diarrhea and measles.

Iodine deficiency, another form of malnutrition, can cause mental retardation, delayed development, and even blindness in severe cases.

Iron deficiency can cause a person to be less active and less able to concentrate. Students who are malnourished often have trouble keeping up in school.

Fortunately, many of the harmful effects of malnutrition can be reversed, especially if a child is only mildly or briefly malnourished. To correct problems related to malnutrition, a doctor or dietitian will recommend specific changes in the types and quantities of foods that a child eats. Sometimes he or she will prescribe dietary supplements, such as vitamins and minerals. Other treatment may be necessary for children who are found to have a specific disease or condition causing their malnutrition.

Few teens in the United States and other developed nations suffer from serious malnutrition like that seen in Third World countries. Over time, even children who are very finicky eaters usually will get enough calories and nutrients to develop a healthy body.

B complex – helps correct deficiencies. B vitamins need to be replaced daily and are needed for normal digestion and to prevent anemia.

Calcium – is needed for healthy bones.

Amino Acid Complex – to help protein break down in the body, because protein is needed for all body functions.

DHA and EPA - is being added to baby cereal and formula because it is so good for the brain and their development. It is a very good essential fatty acid.

Garlic – aids in digestion and promotes healing.

Magnesium – is important for energy production and helps calcium break down.

Vitamin C – is needed to stimulate the immune system.

Essential Fatty Acid – repairs the cells along the intestinal walls and the proper break down of fats.

zinc – aids in the break down of digestive enzymes and proteins.

Alfalfa – helps the body absorb nutrients.

Fennel seed tea – helps the body absorb nutrients.

Irish moss – are good for colon disorders.

Yellow dock – improves colon and liver function.

Pineapple – high in enzymes and helps food break down.

Measles

Measles, also called rubeola, is a highly contagious respiratory infection that's caused by a virus. It causes a total-body skin rash and flu-like symptoms, including a fever, cough, and runny nose. Since measles is caused by a virus, symptoms typically go away on their own without medical treatment once the virus has run its course. But a child who is sick should be sure to receive plenty of fluids and rest, and kept from spreading the infection to others.

While measles is probably best known for the full-body rash that it causes, the first symptoms of the infection are usually a hacking cough, runny nose, high fever, and watery red eyes. Another marker of measles are small red spots with blue-white centers that appear inside the mouth. The measles rash typically has a red or reddish brown blotchy appearance, and first usually shows up on the forehead, then spreads downward over the face, neck, and body, then down to the feet. When someone with measles sneezes or coughs, he or she can spread virus droplets through the air and infect others.

Measles is very rare in the United States. Due to widespread immunizations, the number of U.S. measles cases has steadily declined in the last 50 years. There were thousands of cases of the measles in 1950, but in 2002 there were just 44. Most of the time, the cases occur in settings where there are lots of kids, some of whom haven't gotten vaccinated or whose immunity has diminished since they got the vaccine.

Infants are generally protected from measles for 6 to 8 months after birth due to immunity passed on from their mothers. Older children are usually immunized against measles according to state and school health regulations. For most children, the measles vaccine is part of the measles-mumps-rubella immunizations (MMR) given at 12 to 15 months of age and again at 4 to 6 years of age. Measles vaccine is not usually given to infants younger than 12 months old. But if there's a measles outbreak, the vaccine may be given when a child is 9 months old, followed by the usual MMR immunization at 12–15 months.

The vaccine shouldn't be given to children who have a history of severe allergic reaction to gelatin or to the antibiotic neomycin, as they are at risk for serious reactions to the vaccine. These children can be protected from measles infection with an injection of antibodies called gamma globulin if it's given within 6 days of exposure. These antibodies can either prevent measles or make the symptoms less severe. Measles vaccine occasionally causes side effects in children who don't have any underlying health problems. In about 10% of cases the measles vaccine causes a fever between 5 and 12 days after vaccination, and in about 5% of cases the vaccine causes a rash, which isn't contagious and usually fades on its own.

Vitamin A – helps reduce infection and helps with tissue repair.

B complex – is necessary for cell repair, healing, and immune response.

Vitamin C – has antiviral properties, fights fevers, and helps immune function.

zinc – helps speed healing and tissue repair.

Lobelia tea – helps relieve pain.

Spirulina – is a single cell food that helps build a healthy immune system.

Meningitis

The central nervous system (brain and spinal cord) is surrounded by cerebro spinal fluid. This fluid acts to cushion and protect the central nervous system when you move around. Even more protection is given by the meninges, which are the membranes that cover the brain and spinal cord. Meningitis is a disease involving inflammation, or irritation, of the meninges. There are different kinds of meningitis, but most of the time it is caused by germs, especially viruses.

Meningitis gets attention because it not only makes a person feel sick, it can have lasting effects on a person's ability to think and learn. It also can cause hearing loss. But many children recover from the infection without permanent damage. And the illness is so rare, you may never know anyone who gets it. Many viruses can cause viral meningitis. They include a family of viruses known as enteroviruses. Like most viruses, enteroviruses infect your body through saliva, feces, and nasal discharge. This is why washing your hands after you go to the bathroom, after you sneeze, and before you eat is so important. Bacterial meningitis is contagious also, and it can be spread when you sneeze or cough, when you share cups or utensils, or when you kiss someone

Usually, a child with meningitis will have a headache, neck stiffness, back stiffness, eyes are sensitive when exposed to light, nausea, vomiting, body aches, fever, unable to fully wake up and feeling confused. A spinal tap allows the doctor to collect some of the cerebrospinal fluid that surrounds the brain and spinal cord. During a spinal tap, a child usually lies on his or her side curled into a ball. First, the doctor will numb the skin with medication. The child needs to lie very still while the doctor inserts a very thin needle into the spinal column. The needle is placed between two vertebral bones in the lower back away from the spinal cord. Fluid is removed and collected in some tubes. Then the needle is removed and the doctor puts a bandage over the area.

After it is collected, the spinal fluid will be examined under a microscope to see if any bacteria, cells, or substances that indicate inflammation or infection are there. The fluid will also be sent to a laboratory to be tested for bacteria and sometimes for viruses. Once the doctors know what germ is causing the meningitis, they can choose the best medicine to treat the infection. Bacterial meningitis is very serious and a person will need to be in the hospital during treatment. Strong antibiotic medicine will be given through an IV to get rid of the bacteria. Fluids containing glucose and minerals may also be given through the IV to help a child recover.

Viral meningitis can also be serious, but usually is not as bad as meningitis caused by bacteria. A child with viral meningitis may still need to be in the hospital for a few days and it may take weeks before he or she is feeling better. Antibiotics do not work against viruses, so a child with viral meningitis will need lots of rest to fight off the infection.

Olive leaf extract – fights viral infections.

Colloidal Silver – fights against many disease causing organisms and has antifungal properties.

Garlic – builds the immune system, antibacterial and antiviral.

Vitamin C – helps reduce fever, infection and helps clean the bloodstream.

Mononucleosis

Infectious mononucleosis, sometimes called "mono" or "the kissing disease," is an infection usually caused by the Epstein-Barr virus (EBV). EBV is very common, and many people have been exposed to the virus at some time in childhood. Not everyone who is exposed to EBV develops the symptoms of mono, though. As with many viruses, it is possible to be exposed to and infected with EBV without becoming sick. People who have been infected with EBV will carry the virus for the rest of their lives even if they never have any signs or symptoms of mono. People who do show symptoms of having mono probably will not get sick or have symptoms again.

One common way to "catch" mono is by kissing someone who has been infected, which is how the illness got its "kissing disease" nickname. If you have never been infected with EBV, kissing someone who is infected can put you at risk for getting the disease. You can also get mononucleosis through other types of direct contact with saliva from someone infected with EBV, such as by sharing a straw, a toothbrush, or an eating utensil.

Some symptoms of mono are constant fatigue, fever, sore throat, loss of appetite, swollen lymph nodes, headaches, sore muscles, skin rash, and abdominal pain. People who have mono may have different combinations of these symptoms, and some may have symptoms so mild that they hardly notice them. Others may have no symptoms at all. Even if you have several of these symptoms, don't try to diagnose yourself. Always consult your doctor if you have a fever, sore throat, and swollen glands or are unusually tired for no apparent reason.

Because the symptoms of mono are so general and can be signs of other illnesses, it's possible to mistake mononucleosis for the flu, strep throat, or other diseases. In fact, occasionally some people may have mono and strep throat at the same time.

There is no cure for mononucleosis. But the good news is that even if you do nothing, the illness will go away by itself, usually in 3 to 4 weeks. Because mono is caused by a virus, antibiotics such as penicillin won't help unless you have an additional infection like strep throat. In fact, certain antibiotics can even cause a rash if you take them while you have mono.

Astragalus – helps build up the immune system.

Echinacea – helps build up the immune system.

Cat's Claw – fights against viral infections and builds the immune system.

Dandelion – helps protect the liver.

Olive leaf extract – helps inhibit the growth of viruses.

Acidophilus – builds up the friendly flora and protects the body from bacterial infection.

Vitamin A – helps fight against infection.

Vitamin C – has antiviral properties and boost the immune system.

Garlic – has antibacterial, antiviral properties, and builds the immune system.

B Complex – increase energy and is needed for all body functions.

zinc – speeds healing and is an antioxidant.

Motion Sickness

If you've ever been sick to your stomach while riding in a car, train, airplane, or boat, you know exactly what motion sickness feels like. If you're riding in a car and reading a book, your inner ears and skin receptors will detect that you are moving forward. Yet, your eyes are looking at a book that isn't moving, and your muscle receptors are telling your brain that you're sitting still. The brain gets an instant report from these different parts of your body and tries to put together a total picture about what you are doing just at that moment. But if any of the pieces of this picture don't match, you can get motion sickness.

So the brain gets a little confused. Things may begin to feel a little scrambled inside your head at that point. When this happens, you might feel really tired, dizzy, or sick to your stomach. Sometimes you might even throw up. And if you're feeling scared or anxious, your motion sickness might get even worse.

But for typical motion sickness, you may be able to take medicine before travel. For some children, it may help to wear pressure bracelets that can be bought at the pharmacy or drugstore.

If your child is getting sick while they are traveling in a car, it might help if the driver finds a safe spot, where the child can get out and walk around a little bit. If you can't pull over, make sure you have a plastic bag in the car just in case. Many natural remedies have been used with great success for motion sickness. Motion sickness is far easier to prevent than it is to cure. Once excess salivation and nausea set in, it is usually to late to do anything but wait for the trip to be over.

Black horehound – reduces nausea.

Butcher's broom tea – helps relieve vertigo.

Motherwort – helps relieve vertigo.

Ginger – helps with nausea and sooths an upset stomach.

Peppermint tea – calms the stomach.

Magnesium – helps relieve nausea.

Vitamin B6 – helps relieve nausea.

Calcium & Magnesium - This has a calming effect. It is best to take Calcium with Magnesium because they work synergistically well together to relieve anxiety and nervousness.

Multivitamin and mineral complex – is needed to correct chemical imbalances due to poor nutrition.

B - Complex - It helps with stress, nerves and provides energy.

Vitamin C – helps with anxiety, stress, and immune system.

Catnip – helps with anxiety and to relax.

Passion Flower – helps with stress and anxiety. Also has a calming effect.

Skullcap – helps with sleep, stress and anxiety.

Multiple Sclerosis

Although multiple sclerosis has long been considered an adult disease, doctors are now starting to diagnose more cases in children, according to a report in The Wall Street Journal. Multiple sclerosis, or MS, is an autoimmune disorder in which myelin, the protective coating surrounding the brain and spinal cord, becomes inflamed. That inflammation can affect the person's speech, vision, movement, and bladder function. There is no cure for MS, but treatment can reduce the symptoms, and help slow the progression of the disease. The exact cause of MS isn't known, but doctors suspect that a combination of genetic and environmental factors may trigger the disease.

MS affects approximately 10,000 children between the ages of 10 and 17. Experts believe that the condition may be going undiagnosed in many children because MS isn't among the usual suspects of pediatric diseases doctors consider, the Journal said. Doctors have long known that MS can affect children. But there's a drive to diagnose the disease earlier now as advancements in technology have given doctors more tools to make the diagnosis, and new research is showing that many adults with MS had symptoms as children.

Many of the symptoms of MS are the same in children and adults, but for children, some of the symptoms, such as memory lapses and reading difficulty may have a bigger impact because their brains are still under development. Doctors are hoping to better understand what kinds of environmental triggers contribute to MS in children .

There is no single test to diagnose MS. In children with symptoms pointing to MS, doctors typically diagnose the condition by performing a series of tests over time and ruling out other causes for the child's symptoms. The symptoms of MS affect different children in different ways. But they generally include extreme fatigue, numbness and tingling, vision problems, loss of balance and muscle coordination, slurred speech, tremors, stiffness, and bladder control problems. Some symptoms may come and go, while others may be long lasting.

If your child has any of these symptoms, it's important to talk with your child's pediatrician.

CoQ10 – helps with circulation, tissue oxygenation, strengthening the immune system, and a strong antioxidant.

MSN – helps with pain and nutrients to get into cells and helps remove toxins.

Essential Fatty Acid - repairs the cells along the intestinal walls and the proper break down of fats.

Amino Acid Complex – nutrients needed for the muscles.

L-glycine – helps strengthens the myelin sheaths.

Calcium and magnesium complex – to prevent deficiencies and helps minerals absorb in body.

Grape Seed Extract - is a strong antioxidant and anti inflammatory.

Grapefruit seed extract - Rids the body of harmful micro organisms.

Colostrum - A very strong immune builder.

Mumps

Mumps is a disease caused by a virus that usually spreads through saliva and can infect many parts of the body, especially the parotid salivary glands. These glands, which produce saliva for the mouth, are found toward the back of each cheek, in the area between the ear and jaw. In cases of mumps, these glands typically swell and become painful.

Mumps was common until the mumps vaccine was licensed in 1967. Before the vaccine, more than 200,000 cases occurred each year in the United States. Since then the number of cases has dropped to fewer than 1,000 a year, and epidemics have become fairly rare. Most cases of mumps are still in children ages 5 to 14, but the proportion of young adults who become infected has been rising slowly over the last two decades. Mumps infections are uncommon in children younger than 1 year old. After a case of mumps it is very unusual to have a second bout because one attack of mumps almost always gives lifelong protection against another.

Cases of mumps may start with a fever of up to 103 degrees Fahrenheit, as well as a headache and loss of appetite. The well-known hallmark of mumps is swelling and pain in the parotid glands, making the child look like a hamster with food in its cheeks. The glands usually become increasingly swollen and painful over a period of 1 to 3 days. The pain gets worse when the child swallows, talks, chews, or drinks acidic juices.

Both the left and right parotid glands may be affected, with one side swelling a few days before the other, or only one side may swell. In rare cases, mumps will attack other groups of salivary glands instead of the parotids. If this happens, swelling may be noticed under the tongue, under the jaw, or all the way down to the front of the chest. Mumps can lead to inflammation and swelling of the brain and other organs, although this is not common.

Mumps in adolescent and adult males may also result in the development of orchitis, an inflammation of the testicles. Usually one testicle becomes swollen and painful about 7 to 10 days after the parotids swell. This is accompanied by a high fever, shaking chills, headache, nausea, vomiting, and abdominal pain that can sometimes be mistaken for appendicitis if the right testicle is affected. After 3 to 7 days, testicular pain and swelling subside, usually at about the same time that the fever passes. In some cases, both testicles are involved. Even with involvement of both testicles, sterility is only a rare complication of orchitis.

The mumps virus is contagious and spreads in tiny drops of fluid from the mouth and nose of someone who is infected. It can be passed to others through sneezing, coughing, or even laughing. The virus can also spread to other people through direct contact, such as picking up tissues or using drinking glasses that have been used by the infected person. People who have mumps are most contagious from 2 days before symptoms begin to 6 days after they end. The virus can also spread from people who are infected but have no symptoms. Mumps can be prevented by vaccination. The vaccine can be given alone or as part of the measles-mumps-rubella (MMR) immunization, which is usually given to children at 12 to 15 months of age.

Vitamin C – has antiviral properties and helps get rid of toxins.

Echinacea tea – helps build the immune system and cleanses the lymphatic system.

Slippery Elm tea – is nourishing to the body and sooths a sore throat.

Muscle Cramps
Growing Pains

Growing pains is not a disease. But they can hurt. Usually they happen when children are between the ages of 3 and 5 or 8 and 12. Growing pains stop when children stop growing. By the teen years, most children don't get growing pains anymore. Children get growing pains in their legs. Most of the time they hurt in the front of the thighs, in the calves, or behind the knees. Usually, both legs hurt.

Growing pains often start to ache right before bedtime. Sometimes a child will go to bed without any pain, but wake up in the middle of the night with their legs hurting. The best news about growing pains is that they go away by morning.

Growing pains don't hurt around the bones or joints, the flexible parts that connect bones and let them move, but in the muscles. For this reason, some doctors believe that children might get growing pains because they've tired out their muscles. When you run, climb, or jump a lot during the day, you might have aches and pains in your legs at night.

If your child has a fever, or limping when they walk, or their leg looks red or is swollen, you should go to the doctor. Growing pains should not keep your child from running, playing, and doing what they normally do.

Vitamin A – needed for proper growth.

Vitamin D – needed for proper growth and strong bones.

Cod liver oil – contains vitamin A and D and are needed for proper growth and strong tissues and bones.

Lysine – is needed for normal growth and bone development.

Essential Fatty Acids – needed for normal growth.

Calcium and magnesium – is for normal bone growth.

Amino Acid complex – needed for proper growth.

L-Ornithine – promotes the release of growth hormone. Use under a doctor's supervision.

Diet – Make sure you child gets good sources of protein since it is necessary for proper growth. Nothing with dyes, preservatives, processed or sugar. Lots of fruit, vegetables, whole grains, fish, salmon, herbal ice teas in place of fruit juices and soda. Make a rinse with food grade hydrogen peroxide and water and rinsed all fruits and veggies to get rid of pesticide residue and bacteria. Let your child help pick out healthy foods to eat, this way they are more likely to enjoy trying it.

DHA and EPA - is being added to baby cereal and formula because it is so good for babies brains and their development. It is a very good essential fatty acid.

Multivitamin and mineral complex – is needed to correct chemical imbalances due to poor nutrition.

Sleep – is very important for good health and proper growth when you get the proper amount.

Nails

The hard surface of your nails helps to protect the tips of your fingers and toes. And your fingernails make it easier to scratch an itch or remove a dog hair from your sweater. Nails themselves are made of Keratin. This is the same substance your body uses to create hair and the top layer of your skin. Nails start in the nail root, hidden under the cuticle.

When cells at the root of the nail grow, the new nail cells push out the old nail cells. These old cells flatten and harden, thanks to keratin, a protein made by these cells. The newly formed nail then slides along the nail bed, the flat surface under your nails. The nail bed sits on top of tiny blood vessels that feed it and give your nails their pink color.

Your fingernails grow slowly, they grow about one tenth of an inch each month. At that rate it can take about 3 to 6 months to completely replace a nail. Where your nail meets your skin is your cuticle. Cuticles help to protect the new nail as it grows out from the nail root. Most of the time, your nails are pink and healthy, but sometimes nails have problems. Some of the most common for children are ingrown nail, when the nail curves down and into the skin, causing pain and sometimes infection. Children can also cause injury to their nail when they drop something on their toe nail or shut their finger in a door. Sometimes a child can chew their nails so short that is causes the nail to become deformed.

Some of these problems, such as a minor nail injury or hangnail, can be handled at home. But infections and more serious nail injuries need a doctor's care. Signs of a nail infection include pain, redness, puffiness, and maybe some pus. Don't be surprised if your doctor takes a look at your nails at your next checkup, even if you're having no problems with them. Fingernails provide good clues to a person's overall health. When the doctor presses your nails, he or she is checking your blood circulation. By looking at your nails, a doctor may find changes that may be associated with skin problems, lung disease, anemia, and other medical conditions.

Acidophilus – promotes the growth of friendly bacteria and inhibits the harmful bacteria that causes fungal infection.

Silica – is needed for strong hair, skin, and nails.

Black Currant Seed Oil – is helpful for weak, brittle nails.

Essential Fatty Acids – are important for healthy hair, skin, and nails.

Biotin – is helpful for brittle nails.

Folic Acid – helps with splitting nails.

Vitamin C – deficiencies cause weak nails.

Horsetail – is a good source of silica.

Oat straw tea – is a good source of silica.

Turmeric – is good for circulation and nourishes the nails.

Ginko Biloba tea – is good for circulation and nourishes the nails.

Protein – is needed for healthy nails.

Nightmares

Sometimes it's hard for a child to fall asleep when they are afraid of having a scary dream that feels way too real. If the fear of nightmares is keeping a child awake, try talking to them. Sometimes talking about the nightmares can help your child to stop having them.

By the way, children have more bad dreams when they watch scary or violent TV shows or movies or read scary books or stories before bedtime. Instead of doing those kinds of things, try thinking good thoughts before bed. Reading a peaceful book before bed or playing soothing music can help.

Insomnia also can happen when your child is worried about things. It's easy to feel stressed when you have tests at school, after-school activities, team sports, and chores around the house. A major change in your child's life or daily routine can easily cause sleep problems. Changes like divorce, death, illness or moving to a new town can affect your child's ability to sleep through the night. Try putting a comforting object to bed with your child, like a blanket a relative made for them or a favorite stuffed animal.

If they feel too hot, too cold, hungry, or crowded, your child won't get to sleep like they should. Limit foods and drinks that contain caffeine, like sodas, ice tea, and other drinks. If a child has really tough sleep problems, he or she might need extra help. Some hospitals even have sleep labs, where patients come in and go to sleep so doctors can monitor their sleep and see what might be wrong.

Multivitamin and mineral complex – is needed to correct chemical imbalances due to poor nutrition.

B - Complex - It helps with stress, nerves and provides energy.

Vitamin C – helps with anxiety, stress, and immune system.

Melatonin - Is a great sleep aid and especially helps when a child is having night fears and night anxiety.

Calms Forte - It is a homeopathic blend by Hyland's. We have used this for years. It helps with nervousness and sleeplessness.

Catnip – helps with anxiety and to relax.

Passion Flower – helps with stress and anxiety. Also has a calming effect.

Skullcap – helps with sleep, stress and anxiety.

Valerian - Helps with sleeplessness and anxiety.

Fennel – helps with stomach upset caused by anxiety and has a nice licorice taste.

Calcium & Magnesium - This has a calming effect. One of my favorite ways to use it is to heat purple grape juice on the stove then add powered Cal/Mag to it and stir. It taste like a cream cycle and has an immediate calming effect on the children. It is best to take Calcium with Magnesium because they work synergistically well together to relieve anxiety and nervousness.

Nose Bleed

Most nosebleeds look worse than they are. In other words, nosebleeds are messy, a little uncomfortable, and sometimes even scary, but they are usually no big deal. Children can get nosebleeds once in a while or more often. The nosebleeds that are most common in children usually occur near the front of the nose, on the wall separating the two sides of the nose (the septum), and usually start from just one nostril.

Most nosebleeds occur when little blood vessels that line the inside of your nose break and bleed. Sometimes when a child picks his nose it will start bleeding, or when they sneeze, and when the air is dry. These blood vessels are very fragile and lie very close to the surface, which makes them easy targets for injury. Injuries to the outside of the nose, face, or head can cause nosebleeds, also. If this happens, you need to see a doctor right away. You can help prevent your child from getting these types of nosebleeds by wearing protective gear, such as helmets for hockey, football, and baseball.

If a nosebleed is not caused by any injury to the face and just starts to bleed on it's own, have the child sit down and put the head forward so that the blood does not run down the throat and the child start coughing and chocking. Apply a damp washcloth to the nose to absorb the blood. Gently pinch the soft part of the nose together just below the bony part of the nose for 10 minutes. Do not let the child pick, rub, or blow the nose because this could cause the nose to bleed more.

Aloe Vera - If you find that your nose is dry inside try rubbing a small amount of Aloe Vera inside the nostril. It is a wonderful healer.

Saline (saltwater) – use saline nasal spray or saline nose drops two or three times a day.

Humidifier - sends a fine mist of water into the air and this keeps the air from being too dry. When the air is damp your nose is less likely to feel dry inside.

Homeopathic - phosphmus 6 c works fast and effectively in stopping a bloody nose.

Crushed ice - apply ice in a baggie or washcloth to the bridge of your nose.

Diet - Eat plenty of foods high in vitamin K which is essential for normal blood clotting. Sources of vitamin K are your dark green leafy veggies.

Alfalfa - has many minerals and vitamin K. You can get it in a tablet form from your health food store.

White vinegar - on a gauze and placed gently up the nose, stops a bleeding nose.

Bioflavonoid complex – helps prevent bloody noses.

Rutin – helps prevent bloody noses.

Vitamin C with bioflavonoids – speeds healing and builds the immune system.

Comfrey salve – rub a small amount inside the nostril to help with dryness.

Calendula ointment – rub a small amount inside nostril after is has stopped bleeding to speed healing.

Obesity

In the last 30 years, a growing number of children and teenagers have developed weight problems. Today, 1 out of 3 children and teens between the ages of 2 and 19 are overweight or obese, which is a word that means very overweight. Many adults understand what it's like to have weight problems. More than half of adults are overweight or obese. For children and adults, weighing too much can lead to illnesses and health problems. And a child who is overweight might get teased or find it hard to keep up with friends on the playground.

When people talk about being overweight they mean that someone has more body fat than is healthy. Everyone has some body fat, but when a child has excess fat, it can affect the child's health and ability to walk, run, and get around. It also affects the way they look and may cause them to be bigger and rounder than other children.

A child can be overweight, underweight, or at an ideal weight. There is no one perfect weight for a child to be, but there are ideal weight ranges for children based on height and whether the child is a girl or a boy. Though healthy children can weigh more or less, a good weight range is about 50 to 70 pounds for a child who's 8 years old. But being overweight is more than a number on the scale. A doctor is a good person to make a judgment about a child's weight. The doctor can look at a child's ideal weight range while also taking the child's height into account. A taller child naturally could weigh more than a shorter child and not be overweight. Perhaps the best way to determine if a child is overweight is to use something called body mass index, or BMI.

BMI uses a child's height and weight in a calculation that results in a number. That number can be plotted on a chart that also considers the child's age and if the child is a girl or boy. BMI is an indicator of how much body fat the child has, but it's only an estimate. Because muscle weighs more than fat, it's possible for a muscular child to have a high BMI, but that doesn't mean he or she is overweight. Likewise, it's possible for a child to have a low or ideal BMI but still have too much body fat. Most of the time, children become overweight because the body gets more calories from foods and drinks than it burns through physical activity, such as playing soccer or walking to school. Extra calories are stored as fat. The more extra calories a child consumes, the more fat is stored. This happens very easily in modern life. Children spend more time in front of TVs or computers and less time exercising. We drive everywhere instead of walking or riding bikes. Fewer schools offer gym classes; more children play video games than active ones like dodge ball. Even grown-ups spend more time sitting at desks and in cars than they once did. People also lead busier lives so they have less time to cook healthy meals. We eat more restaurant meals and ready-made food from a box.

Fiber – gives a full feeling and helps cut down hunger pangs.

Chromium picolinate – metabolizes blood sugar and reduces sugar cravings.

Essential Fatty Acids – helps break down fat and helps with appetite control.

Kelp – is full of minerals and aids in weight loss.

Lecithin granules – breaks down fats.

Spirulina – is a good source of protein and balances blood sugar.

Obesity - Continued

It's hard to feel good when your body has too much weight to carry. Being overweight can make it harder to breathe and sleep. It can make a person feel tired and cause aches or pains. Being overweight also can make a child feel embarrassed, sad or even angry. And when children feel bad, they may eat more because food can be comforting. This isn't a good idea, especially if the child is already overweight. Getting help is important because being overweight can make you sick. Overweight children have a greater chance of getting type 2 diabetes. And later in life, an overweight child has a higher risk of getting heart disease. The best way to stay at a healthy weight is to be active. Your child can join a sports team. Or, if they don't like team sports, try swimming, tennis, martial arts, or just being active in their own backyard. Jumping rope, dancing, and walking will get their heart pumping. Getting some extra exercise can be as easy as taking the stairs instead of the elevator or walking, when it is safe, instead of having their parents drive them. Being active also means watching less TV and playing fewer video games.

Eating healthy is another part of staying fit. Aim to eat a variety of foods and get five servings of fruits and vegetables a day. Choose water and low-fat milk over soda and other sugary drinks. No food is off limits, but try eating smaller portions of high-calorie and high-fat foods. In general, children don't need to diet. But a child who is very overweight may need some expert help from a dietitian or a doctor who specializes in weight management. Together, you'll be able to come up with a safe and healthy plan that should include eating nutritious foods and exercising regularly.

Exercise at least an hour a day is very helpful. That seems like a lot, but truly, it is not. Children need to be active, riding their bikes, playing, just having fun. In our society today, our children are bombarded with bad eating habits. The new moms of today are so overloaded with jobs, education and mom duties that fast foods sometimes seem like an easy fix. Fast food is the worst thing you could do on a regular basis. There is so little nourishment and tons of fat in todays fast foods. The only good thing is some fast food restaurants are starting to add some child friendly healthy foods to the menu.

Bee pollen - suppresses appetite speeds metabolism.

Choline and Inositol – helps the body burn fat.

GABA – stops cravings.

L-Carnitine – breaks up fat deposits.

L-Glutamine – helps with carbohydrate cravings.

L-Tyrosine – suppresses cravings.

B complex – aids in proper digestion.

Corn silk tea – works as a diuretic.

Aloe Vera juice – improves digestion and cleanses the digestive tract.

Borage seed – helps improve thyroid function.

Periodontal Disease

Gum disease is also known as periodontal disease. Periodontal disease is an infection of the tissues and bone that support the teeth. Untreated gum disease can become very serious, causing teeth to become loose or fall out. Gum disease is usually caused by a buildup of plaque, an invisible sticky layer of germs that forms naturally on the teeth and gums. Plaque contains bacteria, which produce toxins that irritate and damage the gums. Hundreds of types of bacteria live in the mouth, so keeping plaque at bay is a constant battle. That's why brushing and flossing every day and regular trips to the dentist are so important.

Certain things can make teens more likely to develop gum disease. Some may inherit this tendency from their parents. The snacks you eat also can put you at risk of developing gum disease, especially if you grab fries and a soda in the mall after school and aren't able to brush immediately after eating them. You probably know that sugar is bad for your teeth, but you may not know that starchy foods like fries also feed the acids that eat into your tooth enamel.

If you have braces, fending off plaque can be tougher. Plus, some medical conditions including diabetes and Down syndrome, and certain medicines increase the risk of gum disease. Girls have a higher risk of gum disease than guys. Increases in female sex hormones during puberty can make girls' gums more sensitive to irritation. Some girls may notice that their gums bleed a bit in the days before their periods. Bleeding gums are usually a sign of gingivitis, the mildest form of gum disease. Other warning signs of gingivitis include gum tenderness, redness, or puffiness.

Gum disease progresses in stages. Believe it or not, more than half of teens have some form of gum disease. If plaque from teeth and gums isn't removed by good daily dental care, over time it will harden into a crust called calculus or tartar. Once tartar forms, it starts to destroy gum tissue, causing gums to bleed and pull away from the teeth. This is known as periodontitis, a more advanced form of gum disease.

With periodontitis, gums become weakened and form pockets around the base of teeth. Bacteria pool in these pockets, causing further destruction of the gums. As periodontitis spreads, it damages deeper gum tissue and can eventually spread to areas of the jawbone that support the teeth. This can cause teeth to become loose and fall out. Though periodontitis is rare in teens, it can happen.

Brush - twice a day for at least 3 minutes each time, about the length of your favorite song, and floss daily. If you're not sure whether you're brushing or flossing properly, your dentist or dental hygienist can show you the best techniques.

Diet - Eat a healthy diet. Avoid snacks and junk foods packed with sugar that plaque-causing bacteria love to feed on.

Vitamin C with bioflavonoids – promotes healing and helps with bleeding gums.

Vitamin A – helps the gums to heal.

Calendula flower tea – helps gums to heal quickly.

Myrrh gum – gently rubbed on gums helps inflammation and builds the immune system.

Pica

Many young children put nonfood items in their mouths at one time or another. They're naturally curious about their environment, and they may, for instance, eat some dirt out of the sandbox. Children with pica, however, go beyond this innocent exploration of their surroundings. As many as 25% to 30% of children and 20% of those seen in mental health clinics have an eating disorder called pica, which is characterized by persistent and compulsive cravings to eat nonfood items for one month or longer.

The word pica comes from the Latin word for magpie, a bird known for its large and indiscriminate appetite. Pica is most common in children with developmental disabilities, including autism and mental retardation, and in children between the ages of 2 and 3. Although children younger than 18 to 24 months can try to eat nonfood items, it isn't necessarily considered abnormal at that age. Pica is also a behavior that may surface in children who've had a brain injury affecting their development. It can also be a problem for some pregnant women, as well as people with epilepsy.

Children with pica frequently crave and consume nonfood items such as dirt, clay, paint chips, plaster, chalk, cornstarch, laundry starch, baking soda, coffee grounds, cigarette ashes, burnt match heads, cigarette buts, feces, ice, glue, hair, buttons, paper, sand, toothpaste, and soap to name a few. Although consumption of some items may be harmless, pica is considered to be a serious eating disorder that can sometimes result in serious health problems such as lead poisoning and iron deficiency anemia.

The specific causes of pica are unknown, but certain conditions and situations can increase a person's risk for pica such as iron or zinc nutritional deficiencies. However, the nonfood items craved usually don't supply the minerals lacking in the person's body. Malnutrition, especially in underdeveloped countries, where people with pica most commonly eat soil or clay, and parental neglect, lack of supervision, or food deprivation, often seen in children living in poverty, can be causes of pica. There can also be developmental problems, such as mental retardation, autism, other developmental disabilities, or brain abnormalities, mental health conditions, such as obsessive compulsive disorder or OCD and schizophrenia.

Theories about what causes pica abound. One is that a nutritional deficiency, such as iron deficiency, can trigger specific cravings. Evidence supports that at least some pica cases are a response to dietary deficiency. Nutritional deficiencies often are associated with pica and their correction often improves symptoms. Some pregnant women, for example, will stop eating nonfood items after being treated for iron deficiency anemia, a common condition among pregnant women with pica. However, not everyone responds when a nutritional deficiency is corrected, which may be a consequence of pica rather than the cause, and some children with pica don't have a documented nutritional deficiency.

Fortunately, pica is usually a temporary condition that improves as children get older or following pregnancy. But for individuals with developmental or mental health issues, pica can be a more prolonged concern. Remember that patience is key in treating pica because it can take time for some children to stop wanting to eat nonfood items.

Pneumonia

Pneumonia is an infection of one or both lungs. When you breathe in, you pull oxygen into your lungs. That oxygen travels through breathing tubes and eventually gets into your blood through the alveoli. Alveoli are tiny air sacs covered in tiny blood vessels called capillaries. When oxygen-rich air reaches the alveoli, it can be absorbed into the blood. Then your red blood cells can carry oxygen all over your body. The body needs oxygen to keep working properly and to stay alive.

If a child has pneumonia, his or her lungs can't do this important job very well. This kind of infection creates fluid that blocks the alveoli. This makes it hard for oxygen to get deep into the lungs, where it can be passed through to the blood. The child can still breathe, but it might be hard to breathe, especially if the pneumonia affects both lungs. Pneumonia can happen to people at any age, from tiny babies to elderly people. Getting wet doesn't cause pneumonia, but an infection from bacteria or a virus does. A cold or flu that gets worse can turn into pneumonia. That's because the cold or flu will irritate the lungs, creating an environment where it's easier for pneumonia germs to move in and start an infection.

The symptoms can vary depending on a child's overall health and whether it's caused by a virus or bacteria. With bacterial pneumonia, a child might feel sick suddenly and often has a high fever with chills. The viral kind of pneumonia might happen more slowly and take longer to go away. Either way, a child might feel like he or she has the flu with a headache, fever, muscle aches, and a cough. Pneumonia often causes chest pain, and a feeling like you can't quite catch your breath. The child might be breathing faster than usual and may cough up mucus.

If your doctor thinks your child could have pneumonia, he or she may order a chest X-ray. On an X-ray, the doctor might be able to see signs of the pneumonia infection. Any buildup of fluid or infection often shows up as a cloudy, patchy white area in the usual see-through spaces of the lungs The X-ray can help to tell if the infection is from bacteria. Antibiotics won't work on viruses, so if that's the cause of the pneumonia, only fever reducers and sometimes cough medicine will be given. No matter which germ caused the pneumonia, getting rest and drinking plenty of fluids is always recommended. Regularly washing hands with soap and water can keep your child from getting colds, the flu, and picking up other nasty germs that can cause pneumonia.

Colloidal Silver – helps with inflammation and speeds healing of lung tissue, also works as a natural antibiotic.

Garlic – protects the lungs against respiratory infections and is antiviral and antibacterial.

Vitamin A – helps the immune system to speed healing in the lungs.

Pycnogenol – boosts the immune system and protects the lungs.

Essential Fatty Acids – helps build new lung tissue and reduces inflammation.

Quercetin – helps you breath easier when lungs are compromised.

Maitake extract – is a mushroom that helps build the immune system and fight infection.

Poison Ivy
And all the other
Poison plants

The leaves of poison plants release urushiol if they get bumped, torn, or brushed up against. Once the urushiol has been released, it can easily get on a child's skin, where it often causes trouble. When the oil is released, the leaves may appear shiny or you may see black spots of resin on them. It's also possible to get this kind of rash without ever stepping into the woods or directly touching one of the plants. Urushiol can be transferred from one child to another. Plus, a child can pick it up from anything that's come in contact with the oil, including their dog that likes to roam the woods. Urushiol even can travel through the air if someone burns some of the plants to clear brush.

Urushiol is considered an allergen because it causes an allergic reaction. Not everyone will get a reaction, but about 60% to 80% of people will. This reaction can appear within hours of touching the plant or as late as 5 days later. Typically, the skin becomes red and swollen and blisters will appear. It's itchy, too. After a few days, the blisters may become crusty and start to flake off. It takes 1 to 2 weeks to heal.

It's a good idea to consult with your doctor if your child has any kind of rash, especially if it is accompanied by a fever. If their rash was caused by poison ivy or a similar plant, the doctor may prescribe cool showers and calamine lotion. In more severe cases, an antihistamine may be needed to decrease itching and redness. A steroid may be prescribed in some cases. This medicine may be applied directly to the rash or taken in a pill or liquid form. Learn to identify poison ivy, oak, and sumac, so you can teach your child to steer clear of them. Have your child wear long sleeves and long pants when they are in areas that could contain poison plants.

If your child comes into contact with urushiol oil, try to wash it off their skin right away. But don't give them a bath because the oil can get in the bath water and spread to other areas of their body. Have them take a shower instead, and be sure to use soap.

Vitamin C – helps prevent infection and is a natural antihistamine.

Calamine lotion – apply topically, speeds healing and has drying properties.

Vitamin A – needed for healing of skin.

zinc – speeds healing and for repair of skin.

Aloe Vera gel – is very soothing to skin and helps with itching and burning.

Marshmallow root tea – soothes and heals skin.

Tea Tree Oil – is a natural antiseptic, antiviral, antibacterial, disinfects, and heals skin conditions.

Black walnut – has antiseptic properties and helps fight infection.

Witch hazel – stops itching and aids in healing.

Poisoning

From fertilizer to antifreeze and medicines to makeup and certain foods that have gone bad, there are poisonous items located throughout our homes. Children have a way of finding and getting into things that you don't want them in to. Child-resistant packaging does not mean childproof packaging. It is important to never leave vitamin bottles, aspirin bottles, or other medications on kitchen tables, counter tops, bedside tables, or dresser tops. Small children may decide to try to copy adults and help themselves. Even items that seem harmless, such as toothpaste, can be extremely dangerous if ingested in large quantities by children. Also, just because cabinets are up high doesn't mean children can't get their hands on what's in them. Children will climb up using the toilet and counter top to get to items in the medicine cabinet.

Use safety latches for all cabinets containing hazardous substances. When you're cleaning or using household chemicals, never leave the bottles unattended if there's a small child present. Children seem to like to drink the oddest things. Because of this, special care should be taken during parties. Guests may not be conscious of where they've left their drinks. Clean up promptly after a party. Keep mouthwash out of the reach of children. Many mouthwashes contain substantial amounts of alcohol.

If you're expecting a baby or you already have a child, it's a good idea to be prepared. Learn cardiopulmonary resuscitation (CPR) and the Heimlich maneuver and keep the poison control number programmed in your phone or within close reach of the phone. To check your childproofing efforts, get down on your hands and knees in every room of your home to see things from a child's perspective. Be aware of your child's surroundings and what might be potentially dangerous. Even the most vigilant parent can't keep a child 100% safe at all times, so don't be to hard on yourself if your child does get into something, because touching, holding, climbing, and exploring are the activities that develop your child's body and mind.

Keep the number of your local Poison Control Center near your telephone.

<u>**Ipecac**</u> – will cause vomiting. Only use it after talking to the Poison Control Center or your doctor. You can get ipecac from your local drug store.

<u>**Activated Charcoal**</u> – absorbs toxins. Only use it after talking to the Poison Control Center or your doctor. You can get Activated Charcoal from your local Health Food Store or drug store.

<u>**Garlic**</u> – detoxes the body and works like a natural antibiotic.

<u>**Vitamin C**</u> – is an immune builder and detoxifier.

<u>**Apple Pectin**</u> – helps remove heavy metals from the body.

<u>**Colloidal Silver**</u> – is a natural antibiotic. Kills fungi, viruses and bacteria. Helps in healing.

<u>**Minerals**</u> – to replace the ones lost during diarrhea and to balance the electrolytes in the body.

<u>**Fiber**</u> – removes bacteria from the colon walls so that they do not enter the bloodstream.

<u>**Kelp**</u> – high in minerals that are needed to restore electrolyte imbalance.

<u>**Hydration**</u> – is important is there has been vomiting and diarrhea. Add electrolytes that have been especially designed to rehydrate to water and sip.

Protein

We all know we need protein in our diets for optimal health. Many foods contain protein, but the best sources are beef, poultry, fish, eggs, dairy products, nuts, seeds, and legumes like black beans. Protein builds up, maintains, and replaces the tissues in your body, your muscles, your organs, and your immune system are made up mostly of protein.

Your body uses the protein you eat to make lots of specialized protein molecules that have specific jobs. For instance, your body uses protein to make hemoglobin, the part of red blood cells that carries oxygen to every part of your body. Other proteins are used to build cardiac muscle. In fact, whether you're running or just hanging out, protein is doing important work like moving your legs, moving your lungs, and protecting you from disease.

When you eat foods that contain protein, the digestive juices in your stomach and intestine go to work. They break down the protein in food into basic units, called amino acids. The amino acids then can be reused to make the proteins your body needs to maintain muscles, bones, blood, and body organs.

Proteins are sometimes described as long necklaces with differently shaped beads. Each bead is a small molecule called an amino acid. These amino acids can join together to make thousands of different proteins. Scientists have found many different amino acids in protein, but 22 of them are very important to human health.

Of those 22 amino acids, your body can make 13 of them without you ever thinking about it. Your body can't make the other nine amino acids, but you can get them by eating protein-rich foods. They are called essential amino acids because it's essential that you get them from the foods you eat.

Protein from animal sources, such as meat and milk, is called complete, because it contains all nine of the essential amino acids. Most vegetable protein is considered incomplete because it lacks one or more of the essential amino acids. This can be a concern for someone who doesn't eat meat or milk products. But people who eat a vegetarian diet can still get all their essential amino acids by eating a wide variety of protein-rich vegetable foods.

For instance, you can't get all the amino acids you need from peanuts alone, but if you have peanuts or peanut butter on whole-grain bread you're set. Likewise, red beans won't give you everything you need, but red beans and rice will do the trick. The good news is that you don't have to eat all the essential amino acids in every meal. As long as you have a variety of protein sources throughout the day, your body will grab what it needs from each meal.

You can figure out how much protein you need if you know how much you weigh. Each day, a child needs to eat about 0.5 grams of protein for every pound they weigh. That's a gram for every 2 pounds they weigh. Their protein needs will grow as they get bigger, but then they will level off when they reach adult size. Adults, for instance, need 60 grams per day.

To figure out their protein needs, multiply their weight in pounds times 0.5 or you can just take their weight and divide by 2. For instance, a 56-pound child should have about 28 grams of protein every day. You can look at a food label to find out how many protein grams are in a serving. But if they are eating a balanced diet, you don't need to keep track of it. It's pretty easy to get enough protein.

Respiratory Virus

Respiratory syncytial virus (RSV) is a major cause of respiratory illness in young children. RSV causes infection of the lungs and breathing passages. In adults, it may only produce symptoms of a common cold, such as a stuffy or runny nose, sore throat, mild headache, cough, fever, and a general feeling of being ill. But RSV infections can lead to other more serious illnesses in premature babies and children with diseases that affect the lungs, heart, or immune system.

RSV is highly contagious, and can be spread through droplets containing the virus when a child coughs or sneezes. The virus can also live on surfaces such as counter tops or doorknobs, and on hands and clothing. RSV can be easily spread when a child touches an object or surface contaminated with the virus. The infection can spread rapidly through schools and childcare centers. Infants often get it when older children carry the virus home from school and pass it to them. Almost all children are infected with RSV at least once by the time they are 2 years old.

RSV infections often occur in epidemics that last from late fall through early spring. Respiratory illness caused by RSV, such as bronchiolitis or pneumonia usually lasts about a week, but some cases may last several weeks. Because RSV can be easily spread by touching children or surfaces that are infected, frequent hand washing can go a long way toward preventing the virus from spreading around a household. It's best to wash your hands after having any contact with someone who has any cold symptoms. And keep your school-age child with a cold away from younger siblings, particularly infants, until the symptoms pass.

Fortunately, most cases of RSV are mild and require no specific treatment from doctors. Antibiotics aren't used because RSV is a virus and antibiotics are only effective against bacteria. Medication may sometimes be given to help open airways. RSV infection can be more serious in an infant and may require hospitalization so that the baby can be watched closely, receive fluids, and, if necessary, be treated for breathing problems.

Fenugreek tea – helps get rid of mucus.

Eucalyptus – helps relieve congestion. Add a few drops to a humidifier.

Vitamin C – is antiviral, shortens the life of a cold, and helps build the immune system.

Colostrum – is an immune system builder and speeds healing.

Multivitamin and mineral complex – very important for normal immune system function. Use a whole food supplement.

B Complex - important for cell repair, immune system, and stress.

Homeopathy is based on the theory of "like cures like." I like homeopathic medicines because they do not have harmful side effects. The kids do not get drowsy or act spacey. A few favorites we have used for colds are **Apis mellifica**, **Rhus toxicodendron** and **Pulsatilla** (the last one mentioned has stopped a runny nose very quickly).

Acidophilus - is an active good bacteria found in the intestinal track which increases the good flora and promotes a healthy immune system.

Reye Syndrome

Reye syndrome is still not well understood. It predominantly affects children between 4 and 16 years of age, and occurs more frequently when viral diseases are epidemic, such as during the winter months or following an outbreak of chickenpox or influenza B. The use of salicylates like aspirin during viral disease appears to be statistically linked to the incidence of Reye syndrome, even though there is no conclusive proof.

The signs and symptoms of Reye syndrome are almost always preceded by a viral illness. This could be an upper respiratory tract infection, diarrhea of infectious origin, or chickenpox. Reye syndrome symptoms usually appear 3 to 5 days after the onset of the chickenpox rash. Many cases are mild and may even go undetected, while others may be severe, requiring aggressive care.

Symptoms include nausea, vomiting, lethargy, and indifference. The child may exhibit irrational behavior or delirium, and rapid breathing. In the later stages, breathing becomes sluggish and the child becomes comatose, with dilated pupils. The liver may be enlarged, but there is usually no jaundice or fever. Reye syndrome is rare, approximately 0.1 cases per 100,000 population. It is often thought of when a child has continual vomiting or change of mental status, particularly after a recent viral illness.

Although severity varies, Reye syndrome should be considered an acute disorder that is potentially life threatening. Aspirin and other salicylate drugs should never be used in the treatment of chickenpox, influenza, and other viral diseases. In general, aspirin should not be used for children or teenagers except on the advice of a doctor for certain conditions. The duration varies with the severity of the disease. Reye syndrome can be mild and self-limiting or, rarely, can progress to death within hours. But the progression may stop at any stage, with complete recovery in 5 to 10 days. The viral illnesses that lead to Reye syndrome are contagious. The syndrome itself is noncontagious.

Children with Reye syndrome are usually treated in a hospital, if seriously ill, in the intensive care unit. The prognosis for children with Reye syndrome has improved. Earlier diagnosis and better treatment have reduced the mortality rate to about 20% in recent years. The earlier the syndrome is detected, the better the chances for survival. Children who progress to the late stages of the syndrome may have continuing neurological defects. Here are some nutrients that will help before and after a viral infection.

Beta Carotene - very good for the immune system and repairs tissue damage.

Vitamin E – is a free radical scavenger and promotes healing. Make sure you use a food grade supplement and not one with petroleum in it.

Vitamin C with bioflavonoid – builds the immune system.

Multivitamin and mineral complex – all nutrients are need for proper body function and healing.

Catnip tea – is good for fever.

Antiviral medication – you can receive an antiviral medication from your doctor to shorten the duration of viral infection.

Scabies

Scabies is an itchy skin condition caused by teeny, tiny mites that dig tunnels underneath the skin's surface. Mites are part of the arachnid family, the same family that includes spiders and ticks. Scabies mites have eight legs and a round body and are pretty hard to see. When they're fully grown, each mite is no bigger than the size of the point of a pin.

When you get scabies mites, the female mites dig under the top layer of your skin. There they lay eggs and die after about a month. The eggs hatch, and the new mites grow up and come to the skin's surface. The females mate with the males, then the males die and the females dig back under the skin to lay new eggs. This life cycle takes only 2 to 3 weeks.

Anyone can get scabies, little babies, adults, and children. The mites are not picky. They don't care if you're clean, dirty, rich, or poor. All they want is to live on or in the skin of a human being. Mites are more common in places where there are lots of people, like college dorms, camps, classrooms, and child-care centers. In crowded places like these, people are often in close contact with each other. When people get close enough, mites move from skin to skin. That's how you can get scabies, from someone who already has them. Sometimes the mites may move onto a person from a towel, clothing, or sheets recently used by someone who has scabies, but this is not common.

After scabies make your skin their home, your body may react to them with a dry, itchy, reddish rash of bumps. You may also see thin, slightly raised light lines on your skin where the mites have been digging. These signs of scabies usually appear in places where there are skin folds, such as between your fingers and toes, on your wrists, behind your knees, under your arms, or around your groin or rear end. When you have scabies you may have lots of itching at night and sores from scratching, too. It takes about 4 to 6 weeks for the rash to show up. If you've had scabies before, your body will recognize the mites more quickly and you'll probably see the bumpy rash in just a few days.

If a child with scabies scratches the itchy areas of skin, it increases the chance that the injured skin will also be infected by bacteria. Impetigo, a bacterial skin infection, may occur in skin that is already infected with scabies.

If you think you child has scabies, your doctor will probably give them a cream to spread on their body that will kill the mites. Many of these creams are left on overnight and washed off the next morning in the shower. After they rub on the cream, don't wash their hands. The skin between fingers is one of mites' favorite places, and you want to make sure the cream is there, too. If any spaces are left uncovered the mites will go there and start all over.

The doctor will probably treat everyone else in the house with the scabies medicine, just in case. To kill all other mites, you will need to use hot, soapy water to wash all clothing, towels, or bedsheets used by anyone who has scabies. Then the laundry should be dried on high heat. You can also place other personal items in airtight plastic bags for 2 weeks and vacuum the house. After vacuuming, the vacuum cleaner bag should be thrown away.

Garlic – kills parasites, and works as a natural antibiotic.

Rhubarb tea – rids the body of parasitic infections.

Scars

A scar is a pale pink, brown, or silvery patch of skin that grows in the place where you once had a cut, scrape, or sore. A scar is your skin's way of repairing itself from injury. Your child probably has one or two scars already. Most children do, because a lot of things do leave scars from falls, to surgeries. Scars are part of life and they show what you've been through.

No matter what caused your child's scar, here's how the skin repaired the open wound. The skin sends a bunch of collagen, which are white protein fibers that act like bridges, to reconnect the broken tissue. As the body did its healing work, a dry, temporary scab formed over the wound. The scab's job is to protect the wound as the damaged skin heals underneath. Eventually, a scab dries up and falls off on its own, leaving behind the repaired skin and, often, a scar.

The best way to prevent scars is to prevent wounds. You can reduce your child's chances of getting hurt by wearing kneepads, helmets, and other protective gear when your child plays sports, rides their bike, or goes in-line skating. But even with protective gear, a child can still get hurt once in a while. If this happens, you can take steps to prevent or reduce scarring. You can help their skin heal itself by treating it during the healing process.

Keep the wound covered as it heals so you can keep out bacteria and germs. Avoid letting your child pick at the scab because it tears at the collagen and could introduce germs into the wound. Some doctors say vitamin C helps by speeding up the creation of new skin cells and the shedding of old ones. Also, some people believe rubbing vitamin E on the wound after the scab begins forming can aid the healing process. Some scars fade over time. If your child's doesn't and it bothers you, there are treatments that can make a scar less noticeable, such as skin-smoothing medicated creams, waterproof makeup, or even minor surgery.

B Complex – is needed for cell repair and makes healthy skin.

Essential Fatty Acid – is good for the skin.

Vitamin C with bioflavonoids – has anti inflammation properties.

Vitamin E – is an antioxidant and relieves dry, itchy skin and also lightens the appearance of scars over time.

Flaxseed oil – is good for the hair, skin, and nails. It helps the skin retain moisture.

Shark cartilage – reduces inflammation.

Vitamin A – is good for the skin and when applied topically lightens the appearance of scars over time.

Emulsified Cod Liver Oil – is good for smooth skin and prevents dryness.

Beta Carotene – helps with skin repair.

Protein – is needed for healthy skins.

Silica – is needed for healthy skin.

Horsetail – is used for healthy skin.

Sinusitis

The sinuses are air-filled spaces found in the bones of the head and face. Sinuses start developing before you are born and some of them keep growing until you're about 20. There are four pairs of sinuses, or eight in all. They are located on either side of the nose in your cheeks, behind and between the eyes, in the forehead, and at the back of the nasal cavity.

Like the inside of the nose, the sinuses are lined with a moist, thin layer of tissue called a mucous membrane. The mucous membranes help moisten the air you breathe in. The mucous membrane also makes mucus. The mucus traps dust and germs that are in the air we breathe. On the surface of the cells of the mucous membrane are microscopic hairs called cilia.

The cilia beat back and forth in waves to clear mucus from the sinuses through a narrow opening in the nose and then move the mucus toward the back of the nose to be swallowed. If you have a cold or allergies, the membrane gets irritated and swollen and produces even more mucus. No one is completely sure why we have sinuses, but some researchers think they keep the head from being too heavy. Sinuses are pockets of air, and air doesn't weigh very much. If those pockets were solid bone, your head would weigh a lot more than it does. Sinuses also give you the depth or tone of your voice.

A cold virus can damage the delicate cilia so that mucus is not swept away and cause the mucous lining of the nose to become swollen, which narrows and blocks the small opening from the sinuses into the nose. A cold virus can also lead to the production of more mucus, which is often thicker and stickier, making it harder to flow out of the sinuses. When the tiny openings that drain the sinuses get blocked, mucus becomes trapped in the sinuses. Like water in a stagnant pond, it makes a good home for bacteria, viruses, or fungi to grow.

If a cold lasts for more than 10 to 14 days, you may have sinusitis. This means an infection of the sinuses. Sinusitis is a pretty common infection. Acute sinusitis may be diagnosed when a cold lasts more than 10 to 14 days. Chronic sinusitis means a person has had symptoms for more than 3 months. Symptoms may be similar to acute sinusitis, but typically are less severe and not associated with fever. Sometimes a child could have headache or pain behind the eyes, forehead, and cheeks. The good news about sinusitis is that it's not contagious, so if your child is feeling well enough, then they can go to school or go outside and play.

Flaxseed oil – reduces pain and inflammation.

Quercetin – increases immunity.

Vitamin A – boosts the immune system and helps protects against colds and infection.

Fenugreek tea – helps to loosen phlegm and clear congestion.

Marshmallow tea – helps to loosen phlegm and clear congestion.

Bayberry tea – is a decongestant and astringent.

Olive leaf extract – has antibacterial, antiviral, and anti inflammatory properties.

Neti pot – is a small teapot like device designed for nasal irrigation. Fill pot with sea salt and water to make a saline solution and rinse out your nose with solution. This will reduce inflammation and congestion.

Skin Rash

A rash can also be called dermatitis, which is any swelling or irritation of the skin. It can be red, dry, scaly, and itchy. Rashes also can include lumps, bumps, blisters, and even pimples. Most people have had a rash or two, including a diaper rash when they were babies. But some rashes, especially combined with a fever, can be signs of serious illnesses. Hives, also called urticaria, can be serious because they can be a sign of an allergic reaction and the child may need immediate medical attention.

Hives, which are reddish or pale swellings, appear on a child's body when a chemical called histamine is released in response to an allergen. The trigger could be a certain food, medicine, or an insect bite. A virus can also cause hives. Eczema, also called atopic dermatitis, is a common rash for children. Eczema can cause dry, chapped, bumpy areas around the elbows and knees. More serious cases cause red, scaly, and swollen skin all over the body.

Irritant contact dermatitis is caused by contact with something irritating, such as a chemical, soap, or detergent. It can be red, swollen, and itchy. Even sunburn can be a kind of irritant dermatitis because it's red and may itch while it's healing. Allergic contact dermatitis is a rash caused by contact with an allergen. An allergen is something you are allergic to, such as rubber, hair dye, or nickel, a metal found in some jewelry. If you have nickel allergy, you might get a red, scaly, crusty rash wherever the jewelry touched the skin, like around your finger if you were wearing a ring. Urushiol, an oil or resin contained in poison ivy, oak, and sumac, also can cause this kind of rash.

Some rashes form right away and others can take several days to occur. When a rash appears, you usually know it because it will start to bother you. Try not to scratch. If you do, the rash may take longer to heal and you'll be more likely to develop an infection or scar.

A visit to the doctor is a good idea if you have a rash. Although all rashes may look alike to you, a skin doctor called a dermatologist knows the difference. And knowing which kind of rash your child may have can help the dermatologist choose the best treatment to heal their rash.

Betaine – is a form of hydrochloric acid and people with dermatitis usually have low levels of this acid.

B Complex – is needed for cell repair and makes healthy skin.

Essential Fatty Acid – is good for the skin.

Vitamin C with bioflavonoids – has anti inflammation properties.

Vitamin E – is an antioxidant and relieves dry, itchy skin.

Flaxseed oil – is good for the hair, skin, and nails. It helps the skin retain moisture.

Vitamin A – is good for the skin.

Emulsified Cod Liver Oil – is good for smooth skin and prevents dryness.

Oregon grape root – detoxifies and reduces inflammation.

Gluten free diet – eliminate gluten for a few days to see if rash clears up.

Sleep Walking

Not all sleep is the same every night. We experience some deep, quiet sleep and some active sleep, which is when dreams happen. You might think sleepwalking would happen during active sleep, but a person isn't physically awake during active sleep. Sleepwalking usually happens in the first few hours of sleep in the stage called slow-wave or deep sleep.

Not all sleepwalkers actually walk. Some simply sit up or stand in bed or act like they're awake but dazed when in fact, they're asleep. Most, however, do get up and move around for a few seconds or for as long as half an hour.

Sleepwalkers' eyes are open, however, they don't see the same way they do when they're awake and often think they're in different rooms of the house or different places altogether. Sleepwalkers tend to go back to bed on their own and they do not remember it in the morning.

Researchers estimate that about 15% of children sleepwalk regularly. Sleepwalking may run in families and sometimes occurs when a person is sick, has a fever, or is not getting enough sleep, or is stressed. If sleepwalking occurs frequently, it's a good idea to see your doctor. But occasional sleepwalking generally isn't something to worry about, although it may look funny or even scary to the people who see a sleepwalker in action.

Although occasional sleepwalking isn't a big deal, it is important, of course, that the child is kept safe. Precautions should be taken so the child is less likely to fall down, run into something, or walk out the front door while sleepwalking.

Calcium & Magnesium - This has a calming effect. One of my favorite ways to use it is to heat purple grape juice on the stove then add powered Cal/Mag to it and stir. It taste like a cream cicle and has an immediate calming effect on the children. It is best to take Calcium with Magnesium because they work synergistically well together to relieve anxiety and nervousness.

Multivitamin and mineral complex – is needed to correct chemical imbalances due to poor nutrition.

B - Complex - It helps with stress, nerves and provides energy.

Vitamin C – helps with anxiety, stress, and immune system.

Melatonin - Is a great sleep aid and especially helps when child is having night fears and night anxiety.

Calms Forte - a homeopathic blend by Hyland's. We have used this for years. It helps with nervousness and sleeplessness.

Catnip – helps with anxiety and to relax.

Passion Flower – helps with stress and anxiety. Also has a calming effect.

Skullcap – helps with sleep, stress and anxiety.

Valerian - Helps with sleeplessness and anxiety.

Sleep – this way the body does not get run down. Sleep is very important for good health when you get the proper amount. It also helps keep the stress levels down.

Sore Throat

Strep throat is a disease caused by tiny egg-shaped bacteria called Group A streptococci. These bacteria cause 15% to 20% of all sore throats and are found in your throat and on your skin. If a child has strep throat, the doctor will probably give him or her a medicine called antibiotics. These kill the strep bacteria. That's good news because sometimes strep throat can get worse and cause problems which affects other parts of a child's body. In rare cases, untreated strep can cause arthritis or heart problems from a disease called rheumatic fever.

Most of the time children get the medicine they need and recover from strep throat very quickly. After taking the medicine for 24 hours, you will feel a lot better and will no longer be contagious. If someone in your family or at school has strep throat, there is a chance you may get it. Strep throat is spread when healthy people come into contact with people who have it. When a person with strep throat sneezes or blows his or her nose and you are close by, or if you share the same forks, spoons, or straws, the bacteria can spread to you. If you get strep throat, you will start to feel sick within 5 days after you have been around the infected child who gave it to you.

Most of the time, strep will give you a sore throat, headache, stomach ache, and fever. Typically strep will not give you a runny nose or cough, and occasionally it won't give you any specific symptoms. To prove that what you have is strep throat, your doctor may do one or two tests. First he or she can do a rapid strep test to check for strep bacteria. He or she will rub a cotton swab over the back of your throat. With this test, the doctor may be able to find out in less than 1 hour if you have strep throat. If the first test doesn't prove anything, then your doctor may do a longer test called a throat culture. A swab from your throat will then be rubbed on a special dish and the dish will be left to sit for two nights. If you have strep throat, streptococci bacteria will usually grow in the dish within the next 1 to 2 days. If your child has strep throat, your doctor will give them an antibiotic, a medicine that kills bacteria. Usually the antibiotic used for strep throat is a form of penicillin. Your child will take penicillin as a pill, a liquid, or a shot, to make sure the bacteria go away completely and doesn't spread to other parts of your body. Acetaminophen will help to get rid of aches, pains, and fever. You'll want to give your child soothing drinks, like tea and warm chicken soup. It's best to avoid spicy and acidic foods, such as orange juice, because they could irritate your child's tender throat.

Acidophilus – important when taking antibiotics and to help build up good bacteria.

Bee propolis – fights against infections, antibacterial, protects mucous membranes of the mouth and throat. Do not use if allergic to bee stings.

Colloidal silver – is a natural antibiotic with no known side effects.

Maitake mushroom extract – boosts the immune system and fights viral infections.

Licorice tea – soothes a sore throat.

Slippery elm lozenges – soothes a sore throat.

Astragalus – helps build up the immune system.

Cat's Claw – fights against viral infections and builds the immune system.

Snoring

Snoring is a fairly common problem that can happen to anyone, young or old. Snoring happens when a person can't move air freely through his or her nose and mouth during sleep. That annoying sound is caused by certain structures in the mouth and throat, the tongue, upper throat, soft palate, uvula, as well as big tonsils and adenoids vibrating against each other.

People usually find out they snore from the people who live with them. Children may find out they snore from a brother or sister or from a friend who sleeps over. Snoring keeps other people awake and probably doesn't allow the snoring child to get top quality rest, either.

There are many reasons why children snore. Some of the most common reasons are seasonal allergies which can make some children's noses stuffy and cause them to snore, blocked nasal passages or airways, or a deviated septum, which is the tissue and cartilage that separates the two nostrils in your nose. Some children with a very deviated septum have surgery to straighten it. This also helps them to breathe better as well as stopping their snoring. Enlarged or swollen tonsils or adenoids may cause a child to snore. Adenoids are glands located inside of your head, near the inner parts of your nasal passages. Tonsils and adenoids, help trap harmful bacteria, but they can become very big and swollen all of the time. Many children who snore have this problem. Being overweight can cause narrowing of the air passages. Many children who are very overweight snore.

Snoring is also one symptom of a serious sleep disorder known as sleep apnea. When a child has sleep apnea, his or her breathing is irregular during sleep. Typically, a child with sleep apnea will actually stop breathing for short amounts of time, 30 to 300 times a night. It can be a big problem if the child doesn't get enough oxygen.

Children with this disorder often wake up with bad headaches and feel exhausted all day long. They may be very drowsy and have difficulty staying awake while having a conversation or even while driving. Children affected by sleep apnea may be irritable and have difficulty concentrating, particularly in school and with homework.

If your child can't stop snoring or the snoring becomes heavy, it's a good idea to see a doctor. He or she might tell you how to keep your child's nasal passages clear and will check your tonsils and adenoids to be sure they aren't enlarged and don't have to be removed.

Some children need to lose weight, change their diets, or develop regular sleeping patterns to stop snoring. It may be helpful to remove allergy triggers like stuffed animals, pets, and feather, down pillows and comforters from the child's bedroom.

If a doctor suspects a child has sleep apnea, he or she will order a test to monitor the patient while they sleep. This is usually done in a sleep center which is a medical building that has equipment to monitor breathing during sleep. A patient is attached to machines that check heart rate, oxygen and carbon dioxide levels, eye movement, chest wall movement, and the flow of air through the nose.

The doctor can then tell if a patient has a disorder like sleep apnea. The best thing about the test is that it doesn't hurt at all. Once doctors know what's wrong, your child can be treated for it, usually with lifestyle changes, sometimes medicines, or even surgery, if necessary.

Splinters

It might be tempting to ignore a splinter, especially if it doesn't hurt. However, a splinter can become infected, so you should try to get it out as soon as you notice it. Removal of a splinter right away means the skin won't have time to heal over and the splinter will pull out more easily. To remove a splinter clean the area well. Wash your hands, then wash the area surrounding the splinter with soap and warm tap water. Sterilize a needle and some tweezers. The best way to do this is to immerse the ends of the needle and tweezers in boiling water or run boiling water over them or submerse in alcohol. Wipe them off with a clean cotton pad, cotton ball, or alcohol pad after boiling.

Gently pull out the splinter. If the end of the splinter is still poking out of the skin, you should be able to remove it using just tweezers. Be sure the tweezers have a firm grip on the end of the splinter and pull slowly and gently at the same angle as the splinter went into the skin. Pulling too quickly or at the wrong angle can break the splinter and make it harder to remove the part that remains in your child's skin. If there's no end to grab, use the sterilized needle to gently scrape the skin away from the splinter until there's enough of an end to grab with the tweezers.

Clean the wound. Check to be sure all pieces of the splinter came out. Then, wash the area with soap and warm water once more. You can also dab it with an alcohol pad or rubbing alcohol if you wish. If the opening left by the splinter is noticeable, it's a good idea to cover it with a bandage to prevent infection.

Usually, splinters can be handled at home. But in some cases, you might have to visit the doctor. See a doctor if the splinter seems to be too deep or the wound is bleeding a lot and the splinter seems infected . Not all splinters can be prevented. It is a good idea to have your child wear sandals or flip-flops instead of bare footing it over a rough wood boardwalk or deck. It's also a good idea for children to wear water shoes to protect their feet when diving off a dock or wading in water.

Quercetin – good for the immune system, antihistamine, and helps with inflammation.

Vitamin C – protects and helps with infections and inflammation.

Vitamin K – helps the blood to clot.

Garlic – helps fight infection.

Arnica gel – helps with cuts and bruises.

Colloidal Silver – is a natural antibiotic. Kills fungi, viruses and bacteria. Helps in healing.

Emulsified Cod Liver Oil – is good for smooth skin and prevents dryness.

Beta Carotene – helps with skin repair.

Protein – is needed for healthy skins.

Silica – is needed for healthy skin.

Sprains

Muscles contract and relax almost like rubber bands to help your body move. So a strain is exactly what it sounds like, a muscle that has been stretched too far. It's common for people to strain the muscles in their backs, necks, or legs. Bones meet at joints, such as elbows, knees, or shoulders. That's where your body bends and rotates. Strong, elastic bands of tissue, called ligaments, hold bones together in the joints. A sprain happens when those ligaments have been overstretched or torn. Ankles, wrists, and knees sprain easily.

Even though both can hurt a lot, strains are not as serious as sprains. Because a strain is pain in the muscle, it may start to hurt immediately or several hours later. The area will be tender and swollen and may also appear bruised. A sprain will probably start to hurt right away. Usually the injury will swell and look bruised, it may be hard to walk or move the injured part, and you may even think you have broken a bone.

Strains often happen when you put a lot of pressure on a muscle or you push it too far, such as when lifting a heavy object. Strains may be more likely to happen if you haven't warmed up first to get blood circulating to the muscles. They're also common for someone returning to a sport after the off season. That first time playing softball after a long winter off might lead to a strained calf or thigh muscle. Sprains are caused by injuries, such as twisting your ankle. This kind of injury is common in sports, but can also happen any time you trip or fall.

Don't let your child use the part of their body that's hurt. This means not walking on a hurt ankle or using a hurt arm. It can be hard to tell the difference between a sprain and a broken bone, so it's often a good idea to see a doctor. If your child has a sprain, the doctor will probably have you wear a splint or temporary cast to support and protect the injured area. He or she may wrap the injury with an elastic bandage to reduce swelling and provide extra support. If you have a strain, the doctor will probably tell you to rest the injury and possibly take some pain medication. After 24 hours, it's OK to use warm compresses or a heating pad to soothe aching muscles. A strain takes about 1 week to heal. A bad sprain may take longer, as long as 3 to 4 weeks to heal or sometimes even longer. While the strain or sprain heals, have your child take it easy and don't do anything that could cause another injury.

Calcium – important for bone and muscle repair.

Magnesium – balances calcium and helps it absorb in the body.

Boron – increases calcium uptake and helps in healing.

Silica – helps in calcium absorption and connective tissue repair.

Horsetail – helps in calcium absorption and connective tissue repair.

Vitamin D - needed for calcium absorption and bone repair and makes bones stronger.

Amino acid complex – speeds healing, muscle repair and cell repair.

Bromelain – an enzyme that has anti inflammatory properties.

DLPA DL-Phenylalanine – is a pain reliever.

Glucosamine sulfate – is a natural pain reliever and helps with inflammation.

Staph Infection

Staph is the shortened name for Staphylococcus, a type of bacteria. These bacteria can live harmlessly on many skin surfaces, especially around the nose, mouth, genitals, and anus. But when the skin is punctured or broken for any reason, staph bacteria can enter the wound and cause an infection. There are more than 30 species in the staph family of bacteria, and they can cause different kinds of illnesses, for example, one kind of staph can cause urinary tract infections. But most staph infections are caused by the species Staphylococcus aureus.

S. aureus most commonly causes skin infections like folliculitis, boils, impetigo, and cellulitis that are limited to a small area of a person's skin. S. aureus can also release toxins that may lead to illnesses like food poisoning or toxic shock syndrome. In teens, most staph infections are minor skin infections. Children with skin problems like burns or eczema may be more likely to get staph skin infections. Children can get staph infections from contaminated objects, but staph bacteria often spread through skin-to-skin contact. The bacteria can be spread from one area of the body to another if someone touches the infected area.

Staph infections can spread from person to person among those who live close together in group situations such as in college dorms. Usually this happens when people with skin infections share things like bed linens, towels, or clothing. Warm, humid environments can contribute to staph infections, so excessive sweating can increase someone's chances of developing an infection. Although it's very rare, infections caused by S. aureus can occasionally become serious. This happens when the bacteria move from a break in the skin into the bloodstream. This can lead to infections in other parts of the body, such as the lungs, bones, joints, heart, blood, and central nervous system. If a minor infection gets worse and your child starts feeling feverish or ill or the area spreads and gets very red or and hot, it's a good idea to see a doctor.

Staph infections in other parts of the body are less common than staph skin infections. They are more likely in children whose immune systems have been weakened by another disease. Occasionally patients undergoing surgery may get these more serious types of staph infections. The good news is that hospital staff take many precautions to avoid infection in someone having surgery. Cleanliness and good hygiene are the best way to protect your child against getting staph infections. You can help prevent staph skin infections by washing your hands frequently and by bathing or showering daily.

Colloidal Silver – is a natural antibiotic. Kills fungi, viruses and bacteria. Helps in healing.

Garlic – a natural antibiotic and immune enhancer.

Vitamin C – has antibacterial properties and helps build the immune system.

zinc – aids in healing and helps the immune system.

Flax – ground and made into a paste can be used as a compress.

Fenugreek – ground, mix with flax and add warm water to use as a hot compress.

Suma – boosts the immune system.

Tea Tree Oil – antiseptic and antibacterial.

Stitches

Everybody gets cuts, and some cuts are bigger than others. That's why a lot of children need stitches at one time or another, usually on their face, chin, hands, or feet. Stitches aren't for scratches. They are for bigger cuts that probably wouldn't heal well on their own. Your child might take a fall, hit on the head, or step on something sharp, or they may need to have surgery and end up getting stitches.

If your child needs stitches, the doctor will start by cleaning the cut with sterile water, which is squirted into the cut to remove harmful germs and dirt. The doctor will then wipe the edges with a disinfectant, which also helps to keep it from getting an infection. The doctor will also make sure that whatever cut your child, such as glass, isn't still in the cut. The nurse or doctor will first numb the area with a gel or cream or by using a very small shot. These substances, called anesthetics, make them numb so the child doesn't feel pain.

Stitches are loops of string that doctors use to join the edges of a cut on your child's skin. It's a lot like sewing fabric together. Using a very tiny needle, the doctor will sew your child's cut together with the sutures. Although the area will be numb, they might feel a tug as the doctor pulls the stitches together. Stitches are done the same way at the end of surgery. Once the edges are touching, the doctor ties a knot in the string so their skin will stay that way until it heals. After a few days or a week, the skin heals and the stitches come out. Doctors have many different kinds of string called sutures, including some made of nylon, silk, and vicryl. Vicryl string actually dissolves in the skin, so you don't even need to get those stitches removed. This kind of string is used mostly on the lips or in the mouth.

Another way of closing a cut is to use glue. Sometimes, if a cut isn't too long or wide, the doctor will use special skin glue to keep the cut's edges together until it heals. It usually falls off by itself in 5 to 10 days. Another option for tiny cuts is a small sticky strip called a butterfly bandage. It keeps the cut's edges together for a few days, and then it usually comes off in the bath. Different kinds of stitches, sutures, glue, and butterflies, need different kinds of care.

The doctor probably will tell you to keep your child's cut dry for at least 1 to 2 days. Most stitches should not get wet. Some cuts with stitches need to be covered with an antibiotic ointment and a bandage to prevent infection. Glue, on the other hand, shouldn't be coated with ointment. It's important that your child doesn't tug or pull on the stitches, even if they get itchy. And don't ever try to take the stitches out by yourself. If you notice that your child popped or torn a stitch, or if their cut is hot, red, swollen, or oozing pus you may need to take them to the doctor to check if the cut is infected.

B Complex – is needed for cell repair and makes healthy skin.

Vitamin C with bioflavonoids – has anti inflammation properties.

Vitamin E – is an antioxidant and relieves dry, itchy skin and also lightens the appearance of scars over time.

Vitamin A – is good for the skin and when applied topically lightens the appearance of scars over time.

Sunburn

Even though the sun is hot, it does cool things. It keeps us warm. It makes flowers and plants grow. It even gives us vitamin D so we can better absorb calcium into our bodies for strong bones. It does all these things by sending down light, which includes invisible ultraviolet rays. These are also sometimes called UV rays. Some ultraviolet rays pass through air and clouds and penetrate the skin. When your skin's been exposed to too many of these rays, you get what's known as a sunburn.

Some children get a sunburn faster than others because of their coloring. If you have blond or red hair, light-colored skin, and light-colored eyes, you'll tend to get a sunburn more quickly than someone with dark eyes and skin. That's because you have less melanin. Melanin is a chemical in the skin that protects the skin from sun damage by reflecting and absorbing UV rays. Children with darker skin have more melanin, but even if you have dark hair, dark eyes, or darker-toned skin, you can still get a sunburn. It will just take a little bit longer.

Sunburns look bad and feel even worse. They can cause blisters on your child's skin. They can keep them inside feeling sore when everyone else is outside having fun. They increase their chance of getting wrinkly when they get older. And worst of all, sunburn can lead to skin cancer when they get older.

You don't need to hide your child from the sun completely or wrap them up like a mummy to protect them. But you should apply sunscreen and take frequent breaks from the sun by going indoors or moving into the shade. These steps are especially important between 10:00 in the morning and 4:00 in the afternoon, when the sun's rays are strongest.

Use a sunscreen with an SPF rating of 15 or higher. Put on sunscreen 15 to 20 minutes before going out in the sun. If your child is fair skinned, you should use a sunscreen with a higher SPF rating such as SPF 30. The letters SPF stand for sun protection factor, and the number rating tells you how much longer you can stay in the sun without getting sunburned. So if you normally burn after 20 minutes and you put on a sunscreen with an SPF rating of 15, this sunscreen may give you 15 times the protection. That's 15 times 20 minutes, or 300 minutes (5 hours).

But this isn't always true, so reapply sunscreen at least every 2 hours, just to be safe. Do this more often if your child has been swimming or sweating a lot, even if the sunscreen is waterproof. And remember, your child can get sunburned more quickly when they are swimming or boating because the reflection from the water intensifies the sun's rays.

Aloe Vera - apply directly to burn. This helps in pain relief and speeds healing.

Colloidal Silver - a natural antibiotic that helps wounds heal quickly by applying to burn.

Garlic - Natural antibiotic and helps with tissue repair.

Beta Carotene – helps with skin repair.

B Complex - important for skin repair, cell repair and stress.

C with Bioflavonoids – is an antioxidant that helps in the formation of collagen and healing.

Cool water with Apple Cider Vinegar – when applied, helps with the pain and cools the burn.

Swimmer's Ear

Swimmer's ear, sometimes called otitis externa, is different from a regular ear infection. Usually, when people say a child has an ear infection, they mean otitis media, an infection of the middle ear. This might happen when the child gets a cold. But swimmer's ear happens when bacteria grow in the ear canal, which leads to the eardrum. In that canal, you'll find delicate skin that's protected by a thin coating of earwax. Most of the time, water can run in and out of the ear canal without causing a problem.

Bacteria get a chance to grow when water stays in the ear canal and it washes away the protective coating of earwax. A lot of swimming can wash away that wax protection and lead to these wet conditions in the ear canal. Bacteria grow and the ear canal gets red and swollen. Swimmer's ear may start with some itching, but try not to let your child scratch, because this can worsen the infection. Ear pain is the most common sign of swimmer's ear. Even touching or bumping the outside of the ear can hurt. The infection also could make it harder to hear with the infected ear because of the swelling that happens in the ear canal.

The doctor will probably prescribe ear drops that contain an antibiotic to kill the bacteria. Sometimes, the doctor may use a wick. This kind of wick is like a little sponge the doctor puts in your child's ear. The medicine goes into the sponge and it keeps the medicine in contact with the ear canal that's infected.

Use the drops as long as your doctor tells you to, even if your child's ear starts feeling better. Stopping too soon can cause the infection to come back. If your child has a big problem with swimmer's ear or they are a child who's always in the water, the doctor may suggest ways for you to protect their ears. For instance, you can get some special drops to put in the ears after swimming to dry up the water in there. If it's treated with medication, external otitis is usually cured within 7 to 10 days, but you'll probably need to keep water out of the infected ear for a longer period. Your child's ear pain actually may increase for the first 12 to 24 hours after treatment begins. After that time, the pain should lessen.

You may be able to prevent external otitis by using acid alcohol drops after your child has finished swimming for the day. You shouldn't use these drops if your child has ear tubes or a hole in their eardrum. It's also a good idea to dry their ears thoroughly with a clean towel after swimming, bathing, or showering. Keep all objects out of your child's ear canals, including cotton-tipped applicators or bobby pins and even earplugs, unless your doctor has told you it's OK to use them. Avoiding swims in polluted water also reduces your child's risk of infection. External otitis is not contagious, so you don't have to limit your child's contact with friends as long as they are feeling well enough to socialize.

Warm cotton cloth or heating pad – place against your ear to help relieve the pain. You may also take acetaminophen or ibuprofen.

Garlic - Natural antibiotic and helps with tissue repair. You can get garlic oil from any Health Food Store and apply a few drops in the ear to help kill bacteria.

Ear Candling - can remove the excess wax and relieve pressure.

Colloidal Silver - natural antibiotic, use orally and topically.

Teeth

Taking care of your teeth helps prevent plaque, which is a clear film that sticks to your teeth. The film itself might not sound so bad, but it's very sticky, and it acts like a magnet for bacteria and sugar. Bacteria go crazy over the sugar on your teeth, breaking it down into acids that eat away tooth enamel, causing holes called cavities. Plaque also causes gingivitis, which is gum disease that can make your gums red, swollen, and sore. Your gums are those soft pink tissues in your mouth that hold your teeth in place. If you don't take care of your teeth, it won't be long before cavities and unhealthy gums make your mouth very, very sore. Eating meals will be difficult. And you won't feel like smiling so much. We're lucky that we know so much now about taking care of our teeth. Long ago, as people got older, their teeth would rot away and be very painful. To get rid of a toothache, they had their teeth pulled out. Finally people learned that cleaning their teeth was important, but they didn't have toothpaste right away.

It was only about 100 years ago that someone finally created a minty cream to clean teeth. Not long after that, the toothpaste tube was invented, so people could squeeze the paste right onto the toothbrush. Tooth brushing became popular during World War II. The U.S. Army gave brushes and toothpaste to all soldiers, and they learned to brush twice a day. Back then, toothpaste tubes were made of meta, today they're made of soft plastic and are much easier to squeeze. Today there are plenty of toothpaste choices, lots of colors and flavors to choose from, and some brands are made just for children. There are many natural toothpastes for children without dyes, preservatives, and other additives that you don't want in it. When your child brushes, they don't need a lot of toothpaste, just squeeze out a bit the size of a pea. It's not a good idea to swallow the toothpaste, so be sure to have your child rinse and spit after brushing.

Children can take charge of their teeth by brushing at least twice a day, after breakfast and before bedtime. Have them brush after lunch or after sweet snacks if you can. Brushing properly breaks down plaque. Be sure they brush all of their teeth, not just the front ones. Have them spend some time on the teeth along the sides and in the back. Spend at least 3 minutes each time they brush. If you have trouble keeping track of the time, use a timer or play a recording of a song your child likes to help pass the time. Be sure your child's toothbrush has soft bristles. Get a new toothbrush every 3 months. Some toothbrushes come with bristles that change color when it's time to change them. Teach your child how to floss their teeth, which is a very important way to keep them healthy. It feels weird the first few times, but pretty soon they will be a pro at brushing and flossing. Slip the dental floss between each tooth and up along the gum line. The floss gets rid of food that's hidden where your child's toothbrush can't, no matter how well you brush. It's also important to visit the dentist twice a year. Besides checking for signs of cavities or gum disease, the dentist will help keep your child's teeth extra clean, and he or she can help them learn the best way to brush and floss.

Calcium & Magnesium – very important for strong bones and teeth.

Multivitamin and mineral complex – helps in nutrition imbalance.

Vitamin D3 – needed for proper growth and strong bones.

Tonsillitis

Your tonsils are two lumps of tissue that work as germ fighters for your body. Usually, tonsils do their job well. But sometimes bacteria or viruses get into the tonsils and infect them. When this happens, you have tonsillitis. If you have tonsillitis, your throat usually hurts and it's hard to eat or drink or even swallow and you may also have a fever. Some signs that bacteria or a virus are infecting your tonsils is they will be redder than normal, a yellow or white coating on the tonsils, swollen glands in the neck, fever, and bad breath. If the tonsillitis is caused by strep bacteria, the doctor will prescribe antibiotics, a type of medicine that kills bacteria.

If the tonsillitis is caused by a virus, antibiotics won't work and your body will fight off the infection on its own. Sometimes children get an operation to remove their tonsils, but only if their tonsils get infected a lot during the year or are so big they make it hard for the child to breathe at night. The surgery to remove tonsils is called a tonsillectomy. After this operation, children usually don't have as many sore throats. And, if they were having trouble breathing at night, that problem goes away, too. Without tonsils, a child won't look any different and he or she won't have any scars that anyone can see. Sometimes when a child has their tonsils removed, the doctor may remove their adenoids also. The adenoids are lumpy clusters of spongy tissue that help protect children from getting sick. They sit high on each side of the throat behind the nose and the roof of the mouth. Although you can easily see your tonsils by standing in front of a mirror and opening your mouth wide, you can't see your adenoids this way. A doctor has to use a small mirror or a special scope to get a peek at the adenoids.

Like tonsils, adenoids help keep your body healthy by trapping harmful bacteria and viruses that you breathe in or swallow. Adenoids also contain cells that make antibodies to help your body fight infections. Adenoids do important work as infection fighters for babies and little children. But they become less important once a child gets older and the body develops other ways to fight germs. Some doctors believe that adenoids may not be important at all after children reach their third birthday. In fact, adenoids usually shrink after about age 5, and by the teenage years they often practically disappear.

Because adenoids trap germs that enter a child's body, adenoid tissue sometimes temporarily swells as it tries to fight off an infection. Swollen or infected adenoids can make it tough for a child to breathe and cause a very stuffy nose. So, the child can breathe only through his or her mouth and end up snoring and have trouble getting a good night's sleep. They can also end up with a sore throat and have trouble swallowing, swollen glands in the neck, and ear problems.

Acidophilus – important when taking antibiotics and to help build up good bacteria.

Bee propolis – fights against infections, antibacterial, protects mucous membranes of the mouth and throat. Do not use if allergic to bee stings.

Colloidal silver – is a natural antibiotic with no known side effects.

Maitake mushroom extract – boosts the immune system and fights viral infections.

Licorice tea – soothes a sore throat.

Tooth Decay

Tooth decay quite simply comes from bacteria that slowly eats away at the tooth. Teeth are alive and must have nutrition just like any other part of our bodies. Eating sugars speeds up the bacterial process of the decay because bacteria quite simply loves sugar. Prevention, as always, is the best medicine.

Calcium is absolutely imperative for strong and healthy teeth, as well as a good multivitamin. Because of the bacteria that result in decaying teeth, other parts of the body can also be affected, such as your heart, your digestive system, and your blood stream. It is essential to give your child added nutrition in the form of a vitamin and mineral supplement because our food sources no longer supply the necessary nutrients our bodies require.

A cavity develops when a tooth decays, or breaks down. A cavity is a hole that can grow bigger and deeper over time. Cavities are also called dental caries, and if your child has a cavity, it's important to get it repaired. Plaque is why your child's tooth decays. It is a sticky, slimy substance made up mostly of the germs that cause tooth decay. The bacteria in your mouth make acids so when plaque clings to your teeth, the acids can eat away at the outermost layer of the tooth, called the enamel.

If you don't remove the plaque, the acids can continue to make their way through the enamel, and the inside parts of the tooth can begin to decay. If your child has had a very bad toothache, it may be because there was a cavity that reached all the way inside a tooth, where the nerve endings are.

Your dentist will carefully examine your child's teeth and may take X-rays. If your dentist discovers a cavity, he or she can repair it for your child by first removing the rotted part of their tooth with a special drill. The dentist then fills the hole in the tooth with a special material called a filling. If you are concerned about mercury in your child's filling, many dentist use filling materials that do not have mercury in it.

Though cavities can be repaired, try to avoid them by teaching your child to care for their teeth. Have them brush their teeth with toothpaste each time they eat or at least twice a day. Floss the teeth once a day to remove plaque and food that's stuck between the teeth. Bed time is an important time to brush. It is important to have them gently brush their gums as well to keep them healthy and limit sweets and sugary drinks, like soda.

Calcium & Magnesium – very important for strong bones and teeth.

Multivitamin and mineral complex – helps in nutrition imbalance.

Vitamin D3 – needed for proper growth and strong bones.

Diet - Eat a healthy diet. Avoid snacks and junk foods packed with sugar that plaque-causing bacteria love to feed on.

Vitamin C with bioflavonoids – promotes healing and helps with bleeding gums.

Vitamin A – helps the gums to heal.

Myrrh gum – gently rubbed on gums helps inflammation and builds the immune system.

Urinary tract Infection

Your urinary tract is actually a system made up of six main parts, your two kidneys, two ureters, bladder, and urethra. All day long, the kidneys clean waste products from your blood. The waste becomes urine, which drips into the ureters, which are long, thin tubes, one connected to each kidney. From there, the urine travels through the ureters down to the bladder. When it's empty, your bladder is about the same size as an empty balloon. It looks like one, too. Then the bladder slowly fills up with the urine coming from the kidneys. When you have about a cup of urine in your bladder, your brain tells you it's time to find a bathroom. Once you're ready to urinate, you relax a set of muscles at the bottom of your bladder. That lets the urine rush into the urethra, a tube that leads from your bladder out of your body.

Girls are more likely than boys to get a UTI. That's because their urethra's are much shorter than boys' urethra's. The shorter urethra means bacteria can get up into the bladder more easily and cause an infection there. The bacteria that cause UTIs normally live in your intestines. Each time you have a bowel movement, some of these bacteria come out of your body. If they aren't wiped away properly, they stay on your skin. In girls, this means they can grow near the opening of the urethra because their urethra's are closer to where they wipe. From there, bacteria can get inside the urethra, causing irritation to the urethra. This is called urethritis. If the bacteria go there, they can cause a bladder infection. You may also hear a bladder infection called cystitis, which really means an irritation of the bladder.

Sometimes the harmful bacteria keeps spreading. From the bladder, they may head into one of the ureters and climb up into a kidney. This type of UTI is called a kidney infection, and it's serious because it can damage the kidneys and make you very sick. You may notice signs of a urinary tract infection before anyone else can see there's anything wrong with you. It may hurt when a child urinates, frequent trips to the bathroom, feel pain, pressure, blood in the urine, cloudy urine, and strong order when you urinate. Also there may be symptoms of fever, chills, or pain in their belly or back, just under the lower ribs. These are signs of a kidney infection and you should see a doctor right away.

Prevention is always the best way from getting UTI. Keep clean. Wash your private parts every day when you take a bath or shower. If you're a girl, always wipe from front to back when you go to the bathroom. Don't hold it if you have to go. Water and cranberry juice are two good choices to drink when you child has an infection. Those trips to the bathroom can help wash bacteria out of your child's body and cranberry juice can actually help prevent another infection. If you're a girl, think twice about taking bubble baths because they can bother the urethra. Wear cotton underwear. Nylon underwear traps moisture near your body, especially when it's hot outside. Bacteria love to grow in warm, moist places.

Cranberry – is antibacterial and acidifies the urine and prevents bacteria from sticking to the walls of the bladder. If pure cranberry juice is not available, cranberry capsules can be substituted. Pure cranberry juice will help keep the urine acidic and bacteria don't multiply as well in that kind of environment.

Acidophilus – is needed to restore friendly bacteria. Acidophilus and antibiotics should not be taken at the same time so that they do not cancel each other out. Take acidophilus two hours after you take your antibiotics.

Vegetarian

A true vegetarian eats no meat at all, including poultry and fish. A lacto-ovo vegetarian eats dairy products and eggs, but excludes meat, fish, and poultry. A lacto vegetarian eats dairy products but not eggs. An ovo vegetarian eats eggs but not dairy products. And lots of people won't eat red meat or pork but do eat poultry and/or seafood. Less commonly practiced is the form of vegetarianism known as veganism. A vegan doesn't consume any animal-derived foods or use animal products or byproducts, and eats only plant-based foods.

In addition to not eating meat, poultry, seafood, eggs, or dairy, vegans avoid using products made from animal sources, such as fur, leather, and wool. While those are obvious animal products, many animal byproducts are things we might not even realize come from animals such as gelatin, lanolin, rennet, honey, beeswax, silk, shellac, and cochineal. Veganism, as defined by the Vegan Society, is "a philosophy and way of living which seeks to exclude, as far as is possible and practical, all forms of exploitation of, and cruelty to, animals for food, clothing, or any other purpose." Vegans also avoid toothpaste with calcium extracted from animal bones, if they are aware of it. Similarly, soap made from animal fat rather than vegetable fats is avoided. Vegans generally oppose the violence and cruelty involved in the meat, dairy, cosmetics, clothing, and other industries.

Vegetarian diets offer a number of advantages including lower levels of total fat, saturated fat, and cholesterol, and higher levels of fiber, magnesium, potassium, folate, and antioxidants. As a result, the health benefits of a vegetarian diet may include the prevention of certain diseases, including heart disease, diabetes, and some cancers. A vegan diet eliminates food sources of vitamin B-12, which is found almost exclusively in animal products, including milk, eggs, and cheese. A vegan diet also eliminates milk products, which are good sources of calcium. Vegans must find alternative sources for B-12 and calcium, as well as vitamin D, protein, iron, zinc, and occasionally riboflavin.

Vegans can get vitamin B-12, needed to produce red blood cells and maintain normal nerve function, from enriched breakfast cereals, fortified soy products, nutritional yeast, or supplements. You can get calcium from dark green vegetables such as spinach, bok choy, broccoli, collards, kale, turnip greens, sesame seeds, almonds, red and white beans, soy foods, dried figs, blackstrap molasses, and calcium-fortified foods like fruit juices and breakfast cereals. Vegans can get vitamin D from fortified foods, including vitamin D-fortified soy milk or rice milk, soy, other legumes, nuts, and seeds.

Vegetarian food sources of iron include soy foods like soybeans, tempeh, and tofu; legumes like lentils and chickpeas, and fortified cereals. Iron absorption is enhanced by vitamin C. Zinc plays a role in many key body functions, including immune system response. Vegans can get zinc by eating nuts, legumes, miso and other soy products, pumpkin and sunflower seeds, tahini, wheat germ, and whole-grain breads and cereals. Riboflavin is important for growth and red blood cell production, and can be found in almonds, mushrooms, broccoli, figs, sweet potatoes, soybeans, wheat germ, and fortified cereals and enriched bread. Try some of the wide array of meat alternatives that are found in almost every grocery store. Tasty frozen veggie burgers, chicken and meat substitutes, sausage alternative, fake bacon, and tofu dogs will make the transition to a vegan diet convenient and easy.

Vitamins

Vitamins and minerals are substances that are found in foods we eat. Your body needs them to work properly, so you grow and develop just like you should. When it comes to vitamins, each one has a special role to play. For example, Vitamin D in milk helps your bones, Vitamin A in carrots helps you see at night, Vitamin C in oranges helps your body heal if you get a cut, and B vitamins in leafy green vegetables help your body make protein and energy. There are two types of vitamins, fat soluble and water soluble.

When you eat foods that contain fat-soluble vitamins, the vitamins are stored in the fat tissues in your body and in your liver. They wait around in your body fat until your body needs them. Fat-soluble vitamins are happy to stay stored in your body for awhile, some stay for a few days, some for up to 6 months. Then, when it's time for them to be used, special carriers in your body take them to where they're needed. Vitamins A, D, E, and K are all fat-soluble vitamins.

Water-soluble vitamins are different. When you eat foods that have water-soluble vitamins, the vitamins don't get stored as much in your body. Instead, they travel through your bloodstream. Whatever your body doesn't use comes out when you urinate. So these kinds of vitamins need to be replaced often because they don't stick around. This crowd of vitamins includes vitamin C and the B vitamins, B1 (thiamin), B2 (riboflavin), niacin, B6 (pyridoxine), folic acid, B12 (cobalamine), biotin, and pantothenic acid.

One thing your body can't do is make vitamins. That's where food comes in. Your body is able to get the vitamins it needs from the foods you eat because different foods contain different vitamins. The key is to eat different foods to get an assortment of vitamins. Though some children take a daily vitamin, most children don't need one if they're eating a variety of healthy foods.

Vitamin A plays a really big part in eyesight. It's great for night vision, like when your child is trick-or-treating on Halloween. Vitamin A helps you see in color, too, from the brightest yellow to the darkest purple. In addition, it helps you grow properly and aids in healthy skin.

The B Vitamins, B1, B2, B6, B12, niacin, folic acid, biotin, and pantothenic acid. The B vitamins are important in metabolic activity, this means that they help make energy and set it free when your body needs it. This group of vitamins is also involved in making red blood cells, which carry oxygen throughout your body. Every part of your body needs oxygen to work properly, so these B vitamins have a really important job.

Vitamin C is important for keeping body tissues, such as gums and muscles in good shape. C is also key if you get a cut or wound because it helps you heal. This vitamin also helps your body resist infection. This means that even though you can't always avoid getting sick, vitamin C makes it a little harder for your body to become infected with an illness.

Vitamin D is the vitamin you need for strong bones. It's also great for forming strong teeth. Vitamin D even lends a hand to an important mineral, it helps your body absorb the amount of calcium it needs. Vitamin E is a hard-working vitamin that maintains a lot of your body's tissues, like the ones in your eyes, skin, and liver. It protects your lungs from becoming damaged by polluted air. And it is important for the formation of red blood cells.

Warts

A wart is a small area of hardened skin that usually has a bumpy surface. Warts come in many sizes, colors, and shapes. They can appear anywhere on the body. Children get them most often on the hands, feet, and face. Anybody can get warts, but children get them more often than adults do. Doctors really don't know why some children get warts, but they're sure it's not from touching frogs or toads. It could be that some people's immune systems, which fight infections, make them less likely to get warts.

The good news is that most warts won't make you sick or cause a health problem. Viruses cause warts. They're called human papilloma viruses, or HPV for short. HPV viruses are like other germs. The wart virus loves warm, moist places like small cuts or scratches on your hands or feet. Once the virus finds a nice warm place on the skin, a wart begins to develop. Warts can grow for many months, sometimes a year or more, before they are big enough to see. So if you do get a wart, you may never know where you came into contact with HPV.

If you touch a towel, surface, or anything else someone with a wart has used, you can pick up HPV. Children who bite their fingernails or pick at hangnails get warts more often than children who don't. That's why it's important to avoid picking, rubbing, or scratching a wart, whether it's on another person or on your own body. Most warts don't hurt. But a wart can be annoying if it's on a part of your body that gets bumped or touched all the time. Different kinds of warts grow on different parts of the body. Some warts are smooth and flat. Some are big, rough bumps. Others are tiny and grow in clusters.

Although most warts are painless, a wart on the bottom of the foot, called a plantar wart, can really hurt. It can feel like you have a stone in your shoe. To prevent plantar warts, do not walk barefoot in public places, like a gym locker or at a public pool. Also, change your shoes and socks every day and keep your feet clean and dry. For some kinds of warts you don't need medicines to make them go away. In time, these warts will disappear on their own. Warts can be hard to get rid of because the thick layers of skin make it hard for medicine to reach the virus that causes them. There are many ways to treat warts, but treatments can sometimes be tricky. After a wart seems to be removed, it might come right back.

Vitamin E - 400 IU cut open and apply directly to the wart and cover with tape. This causes the wart to not be able to breath and it will shrink and eventually go away.

Zinc - 50mg a day speeds healing.

Vitamin C – has antiviral and antibacterial properties.

Astragalus – builds the immune system and has antiviral and antibacterial properties.

Aloe Vera - applied directly 3 - 4 times a day and then cover with a band aid will kill a wart.

Tea Tree Oil – placed directly on a wart and then covered with duct tape will get rid of a wart.

For a plantar wart place duct tape directly on the wart and leave on. Change tape every few days and this gets rid of a wart. We have also used clear nail polish and put on small warts daily and this has gotten rid of warts.

Weakened Immune System

To be immune means to be protected. So it makes sense that the body system that helps fight off sickness is called the immune system. The immune system is made up of a network of cells, tissues, and organs that work together to protect the body. White blood cells, also called leukocytes, are part of this defense system. There are two basic types of these germ-fighting cells, phagocytes which chew up invading germs and lymphocytes, which allow the body to remember and recognize previous invaders.

Leukocytes are found in lots of places, including your spleen, an organ in your belly that filters blood and helps fight infections. Leukocytes also can be found in bone marrow, which is a thick, spongy jelly inside your bones. Your lymphatic system is home to these germ-fighting cells, too. You've encountered your lymphatic system if you've ever had swollen glands on the sides of your neck, like when you have a sore throat. Although we call them glands, they are actually lymph nodes, and they contain clusters of immune system cells. Normally, lymph nodes are small and round and you don't notice them. But when they're swollen, it means your immune system is at work.

Lymph nodes work like filters to remove germs that could hurt you. Lymph nodes, and the tiny channels that connect them to each other, contain lymph, a clear fluid with leukocytes, white blood cells, in it. You have lymph nodes beside your neck, behind your knees, in your armpits, and in your groin, just to name a few.

Sometimes a person has a problem with his or her immune system. Allergies are one kind of problem, the immune system overreacts and treats something harmless, like peanuts, as something really dangerous to the body. With certain medical conditions, such as lupus or juvenile rheumatoid arthritis, instead of fighting germs, the immune system fights the good cells and this can cause problems. Other immune system problems may develop due to an illness like cancer.

Healthy children can help their immune systems by washing their hands regularly to prevent infections, eating nutritious foods, getting plenty of exercise, and getting regular medical checkups. The symptoms of immune deficiency depend on what part of the immune system is affected and can range from mild to life-threatening. One example of a life-threatening immune deficiency is severe combined immunodeficiency (SCID).

SCID, which is believed to be rare, can be successfully treated if it's identified early. Otherwise, it can be fatal within the first year of life. SCID is actually a group of inherited disorders that cause severe abnormalities of the immune system. These disorders lead to reduced or malfunctioning T- and B-lymphocytes, the specialized white blood cells made in the bone marrow to fight infection. When the immune system doesn't function properly, it can be difficult or impossible for it to battle viruses, bacteria, and fungi that cause infections.

Classic signs of SCID include an increased susceptibility to infection and failure to thrive as a result of infections. A baby with SCID may have recurrent bacterial, viral, or fungal infections that are much more serious and less responsive to treatment than would normally be expected. These can include ear infections, sinus infections, oral thrush, skin infections, meningitis, and pneumonia. See page 33 – Cancer Supplementation.

Weakened Immune System - Continued

Infants with SCID may also have chronic diarrhea. If a child has these symptoms, a doctor will test for SCID or other types of immune deficiency. Parents who have a child with SCID or a family history of immunodeficiency might want to consider genetic counseling and early blood testing, since early diagnosis can lead to prompt treatment and improve the chances of a good outcome. It may also be possible to test a high-risk baby for the disease before birth if the genetic mutation causing SCID in a family is known. Babies born with SCID can have a healthy immune system if they are treated early in life.

Most children without a known family history of the disease are not diagnosed until 6 months of age or older. When a child is diagnosed with SCID, a referral typically is made to a doctor who specializes in treating immune deficiencies, usually a pediatric immunologist or pediatric infectious disease expert. It's important to prevent infections in kids with SCID, so your doctor may prescribe antibiotics to prevent infection and advise keeping the child away from crowds and sick people.

Children with SCID should not be immunized with live viruses, like the chickenpox or measles, mumps, and rubella (MMR) vaccines, because they lack the normal defense of antibodies to the viruses. Introducing a virus, even a weakened vaccine virus, can be dangerous. Doctors may also administer an infusion of intravenous immune globulin (IVIG) to help the body fight infection.

The most effective treatment for SCID is a stem cell transplant. This is when stem cells, cells found primarily in the bone marrow from which all types of blood cells develop, are introduced into the body in the hopes that the new cells will rebuild the immune system. To provide the best chances for success, a transplant is usually done using the bone marrow of a sibling. However, a parent's marrow might also be acceptable. Some children do not have family members who are suitable donors, in such cases, doctors may use stem cells from an unrelated donor. The likelihood of a good outcome also is higher if the transplant is done early, within the first few months of life, if possible.

Some SCID patients require chemotherapy before their transplant. Chemotherapy will destroy cells in the bone marrow to make room for the donated cells and help prevent the child's immune cells from attacking the donated cells. Other children with SCID may not need such treatment, especially if they have very few immune cells to start with. In cases of SCID caused by a missing enzyme, the enzyme can be replaced via a weekly injection. This is not a cure and these children must receive the injections for the rest of their lives.

Babies who have had bone marrow transplants may need additional treatment with antibiotics or immunoglobulins. Your doctor will advise you about these. Until your child's immune system develops adequate protection after a bone marrow transplant, you can help reduce the risk of infection by having your child wear a mask. A mask can also serve as a signal to others that your child is trying to avoid infection. Understand that infants with SCID may have to endure many painful procedures and repeated hospital stays. And that can be stressful and difficult for the entire family. Luckily, this doesn't have to be handled alone. Support groups, social workers, and family friends often can lend a helping hand. It's important to reach out for support during this time.

Weight

Body mass index is a calculation that uses your height and weight to estimate how much body fat you have. Too much body fat is a problem because it can lead to illnesses and other health problems. BMI, although not a perfect method for judging someone's weight, is often a good way to check on how a child is growing. BMI is not the whole story when it comes to someone's weight. A more muscular child may have a higher weight and BMI but not have too much body fat. Also, a smaller child could have an ideal BMI, but might have less muscle and too much body fat. Because of these and other considerations, it's a good idea to talk to your doctor if you have questions about whether your child is at their ideal weight.

If your doctor tells you your child's BMI is high, don't let it get you down. Instead, talk to your doctor about what you should do to lower their BMI. Unlike adults, children don't usually need to diet. But by eating healthier and getting more exercise, a child can improve his or her BMI. Controlling a weight problem while still a child can help them avoid becoming an overweight adult and developing health problems like diabetes and heart disease.

Children come in all different shapes and sizes, and the best weight for your child is one that is right for their individual body type and size. It can be unhealthy to be too thin if they are eating less food than what their body needs. Being overweight is not good either. Children who are overweight may not be getting the right nutrition if the food they eat has a lot of fat and calories without the other nutrients needed to stay healthy and strong. Eating a variety of healthy foods, including fruits and vegetables, is the best way to go. A child's genetic makeup, the physical traits that get passed down to them from their parents, plays a big part in determining their size and weight. The same goes for their body type.

Poor eating and exercise habits also run in families and this may be the reason that members of a family are overweight. And even though some children gain weight more easily than others even while they are eating right and exercising, they can be a healthy and happy weight that is just right for them. The way you live can change the way you look. How much you weigh is a balance between the calories you eat and the calories you use. If you eat more calories than your body needs to use, you will gain too much weight. If you spend your free time watching TV, your body won't use as many calories as it would if you played basketball, skated, or went for a walk.

Fiber – gives a full feeling and helps cut down hunger pangs and helps keep you regular.

Chromium picolinate – metabolizes blood sugar and reduces sugar cravings.

Essential Fatty Acids – helps break down fat and helps with appetite control.

Kelp – is full of minerals.

Lecithin granules – breaks down fats.

Spirulina – is a good source of protein and balances blood sugar.

Multivitamin and mineral complex – is needed to correct chemical imbalances due to poor nutrition.

B - Complex - It helps with stress, nerves and provides energy.

West Nile Virus

Even though it was discovered all the way back in 1937 in Africa, the West Nile virus probably didn't make its way to the United States until 1999. But since then, it has been a cause of concern all over the country during the summer months. West Nile virus is caused by a bite from an infected mosquito that's already carrying the virus, but it's important to remember that not all mosquitoes are infected. In many parts of the United States, the risk of being bitten by an infected mosquito is greatest from July to early September. But in some parts of the country, mosquito bites can be a risk all year long.

Not everyone who gets bitten by an infected mosquito will get the virus. And although children can get West Nile virus, it's rare for them to become very sick from it. Symptoms of West Nile virus really depend on the person who becomes infected. Children with normal immune systems, the system of the body that fights off disease and infection, usually get just a mild flu-like illness and may not feel bad at all with the infection. In the most rare and extreme cases, West Nile virus can cause a condition called encephalitis, which is irritation and swelling of the brain.

West Nile virus is not spread from person to person. That means if your child's friend next door just got it, and they played together the day before, your child won't get the virus. And though pets can get the virus, they can't spread it to people. The only way to get it is from the bite of an infected mosquito. Health officials in each state are doing their best to find out where mosquitoes live and kill the eggs of mosquitoes that might carry the virus.

You can do your best to prevent coming in contact with West Nile virus by wearing insect repellent. Repellents that include one of these ingredients are DEET and lemon eucalyptus. Playing outside at midday will help you avoid getting bitten because mosquitoes are most likely to be out during early morning or early evening. When possible, wear socks, long sleeves, and long pants when you're playing outside. Playing near standing water, like creeks or wading pools, are where mosquitoes love to hang out.

Charcoal - Make a paste using a few drops of water added to Activated Charcoal. This will draw out the poison from the bite. A lot of people have used mud with good results.

Tea Tree oil - repels insects, stops itching, add to jojoba oil and apply. Do not get near eyes because it will burn.

Black tea bag - Put a few drops of water so that tea bag is wet. Then put it in a microwave for a couple of seconds until very warm. Then apply it to the bite until the tea bag cools and then reheat and apply again until swelling is reduced. This will draw out the toxins.

Meat tenderizer - Make a paste and apply. This will help with pain and swelling and drawing out poison.

Quercetin - good for the immune system, antihistamine, and helps with inflammation.

Insect repellent - We mix different oils together to make a pretty good insect repellent. We will mix citronella, cedar, tea tree, lemon grass, and jojoba oil together and apply. This works on our pets as well.

Vitamin C – protects lungs, helps with infections and inflammation.

Worms

Now, don't get grossed out. Worms or parasites can be found in many places of the body. However the gastrointestinal tract seems to be the favored housing for most parasites. Parasites are much more common than most people think and most of the time you don't even know they are there. Pin worms are one of the most common parasites and are easily detected. Itchy anus or a child who coughs a lot, and all the other reasons has been exhausted as to why, could have pin worms. Some forms of diarrhea are the result of parasites. Parasites are rarely addressed as the cause behind life threatening illness. But they can be a very real problem in the human body. Parasite infection can make you more prone to many diseases, because they help destroy the immune system. Be sure you wash your veggies good and cook your meat well, and wash your hands after a BM.

Pin worms are really small, about as long as a staple. Their eggs get inside the body through the mouth, and they pass through the digestive system. The eggs hatch in the small intestine, and the baby worms grow and move on to the large intestine. There, the pin worms grab onto the wall of the intestine. After a few weeks, the female pin worms move to the end of the large intestine, and they come out of the body at night to lay their eggs around the anus. The amount of time that passes from when someone swallows the eggs until the worms lay new eggs is about 1 to 2 months.

Pin worm eggs can end up on anything that someone who has pin worms touches, on a counter in the kitchen, in a bed, or on a desk at school. The eggs can also be on clothes, towels, or eating utensils. The eggs can live for about 2 weeks, and when your child accidentally touch them and then put their fingers in the mouth, they can swallow the eggs without even knowing it. The worms do not come from pets, only people. And people who have pin worms are not dirty. Children can get pin worms no matter how often they take a bath or play in the mud.

If your child already has pin worms, they could swallow more eggs if they scratch around their bottom and put their fingers in their mouth. Or a few of the eggs around the anus could hatch while they're on the skin, and the baby worms might crawl back inside the body and grow into adults. The best way to keep from getting pin worms is to have your child wash their hands with warm, soapy water before they eat, after they play outside, and after they use the toilet. Try to keep your child's fingernails short and clean, and don't let them scratch around the bottom or bite their nails. Because pin worm eggs can hang around in clothes, be sure to have your child change their underwear every day and always put on a clean pair.

Multi vitamin and mineral - promotes overall health.

Wormwood (black walnut) - kills parasites.

Garlic – kills parasites, and works as a natural antibiotic.

Rhubarb tea – rids the body of parasitic infections.

Acidophilus - builds friendly flora and replaces important intestinal bacteria.

Grapefruit seed extract - is an antifungal and kills parasites.

Garlic - a natural antibiotic and immune enhancer and kills parasites.

Zits
(Acne)

Acne, also known as pimples or zits, is a totally normal part of growing up. Children get acne because of changes that occur during puberty, the time when children bodies begin the many changes that turn them into adults. Some children feel that popping zits will make them less noticeable and help them heal faster, but they're wrong. Picking pimples pushes germs further under the skin, which could cause more redness, pain, and maybe even an infection. And popping zits can lead to scarring, which could last forever. What your child eats isn't the cause of acne, but that doesn't mean your child should pig out on food that isn't very nutritious. Eating a variety of foods, such as fruits, vegetables, whole grains, and low-fat dairy products, will make your child feel good and keep the rest of their body healthy and strong.

The normal everyday stress of being a child doesn't cause acne. Also, baking in the sun does nothing to improve their acne. When you spend time outside and your skin becomes darker, the redness caused by acne may be less noticeable for a little while. But when your tan fades, you'll still see the zits. And spending time in the sun without the proper protection can cause dry, irritated, or burned skin, not to mention it increases the risk of developing wrinkles and skin cancer later in life.

Before your child heads outdoors, protect their skin with a sunscreen that contains a sun protection factor of at least 15. Use a brand that's marked non-acnegenic, which means it won't clog their pores and worsen acne. And if you ever wondered about tanning beds, here are the facts, they're boring, expensive, and dangerous because they increase the risk of developing skin cancer.

Washing your face regularly is a good idea because it helps remove dead skin cells, excess oil, and dirt from your skin's surface. But over washing or scrubbing your skin too hard can dry out and irritate your skin, which only makes acne worse. Using too much medicine to zap zits can lead to dry, irritated skin. Whether you bought an acne product at your local drugstore or you are using something prescribed by a doctor, be sure to follow the directions carefully.

If over the counter medicine isn't helping the acne problem, your child may need to see a doctor or a dermatologist, who may prescribe other medications to help clear up the skin. It can take as long as 8 weeks before they notice an improvement. Almost all children and teens have to deal with acne at some point, but the good news is that with the right facts and the proper acne treatment, you can help your child's skin and improve acne.

Acidophilus - builds friendly flora and replaces important intestinal bacteria.

Garlic - a natural antibiotic, immune enhancer, antiviral and antibacterial.

Colloidal Silver - is soothing and helps healing, can be applied right to acne.

Grapefruit seed extract - Rids the body of harmful micro organisms.

Colostrum - A very strong immune builder.

Tea Tree Oil – apply directly to acne, antifungal, antibacterial and antiviral properties.

Food Grade Hydrogen Peroxide
Uses of Hydrogen Peroxide

35% hydrogen peroxide is highly concentrated and extremely strong. This is the strength that I usually purchase and dilute myself. You must keep this strength out of the reach of children. If it is spilled on the skin, wash immediately in cold water. Do not allow it to touch the eyes. If this happens, wash and rinse thoroughly with cold water.

3% hydrogen peroxide is the acceptable concentration for personal or household use. It is the strength that is sold in drug stores and supermarkets.

To make 3% H2O2, mix one ounce of 35% food grade to 11 ounces of distilled water or filtered water. Store 35% H2O2 in the freezer. Out of the refrigerator, it will lose strength at the rate of approximately one percent a month.

Athlete's Foot: Soak feet 10 to 20 minutes each night in 3% H2O2 until condition has cleared up.

Bath: To one bathtub half full of water, add one half cup 35% H2O2, half cup salt, half cup baking soda and soak 20 to 30 minutes.

Eye Wash: Use one to five drops per eight ounces water in eye cup with pinch of sea salt so that it taste like tears.

Facial: Wash face with cotton ball soaked with 3% H2O2.

Mouthwash: Rinse mouth with 3% H2O2 then gargle and swish for a few seconds. This will help prevent colds.

Nasal Spray: 3 teaspoons of 3% H2O2 to eight ounces of distilled water. Spray into nasal passages to relieve congestion.

Vaporizer: One ounce of 35% H2O2 per gallon of purified water in a vaporizer improves nighttime breathing and helps clear sinus and bronchial congestion.

Dishwasher: Add two to three ounces of 3% H2O2 to dispenser. Add the same amount for washing dishes in the sink.

Deodorant: Saturate cotton ball with 3% H2O2 and rub under arms.

Treatments

The more a person knows about treatments that are out there, the more empowered you become. This way you can be a large part in making decisions about your health care. The herbs that are being discussed in this book have a long history of being safe and having healing qualities. European Countries, China, Japan, etc., are ahead of the U.S. In using herbs in place of conventional medicine, but the U.S. Is starting to catch up with good results.

Acupressure

Acupressure is a massage technique that combines fingertip massage with pressure to the acupuncture points lying along the meridians which are the channels thought which the life force of the body is thought to flow. Just as acupuncture is thought to stimulate the flow of the life force through the meridians, so acupressure is thought to stimulate energy blockages that lead to disease and pain. However, because acupressure is done with the hands rather than with needles, it is most appropriate for self help. Acupressure is best carried out using the thumb and exerting deep pressure so that the acupressure point feels rather achy or even slightly numb. Using a circular massage motion.

Acupuncture

Acupuncture is the placing of extremely thin disposable needles in points along the meridians which are channels through which the life force of the body flows. This is though to help clear energy blockages that might otherwise lead to disease. Acupuncture is not a self help treatment and it must be performed by a licensed practitioner and is sometimes recommended as a suitable means of professional help. In the West acupuncture is often offered as a treatment in itself, rather than as a part of traditional Chinese medicine. Some acupuncturist make dietary recommendations and prescribe herbs while others do not. Acupuncture is a diverse system of treatment that can be applied to virtually all ailments.

Aromatherapy

Essential oils, obtained from plants, roots, leaves, flowers, and fruit, have been shown to have powerful psychological effects. Research has shown that certain oils, when inhaled, have the power to relax or stimulate. In treatment, aromatherapy can be used to relieve condition such as depression and fatigue. Many essential oils also have antiseptic and anti-inflammatory properties. You can safely use aromatherapy as a self-help treatment if you follow these guidelines: Use the purest oils available from reputable suppliers. Essential oils are highly concentrated. When placed on the skin, they are nearly always diluted with a carrier oil such as sunflower, safflower, or almond. When making up a dilution, add five drops of oil to thirty drops of the carrier oil or lotion and shake well. If you have sensitive skin, test a little of the diluted essential oil on a small area of your skin before you proceed with treatment. Avoid contact with the eyes. Keep essential oils out to the reach of children. Always close your eyes when inhaling essential oil.

Bach Flower Remedies

Flower remedies were first invented and used by Dr. Edward Bach around the turn century. They are now extensively used in the home and are suitable for self help. The remedies are derived from wildflowers and from pure stream water, which Dr. Bach believed provide subtle energy that is effective in treating emotional disharmony. The remedies are made by picking fresh flowers, placing them on the surface of a bowl of water and leaving them in the sun for several hours. It Is thought that the action of the sun on the flowers releases their life force or energy into the water. Each of the remedies is appropriate to specific personality traits, and is administered in liquid form. The most commonly used remedy is Rescue Remedy, a combination of five flower remedies.

Chiropractic

Chiropractors specialize in the diagnosis and treatment of mechanical disorders of joints, particularly joints of the spine. They believe in the circulation of the blood, lymph,and nerve activity to vital organs, because if it is blocked it causes discomfort and sometimes disturbs bodily functions, which may result in disease. Chiropractors usually use X-rays when making a diagnosis, and treatment often involves short, direct manipulations of the spine. Some chiropractors use palpatory diagnostic techniques and use massage, heat treatment, gentle manipulation, and exercise to ease misalignments back into place.

Dietary

The importance of diet in preventive medicine and treatment is becoming increasingly acknowledged. Practically everyday, news hits the headlines regarding something we should or should not eat or drink. Diet is probably the area where we can make the greatest impact on general health and vitality, the prevention of disease, and the treatment of common ailments. Nutritional research gives clinical evidence of the effects of the diet on many different diseases and syndromes. Naturopathic medicine is a complementary treatment founded on the principles that disease occurs when the body's inner force is suppressed through incorrect diet and lifestyle. Naturopathic treatment seeks to provide the body with the strength to heal itself through the elimination of toxins, and dietary rebalancing according to individual needs and life style. Therapy may include a period of fasting, special diets, methods to encourage elimination,and supplementation with vitamins, minerals, amino acids, or other nutrients.

Exercise

When you exercise, you're helping build a strong body that will be able to move around and do all the stuff you need it to do. You may know that your heart is a muscle. It works hard, pumping blood every day of your life. You can help this important muscle get stronger by doing aerobic exercise. Aerobic exercise is a kind of activity that requires oxygen. When you breathe, you take in oxygen, and, if you're doing aerobic exercise, you may notice you're breathing faster than normal. Aerobic activity can get your heart pumping, make you sweaty, and quicken your breathing. When you give your heart this kind of workout on a regular basis, your heart will get even better delivering oxygen to all parts of your body.

Tinctures

There are many different ways to make tinctures. Usually it is done by soaking an herb in alcohol for a period of days. I saw a show once on the discovery channel, where they were making tinctures using snakes, scorpions, and other stuff.

In this book we are dealing with children, so my favorite base to use is Bragg's Apple Cider Vinegar with the mother in it. There are many other apple cider vinegars out there, and they would all do the same thing, you just want to make sure it is good quality.

I use a canning jar that has been sterilized and add half a cup of which ever herb I am working with, or need, and then add two and a half cups of apple cider vinegar. After that I seal the jar and shake it well. Then I put a label on the jar stating what is in there and the date. Then I put it in the cupboard to let is work for about three weeks.

After about three weeks I strain it using a cheese cloth and then put it in smaller jars. Then I seal the smaller jars and store for use. Tinctures are stronger to use than teas, so be sure you are working with a holistic practitioner.

You can use vodka or rum to make tinctures in place of apple cider vinegar. That is how most tinctures are made. But alcohol based tinctures are not recommended for pregnant women or children or people with certain medical conditions.

Do not use rubbing alcohol to make tinctures. Rubbing alcohol is not meant to be consumed. Two of my favorite tinctures to make are catnip and valerian. They help with so many symptoms. Also, did you notice they both mellow and calm children down?

Ear Candling

Ear coning is considered a folk medicine. The practice of using ear cones is actually an ancient art from many other countries such as China, Czechoslovakia, Mexico and Italy. Egyptians have been doing ear candling for thousands of years.

Ear cones are used to clean the ears and are believed to help with various ear disorders. Using ear cones is generally more comfortable and less expensive than conventional ear cleaning where water is forced into the ear canal.

Many people use ear cones once a year or less, but others with chronic ear problems seem to benefit with much more frequent treatments. When using ear cones, the small end of the cone is put into the ear and the other end is lit. As the cone burns, the smoke travels into the ear canal, warming the ear wax and creating a gentle vacuum. This can dislodge the wax or foreign debris and pull it into the ear cone. Many report this as being a rather pleasant sensation. Most often, an improvement in hearing is reported after using ear cones. Ears should not get water in them or be exposed to very loud noises for 24 hours after treatment.

Here is what you will need if you are going to candle a family members ear. You will need a paper plate, towel, cup of water, pair of scissors, cotton swabs, ear candles, and hydrogen peroxide. First you want to make an opening in a paper plate large enough for the ear cone to fit through. Put the small end of the cone through the plate, making certain the opening of the cone is not bent or pressed shut. Lay on your side, light the big end of the cone. Wait to see smoke come through the small end, and then seat the cone into the ear. Leakage of smoke around the ear indicates improper positioning or seating of the cone. Simply adjust the position of the cone until no smoke appears. The person assisting can gently massage around the ear being vary cautious with flame, making certain no one is burned. Let the cone burn about 3 inches above the plate. Take the candle out of the ear, and out of the plate, putting it into the container of water to extinguish. Do not attempt to blow the flame out.

Sometimes it is helpful to use more than one ear cone to obtain desired results. Do use common sense being very careful with the flame. Several users indicate ear cones are very effective. Many people say that they get relief from ear wax build up, hearing problems, ringing in the ears, sinus problems, headaches, and even infections.

Not all the wax at the bottom of the cone is going to be from your ear. Some of the wax residue is from the candle. By carefully examining the residue, you may be able to distinguish between the candle residue and earwax. The most important thing to notice after ear coning is how good your ears feel.

How often you ear candle is an individual decision. It takes about 24 hours to replace their protective coating of wax if it has been removed. Obviously, using ear cones every day would not be advisable. Common sense is the best determining factor.

Ear candling should not be used if the ear drum is perforated or if there are tubes in the ear. If ear wax is very impacted and has been untreated for a long time, ear cones may not give desired results.

Herbal Healing

Dating back 5000 years, written records exist to reveal man's uses of herbs in his efforts to attain better health and healing. The oldest recorded history of herbal uses for health and healing come from China. Because of a long history of experimentation and treatment with herbs and herbal remedies, Chinese Pharmacopoeia and Chinese physicians are further advanced in many areas than their counterparts in the western world using western medicine.

There is evidence of the use of herbs by Stone Age humans, who either cultivated or gathered hundreds of herbs and plants for a variety of uses. In India, the recorded history of herbal medicine dates back almost 3000 years. The Ayurvedic form of treatment from India has now extended into the Western world and is growing every year. The use of herbs for healing has even been recorded in the Bible. Ezekiel 47:12 says, "And the fruit thereof shall be for meat and the leaf thereof for medicine."

In the United States, an interest in herbal uses continues to increase every year. Scientists are devoting much research to understand properties of plants in the rain forests. Many of the drugs used in the U.S. today are derived from herbs. For example, Ephedrine, the number one medicine for allergies, is taken from the Chinese herb Ma Huang. Digitalis comes from the herb Foxglove. Aspirin comes from White Willow Bark.

In the United States our medical science is linked to dollars and profit. Because herbs cannot be patented for exclusive use, the chemical elements contained in an herb are often extracted. In many instances, they are reproduced synthetically. These extracted chemical elements and synthetic chemicals do not contain the God-given ingredients found in the natural herb to buffer and soothe the body without the side effects so often found in the patented medication.

Through modern research and development, many new herbs and uses for them have been discovered. Scientists remove the active ingredients from the plant through the process of extraction, leaving only the fiber. In many instances, this produces a stronger and more effective product. This method is not new, although it has been refined and advanced over the years. Tea, in fact was the original extract and even today, infusing tea is a better process than extraction in many situations.

Another modern practice that is really an ancient art is aromatherapy. Aromatherapy helps promote physical, emotional, and mental well being. When you inhale certain scents, the scent molecules are transported through the brain's olfactory nerve, then received by the limbic system. It is here that many researchers feel that emotions, memory, and learned information are stored. It is here where the right aroma can trigger a desired response.

Having said all this, we must still recognize and understand that the body has its ongoing, everyday work of restoring, healing, replenishing, and refreshing itself. Naturopathic, homeopathic, allopathic, therapeutic and many more procedures as well as herbs only assist the body.

Vitamin and Herbal Supplements

Acidophilus – a type of friendly bacteria that assists in the digestion of proteins. It has antifungal properties, reduces cholesterol levels, aids digestion, and enhances absorption of nutrients.

Acerola – has antioxidant, antifungal, astringent properties, liver, hydrate the skin, diarrhea and fever.

Agrimony – bed wetting, bleeding, bruising, diabetes, diarrhea, jaundice, liver problems, parasitic infection.

Alfalfa – alkalizes, detoxifies, diuretic, anti-inflammatory, antifungal, cholesterol, blood sugar, anemia, arthritis, ulcers, digestive system, and skin.

Aloe – astringent, emollient, antifungal, antibacterial, antiviral, heals burns, wounds, cholesterol, inflammation, soothes stomach, aids healing, laxative, and skin.

American Ginsing – diabetes, high blood pressure, stress, and infertility.

Alpha Linolenic Acid – antioxidant.

Anise – aids digestion, clears mucus from air passages, fights infection, promotes milk production in nursing mothers, indigestion, respiratory infection, and menopausal symptoms.

Arnica – prevents bruising and speeds healing.

Ashwaganda – good for the nervous system, increases physical endurance, anti-inflammatory, and stimulates the immune system.

Astragalus – tonic, immune system, adrenal gland function, digestion, metabolism, promotes healing, energy, colds, flu, and lung weakness.

Avena – attention deficit disorder, eczema, nervousness, and menopause.

Barberry – kills bacteria on skin and stimulates intestinal movement.

Bayberry – decongestant, astringent, circulation, reduces fever, hypothyroidism, eyes, and immune system.

Bilberry – antioxidant, diuretic, blood sugar levels, antibacterial, hypoglycemia, inflammation, stress, anxiety, night blindness, and helps prevent macular degeneration.

Birch – diuretic, anti-inflammatory, pain reliever, joint pain, urinary tract infections, boils, and sores.

Bitter melon – chronic fatigue, herpes, and diabetes,

Bitter Orange – anemia, heart, stress, high blood pressure, indigestion, liver cancer, and obesity.

Black Cohosh – lowers blood pressure, cholesterol, mucus production, induces labor, aids in childbirth, menopausal symptoms, pain, and arthritis.

Black walnut – aids digestion, acts as a laxative, heals mouth sores, parasitic, bruising, fungal infection, herpes, poison ivy, warts, blood pressure, and cholesterol.

Blessed thistle – stimulates the appetite, liver, inflammation, circulation, detox, heart, brain food, and increases milk flow in nursing mothers.

Blue cohosh – muscle spasms, stimulates uterine contractions for childbirth, memory, and nervous disorders.

Boneset – decongestant, laxative, inflammation, diuretic, fever, colds, flu, bronchitis, aches, and pains.

Borage seed – cardiovascular health, healthy skin, and nails.

Boswellia – inflammation, arthritis, antifungal, antibacterial, pain, cholesterol, liver, gout, fibromayalgia, obesity, diarrhea, dysentery, ringworm, and boils.

Bromelain – an enzyme found in pineapple, that helps with digestion and arthritis.

Burdock – antioxidant, diuretic, toxins, antibacterial, antifungal, cleanses the blood, liver, immune system, skin, boils, gout, and menopause.

Butcher's Broom – inflammation, carpal tunnel, edema, obesity, varicose veins, vertigo, bladder, and kidneys.

Calendula – inflammation, fevers, skin disorders, rashes, sunburns, toothache, diaper rash, and neuritis.

Cardamom – indigestion, antibacterial, antifungal, tuberculosis, and urinary incontinence.

Cascara sagrada – colon cleanser, laxative, constipation, and parasitic infestation.

Catnip – fever, gas, digestion, sleep, stress, anxiety, colds, flu, inflammation, and pain.

Cat's Claw – antioxidant, inflammation, immune system, intestines, arthritis, cancers, tumors, and ulcers.

Cayenne – digestion, circulation, bleeding ulcers, heart, kidneys, lungs, pancreas, stomach, arthritis, rheumatism, colds, sinus, and sore throats.

Cedar – antiviral, antifungal, expectorant, lymph cleanser, immune system, and warts.

Celery – blood pressure, relieves muscle spasms, arthritis, gout, kidney, diuretic, antioxidant, and sedative.

Chamomile – inflammation, digestion, sleep, diuretic, nerve tonic, fever, headaches, pain, stress, and anxiety.

Chaparral – chelates heavy metals, fights free radicals, radiation, sun exposure, pain, and skin disorders.

Chaste tree – stress, muscle cramps, PMS, and menopause.

Chickweed – relieves congestion, bronchitis, circulation, colds, coughs, skin diseases, and warts.

Cinnamon – stops diarrhea, nausea, congestion, peripheral circulation, digestion, metabolism of fats, fungal infection, diabetes, weight loss, yeast infection, and uterine hemorrhaging.

Clove – antiseptic, anti-parasitic, digestion, toothache, and mouth pain.

Coltsfoot – congestion, bronchitis, cough laryngitis, and pneumonia.

Comfrey – speeds wound healing, skin conditions, bedsores, bites, stings, bruises, bunions, burns, dermatitis, dry skin, hemorrhoids, leg ulcers, nosebleeds, psoriasis, scabies, skin rashes, and sunburns.

Cordyceps – strengthens immune system, exhaustion, cancer, high cholesterol, and ringing in the ears.

Corn silk – diuretic, bladder, kidney, bed wetting, edema, obesity, and urinary tract.

Cramp bark - muscle spasms, pain, and leg spasms.

Cranberry – antibacterial, kidneys, bladder, skin, anticancer, infections, and urinary tract.

Damiana – energy tonic, hormonal problems, and aphrodisiac for woman.

Dandelion – diuretic, detoxes blood, liver, cholesterol, kidneys, pancreas, spleen, stomach, abscesses, anemia, boils, breast tumors, cirrhosis of the liver, constipation, fluid retention, jaundice, and breast cancer.

Devil's claw – pain, inflammation, diuretic, sedative, digestion, pain, arthritis, rheumatism, diabetes, allergies, liver, kidney, gout, and menopausal symptoms.

Dong quai – sedative, laxative, diuretic, pain reliever, hot flashes, and menopause.

Echinacea – inflammation, bacteria, viral infection, immune system, lymphatic system, allergies, colic, colds, flu, and infections.

Elder berry – inflammation, coughs, congestion, constipation.

Ephedra – relieves congestion, diuretic, helps bronchial spasm, allergies, asthma, colds, and depression.

Eucalyptus – decongestant, antiseptic, swelling, sore muscles, colds, coughs, and breaks up mucus.

Eyebright – helps with eyestrain, irritation, eyewash, allergies, and runny nose.

False unicorn root – helps with infertility, pain, and prostrate disorders.

Fennel – appetite suppressant, eyewash, kidneys, liver, spleen, clears the lungs, abdominal pain, gas, and stomach acid.

Fenugreek – laxative, fever, cholesterol, blood sugar, asthma, sinus problems, eyes, inflammation, and lung disorders.

Feverfew – inflammation, muscle spasms, appetite, stimulates uterine contractions, nausea, vomiting, arthritis, colitis, fever, headaches, migraines, muscle tension, and pain.

Flax – strong bones, nails, and teeth, healthy skin, colon problems, and inflammation.

Garlic – detoxifier, infections, immune system, blood pressure, circulation, blood sugar levels, arthritis, asthma, cancer, colds, flu, digestive problems, heart, insomnia, liver, sinusitis, ulcers, yeast infections, any disease or infection.

Ginger – helps with inflammation, colon, cramps, circulation, antioxidant, wounds, liver, stomach, arthritis, fever, headache, hot flashes, indigestion, morning sickness, motion sickness, muscle pain, nausea, and vomiting.

Ginkgo – brain function, circulation, antioxidant, alzheimer's, leg cramps, asthma, dementia, depression, eczema, headaches, heart, kidney, memory, and ringing in the ears.

Ginseng – immune function, lungs, appetite, bronchitis, diabetes, infertility, energy, and stress.

Goldenseal – infections, inflammation, detoxifier, immune system, colon, liver, spleen, respiratory, digestion, allergies, ulcers, bladder, prostate, stomach, cold, flu, and sore throat.

Gotu kola – diuretic, fatigue, depression, healing, wounds, varicose veins, heart, liver, fatigue, appetite, and sleep disorders.

Green tea – antioxidant, cancer, cholesterol, immune system, tooth decay, blood sugar, mental fatigue, and asthma.

Guarana – tonic, stimulant, intestinal cleanser, stamina, endurance, fatigue, headaches, urinary tract irritation, and diarrhea.

Guggul – acne, heart, and high cholesterol.

Hawthorn – blood pressure, cholesterol, heart, anemia, and cholesterol.

Hops – anxiety, appetite, hyperactivity, insomnia, nervousness, pain, shock, stress, toothaches, and ulcers.

Horehound – bronchial tubes, lungs, immune system, indigestion, appetite, bloating, hay fever, sinusitis, and respiratory.

Horse chestnut – good for varicose veins, diuretic, pain, swelling, and bruises.

Horsetail – diuretic, inflammation, muscle cramps, spasms, calcium absorption, bones, hair, nails, teeth, heart, lungs, arthritis, bronchitis, edema, gout, and muscle cramps.

Hydrangea – kidneys, diuretic, bladder infection, obesity, and kidney stones.

Hyssop – congestion, blood pressure, gas, healing, epilepsy, fever, gout, and weight problems.

Irish moss – expectorant, bronchitis, and intestinal disorders.

Juniper berry – diuretic, inflammation, decongestant, blood sugar, asthma, bladder infection, water retention, gout, obesity, and prostate.

Kava kava – diuretic, antiseptic, muscle spasms, pain, anxiety, insomnia, stress, menopausal symptoms, and urinary tract infections.

Kelp – mild laxative, diabetes, cancer, fibrocystic breasts, cellulite, and constipation.

Kudzu – suppresses alcohol cravings, blood pressure, headaches, colds, and flu.

Lady's mantle – inflammation, diuretic, antiviral, cramps, fever, and promotes healing.

Lavender – stress, depression, skin, burns, headaches, psoriasis, and skin problems.

Lemongrass – astringent, tonic, digestive aid, skin, nails, fever, flu, headaches, and intestinal.

Licorice – inflammation, antiviral, antibacterial, parasites, allergies, asthma, and ulcers.

Maitake – cancer, chronic fatigue, lyme disease, immune function, fights infection, and helps with blood pressure.

Marshmallow – diuretic, heals skin, bladder infection, headache, kidney problems, sinusitis, and sore throat.

Meadowsweet – diuretic, inflammation, colds, flu, nausea, digestive, cramps, and diarrhea.

Milk thistle – protects the liver, repairs liver, kidneys, gallbladder, psoriasis, immune system, and anticancer properties.

Motherwort – helps in childbirth pain, tranquilizer, thyroid, heart, headache, and insomnia.

Muira puama – relieves pain, mild laxative, detoxes, heart, depression, stress, hair loss, asthma, and menopause.

Mullein – laxative, relieves pain, sleep, warts, asthma, bronchitis, earache, hay fever, and inflammation.

Mustard seed – improves digestion and aids in metabolism of fat, inflammation, and joint pain.

Myrrh – antiseptic, disinfectant, expectorant, immune system, antibacterial, helps bad breath, periodontal disease, skin, asthma, bronchitis, colds, flu, sinusitis, sore throat, ulcers, abscesses, boils, sores, and wounds.

Nettle – diuretic, expectorant, pain, tonic, anemia, arthritis, rheumatism, hay fever, allergies, kidney, inflammation, and hair.

Oat straw – antidepressant, nerve tonic, insomnia, bed wetting, depression, stress, and skin.

Olive leaf – antibacterial, antiviral, fungus, parasites, colds, flu, antioxidant, blood pressure, chronic fatigue syndrome, diarrhea, arthritis, and psoriasis.

Oregon grape – detoxes, laxative, skin, acne, and psoriasis.

Papaya – appetite, digestion, heartburn, indigestion, and bowel.

Parsley – gets rid of worms, gas, freshens breath, bladder, kidney, liver, lung, stomach, thyroid, bed wetting, and high blood pressure.

Passionflower – sedative, blood pressure, anxiety, hyperactivity, insomnia, and stress.

Pau d'arco – antibacterial, antiviral, detoxes, yeast, warts, allergies, cancer, inflammation, and tumors.

Peppermint – digestion, colic, diarrhea, headache, heart trouble, nausea, rheumatism, and spasms.

Plantain – diuretic, antibiotic, heartburn, bee stings, and bites.

Pleurisy – inflammation, lungs, expectorant, pneumonia, bronchitis, flu, and coughs.

Prickly ash – stimulates the lymph system, stress, circulatory disorders, gallstones, and parasitic infection.

Primrose – aids in weight loss, blood pressure, alcoholism, arthritis, hot flashes, cramps, and skin.

Psyllium – diarrhea, constipation, hemorrhoids, urinary problems, and irritable bowel syndrome.

Pumpkin – high in zinc, prostate, and bladder.

Pygeum – inflammation, congestion, and prostate.

Quercetin – antioxidant, antiviral, allergies, asthma, emphysema, cancer, hives, canker sores, cataracts, celiac disease, eczema, wrinkles, gout, headache, migraine, and prostate.

Red clover – infections, suppresses appetite, detoxes, expectorant, hot flashes, antibacterial, coughs, bronchitis, lungs, kidney, liver, and skin.

Red raspberry – uterus, healthy nails, bones, teeth, skin, diarrhea, morning sickness, canker sores, and hot flashes.

Rhubarb – infections, worms, constipation, malabsorption, and liver.

Rose hips – bladder, infections, and diarrhea.

Rosemary – inflammation, antibacterial, digestion, astringent, decongestant, circulation, detoxes, anticancer, anti tumor, headaches, blood pressure, and menstrual cramps.

Sage – digestion, hot flashes, menopause, mouth, throat, tonsillitis, and dries up mother's milk when finished with nursing.

St. John's wort – depression, nerve pain, stress, and healing.

Sangre de grado – inflammation, antibacterial, antiviral, antifungal, heals wounds, respiratory, skin, mouth, sore throat, colds, flu, candida, psoriasis, and herpes.

Sarsaparilla – energy, hives, impotence, infertility, nerves, psoriasis, rheumatoid arthritis, and detoxes.

Saw palmetto – diuretic, urinary, and prostate.

Schisandra – adaptogen, stamina, blood sugar, blood pressure, cholesterol, cancer, cirrhosis of the liver, hepatitis, depression, insomnia, restless leg syndrome, stress, and skin cancer.

Skullcap – aids sleep, circulation, heart, pain, spasms, anxiety, fatigue, headache, and rheumatism.

Slippery elm – stomach, urinary tract, diarrhea, ulcers, colds, flu, sore throat, colitis, diverticulitis, and Crohn's disease.

Squawvine – nerves, cramps, and childbirth.

St. John's wort – burns, skin disorders, cancer, carpal tunnel syndrome, Crohn's disease, hemorrhoids, abrasions, depression, diabetes, headaches, and ear infection.

Stinging nettle – allergies, hay fever, anemia, hives, and lupus.

Stone root – diuretic, sedative, astringent, tonic, urinary tract, bronchitis, headache, cramps, indigestion, and hemorrhoids.

Suma – inflammation, immune system, anemia, fatigue, stress, arthritis, cancer, liver, blood pressure, and Epstein Barr virus.

Tea tree oil – disinfects wounds, skin, acne, athlete's foot, boils, cuts, scrapes, earache, antifungal, hair, scalp, herpes, insect bites, scabies, and warts.

Thyme – gas, fever, headache, mucus, antiseptic, cholesterol, asthma, bronchitis, croup, respiratory, and liver.

Turmeric – circulation, cholesterol, antibiotic, anticancer, inflammation, and arthritis.

Uva ursi – diuretic, antibacterial, heart, spleen, liver, intestine, bladder, kidney, and diabetes.

Valerian – sedative, circulation, colds, anxiety, fatigue, blood pressure, insomnia, cramps, and ulcers.

Vervain – liver, gallbladder, stress, increases mother's milk, depression, headache, toothache, wounds, colds, and fever.

Walnut leaf – acne, eczema, and ringworm.

White oak – antiseptic, skin, bee stings, burns, diarrhea, fever, cold, bronchitis, poison ivy, and varicose veins.

White willow – pain, allergies, headache, joint pain, inflammation, cramps, toothache, and injuries.

Wild cherry – expectorant, coughs, colds, bronchitis, asthma, digestive disorders, and diarrhea.

Wild oregano – inflammation, antibacterial, antiviral, antifungal, immune system, acne allergies, animal bites, arthritis, asthma, athlete's foot, bee stings, bronchitis, cold, cough, diarrhea, earache, eczema, fatigue, headache, parasitic infections, psoriasis, sinusitis, skin, and urinary.

Wild yam – muscle spasms, inflammation, colic, gallbladder, hypoglycemia, kidney stones, rheumatism, and menopause.

Wintergreen – pain, inflammation, circulation, arthritis, headache, toothache, muscle pain, and rheumatism.

Witch hazel – astringent, itching, hemorrhoids, mouth, skin, and inflammation.

Wood betony – heart, digestion, hyperactivity, nerve pain, headaches, and anxiety.

Wormwood – mild sedative, eliminates worms, fever, liver, gallbladder, migraine, wounds, skin ulcers, blemishes, and insect bites.

Yellow dock – blood purifier, liver, inflammation, respiratory, anemia, skin, eczema, hives, psoriasis, and rashes.

Yerba mate – detoxes, stimulate, allergies, constipation, and inflammation.

Yohimbe – Increases libido and blood flow.

Yucca – detoxes, arthritis, and inflammation.

Glossary - Definitions

Abdominals - are called abs, these are the muscles in front of your abdomen, the area below your chest and above your belly button.

Abrasion - is when the top layers of the skin gets rubbed away, leaving a scrape or scratch.

Absorption - is a process where nutrients are absorbed through the intestinal tract into the bloodstream and then used by the body. If nutrients are not absorbed well then vitamin deficiencies and sickness can result.

Acidosis – a condition of excessive acid of body fluids.

Acne - is the name for those red bumps called pimples that a lot of kids and teens get on their skin. When your skin's oil glands make too much oil, the tiny holes on your skin called pores get stopped up with oil, dead skin, and bacteria. Then the skin around these clogged pores can swell and look lumpy or red. Usually, this happens during puberty when your body is changing from a kid into an adult.

Acute illness - where symptoms of an illness come on very quickly and seem very severe but does not last for a very long time.

Addiction - is an urge to do something that is hard to control or stop.

ADHD - is short for attention deficit hyperactivity disorder. Children who have ADHD find it difficult to pay attention and are hyperactive, which means they might have trouble sitting still.

Aerobic activity - is any kind of movement that makes your muscles use oxygen. Aerobic activity gets your heart pumping, too. Swimming, dancing, and soccer are all types of aerobic activity.

Airways – When something keeps the air from moving in and out of the airways in your lungs, it's called an airway obstruction. When someone has asthma, the airways may become obstructed, or blocked, because the airways are swollen, narrow, and clogged with thick mucus. Obstructed airways can cause coughing, wheezing, and shortness of breath. The airways in your lungs are like tubes or straws. The air flows in and out of them so you can breathe. They're also called bronchial .

Alignment - means to bring into line. If your teeth aren't straight, their alignment might need a little help. You can get perfect alignment with braces, little metal wires that move your teeth into place.

Allergen - any substance that provokes an allergic reaction in someone. Allergen is a medical word for anything that causes an allergic reaction. Allergens can be many different things, including grass, dust mites, or animal dander, the stuff that flakes off dogs' and cats' skin.

Allergists - are special doctors who help people who are allergic to things like animals, grass, pollen, dust, and even foods. Sometimes they can give you medicine or shots to help you feel better when allergies are bothering you.

Allergy - when the immune system over reacts to a normal harmless substance. Allergies can come in the form of a rash, hives, runny nose and asthma flair ups, to name a few. Many things can trigger allergies, like pollen, certain animals, foods, or a bee sting. Allergies can make your eyes water and your nose run, make your skin itchy and bumpy, make your throat and ears sore. With allergy triggered asthma, someone's asthma symptoms like coughing and trouble breathing occur when the person comes in contact with an allergen. But not all asthma is caused by allergies, and not all allergies cause symptoms of asthma.

Allyl sulfides – are phytochemicals found in leeks, onions, garlic and chives that detoxify the body.

Alopecia – is hair loss.

Alternative medicine - using vitamins, herbs and other methods to heal sickness besides using the medical profession, prescriptions or surgery.

Amino acid – one of twenty two nitrogen containing organic acids from which proteins are made.

Analgesic - substance in a cream or lotion to relieve pain.

Anaphylatic shock – severe allergic reaction to an allergen, such as a bee sting, where within seconds there is difficulty with breathing and swelling.

Anemia - the blood's inability to carry oxygen to body cells due to low iron. Red blood cells carry oxygen all over our bodies. People who have anemia have fewer red blood cells than normal, which can make them feel tired because not enough oxygen is getting to their bodies' cells. There are a lot of reasons why a person may have anemia, but a common reason why some children get anemia is because they don't get enough iron in the foods they eat. Iron is needed for red blood cells to work.

Anesthesia - is medicine that doctors give to make people feel comfortable when they're having surgery, stitches, or other things that might be painful. General anesthesia helps you fall asleep for a little bit so you don't feel any pain while the doctors are fixing something. A doctor can give you general anesthesia with a shot or by letting you breathe a special kind of air. The medicine wears off and you wake up a while later. Local anesthesia doesn't make you fall asleep, but it numbs the area so you won't feel pain while you get stitches or minor surgery to remove something like a wart.

Antacid - neutralizes acid in the stomach.

Antibiotics – attack bacteria that make you sick and destroys the growth of bacteria or fungi in or on the body.

Antibody – a protein molecule made by the immune system that is designed to intercept and stop a specific invading organism or other foreign substance.

Antigen - is a substance that can raise the formation of an antibody when introduced into the body.

Antihistamine - blocks histamines. Antihistamines are medicines that block allergy symptoms. They can make you stop sneezing, and stop your nose from running when your allergies are acting up. When you are itchy or have hives, they can work, too.

Antioxidant - stops or inhibits oxidation in cells. Vitamin C, E, Co Q 10 are examples of antioxidants.

Antivenin – a serum that contains antitoxin specific for an animal or insect venom.

Arrhythmia – is an abnormal heart beat.

Arteries and Veins - your body has a highway system all its own that sends blood to and from your body parts. It's called the circulatory system and the roads are called arteries and veins. Arteries, which usually look red, carry blood away from the heart. Veins, which usually look blue, return blood to the heart.

Ascorbate - a mineral salt of vitamin C. It is less acidic and irritating than pure ascorbic acid.

Ascorbic acid - Vitamin C.

Asthma - someone with asthma can have trouble breathing because of problems with the airways, the tubes that carry air into the lungs. The airways can get irritated, swollen, and narrow like a pinched straw, which makes it difficult to breathe. Many things can trigger an asthma attack, like viruses, allergies, smoke, and even exercise. Of course, breathing is really important, so someone who has asthma may need to see a doctor regularly and carry special medicine to make it easier to breathe.

Asthma Action Plan - Lots of stuff goes more smoothly when you have a plan and that includes dealing with asthma. An asthma action plan is a set of written instructions that can help a person manage breathing problems. That way, the person doesn't have to go to the doctor or hospital all the time. A doctor designs the action plan together with his or her patient. It may include triggers, problems to watch for, information about medicine, and important phone numbers. The plan also may tell the person what to do in an emergency.

Asthma Flare-Up - A person who has asthma may go through times when he or she breathes just fine or has only a little trouble. But when a person has a lot of trouble with wheezing, coughing, or shortness of breath, it's called an asthma flare-up, or attack. Allergies, a cold, cigarette smoke, exercise, or even cold air can trigger an asthma flare-up.

Astigmatism - If you take a good look at your eye, you might barely see your cornea, the clear outer covering of the eye. For someone with astigmatism, the cornea is uneven, which changes how light enters the eye and may make things look funny. Things may look blurry, like making the letter "D" look like a "B," or wavy, like looking in a fun house mirror.

Astringents - If your skin is oilier than normal, you might want to use an astringent. Astringents clean up skin by decreasing the amount of oil that causes pimples and causes the pores to contract after you apply astringent.

Auto immune disease – is when your immune system attacks it's own body's tissue.

Aura – a sensation that precedes an attack of migraine or epilepsy.

Autoimmune disorder – any condition in which the immune system reacts inappropriately to the body's own tissues and attacks them.

Automatism – an automatic behavior or action without conscious knowledge or control such as certain types of epileptic seizure.

Autoimmunity - Your immune system fights infections and illnesses. It prevents you from getting sick, or, if you do, it helps you get better. It's called the immune system because it's not just one body part. It's a system of different organs, cells, and proteins known as antibodies. Together, they identify, attack, and destroy germs and other foreign substances. But sometimes the immune system makes a mistake and attacks part of the body. This is called autoimmunity. One example of an autoimmune disease is type 1 diabetes, in which the immune system destroys the cells in the pancreas that produce insulin.

Bacteria - a single celled micro organism that given the type can have very bad effect on the body. Bacteria are so tiny that you can't see them with just your eyes, but there are thousands, millions, even billions of them all over you, inside and out. Lots of bacteria actually help our bodies. The good bacteria, like the kind you get from yogurt, can be very good for the body by aiding digestion and prevent harmful bacteria from taking over, and the bad bacteria can make us sick. They may be to blame for your next sore throat or ear infection.

Benign - is something that is harmless.

Beta Carotene - is a substance that the body uses to make vitamin A.

Bile – is a bitter, yellowish substance that is released by the liver into the intestines for the digestion of fats.

Bioflavonoid - is used for the absorption of vitamin C. It comes from just below the skin of citrus fruit.

Biopsy - Sometimes, when doctors are not sure what's wrong with a part of your body, they might decide to do a test called a biopsy. This means they remove a tiny piece and look at it under a microscope. A common kind of biopsy is of the skin, but a doctor also can take a biopsy almost anywhere, including from a muscle, lung, or kidney. The biopsy gives doctors a closer look at what's going on inside and will help make the diagnosis so the doctor can choose the right treatment. A doctor will give you medicine called anesthesia that will keep you comfortable while the biopsy is done.

Biotin - is in the B family and is important for cell growth, metabolism, healthy skin and hair. Babies with cradle cap may have a biotin deficiency.

Blackhead - People with acne may have different types of bumps on their skin. These can be whiteheads, blackheads, pimples, and cysts. Your skin is full of tiny holes called pores. If a pore gets clogged with oil, dead skin, and bacteria, the top surface can darken and you're left with a blackhead. With a blackhead, the pore stays open. But if the pore closes, a whitehead forms.

Blood count – a basic diagnostic test in which a sample of blood is examined and the number of red blood cells, white blood cells, and platelets are examined.

Blood brain barrier – cells of the brain that keep many substances from passing out of the blood vessels to be absorbed by the brain tissue.

Blood Glucose Level - Blood glucose level is the amount of glucose in the blood. The body gets glucose, a sugar, from the food we eat. Glucose is carried through the bloodstream to all the cells in the body. Like gas for a car, glucose is fuel for the body's cells and gives them energy.

Blood Sugar - is the amount of sugar or glucose in the blood.

Blood Type - Every person has a blood type. There are four major types, each with a different chemical marker that's attached to a person's red blood cells. These markers determine if someone has type A blood, type B blood, type O blood, or type AB blood. Each blood type can also be positive (+) or negative (-). It's important that doctors know which blood type you have if you're going to have surgery, just in case you need some extra blood. But in an emergency, anyone can safely receive O-negative blood, regardless of his or her blood type.

Bronchi – the two main branches of the trachea that lead to the lungs.

Bronchial Tubes - When a person breathes, air comes in through the nose or mouth and then goes into the trachea (windpipe). From there, it passes through the bronchial tubes, which are in the lungs. These tubes, or airways, let air in and out of your lungs, so you can breathe. The bronchial tubes branch into smaller tubes called bronchioles.

Bruise - When you bang a part of your body against something, your skin might turn different colors. That splotch of purple, green, blue, and black is called a bruise, and it's caused by blood leaking from broken blood vessels under your skin. Because you didn't cut yourself, the blood from the damaged blood vessels can't come out and instead gets trapped under the skin.

Candida Albicans - a yeast over-growing the friendly flora of the intestines especially after taking antibiotics. It can infest all cavities like mouth, throat, bronchial tubes, ear canal, vagina, etc. It may eventually become systemic, invading the blood stream and going to all parts of the body.

Cancer - is a disease that happens when the body makes cells that are not normal. These cells grow very quickly to take over the normal cells and can spread to different parts of the body if a doctor doesn't treat it. People can get very sick from cancer and even die. There are many different types of cancer, but you can't get any of them from being near someone who has it. But you can get some kinds of cancer from smoking, so that's another good reason to not start or quit.

Capillaries – are tiny blood vessels that allow the exchange of nutrients and wastes between the bloodstream and the body's cells.

Carbohydrate - Like proteins and fats, carbohydrates are one of the three main nutrients in food. Carbohydrates (carbs) are the body's major source of energy. There are two main types of carbohydrates - sugars (like the kinds in milk, fruit, table sugar, and candy) and starches, which are found in grains, breads, crackers, and pasta. The body breaks down carbs into the sugar glucose, which the body's cells need. Glucose is absorbed into the bloodstream, which makes the sugar level in the blood go up. As the sugar level rises in the body, the pancreas releases a hormone called insulin. Insulin is needed to move glucose from the blood into the cells, where it can be used as a source of energy.

Carcinogen – an agent that is capable of inducing cancerous changes in cells.

Cardiologist - This kind of doctor knows all about the heart and how it works. If a child has a heart problem, he will visit a pediatric cardiologist, who mainly treats children. Cardiologists treat all kinds of heart problems, from heart murmurs to hearts that miss a beat.

Cartilage - Touch the tip of your nose or the top of your ear - that's cartilage. It's bendable, not hard like bone. This flexible material can be found in various parts of your body, including between bones so they don't rub together.

Cast - If you ever break a bone you'll probably need a cast to hold the pieces of bone steady while they're healing. Casts wrap around the broken area and can be made out of plaster, fiberglass, or even plastic and air (called an air cast). When you get a cast, you need to keep it away from water the entire time it's on. It lets your broken bone grow back together again.

CT Scan or CAT Scan - CT stands for computed tomography, so you can see why people prefer to say CT. CT scans are a kind of X-ray, except they give doctors much better pictures of the inside of your body. Regular X-rays show mainly your bones but CT scans show a lot more.

Catatonia – is a state in which an individual becomes unresponsive.

Cauterization – a technique used to stop bleeding that involves applying electrical current or a chemical to a broken blood vessel.

Cell – is a very small but complex organic unit consisting of a nucleus, cytoplasm, and a cell membrane.

Cellulose – an indigestible carbohydrate found in the outer layers of fruits and vegetables.

Cerebellum - The cerebellum controls balance, coordination, and movement. It's way in the back of the brain, down low and near the spinal cord.

Cerebral Cortex - Also known as gray matter, this term describes the brain's outer layer. The cerebral cortex is involved in complex brain functions, such as language and information processing.

Certified Diabetes Educators (CDEs) - Is a certified diabetes educator. They know a lot about the illness. They also know how to teach people with diabetes to take care of themselves. Nurses, dietitians, pharmacists, doctors, social workers, or other professionals can be certified diabetes educators.

Cerumen - This word means wax. Sticky cerumen lines the outer ear canal and helps trap dirt, germs, and other stuff that gets in your ear.

Chelation therapy – is the introduction of certain substances in the body so that they will chelate, and then remove, foreign substances such as lead, cadmium, arsenic, and other heavy metals.

Chemotherapy - Chemotherapy is the use of special medicines to treat cancer. They can be given alone, but often several chemotherapy drugs are combined to attack the cancer cells in different ways. The exact combination depends on the type of cancer and whether the cancer has spread to other parts of the body. These medicines are very powerful and sometimes get the normal cells, too. That's why people with cancer often lose their hair. The good news is that when a person finishes chemotherapy, the normal cells come back and so does your hair.

Chiropractic – a system of healing based on the belief that many disorders result from misalignments of the spinal vertebrae and other joints. Chiropractors primarily treat illness by using physical manipulation techniques to bring the body into proper alignment and thus restore normal health and functioning.

Chlorophyll – the pigment responsible for the green color of plant tissues. It can be taken in supplement form as a source of magnesium and trace elements.

Cholesterol – a crystalline substance that is soluble in fats and that is produced by all vertebrates. It is a necessary constituent of cell membranes and facilitates the transport and absorption of fatty acids. Excess cholesterol is a potential threat to health.

Chromosomes - Your body is made up of billions of cells, which are too small to see without a strong microscope. Inside most of those cells are chromosomes, which are thread-like strands that contain hundreds, or even thousands, of genes. Genes determine physical traits, such as the color of your eyes. Most people have 23 pairs of chromosomes, and you received half your chromosomes from your mother and the other half from your father. Even after you're born, your 46 chromosomes continue to guide the way your body grows and develops.

Chronic - This word refers to an illness that a person has for a long time or an illness that goes away and keeps coming back. Diabetes and juvenile rheumatoid arthritis are examples of chronic illnesses.

Citric acid – an organic acid found in citrus fruits.

Clotting factor – one of several substances that are present in the bloodstream and are important in the process of blood clotting.

Cochlea - The cochlea looks like a spiral-shaped snail shell deep in your ear. And it plays an important part in helping you hear. It changes sounds into nerve messages and sends them to your brain. After the eardrum takes in a sound, the sound gets turned into a vibration that travels to the cochlea. There, the tiny hairs that line the cochlea move and shake, sending messages to your brain that you hear a sound.

CO-Q10 or Co-enzyme Q10 - is an energizing enzyme useful in regulating the use of oxygen in the cells.

Cold pressed – a term used to describe food oils that are extracted without the use of heat in order to preserve nutrients and flavor.

Colic – sharp abdominal pains that result from spasm or obstruction of certain organs or structures.

Colonoscope – an instrument for examining the colon.

Colonoscopy – a procedure in which a long flexible tube is threaded up through the rectum for the purpose of examining the entire colon and rectum and , if there is an abnormality, taking a biopsy or removing it.

Complete protein – a source of dietary protein that contains a full complement of the eight essential amino acids.

Complex carbohydrate – is a type of carbohydrate that releases its sugar into the body relatively slowly and also provides fiber.

Complete Blood Count (CBC) - Blood is made up of different parts, such as red blood cells, white blood cells, and platelets. Red blood cells are like trucks zooming around on the blood vessel highway in your body, carrying oxygen to the rest of your body. White blood cells are the warriors of the blood, defending your body against germs that try to make you sick. And platelets are like repair people because when you get a cut, platelets stick together to form a plug to stop bleeding. Doctors sometimes do blood tests to count how many of each type of blood cell you have. In a complete blood count, the numbers of red blood cells, white blood cells, and platelets in your blood get counted.

Compress – is used to add ice or heat to an injury on the body.

Congenital – present from birth, but not necessarily inherited.

Congestion - Congestion happens when your nose gets stuffy and makes it hard to breathe. Usually, you have congestion when you have a cold or allergies and your nose gets plugged up with mucus.

Conjunctivitis - This is when the conjunctiva, the covering of your eye and inside your eyelids, gets infected. Your eye may feel itchy and like you have a grain of sand caught in it. Your eye may be teary or gunky, especially when you wake up in the morning.

Constipation - Sometimes your bowel movements might be hard and dry. One way to fight constipation is to eat more fiber which are found in fruits and vegetables, and drink more water and juice.

Contagious - When an illness is contagious, it means one person can catch it from another. By covering your mouth when you sneeze or cough, you can prevent bacteria and viruses from getting in the air. It's also important to wash your hands, whether you are sick or well, to prevent the spread of germs on objects that other people will touch. Some contagious sicknesses that children get are colds, flu, and chicken pox.

Contusion – a bruise, injury in which the skin is not broken.

Convulsion – a seizure characterized by intense, uncontrollable contraction of the voluntary muscles that results from abnormal cerebral stimulation.

Cornea - is part of your eye, but you've probably never noticed it before. The cornea is thin, clear and covers your eye. It's important because it helps you see by focusing light as it enters the eye.

Corticosteroids - are an important kind of asthma medication. They are a type of controller medication. Controllers keep the airways in the lungs open and clear so you can breathe.

Cough - A cough is a reflex that helps your body clear your throat and lungs. A cough is a common symptom in people who have asthma, although it can occur for many other reasons, like when you have a cold. Someone who has asthma may cough because the airways are irritated. For some children, coughing may be the only clue that they have asthma. The coughing may happen only at night or while exercising.

Cradle cap – a type of seborrheic dermatitis found on infants, usually appearing on the scalp, face, and head, and consisting of thick, yellowish, crusted lesions. Scaling or fissuring often appears behind the ears and the face.

DNA - deoxyribonucleic acid. DNA can be found inside the billions of cells that make up your body. And if you could see it, which you can't without a very strong microscope, it would look like a twisting ladder.

Dander - All warm-blooded animals shed tiny flakes from their skin, fur, or feathers. This is called dander. It's like dandruff in humans but much harder to see. When someone is allergic to animals, it could be dander that's causing the problem. Pet dander can be trouble for people who have asthma because, if they're allergic to it, it can worsen breathing problems.

Dandruff - Dandruff is flakes of dead skin on your head that come loose all the time, but especially when you scratch your head, brush your hair, or pull a shirt over your head. Sometimes, during puberty, your oil glands go a little wild and you develop a lot more dandruff than normal. But with the right shampoo or medicine, you can fight that flaky feeling.

Decongestants - They're medicines that keep your nose from being stuffy. When you have a cold, your nose gets a little swollen inside and can fill up with mucus. Decongestants stop your nose from becoming swollen so it doesn't feel as plugged up.

Dehydration - It describes what happens when there's not enough water in your body.

Dementia – a permanent acquired impairment of intellectual function that results in a marked decline in memory, language ability, personality, and cognition.

Depressant - are a kind of drug that, when used as prescribed by a doctor, can help relax muscles or calm nerves. Larger or improperly used doses of depressant drugs can cause confusion, lack of coordination, and shaking. Someone who takes them may have slurred speech, inability to concentrate, and may fall asleep at work or school. Very large doses of depressant drugs can stop your breathing and kill you.

Depression - It's normal to feel sad sometimes, but if you feel that way for a long time, and you never feel happy, it's called depression. Sometimes, it's hard to figure out what's causing a person's depression.

Dermatitis – is skin inflammation, rashy skin, dry skin.

Dermatologist - A special doctor called a dermatologist knows a lot about skin. Dermatologists help people who have itchy skin and any other skin problems.

Detoxification – the process of reducing the buildup of various poisonous substances in the body.

Diabetes Mellitus - Diabetes mellitus is sometimes called "sugar diabetes." When someone has diabetes, his or her body doesn't use glucose properly. Glucose, a sugar, is the main source of energy for the body. Glucose levels are controlled by a hormone called insulin, which is made in the pancreas. In diabetes, the pancreas does not make enough insulin such as in type 1 diabetes or the body can't respond normally to the insulin that is made as in type 2 diabetes.

Diagnosis - The word diagnosis is a fancy name for how doctors figure out what's making you sick by asking questions and ordering tests, like blood tests or x-rays.

Diaphragm - This thin, dome-shaped muscle helps you breathe and separates the lungs from your stomach and intestines. When it gets irritated, the diaphragm forces the air out of your lungs and causes you to have hic ups.

Diarrhea - Diarrhea happens when there's too much water in your bowel movements. With diarrhea, you have to go to the bathroom a lot and your stool is runny and watery.

Dietitian - A dietitian knows a lot about food and healthy eating. That's because dietitians are people who are experts in food. Dietitians can help you decide what to eat, when to eat, and almost anything else about eating right.

Disinfectants - are germ busters. Disinfectants, such as bleach and antibacterial soap, kill germs, such as bacteria and viruses. You have disinfectant cells in your body that kill germs, too.

Dislocation - when a bone gets pulled out of its joint from a fall or some other accident, it's called a dislocation. To fix it, a doctor has to put the bone back into the joint and let it heal.

Diuretic – an herb or medicine that increases urine output.

DNA – deoxyribonucleic acid. Substance in the cell nucleus that genetically contains the cell's genetic blueprint and determines the type of life form into which a cell will develop.

Dust Mites - tiny bugs that live in household dust. You actually need a microscope to see them. People can be allergic to dust mites and their droppings. This stuff gets into the air, and without a person knowing it, the dust mites can get into a person's lungs. Dust mites don't bother most people, but if the person has asthma, they can worsen breathing problems. It's also tough to get rid of dust mites because they work themselves into soft places like pillows, blankets, mattresses, and stuffed animals.

Dysentery – loose, fluidy, bloody bowel movements with cramping.

Dyslexia – is the name of a learning problem some children have with reading and writing. It can make words look jumbled and make it difficult to read and remember what was read.

EEG (Electroencephalogram) - Doctors use electroencephalograms to figure out what's going on in your brain. A special machine measures your brain waves to create an electroencephalogram. No matter what you're doing (even sleeping), your brain gives off electric waves. An electroencephalogram machine measures these electric waves and shows where and how big they are. Some children have a lot of extra electricity flowing inside their brain, which can cause things called seizures. An electroencephalogram does not hurt and it can help doctors decide how to treat these children.

Ear Canal - The ear canal lets in sound so you can hear. Glands in the ear canal make cerumen, or earwax.

Eardrum - Sound waves travel through the ear canal to reach the eardrum. The eardrum is a thin flap of skin that is stretched tight like a drum and vibrates when sound hits it. These vibrations move the tiny bones of the middle ear, which send vibrations to the inner ear. From the inner ear, the message is sent to the brain.

Eczema - your skin is itchy, red, and dry, and eczema is sometimes caused by allergies.

Edema – body retaining to much fluid causing swelling.

Elastin – a protein that gives tissue its elasticity.

Electrolytes – minerals in the body that help balance body fluid, body, heat, etc.

Embolus – a loose particle of tissue, blood clot, or tiny air bubble that travels through the bloodstream and, if it lodges in a narrowed portion of a blood vessel, can block blood flow.

Emulsion – a combination of two liquids that do not mix with each other, such as oil and water, one substance is broken into tiny droplets and is suspended within the other. Emulsification is the first step in the digestion of fats.

Enamel - Enamel is the hardest substance in your whole body, and it covers and protects your teeth.

Endocrine system – the system of glands that secrete hormones into the bloodstream. Endocrine glands include the pituitary, thyroid, thymus, and adrenal glands, as well as the pancreas, ovaries, and testes.

Endorphin – one of a number of natural hormone like substances found primarily in the brain. One function of endorphins is to suppress the sensation of pain, which they do by binding to opiate receptors in the brain.

Endoscope – an instrument for examining the interior of a hollow organ.

Enuresis - is the fancy name for peeing your pants. It can mean accidents that happen in the day or night, but most of the time enuresis refers to wetting the bed while sleeping. Not many children talk about it, but many children do it. The good news is that some children will stop wetting the bed without any special treatment. Others may need to train their bodies to hold the pee longer and can get encouragement from a chart that tracks their dry nights. There is also medication that can help with bed wetting.

Enzyme – one of many specific protein catalysts that initiate or speed chemical reactions in the body without being consumed.

Epidemic – an extensive outbreak of a disease, or a disease occurring with an unusually high incidence at certain times and places.

Epidermis - is the fancy name for the outermost layer of your skin.

Epiglottis - It's the part of your body that flops down over the windpipe when you swallow to keep food from going into your lungs. Without your epiglottis, you would cough or choke every time you eat.

Epinephrine – a hormone that increases heart rate, acts as adrenaline in the body.

Epstein Barr Virus – EBV – a virus that causes infectious mononucleosis and that may cause other health problems as well, especially in people with compromised immune systems.

Eustachian Tube - It runs between the inside of the ear and the throat, and its job is to make sure the pressure is the same on either side of the eardrum.

Essential Fatty Acid – EFA – fatty acids your body needs but cannot make itself. Omega 3 from flax is an example of an essential fatty acid.

Essential oil – oils extracted from a plant, seed, or fruit.

Exercise-Induced Asthma - Some people have asthma symptoms such as coughing, wheezing, or trouble breathing only when they're doing sports or being active. Being active may be the only cause of their breathing trouble, or it can be just one trigger that causes problems. Children who have this kind of asthma need to see a doctor and find out how to treat it. But once they do, they usually can be active and do sports like anyone else. In fact, more than 10% of Olympic athletes have exercise induced asthma that they've learned to control.

Epstein Bar - a low immune system virus characterized by extreme fatigue, fever, sore throat, etc.

Expectorant – a medicine that causes elimination of mucus from the respiratory tract.

External Otitis - Many children have had an ear infection known as external otitis. It is often called swimmer's ear, but you don't have to be a swimmer to get it. The ear is divided into three parts, the outer, middle, and inner ear. When the ear canal, which is part of the outer ear, gets infected, you have external otitis. It can make your ear hurt, especially when you touch it.

Farsighted - If it's easy for you to see things far away but you have trouble seeing things that are close, you might be farsighted. A lot of children who have trouble reading books are farsighted. Being farsighted is the opposite of being nearsighted which means you're able to see things that are up close.

Fat – necessary for normal brain development and concentrated energy.

Fats – Like carbohydrates and proteins, fats are one of the three main components of the food you eat. The body uses fat as a fuel source, and fat is the major storage form of energy in the body. Fat also has many other important functions in the body. You need some fat in your diet for good health. Too much fat or too much of the wrong type of fat can be unhealthy. Oil and butter contain fat. Nuts, meat, fish, and some dairy products contain fat, too.

Fatty Acids - Like gas for a car, glucose is fuel for your cells. But if glucose isn't available, fatty acids may be used instead. Fatty acids are the building blocks of the fat in our bodies. They also can be found in the food we eat. When we digest fats, they are broken down into fatty acids. These fatty acids can then be absorbed into the blood.

Fever - sometimes when you're sick, you feel really hot one minute and then freezing cold the next, chances are you have a fever. A fever is when your body gets a little hotter than normal on the inside. When germs get inside your body, your body tries to get rid of them by turning up the heat. So a fever means your body is trying to get better again.

Fiber - Fiber is found in plants and can't be digested so it helps clean out your intestines by moving bowel movements along. It's important to eat fiber so try some bran muffins instead of chocolate. Another way to get fiber is to eat more brown rice, fruit, and oatmeal.

Fracture - When a bone breaks, it's called a fracture. If you ever hurt yourself and think you might have a fracture, don't move. Wait until someone comes to help you because fractures only get worse when they're moved around. Usually, a doctor will put a cast around the fracture to protect the area and help it heal.

Free Radical – An unstable molecule that can cause damage to tissue. A stable compound such as oxygen, has paired electrons. An unstable, reactive compound contains an unpaired electron. A highly reactive electron will seek out and attach itself to another electron to stabilize itself. A compound or element with an unpaired or extra electron is called a free radical.

Free Radical Scavenger – is a supplement that eliminates free radicals.

Flora - bacterial in the intestine.

Frostbite - Frostbite is what happens when skin is exposed to cold temperatures and freezes. This can damage your skin and parts of your body, such as fingers and toes.

Fungus – one of a class or organisms that includes yeasts, mold, and mushrooms. A number of fungal species, such as Candida albicans, are capable of causing severe disease in immune-compromised hosts.

Gastric Juices - These juices are in the stomach, and their job is to begin breaking down food after you've swallowed it so it can be digested.

Gastroenteritis - sometimes called stomach flu. This illness can make you feel nauseous and cause you to throw up and have diarrhea.

Genes - hang out all lined up on thread-like things called chromosomes. Genes are made up of segments of DNA and they determine physical traits, including the color of your eyes and whether your hair is straight or curly. You inherited your genes from your parents, which is why someone might say you have your mother's smile.

Genetics - Genetics is the study of the way physical traits and characteristics get passed down from one generation to the next. This is also called heredity. Genetics includes the study of genes, which have a special code called DNA that determines what you will look like and whether you are likely to have certain illnesses.

Gingivitis - the word for gum disease, inflammation of the gums.

Gland – an organ or tissue that secretes a substance for use elsewhere in the body rather than for its own functioning.

Globulin – a type of protein found in the blood. Certain globulins contain disease fighting antibodies.

Glucose - When you eat, your body turns the food into a sugar called glucose. Like gas for a car, glucose provides fuel for your cells. It's carried to them by the bloodstream. The hormone insulin helps the glucose get to the cells, so it can be used for energy. Glucose is just a simple sugar which the body uses for energy.

Gluten – a protein found in many grains, including wheat, rye, barley, and oats.

Glycogen – A complex carbohydrate that is the main form in which glucose is stored in the body, primarily in the liver and muscles. It is converted back into glucose as needed to supply energy.

Gluteus Maximus - This is the fancy name for the muscles of your rear end.

Glycemic Index - The body breaks down most carbohydrates from the foods we eat and changes them to a type of sugar called glucose. Glucose is the main source of fuel for our cells. The glucose travels through the bloodstream to reach the cells. After we eat, the glucose from the food gets into the bloodstream fast, slow, or somewhere in between. It depends on the type of carbohydrate and the food that contains it. The glycemic index is a way of measuring how fast this occurs and how a food affects blood glucose levels. Foods with higher index values raise blood sugar more rapidly than foods with lower glycemic index values do.

Grieving - If you've ever been really sad, you might have been grieving. You may grieve because your dog died or because you had to say good-bye to someone you loved a lot. Grieving is OK, though, because it means that you really cared about something. And after a while, you should be ready to feel happy again.

Growth Hormone - Growth hormone is a major player in normal growth, like when your legs get longer and suddenly all your pants are too short. There are special tests to find out if children don't produce enough growth hormone. If they don't, daily shots of growth hormone can often help these children grow to be average-sized adults.

Gums - help keep your teeth in place.

Hair analysis – a method of determining the levels of minerals, including both toxic metals and essential minerals, in the body by measuring the concentrations of those minerals in the hair. Unlike mineral levels in the blood, those in the hair reflect the person's status over several preceding months.

Hay Fever - the name of a type of allergy that people have to natural things like pollen from plants and flowers. If you have hay fever, you don't really get a fever, but you will experience a runny, red, itchy nose and eyes.

HDL Cholesterol – a type of lipoprotein that is commonly referred to a good cholesterol because high levels normally indicate a low risk for hear disease.

Heat Exhaustion - it's what happens when the body is not able to cool itself down. So don't get exhausted and guzzle some water, hit the shade, or go inside and enjoy the air conditioning.

Heavy metal – a metallic element whose specific gravity is greater than 5.0. Some heavy metals, such as arsenic, cadmium, lead, and mercury, are extremely toxic.

Hematocrit – is the percentage of blood that is composed of red blood cells.

Hematoma - Hematoma is just a medical word for bruise, or black and blue mark. The "hema" part of the word means blood, which is what you see under your skin if you get a bad bump. When you get a bad bump, the blood vessels break and the blood leaks out. But then your body goes to work to clean things up. Before you know it, the black and blue color has faded to green or yellow and then it's gone.

Hemoglobin – the iron containing red pigment in the blood that is responsible for the transport of oxygen.

Hemorrhage – profuse bleeding.

Hepatitis – a general term for inflammation of the liver.

Herbal Therapy – the use of herbal combinations for healing or cleansing purposes. Herbs can be used in tablet, capsule, tincture, or extract form, as well as in baths and poultices.

Heredity - If people say you look like your parents, they're probably talking about heredity. Maybe you've noticed that you have the same color eyes as your mom or you're tall like your dad. Your parents pass these physical traits to you through your genes.

Hernia – a condition in which part of an internal organ protrudes, inappropriately, through an opening in the tissues that are supposed to contain it.

Herpes – a virus responsible for chickenpox, cold sores, shingles, etc.

Histamine - Histamine is a substance in the body that's released during an allergic reaction. It can cause allergy symptoms that affect the eyes, nose, throat, skin, digestive system, and lungs. When histamine affects the lungs, a person who has asthma may have breathing problems.

Homeopathy – a medical system based on the belief that 'like cures like'. Homeopathy is a belief that the illness can be cured by taking a minute dose of a substance that, if taken by a healthy person, would produce symptoms like those being treated.

Hormone - Hormones are special chemicals your body makes to help it do certain things like grow up. Hormones are very important when you start to go through puberty, which is when you begin growing and developing into an adult. During this time, you're loaded with hormones that tell your body that it's time to start changing.

Host – an organism in or on which another organism lives and from which the invading organism obtains nourishment.

Humidifier - A humidifier is a machine that makes the air around you a little wetter, so your nose and skin don't dry out as much.

HIV – Human Immunodeficiency Virus.

Hyaluronic acid – an organic acid known as the most effective natural skin moisturizer. It is present in human skin and is able to hold five hundred times its own weight in water.

Hydrochloric acid – a strong, corrosive inorganic acid that is produced in the stomach to aid in digestion.

Hydrocortisone - Hydrocortisone is medicine that helps itchy skin feel better. Poison ivy, bug bites, and eczema all can make you want to scratch. Hydrocortisone cream can help control the itching so you won't scratch as much.

Hydrogen Peroxide - Hydrogen peroxide is a chemical that can clean your cuts and scrapes. When it's poured on a cut, it bubbles a little, making oxygen and killing germs. It may also may use it to clear earwax from your ear.

Hypertension – High blood pressure.

Hypoallergenic – low capacity for inducing hypersensitive reactions.

Hypoglycemia - Glucose is the body's main energy source. Hormones, such as insulin, control the level of glucose in the blood. It's unhealthy if a person's glucose levels get too high, or too low. Hypoglycemia occurs when the levels get too low. This can happen to people who have diabetes. It can occur if the person doesn't eat enough or if the person takes too much insulin, which lowers glucose levels. A person with hypoglycemia may feel hungry, shaky, sweaty, weak, drowsy, or dizzy. If left untreated, hypoglycemia may even make someone faint or pass out.

Hypotension – low blood pressure.

Hypothalamus – a portion of the brain that regulates many aspects of metabolism, including body temperature and the hunger response.

ICU - Short for intensive care unit, this is a place in the hospital where people can recover from very serious illnesses, accidents, or operations. In the ICU, a patient can get extra help from machines and extra attention from doctors, nurses, and other caring people.

IV - IV is actually short for intravenous. You can get nourishment, fluids, and medicine through your veins. In some cases, it can be the best way to deliver the fluid or medicine that a person needs. IVs might be used if a person is having surgery, is very sick, or can't eat and drink normally. Whatever the reason, an IV can help the person get better again.

Ibuprofen - Ibuprofen is a kind of pain reliever that helps ease aches and pains. After you take ibuprofen, it keeps the nerves in your body from sending messages that say to your brain, that you have pain, so you won't hurt as much.

Immune Globulin – a protein that functions as an antibody in the body's immune response. Immune globulins are manufactured by certain white blood cells and found in body fluids and on mucous membranes.

Immune System - This body system, which includes white blood cells and lymph nodes, helps protect your body from disease. The immune system has different parts, all of which work together to fight off outside invaders like germs. Every day your immune system does battle to keep you healthy and feeling your best.

Immunity – the condition of being able to resist and overcome disease or infection.

Immunizations - This is the long word for what most children know as shots. Even though getting immunizations at the doctor's office isn't fun, they are very important because they help protect you against diseases.

Infection - When germs get inside your body, they can multiply and cause an infection. Your body's immune system fights off the germs with special cells. It can become a full-on fight against the nasty invaders and you won't feel better until your body wins. Sometimes when you get sick, it's because you have some kind of infection. If your body's having a little trouble fighting the infection by itself, your doctor may prescribe medicine like antibiotics to help, so just let your body do the work.

Inflammation – swelling, warmth and redness caused by injury, arthritis, etc.

Influenza - Influenza is a type of germ called a virus that can make you sick. You'll feel better if you rest, drink plenty of liquids, and take acetaminophen or ibuprofen and some herbal teas to make you feel more comfortable.

Inhaler - An inhaler is a device that can get asthma medicine directly into a person's lungs. The medicine is a mist, spray, or powder that the person breathes in. In the lungs, this medicine can go right to work, opening narrowed airways. When the tubes are open and clear, the person can breathe more easily, without as much coughing or wheezing.

Insomnia – inability to sleep.

Insulin - If someone has diabetes, he or she has trouble with a hormone called insulin. Insulin, which is made in the pancreas, lowers the level of glucose (a type of sugar) in the blood. It does this by helping glucose enter the body's cells. Glucose is the main source of energy for the cells. And because you're made up of cells, you want those cells to get the fuel they need. Your body gets glucose from the food you eat, and it travels through the bloodstream. But without insulin, glucose can't get into the cells. In diabetes, the pancreas doesn't make enough insulin or the body can't respond normally to the insulin that is made. This causes the glucose level in the blood to rise.

Insulin Injections - Insulin is an important hormone that keeps your body working. If a person doesn't make enough of this substance, he or she may need to get insulin injections, or shots. There are many types of injectable insulin, both short and long acting. Most people with diabetes take insulin injections based on their blood glucose levels, according to a plan that they've worked out with their doctor.

Insulin Pump - A person needs the hormone insulin so the body can function properly. If a person's body doesn't make enough insulin, one way to get it is through an insulin pump. Some people with diabetes use this. The pump is a small battery-operated device that can be worn on a belt or put in a pocket. It's connected to a narrow plastic tube that's inserted just under the skin and taped in place. The pump can be programmed to deliver insulin throughout the day and to release extra insulin when needed, such as after eating.

Insulin Resistance - Children who are starting to get type 2 diabetes are still able to make insulin, but the insulin can't work the way it should. Even though the pancreas is still making insulin, the body doesn't let insulin do its job as well and it's harder for glucose to get into the cells. This is called insulin resistance. People who have insulin resistance may or may not develop type 2 diabetes.

Intensive Care Unit - The intensive care unit, or ICU, is a special place in the hospital where people can recover from very serious illnesses, accidents, or operations. In the ICU, a patient can get extra help from machines and extra attention from doctors, nurses, and other caring people.

Involuntary Muscle - One very important involuntary muscle is your heart, which keeps beating all day and night. Other involuntary muscles help digest food and are found in your stomach and intestines.

Iris - Your iris is the colored part of your eye. So if someone has brown eyes, it means that person's irises are brown. The iris is about more than looks, though. Your iris controls the size of the pupil which is the black dot in the center of your eye, and how much light is let into your eye.

Jaundice – a condition where to much bilirubin in in the blood and causes the skin and eyes to look yellow.

Keratin - This is the hard protein that hair is made of, whether you've got straight red hair, blond curly locks, or black twisty braids. Keratin is also an important part of nails and skin.

Ketoacidosis - Ketoacidosis, a condition that can happen to people with diabetes, occurs when the body uses fat instead of glucose for fuel. When fat is broken down, chemicals called ketones are produced. They get into a person's blood and urine. High levels of ketones cause the blood to become more acidic. Symptoms of ketoacidosis include nausea, vomiting, belly pain, fast breathing, and, in severe cases, unconsciousness. People with ketoacidosis need to get emergency medical treatment.

Ketones - Glucose (a type of sugar) is the body's main energy source. But when the body can't use glucose for energy, it uses fat instead. When fat is broken down, chemicals called ketones are produced. They get into a person's blood and urine. High levels of ketones cause the blood to become more acidic. This can occur when not enough food has been eaten to provide glucose for energy, or it can occur in diabetes, when the body can't use glucose normally.

Kidney - The kidneys are a pair of organs that filter waste materials out of the blood. The waste is passed out out of the body as urine. Kidneys produce important hormones and regulate blood pressure and the levels of water, salts, and minerals in the body. Kidney damage can occur in someone who has had diabetes for many years, especially if the diabetes isn't controlled. You'll find your kidneys on either side of your spine, just below the rib cage.

Melanin - This natural pigment is what gives your skin its special hue. The darker your skin, the more melanin you have.

Lactase – an enzyme that converts lactose into glucose and galactose. It is necessary for the digestion of milk and milk products.

Lactic Acid – is present in certain foods, including certain fruits and sour milk. Lactic acid is also produced in the muscles during anaerobic exercise.

Lactobacilli – any of a number of species of bacteria that are capable of transforming lactose into lactic acid through fermentation. Lactobacilli are naturally present in bacteria because they aid in digestion and fight certain disease causing microorganisms.

Laser – light amplification by stimulated emission of radiation. An instrument that focuses highly amplified light waves. Lasers are used in surgical procedures, especially eye surgery.

LDL Cholesterol – a type of lipoprotein that is commonly referred to as bad cholesterol because high levels normally indicate a high risk of heart disease.

Laxative – a substance that causes the bowels to move.

Lecithin – a mixture of phospholipids that is composed of fatty acids, glycerol, phosphorus, and choline or inositol. All living cell membranes are largely composed of lecithin.

Leukemia – cancer of the blood producing tissues, especially the bone marrow and lymph nodes, resulting in an over abundance of white blood cells.

Lipids - fat soluble substance.

Lipoprotein – a type of protein molecule that incorporates a lipid. Lipoproteins act as agents of lipid transport in the lymph and blood.

Lutein – a phytochemical found in kale, spinach, and other dark green leafy vegetables that is beneficial for the eyes. It may help protect against macular degeneration.

Lycopene – a phytochemical found in tomatoes that appears to afford protection against prostate cancer and to protect the skin against harm from ultraviolet rays.

Lymph – a clear fluid derived from blood plasma that circulates throughout the body, is collected from the tissues, and flows through the lymphatic vessels, eventually returning to the bloodstream. Its function is to nourish tissue cells and return waste matter to the bloodstream.

Lymph nodes – organs located in the lymphatic vessels that act as filters, trapping and removing foreign material. They also form lymphocytes, immune cells that develop the capacity to seek out and destroy specific foreign agents.

Lymphocyte – is a type of white blood cell found in lymph blood, and other specialized tissues, such as the bone marrow and tonsils.

Lymphoma – cancer of the lymphatic tissues.

Macrophage – a cell that eats abnormal cells.

Malignant – cell that is cancerous.

Malabsorption – nutritional defect in the absorption of nutrients from the intestinal tract into the bloodstream.

Melanoma – a malignant tumor originating from pigment cells in the deep layers of the skin.

Melatonin – hormone that helps with sleep cycle.

Metabolism – the physical and chemical processes necessary to sustain life, including the production of cellular energy, the synthesis of important biological substances, and degradation of various compounds.

Metastasis – the spread of cancer to a site or sites away from the original tumor.

Microscope - A microscope is a very powerful magnifying glass. The entire world, our bodies included, are made up of billions of tiny living things that are so small you can't see them with just your eyes. But with a microscope, it's possible to examine the cells of your body or a drop of blood. By using a microscope to see these things up close, a doctor can spot cancer cells, bacteria, and other problems that could be causing a person's illness.

Mineral – an inorganic substance required by the body in small quantities.

Mucous Membrane - Just as skin lines and protects the outside of the body, mucous membranes line and protect the inside of your body. You can find mucous membranes inside of your nose, mouth, lungs, and many other parts of the body. Mucous membranes make mucus, which keeps them moist.

Mucus - You will find mucus in your mouth, lungs, stomach, and intestines. Wherever you find mucus, it protects and lubricates mucous membranes in your body.

Myelin Sheath – a fatty covering that protects nerve cells. Myelin sheaths are noticeably damaged or missing in people with multiple sclerosis.

Myopia - Myopia is also known as nearsightedness, which means you can see things up close, but have trouble seeing objects far away, like the words on a chalkboard. A lot of people have myopia, which is usually corrected by wearing glasses.

Nasal Cavity - The nasal cavity is the inside of your nose. It is lined with a mucous membrane that helps keep your nose moist by making mucus so you won't get nosebleeds from a dry nose. There are also little hairs that help filter the air you breathe in, blocking dirt and dust from getting into your lungs.

Naturopathy – a form of health care that uses diet, herbs, and other natural methods and substances to cure illness. The goal is to produce a healthy body state without the use of drugs by stimulating innate defenses.

Nausea - Nausea is the feeling you get when you feel like you're going to throw up.

Nearsighted - You might be nearsighted if you have no problems seeing things up close but have trouble seeing things that are far away, like the chalkboard when you sit in the back of the classroom. Being nearsighted is the opposite of being farsighted, which is the ability to see things far away.

Nebulizer - A nebulizer is a machine that turns liquid medicine into a mist that can be breathed in. So it's a great way for people with asthma to get their medicine right where they need it, in their lungs. Lots of children with asthma use nebulizers to help them breathe easier.

Nephropathy - Having diabetes for many years can damage small blood vessels throughout a person's body. This can affect several organs, including the kidneys. It is more likely to happen if a person's diabetes isn't well controlled. Kidney disease caused by diabetes is called diabetic nephropathy

Nervous System - The nervous system controls everything you do, including breathing, walking, thinking, and feeling. This system is made up of your brain, spinal cord, and all the nerves of your body. The brain is the control center and the spinal cord is the major highway to and from the brain. The nerves carry the messages to and from the body, so the brain can interpret them and take action.

Neurologist - A neurologist is a doctor who studies the nervous system. Neurologists help people who have epilepsy (seizures), severe headaches, trouble moving arms or legs, and many other problems that can affect the nervous system.

Neuropathy - Having diabetes for many years can damage the nervous system. Neuropathy is the medical word for disease of the nervous system. When this is caused by diabetes, it's called diabetic neuropathy.

Nits - These are the eggs that lice lay. A nit is smaller than a sesame seed and is firmly attached to a strand of hair.

Nutrition - is the study of food and how it works in your body. Nutrition includes all the stuff that's in your food, such as vitamins, protein, fat, and more. It's important to eat a variety of foods, including fruits, vegetables, dairy products, and grains, so you have what you need to grow and be healthy.

Occupational Therapist - An occupational therapist can help children who have trouble doing everyday things, like writing, eating, or getting dressed. An occupational therapist uses exercises and activities to teach children how to do these things better. If a child has trouble eating, the therapist can provide special forks and spoons that are longer, shorter, or have easy-to-hold rubber grips. If a child needs help with writing, the therapy might be strengthening the pointer finger by finger painting or squirting a water gun.

Oncologist - This is a doctor who treats patients who have cancer. Oncologists who treat children who have cancer are called pediatric oncologists.

Operation - An operation is also called surgery, and it's when doctors fix something inside the body to make the person feel better. The doctor may take out a burst appendix, close up a hole in the heart, or even put in a new kidney. The good part about surgery is that it usually means the person is on the road to feeling better.

Ophthalmologist - An ophthalmologist is an eye doctor. This type of doctor helps people with all kinds of eye problems and does surgery on the eye if needed.

Optometrist - An optometrist examines your eyes and tests your vision. If you need glasses, an optometrist can tell what kind of glasses or contact lenses are right for you.

Organic – a term used to describe foods that are grown without the use of synthetic chemicals, such as pesticides, herbicides, and hormones.

Orthodontist - An orthodontist is a dentist who specializes in making teeth straight, instead of fixing cavities. An orthodontist knows how to put on braces and make retainers.

Otitis Media - Most children have had an ear infection, also known as otitis media. Media means middle, so when you get an ear infection, germs get into the middle part of the ear causing fluid or pus to build up in the space behind the eardrum.

Oxidation - a chemical reaction of oxygen. A process by which the body rids itself of waste.

Palate - it's the fancy name for the roof of your mouth.

Pancreas - The pancreas is a long, flat gland in your belly. It sits behind the stomach and produces enzymes that are important for digestion. Insulin and glucagon, which help control the level of glucose (a type of sugar) in the blood, are also made in the pancreas.

Parasite – an organism that gets nutrients off another. Lice and scabies are two different types of parasites.

Pathogen – a toxin or small organism that can cause disease.

Pediatric Endocrinologist - This is the name for the type of doctor who deals with hormones, those special chemical substances your body produces. Hormones make things happen all over the body, especially during puberty. Pediatric endocrinologists help children with diabetes, growth problems, and more.

Peroxide - A chemical compound containing two oxygen atoms, each of which is bonded to the other and to some other element other than oxygen such as hydrogen, magnesium, calcium.

Pathogens - a specific cause of disease such as bacterium or virus.

Papillae - Papillae are the little bumps on the top of your tongue that help grip food while your teeth are chewing. They contain your taste buds, the things that help you taste everything from sour lemons to sweet peaches.

Perspiration - Perspiration is another name for sweat, the stuff that comes out of your skin through tiny holes called pores. Perspiration, which is mostly water, is your body's tool for keeping you cool when you get hot from exercise or hot weather.

Pimple - Your skin has many tiny holes called pores. When you go through puberty, your skin makes a lot of extra oil that might clog up those pores. Too much oil may combine with dead skin and bacteria to create a pimple.

Pituitary – a gland located at the base of the brain that secretes a number of different hormones. Pituitary hormones regulate growth and metabolism by coordinating the actions of other endocrine glands.

Placebo – a fake substance usually used along side a real substance, to test to see how and if a substance works.

Plaque - Plaque is a sticky substance made up mostly of the germs that cause tooth decay. That's why it's important to brush your teeth at least twice every day and floss daily. If too much plaque builds up on and between your teeth, you'll get cavities or gum disease. Plaque can also deposit and build up on arteries.

Platelets - Your blood contains many tiny cells called platelets. They help your blood clot, which means that if you get a cut, some of your platelets stick together to plug the hole in the blood vessel wall caused by the cut. Eventually, the clot dries out to form a scab to protect the healing skin underneath.

Pneumonia - is an infection of the lungs, usually caused by viruses or bacteria. A person with pneumonia may have a fever and cough, and it may be hard to breathe for a little while. A doctor can tell you have pneumonia by listening to your lungs or looking at a chest X-ray.

Pollen - Pollen is a fine powder produced by certain plants. During the spring, summer, and fall seasons, it is released into the air and picked up by the wind. The wind carries it to other plants so they can make seeds. But while it's traveling in the wind, pollen gets into the air we breathe. Many people are allergic to it, including people who have asthma. When they breathe in pollen, it can trigger their asthma symptoms.

Poultice – a soft wrap that could include herbs and is applied to skin.

Precancerous lesion – abnormal tissue that is not malignant, but that may be in the process of becoming so.

Probiotics – elements that encourage the growth of beneficial bacteria in the body.

Protein – essential for growth and development. It provides the body with energy, and is needed for the manufacture of hormones, antibodies, enzymes, and tissue.

Puberty - It's that period of time when your body changes and matures, turning you from a child into an adult. Although everyone is different, puberty usually starts between age 8 and 13 for girls and age 10 and 15 for boys.

Pulmonologist - A pulmonologist is a doctor who specializes in lungs and breathing.

Pulse - Your beating heart creates a pulse. Your heart has to push so much blood through your body that you can feel a little thump in your arteries each time the heart beats. The most common places to feel a pulse is on your wrist and your neck.

Pupil - Pupils are in charge of how much light goes into your eye. That's why your pupils get larger in the dark (to let more light in) and smaller in the light (to keep some light out).

REM - This is short for rapid eye movement, the stage of sleep when your eyes move back and forth under your closed eyelids and you have dreams.

Radiation therapy – is used to treat cancer.

Radiologist - When a child gets an X-ray or a CT scan, a radiologists will come in and read them. They are doctors who are specialists in reading and making sense of these pictures, and they help other doctors figure out what's going on inside you.

Red Blood Cells - Red blood cells have the important job of carrying oxygen. These cells, which float in your blood, begin their journey in the lungs, where they pick up oxygen from the air you breathe. Then they travel to the heart, which pumps out the blood, delivering oxygen to all parts of your body.

Remission – the ceasing or healing of cancer.

Renal – pertaining to the kidneys.

Rescue Medications - Rescue medications are a type of asthma medicine that works quickly. They rescue the person from wheezing, coughing, and shortness of breath. Most rescue medications are inhaled and work by relaxing the muscle around the airways. When the muscles are relaxed, the airways are wider, which makes it easier to move air in and out of the lungs. But rescue medications won't prevent future asthma flare ups and may not be enough to keep someone's asthma under control. Controller medicine, taken daily, is often needed as well to keep the airways from getting swollen and narrow in the first place.

Retina - The retina is at the back of your eye and it has light sensitive cells called rods and cones. When you look at something, light hits the retina, the rods and cones send electrical signals to the brain along the optic nerve. The brain uses these signals to interpret what you are seeing.

Rhinovirus - It's the name for a virus that causes the common cold in people.

Saliva - is spit, the clear liquid in your mouth that's made of water and other chemicals. Saliva helps keep the mouth moist and contains an enzyme that starts to break down food even before it hits your stomach.

Saturated fat – a fat that is solid at room temperature. Most saturated fats are of animal origin, although a few, such as coconut oil and palm oil, come from plants.

Scar - A scar is a mark left on your skin from a cut or wound that has healed. You're most likely to get a scar if there is a lot of damage to the skin or the edges of a cut are too far apart to heal properly. You can help prevent scars by keeping germs out by cleaning and covering your cuts and scrapes.

Scratch test – a procedure in which a small amount of a suspected allergen is applied to a lightly scratched area of skin to test for an allergic reaction.

Scoliosis - is an abnormal curve of the spine, also known as the backbone. Most scoliosis is mild, but for those who need it, back braces and special surgery can help many children .

Sebaceous glands - Sebaceous glands make oil to keep skin soft and smooth. If they make too much oil, your pores can get clogged, and you can get bumps and red spots called pimples.

Sebum - Sebum is your skin's natural oil, and it keeps your skin soft and makes it a bit waterproof.

Sedative – medicine or herb to quiet the nerves.

Seizure - You might hear a seizure called a convulsion, fit, or spell. Most people think of a seizure as shaking all over and losing control of your body. But there are different kinds of seizures, and all of them are caused by abnormal electrical activity in the brain. Your brain uses electrical signals and if those signals go a little haywire, a person can have a seizure. Some people may have only one seizure in their whole life or seizures may recur as part of a condition called epilepsy. People with epilepsy usually need medicine to control their seizures.

Semicircular Canals - Your semicircular canals are three tiny, fluid-filled tubes in your inner ear that help you keep your balance. When your head moves around, the liquid inside the semicircular canals sloshes around and moves the tiny hairs that line each canal. These hairs translate the movement of the liquid into nerve messages that are sent to your brain. Your brain then can tell your body how to stay balanced. If you spin around and then stop, the liquid inside your semicircular canals moves awhile longer and the hairs continue to send the message that you are spinning even though you're not. That's why you feel dizzy after carnival or amusement park rides.

Skin Test - If you think that you might have allergies, a special doctor called an allergist can help figure out what you are allergic to by giving you a skin test. For this test, the doctor will use different liquids, each containing a small amount of stuff that a person can be allergic to, such as pollen or certain foods. The doctor puts a drop of each liquid on your arm or back and then lightly pricks the skin. If you get a red, itchy bump there, you'll know you're allergic.

Spasm – muscle contracts involuntary.

Strep Screen - This is a quick test and your doctor can tell you in minutes if you have strep throat. If you do, the doctor will give you a prescription for an antibiotic, which will help you get better.

Stress - Stress is the feeling you get when you're worrying. Sometimes, you'll feel like you have an upset stomach, sweaty hands, or have trouble sleeping. Exercising or talking about your feelings can help relieve stress.

Stroke – an attack in which the brain is suddenly deprived of oxygen as a result of interrupted blood flow. If it continues for more than a few minutes, brain damage and even death may result.

Sublingual – sublingual medications and supplements often look like tablets or liquids meant for swallowing, but they are designed to be held in the mouth while the active ingredient is absorbed into the bloodstream through the mucous membranes.

Suture - This is the string that doctors use to sew things together. Stitches hold the edges of your skin together so a cut can heal properly. When you have stitches in your skin, usually you have to go back to the doctor to get them removed. When you have surgery, the doctor may use a different kind of suture, which dissolves on its own.

Symptoms - When you're sick, you usually have symptoms in your body, changes like a fever that let you know something is not right. Think of symptoms like clues you need to solve a mystery. If you have enough of them, it can be easy to figure out what's going on. For example, if you have an achy ear and a fever, you might have an ear infection. And if you're throwing up and your stomach hurts, maybe you have a stomach virus.

Syndrome – a group of signs and symptoms that together are known or presumed to characterize a disorder.

Synergy – an interaction between two or more substances in which their action is greater when they are together than the sum of their individual actions would be.

Synthesize – to create a complex substance by combining simpler elements or compounds.

Systemic – pertaining to the entire body.

T Cells – kills cancer cells and other infectious microbes and helps defend the body.

Tea – infusion of water and plant.

Tendons - For keeping things together, tendons come in handy. These special cords made of tough tissue attach your body's muscles to your bones.

Thrush – a fungal infection caused by Candida albicans that is characterized by small whitish spots on the tongue and the insides of the cheeks. It occurs most often in infants.

Tincture – herbs prepared in alcohol solution.

Tinnitus - it's the word for a ringing sound in the ears. Tinnitus can be caused by loud noises or ear infections.

Tonic – promotes wellness and energy.

Tonsillectomy - Tonsils are those two bumps on each side of the back of your throat. Your tonsils are germ catchers for your body. Sometimes, though, these germs multiply, hang out on your tonsils, and make them swollen, red, and painful. If you keep getting tonsil infections, called tonsillitis, doctors can help by performing an operation called a tonsillectomy, where the doctor removes your tonsils.

Topical – applying substance to surface of body.

Toxic waste - poisonous waste.

Toxin - poison, pollutant, contaminant.

Trace elements – a mineral required by the body in extremely small quantities.

Tremor – involuntary trembling.

Triggers - With asthma, a trigger is anything that brings on asthma symptoms, such as coughing, wheezing, and trouble breathing. Triggers can vary from person to person and from season to season. They also can change as a child grows older. Some common triggers include colds, smoke, cold air, exercise, and anything that causes an allergic reaction, such as dust mites or pollen.

Tumor – an abnormal mass of tissue that serves no function. Tumors are usually categorized as either benign or malignant.

Tympanogram - Tympanic membrane is the fancy name for eardrum, so when a doctor wants to find out how your eardrum is working, he or she may get a tympanogram. In this test, a doctor uses a special machine that is small enough to be inserted into your ear. It makes a quiet noise that should get your eardrum moving. The result of this test is known as a tympanogram.

Type A personality – a personality that tends to be impatient and aggressive. Persons with type A personalities tend to have stronger stress reactions and may be more susceptible to cardiovascular disease.

Type B personality – a personality that tends to be relaxed and patient, and less reactive to stress. Those with type B personalities may be less prone to develop stress related illnesses such as high blood pressure and heart disease.

Ulcer – is a lesion.

Ultrasound – Ultra high frequency sound waves. Ultrasound technology is used in a number of different medical diagnostic and treatment tools.

Umbilical Cord - This is the name for the long tube that runs between a mother and her unborn baby. It carries oxygen and nutrients to the baby and waste away from the baby. When the baby is born, the doctor cuts the umbilical cord and a small piece is left attached to the baby.

Urinalysis - Urinalysis helps a doctor learn more about what's going on inside your body. Sometimes your urine has stuff in it that shouldn't be there, like sugar, which may mean you have diabetes. If you have a bladder infection, a doctor might find bacteria or white blood cells in your urine.

Urine – The kidneys remove waste from the blood and make urine. Urine is mostly water so if you don't take in a lot of fluids or if you sweat a lot, your urine has less water in it and it appears darker. If you drink lots of fluids, the extra fluid comes out in your urine, and it will be lighter. Urine is stored in the bladder until it's peed out.

Urticaria - Urticaria is the fancy name for hives. Hives are those itchy, red bumps people get on their skin when they're allergic to something, like certain foods or medicines. Allergies are not the only reason someone might get hives. Some infections, hot or cold temperatures, or even stress can make those bumps appear.

Vaccine - A vaccine is another word for what most children call a shot. Even though getting vaccines isn't fun, they are very important because they help protect you against diseases.

Varicella Zoster - This is the medical name for the virus that causes chicken pox, which is known for its red, itchy bumps. Lots of children get chicken pox, but now there's a shot that can help prevent this itchy illness.

Veins and Arteries - Your body has a highway system all its own that sends blood to and from your body parts. It's called the circulatory system, and the roads are arteries and veins. Arteries, which usually look red, carry blood away from the heart. Veins, which usually look blue, return blood to the heart.

Venom – a poisonous substance produced by an animal, such as certain snakes and insects.

Vertebrae - is a bone called a vertebra and there are 33 vertebrae that make up your spine.

Virus - Viruses are a type of germ. They are a single cell that cannot reproduce on it's own, so it attaches to other cells and takes over in a host. They're very tiny, and when they get inside your body, they can make you sick. Viruses cause colds, chicken pox, measles, flu, and many other diseases. Unfortunately, antibiotics don't work on viruses like they do on bacteria. Wash your hands often to help prevent the spread of viruses, especially before you eat and after you use the bathroom.

Vital signs – basic indicators of an individual's health status, including pulse, breathing, blood pressure, and body temperature.

Vitamin – one of approximately fifteen organic substances that are essential in small quantities for life and health. Most vitamins cannot be manufactured by the body and so need to be supplied in the diet.

Water soluble – capable of dissolving in water.

White blood cell – a blood cell that functions in fighting infection and in wound repair.

Wheeze - A wheeze is the whistling sound air makes when your breathing tubes are narrowed. This is what happens during an asthma flare up. If the breathing tubes get too narrow, a person may have trouble breathing. Sometimes you can hear someone wheeze, but usually a doctor needs to listen to a person's lungs with a stethoscope to hear wheezing.

White Blood Cells - White blood cells are part of the germ-fighting immune system. They are like little warriors floating around in your blood waiting to attack invaders, like viruses and bacteria. You have several types of white blood cells and each has its own special role in fighting off the different kinds of germs that make people sick.

Whitehead - People with acne may have different types of bumps on their skin. These can be whiteheads, blackheads, pimples, and cysts. Your skin is full of tiny holes called pores. If a pore gets clogged with oil, dead skin, and bacteria, the pore may close and form a whitehead. If a pore gets clogged but stays open, the top surface can darken and you're left with a blackhead.

Wisdom Teeth - Between the ages of 17 and 21, most people get four more molars all the way in the back of the mouth, one in each corner. If wisdom teeth don't grow in properly, they may have to be removed.

X-ray - X-rays are special pictures of the inside of your body. A doctor will decide when you need an X-ray and what body part needs to be X-rayed. An X-ray machine, not a camera, is used to take these pictures. Doctors can see broken bones, lung infections, and more.

Yeast – single cell fungi.

Zoonosis - Zoonosis means a disease that people can get from animals. Some examples of zoonosis include ringworm, salmonella infection, and rabies. You can prevent zoonoses by keeping your pet healthy, staying away from wild animals and always washing your hands after touching animals.

Sources for Herbal Supplements and Information

People often ask me what brand of supplements do I use or like. There are so many good companies out there, but I am in the habit of buying from certain companies. It is not because one supplement is better than another, it is just my preference. So I recommend you try several high quality supplements and make your own decision on which one you like.

Starwest Botanicals, Inc.
11253 Trade Center Drive
Rancho Cordova, CA 95742
916/638-8100
800/800-4372
Bulk herbs
www.starwest-botanicals.com

Nutraceutical Corporation
1500 Kearns Blvd.
Park City, UT 84060
800/767-8514
www.nutraceutical.com

Now Foods
395 S. Glen Ellyn Rd.
Bloomingdale, IL 60108
800-999-8069
www.nowfoods.com

Home Comfort Farms
1865 Roby Road
Johannesburg, MI 49751
989-619-3333
garden herbs and medicine herbs

My favorite books that I feel should be a part of everyone's home library and I constantly pour over and have learned so much from over the years are:

Aromatherapy for Everyone
by PJ Pierson and Mary Shipley

The Family Guide to Homeopathy
By Dr. Andrew Lockie

Prescription for Nutritional Healing
By Phyllis Balch, C.N.C.

The Tea Tree Oil Bible
By Drs. Ali, Grant, Nakla, Patel and Vegotsky

Herb Bible
By Earl R. Maindells, PhD.

What Every Parent Should Know About
Childhood Immunization
By Jamie Murphy

Index